# ALL FALL DOWN

Louise Voss &
Mark Edwards

**WINDSOR**
**PARAGON**

First published 2013
by Harper
This Large Print edition published 2013
by AudioGO Ltd
by arrangement with
HarperColllins*Publishers*

Hardcover     ISBN: 978 1 4713 4396 4
Softcover     ISBN: 978 1 4713 4397 1

British Library Cataloguing in Publication Data available

Printed and bound in Great Britain by
MPG Books Group Limited

# ACKNOWLEDGEMENTS

Our first thank you goes to Dr Jennifer Rohn who acted as our chief scientific advisor, helped us create our deadly virus and pointed out exactly how many ways there are to kill someone in a lab. If you enjoy science-based fiction, you should visit Dr Rohn's excellent site, Lablit.com. Also, thanks to Professor Julius Weinberg at Kingston University and to Bob Crewley for checking helicopter accuracy!

For reading the manuscript and checking our Americanisms, thanks to Amy Welch—mistakes, as with the aforementioned 'science bits' are our own—and thanks too to Julie Baugh for being our first (and constant) reader.

This book would be half the book it is—though probably twice as long—were it not for the editorial perspicacity of Kate Bradley. Huge thanks too to Anne O'Brien for the ruthless copy edit. We extend our thanks to the whole team at HarperCollins including Hannah Gamon and Louise Swannell.

Thanks to our agent Sam Copeland for great support and enthusiasm as ever.

The world of crime fiction and thrillers is a warm and friendly one, especially for a group of people who spend their days dreaming up grisly murders, and it is hard to single out individuals from that community. But special thanks go to the following: Peter James, Elizabeth Haynes, Alex Marwood, Emlyn Rees, Stav Sherez, Claire McGowan, Erin Kelly, Mel Sherratt, Mark Billingham, Rhian Davies, Rachel Abbott, J Carson Black, Keith B Walters, Nikki-Ann Trow, Mari Hannah, Jennifer Hillier and everyone involved in the Harrogate Crime Festival. Also, thanks to everyone at Waterstones Wolverhampton, Kingston, and Mary Kennedy at Teddington Waterstones.

Mark would like to thank an assortment of lovely people who would be first into the bunker should a deadly pandemic ever devastate the planet: the whole Baugh clan, Jo Johnston-Pope, Martin Johnston, Louise and Dominic Compagnone, Jonathan Pye, Mark Nunney, Susan Smith and Darren Biggs, Andrew and Vicky Wallace, Oliver Brann, Charlotte Staunton and the studentbeans. com crew. Last but most importantly, his family, especially his mum for starting all of this by letting him read that James Herbert book at a very young age; and huge amounts of love and gratitude to his lovely children Poppy, Archie and Ellie, and to Sara, who inspires him every day.

Thanks from Louise to her fantastic friends and family, for all the emotional and practical support during the writing of this one, particularly to Louise Green, Roxana Ziolkowski, Liz Lewis, Sarah Freestone, Pete Aves, Julie Lane, Kate Blumgart, Paul Cavin, Jacqui Lofthouse, Stephanie Zia, David Osbon, Alex Evans, Alex McPherson, Richard and Clare Jackson, and Nick Laughland.

# AUTHOR'S NOTE

Watoto, the virus featured in *All Fall Down*, is of course made up. However, it does also happen to be the name of an amazing holistic care programme in Uganda set up in 1994 from the Watoto Church in Kampala in response to overwhelming numbers of orphaned children and vulnerable women in the war-torn and AIDS-stricken country. They provide medical treatment, education, housing, counselling and spiritual discipleship. To find out more, or to sponsor a child, please go to www.watoto.com.

*For Claire Finch and Ali Cutting*

# PROLOGUE: PATIENT ZERO

## CALIFORNIA

John Tucker sneezed violently, jerking the steering wheel to the left, the car swerving and almost clipping the median strip. A truck rumbled past in the outside lane, its horn blaring deep and low, and John raised his middle finger and shouted a curse that nobody could hear.

He was twenty-eight years old and had nothing. No woman, no job, no apartment and no money—apart from the five hundred bucks Cindy had given him.

He'd met her in Hollywood, only a few days ago, though it felt like weeks. He had just spent the last of his money on a night in that sleazy pit, the Capitol Hotel. On that hot summer's evening he'd been contemplating a night on the streets unless something miraculous happened.

John had been sitting in a bar, the last of his cash gone on a beer that was warm from where he'd been nursing it so long, staring down at the tabletop, his long greasy hair blocking out the world. He became aware of a presence by the table and a female voice. 'Mind if I join you?'

She was beyond beautiful. Long dark brown hair, a heart-shaped face, hypnotic eyes. She was wearing a leather biker jacket over a white T-shirt that hugged her breasts. He managed to croak, 'Sure.'

She sat down opposite him. 'Thanks.' Her voice was soft and southern, from someplace like Alabama or Georgia. 'I'm Cindy.'

1

'Are you an angel?' he asked.

And she'd laughed, the sweetest laugh he'd ever heard.

'Well . . .' was all she said.

That night, during which she bought him several beers, shrugging off his half-hearted protests, he told her his pathetic story. About coming to LA to be a rock star, about how the band never took off and his bandmates had either drifted into regular employment or embraced drugs and booze, leaving him to his own addiction.

Not alcohol. Not smack. No, he got dizzy from the spin of the roulette wheel, the whirl of the slots, the roll of the dice. The weekend after the band finally broke up, he'd taken off to Vegas and hadn't surfaced until he'd lost everything, emerging in a daze into the desert heat without a cent left to his name.

It had been the same for years. Everything he earned, he threw away in Vegas, driving to Nevada with that sick feeling deep inside him, the itch he had to scratch. But Lady Luck never favoured him. She'd tease him, sure, then snatch it all away.

He told Cindy all this, his eyes stinging with the shame of it, and she reached across the table and stroked the back of his hand with long gold-painted fingernails. Her own eyes were wide and shining with compassion, but she kept smiling.

'You can be saved, John Tucker,' she said. 'All you need to do is open your heart.' She squeezed his hand and leaned forward, dipped her face coyly and looked up at him through her lashes. 'Will you come with me, John? I feel like you shouldn't be alone tonight.'

2

They had left the Capitol Hotel bar around midnight. In the parking lot, John had whistled when Cindy opened the door of a gleaming white Porsche Cayman. He moved to open the passenger door but Cindy shook her head. 'Take your car and follow. Don't worry, I'm gonna to take it nice and slow.'

The way she looked at him as she said this made him wobbly with lust.

He'd followed her for two whole hours along the highway until, finally, she'd pulled up to the gates of a large house. All the lights were off so he couldn't see well with only starlight to go by, but it looked like some kind of ranch house. The kind of place he'd expect a woman who drove a Porsche to live.

She opened the gates and he followed her through. When the cars drew to a standstill all he could hear was the throbbing of crickets and his own heartbeat. Cindy opened the door of his car and leaned inside, putting her hands behind his head. He thought she was going to pull him into a kiss. Instead, she tied a blindfold around his eyes.

'What's this?' he asked, excited.

'Shush . . .' She took him by the hand and led him across a crunchy path and into the house. All was silent. She steadied him as she led him up a staircase, then he heard a door open with the faintest creak, then shut behind them.

'Can I take this off now?' he asked.

She put her finger to his lips. He tried to put his arms around her, to grab her butt and press himself

3

against her, but she slipped out of his embrace like a wisp of smoke.

'Cindy?'

'Sleep,' she whispered, and before he could say a word she had gone, closing the door behind her.

Shocked, he pulled off the blindfold. He was in a small room with a single bed. A candle burned on a low table. He tried the door. It was locked. There was a narrow adjoining room that contained nothing but a toilet and a basin. No way out.

He knocked, shouted, tried knocking on the window too. What the fuck was this? Some kind of kinky game?

Or was some guy—Cindy's boyfriend—about to arrive with a gun or a hunting knife?

He felt in his pocket for his cellphone, then remembered he'd left it in the car.

After a while he stopped yelling and sat down on the bed. He didn't feel horny any more. Eventually, he went to sleep.

\*        \*        \*

In the night, he thought he sensed someone standing over him, felt something on his face. But when he opened his eyes, there was no one there. Just the locked door.

\*        \*        \*

When he woke up, there was a basket of food on the floor: fresh bread and fruit, a pitcher of OJ. He ate and drank greedily. Then he banged on the door again, not really expecting anyone to answer.

4

But within seconds, Cindy stood before him, as beautiful as he remembered.

'What in hell is going on here?' he demanded, but she simply smiled that beatific smile of hers and said, 'Relax, John. You're here to rest. To get better.'

'But I'm not sick,' he protested. 'There's nothing wrong with me.'

She shook her head like that was the saddest, most misguided thing she'd ever heard.

Then she'd sat with him for an hour, talking to him, soothing him with words that he was barely listening to. He was too busy staring at her, aching to touch her creamy skin, to stroke that hair. Aching to fuck her. He felt like a teenage boy on a first date.

But she wouldn't let him touch her. After that hour, she went away. Later, she came back with another tray of food, which she set on the floor before leaving without a word. He banged on the door some more but nobody came.

This pattern continued for three days. Evenings alone in the room, going mad with his thoughts, before crashing out on the bed. Fresh food and drink left by his door. And that sense, in the night, of someone standing over his bed.

On the morning of the third day, he awoke with a scratch in his throat and a different kind of ache that made his skin shiver and feel sore to the touch. His head hurt too, and he kept sneezing.

He tried knocking on the door but he felt too rough. He wanted to go back to bed.

Funny, he'd thought as he lay down, if my life wasn't so shit maybe I'd be busting my balls trying to get out of here. But he actually liked it here—

5

especially the hour when Cindy came and sat with him. It was a kind of instant Stockholm syndrome.

And then, that evening, she came and told him it was time to leave.

'What?' he asked, sniffing.

'You'll be better now,' she said.

'What the fuck are you talking about?'

Then she held out the money. Five hundred bucks. He looked at it like a dog eyeing a steak.

She put the blindfold back on him and led him down the stairs. He had a feeling there were other people around, could hear them breathing. But by the time he was seated in his car, and Cindy removed the blindfold, the door was shut and there was nobody in sight.

'Go, John Tucker,' she said, pressing the money into his hand.

'Come with me?' he asked, though he knew she would say no.

'*Om Shanti*, John.'

\*       \*       \*

The highway was dark, the moon full overhead. One day, he guessed, he'd look back at this strange episode and laugh. For now, though, he only felt confused and sick. He wanted to get back to LA, find a beer and a bed. Maybe rent himself one of those crack whores to unleash his frustration on. He turned up the radio when an old Nirvana tune came on. Then he saw the sign.

## EEL CREEK RESERVATION AND CASINO.
## 1 mile.

Like an alcoholic watching whisky splash into a tumbler, the compulsion hit him in the gut.

*Casino.*

He'd been to casinos on Indian reservations before. They were a poor substitute for the Class A drug that was Vegas, but they were still places where men like him could change their lives with one stroke of luck, one clever play.

He became acutely aware of the five hundred dollars burning in his pocket.

No, he told himself. Keep driving. Get to LA, get yourself holed up, you're going to need that money. It's all you have.

But the itch had started. By the time he was only half a mile from the reservation, his whole body was crawling with it. Surely, whispered the devil on his shoulder, there's no harm in dropping in, seeing what it's like? He could set himself a limit of fifty dollars, leave the rest locked in the glovebox.

Here was the turning. The moment to decide. He sneezed yet again. Didn't he deserve some pleasure, some fun, especially when he was feeling so lousy, after spending half a week imprisoned in a tiny room? Just a couple of spins of the roulette wheel and then he'd be out of there. There was no harm in it.

He signalled right.

\*     \*     \*

He entered the casino with the whole five hundred dollars in his pocket. He wasn't going to spend it all though, no way. Besides, he felt lucky tonight. He was tingling.

7

Bored staff looked him over coolly as he passed into the dark interior of the casino, the electronic clatter of the slot machines making the tingles turn to tremors.

He paused by a slot machine, where an obese woman sat in a motorised wheelchair, joylessly feeding coin after coin into its hungry mouth. Across the other side of the dim room lay the object of his desire. He strode over, trying to ignore the scratching in his throat, the heat around his temples. Since getting out of the car and into the air-conditioned building, his flu had felt considerably worse. But, fuck it. Nothing was going to stop him enjoying tonight.

The dealer at the roulette table was a tall, good-looking Indian guy of about thirty. He looked impassively at John as he took a seat. A waitress came over and took his order, JD on the rocks.

'Evening, sir,' said the dealer.

'Evening.'

John exchanged one hundred dollars for chips. As he handed over the cash, he sneezed, spraying the dealer with spittle.

'Shit, I'm sorry, dude.'

The dealer blinked but didn't show any emotion. John sipped his drink, the burn of the whisky easing the soreness in his throat, thought about his strategy, and ended up doing what he always did.

Bet on black.

\*       \*       \*

Two hours later, he emerged from the casino in a daze. He felt hot and dizzy. His nose was blocked

8

and his throat burned like he'd swallowed a razor. His skin was damp and clammy and his head was pounding.

But he didn't give a damn.

He unlocked his car and flopped on to the front seat, pulling the wad of dollars from his jeans pocket. He couldn't believe it. He'd walked into the casino a broke bum and come out, if not a tycoon, then considerably richer.

Five thousand bucks. He'd got back ten times his stake. He'd never been so lucky in his whole miserable life. The ball kept falling on black, black, black again.

It was freaking unbelievable.

He let out a hoarse whoop that turned into a cough. With this money he could set himself up in LA, get a place, a job, actually do something with his life. Screw you, Cindy. John Tucker didn't need you.

Tomorrow, his new life would begin. But right now, he needed somewhere to crash. The Capitol Hotel was a ninety-minute drive away. A good night's rest there and he'd be raring to go in the morning.

He put the five thousand in the glovebox and locked it, pausing a moment to stroke the cash and murmur a final, '*Un*believable.'

*          *          *

Tucker never made it back to the Capitol Hotel. Nine days later he was found in a boarded-up deserted diner on the outskirts of LA. Too sick to face the gridlock of the city or to find a motel, he'd managed to break in through a window at the rear of the building, presumably to use the facilities—which had been well and truly utilised—Tucker had covered every inch of it with his bodily functions: toilet, basin, tiled floor, mirrored walls, before the final seizure that ended his life. A highway patrolman called Michael Vane who had spotted Tucker's abandoned car found him dead on the floor, fifty-dollar bills glued with bubbles of black matter to the tiles around him, and the green skin of his cheeks stretched in a taut rictus of agony over his face. Flies buzzed around the cadaver; one landed on Vane's face, on his lip, and he batted it away with disgust.

As he pulled out his radio to call for assistance, Vane paused. There were more fifty-dollar bills scattered beside the body, some of them splattered with drops of mucus but most of them clean. He quickly counted the notes: just under five thousand dollars.

Vane, who had debts close to that amount and a pregnant wife, thought about it for a minute. Nobody knew he was here. Nobody need ever know he'd found this poor bastard. Heart pounding, he stuffed the dollar bills into his pockets, including some of the stained ones. He slipped out of the building, checking to make sure there was nobody around to see him sneak back to his patrol car, trying his hardest to shake off the sight of the corpse and ignore the rank smell that wafted from the diner. Before heading back to the precinct he would first go home, hide the money in his closet.

And so he left, headed onto the freeway, nauseous and blissfully ignorant of the death sentence he had imposed upon not only himself and his pregnant wife but many of his Highway Patrol

10

colleagues; a death sentence that they in turn would spread into the air, like the noise from the siren on their patrol cars, into the great, shining city of angels.

# 1

A poster on the door read: TODAY 7 P.M.—
THE FACULTY OF SCIENCE PRESENTS
A FREE LECTURE—'A NEW BREED OF
AIRBORNE VIRUSES: THE STUFF OF SCI-FI
OR A REAL AND PRESENT DANGER TO US
ALL?' GUEST SPEAKER: DR KATE MADDOX
FROM OXFORD UNIVERSITY.

MI6 officer Jason Harley had intended to wait
outside for her, but heavy rain had begun to splatter
the pavement around him, and was already starting
to soak into the shoulders of his suede jacket. He'd
had to park his elderly Jaguar too far away to be
able to sit inside and listen to cricket on the radio;
not without the risk of missing her, at least, so he
pulled his baseball cap—part rain protection, but
mostly male-pattern baldness disguise—lower over
his forehead and went in.

It was warm and dark in the lecture theatre with
forty or so students in attendance, many of them
pecking away on mobile phones or laptops. As
Harley climbed the stairs to slide into the back row
of raked seating, he noticed that most of the screens
displayed social networking sites and games. He
couldn't prevent a quiet but judgmental sort of tut
slipping out at their seemingly total lack of interest.
Why bother to show up if you were going to sit and
play Angry Birds instead of listening?

'Of course, what is of primary concern to us
virologists is the *way* in which West Nile disease is

13

transmitted. It's not airborne, as I'm sure you know, and therefore not strictly relevant to my lecture today, but I'll talk about it for a few minutes, because it's really fascinating . . .'

The speaker was a slim woman with long, shiny brown hair and a mid-Atlantic accent. She stood on the stage with her back to the audience, and Harley admired her high heels and tight pencil skirt as she pointed to a PowerPoint slide of the map of the world, dotted in various locations with outsize illustrations of mosquitoes, their long thin legs dangling like a toddler's faint scribbles. Kate Maddox, he thought, you are damn lucky to be alive.

'Mosquitoes become infected after feeding on virus-carrying birds, such as crows, and the mosquitoes can then infect humans . . .'

He wondered if she remembered him. He was pretty sure that his appearance would not be a welcome one, especially when he explained why he'd been sent to talk to her.

'. . . and this map shows the increase of West Nile encephalitis in the Western world in the last decade . . .'

Kate turned back round to face her audience, and it struck Harley how beautiful she was. She was unrecognisable as the wild-eyed woman she'd been two years previously, when he'd first seen her during the raid on a lab, the secret HQ of a criminal virologist named Gaunt. Kate and her boyfriend Paul had been held prisoner there, a fate doubly painful to her, in the knowledge that her little boy had just been sent out into the world with a deadly virus. It had been a frantic race against time to get them out, find the antivirus—and then find her son,

14

Jack.

'One biotech company has found that blocking angiotensin II can treat the "cytokine storm" of West Nile virus encephalitis—and, even more exciting, of other viruses too. The potential of this is enormous, and I feel we scientists are getting close to developing a vaccine that will work on a variety of strains of similar mosquito-borne viruses.'

A fleeting look of anxiety passed across Dr Maddox's features as she talked, clearly noticing the students shifting in their seats, playing games on their phones, or whispering, but it was so brief that Harley was probably the only one to notice it.

She's losing them, he thought, half sympathetically, half curious to see how she would react. He watched her closely as she pushed back her shoulders and inhaled deeply. A subtle movement, but one that denoted a gathering of control. Harley recalled the last time they'd met: at the funeral of the poor bastard killed in the same lab raid. Stephen Wilson, Paul's twin brother. A weird one, as they all thought Stephen had died years earlier anyway, in a fire. Must have been like burying a ghost. Harley remembered a blistering hot day, with the floral tributes already withering on the grave. Not much body left to bury—the virus had turned it to purée within minutes of being unleashed. He shivered.

'But it's the lab-manufactured ones we need to be more concerned about. "Designer" viruses, created to cause havoc, that could quite conceivably wipe out whole continents if they got into the wrong hands—or rather, remained in the wrong hands.'

The students stopped fidgeting and visibly sat up straighter, as did Harley, even though he was well

15

aware of the facts already. A heavily tattooed boy near the front whistled softly.

'Seriously? So that shit really does go on?'

Dr Maddox smiled at him. 'I shouldn't say that kind of thing—walls have ears, ha ha! But take haemorrhagic viruses, for example, my primary area of expertise. My partner, Dr Isaac Larter—some of you may have heard of him, he's extremely well-known in his field—and I have been studying one particularly virulent strain for years, the Watoto virus, which is similar to Ebola but airborne, making it easier to transmit. Its origins are natural—the word Watoto means "child" in Swahili, as its first victims tend to be children—and there have been several breakouts in West Africa. Fortunately these have been restricted to remote and contained areas, but we always have to be on the lookout for shifts in its genetic make-up. And you may have heard of the recent case in which two sets of researchers found a way to make bird flu infectious through airborne transmission— which could ultimately wipe out half the human race. Because of the fear of bioterrorists stealing the virus, or the new strain escaping from a lab, the researchers agreed to stop research . . .'

\*       \*       \*

Kate Maddox looked out at the now rapt, if slightly blurry faces in front of her. She intentionally never wore her glasses to give lectures, as a means of not allowing herself to get intimidated by her audience—public speaking had never been her strong suit, although she knew it came with the

16

territory. She hadn't needed her specs, though, to discern that they'd been rapidly losing interest up until this point.

Phew, she thought. Got 'em back again. A mention of the threat of global annihilation usually did the trick. This lecture was proving hard work, though. She wished she could be back in the lab in Oxford, bantering with Isaac—her 'work husband' as Paul referred to him, without rancour, for Isaac was a good friend to Paul as well as to Kate. We must have him and Shelley round soon, Kate thought, as she talked through the grisly symptoms of Influenza A virus, subtype H1N1. It's our turn to cook them dinner. Isaac was in the US at the moment, at the big immunology conference, rubbing shoulders with many of the top researchers in the field. Kate was supposed to be there too— had even booked her ticket—but last week Jack, ironically, had come down with chickenpox. He was fine now, just a bit spotty. He'd been lucky and hadn't suffered too much, but Kate hadn't wanted to leave him.

She spoke for another half an hour, until her voice became croaky and her legs ached with the tension. Isaac can bloody well do the next one, she thought, and next time I'll be the one who gets to swan off to a conference in California.

The university was a four-hour journey from her home in Oxfordshire, and she was glad she'd had the foresight to ask them to book her into the local Travelodge. She was looking forward to a large drink and to kicking off the high heels that were making her feet cramp up.

'Well,' she said briskly, 'we're out of time, so I will leave you all to start building your bunkers and never venturing outside again without face masks and biohazard suits on.'

Polite laughter ensued, and the same short, hirsute professor who'd introduced her shambled back on to the stage to thank her and lead a half-hearted round of applause.

As the students filed out, Kate started putting away her laptop. The professor sidled up to her, scratching his beard. He was a full head shorter than her, and seemed to address his comments to her briefcase. Kate thought he looked as though he lived in Middle Earth.

'Wondered if you would like to, er, come for a coffee, Dr Maddox? I would love to discuss your research into the Watoto virus in more detail. It's absolutely fascinating. I could give you a lift?'

Kate had a brief image of them getting on the back of a donkey tethered to the railings outside, the professor with all his possessions tied in a handkerchief to a knotted ash stave that he carried over his shoulder.

'Thank you so much for having me, but I'm actually really tired—and anyway my car is—*oh*!'

Her hand flew to her mouth as she suddenly recognised the remaining person in the lecture theatre, a stocky man in a baseball cap and tatty suede jacket. For a moment she thought her legs were going to give way, and a multitude of emotions and memories flooded through her: this man had been there as she'd looked through the porthole door of the lab and seen the bodies of Stephen and Dr Gaunt locked in there, writhing and dissolving into a pool of black blood on the floor before her eyes, instant victims of Pandora, one of the most deadly viruses on the planet. Then the despair of knowing that the one vial of antivirus that could save her son was also in the same room . . .

What on earth was he doing here now?

# 2

'You remember me, don't you, Kate?' asked Harley, holding out his hand. 'I'm sorry, I didn't mean to shock you. But I wondered if we could have a word, if you're not busy.'

Although outwardly she retained her composure, Kate had turned pale. She shook his hand, and he felt the smooth contact of her skin. 'Yes, of course I remember you. I'm terrible with names, though . . .?'

'Jason Harley,' he said, holding her hand a second too long. The professor looked distinctly annoyed.

'Is everything all right, Dr Maddox?'

'Thank you, Professor, it's fine. This gentleman is an, um, old colleague of mine. And thank you again for hosting the lecture. I do hope your students enjoyed it.' She turned back to Harley, somewhat reluctantly. 'Let's go for a drink, then.'

They drove in convoy out of the campus, Harley following Kate in her shabby red Golf. He could see her eyes darting anxious glimpses at him in the rear-view mirror when they stopped at traffic lights, and felt sorry for her. She pulled into the car park of the nearest pub, and he parked next to her.

'I can't stay long,' she said as she got out and locked the door. It was still raining, more persistently now.

19

'I won't keep you.'

Once they were sitting across from one another on slippery leather sofas in a deserted corner, a glass of Scotch in front of each of them, Harley opened his mouth to explain.

Kate interrupted him before he got the words out. 'Are you here to give me a warning because I mentioned the threat of bioterrorism? I mean, I didn't think that would contravene the Official Secrets Act, I'm really sorry, but everyone knows that it's a danger, look at the anthrax attacks, it's common knowledge—'

He held up a hand. 'That's not why I'm here. Although it's a good thing you didn't mention Gaunt, or the Pandora virus—as you know, we prefer that those particular topics don't become common knowledge . . .' He didn't want to let on to her that his colleagues had kept her and Paul under surveillance for the past two years, and they would certainly have known about it had either of them ever let anything slip.

'Oh. Good. I don't ever. Trust me. So why are you here?'

'I'll tell you, if you'll let me.' He smiled as he said it, trying to put her at ease. A strand of slightly damp hair twisted down below her collarbone, and he felt an urge to reach out and tweak it, before upbraiding himself for behaving like a lovelorn schoolboy. It was clearly too long since he'd had a girlfriend.

'We need your help.'

'Me?' She looked away, but her instant reluctance was imprinted all over her features. You'd make a lousy spy, Dr Maddox, thought Harley, amused.

20

'A situation has arisen in the US. California, to be precise. A new strain of virus that we haven't seen before. It's known as Indian flu, because it has broken out in a Native American reservation.'

Kate nodded and took a big swig of whisky, her interest immediately piqued.

'It's nasty. Really nasty. The first victim was thirty years old, fit, no underlying health issues. He got up one morning, complained to his wife that he had a sore throat and a runny nose. Went to his job on the reservation and apparently spent the whole shift sneezing over his co-workers, so they sent him home. Three days later, he was dead.'

'Go on.'

'A few days after that, his wife was dead too, along with three other people who worked with him. They've contained it, though. The whole reservation has been quarantined, no one in or out. There are no reported cases outside of it, so it seems it's under control.'

Harley felt uncomfortable, misleading Kate in this way, but he had his orders: to recruit her to the team using any means he could, whether ethical or not. If he told her that the first victim worked in a casino, that several men who had been at that casino had died or were in intensive care and that the virus had spread beyond the reservation, she would be immediately aware of the risk faced by any visitor to California.

'What kind of virus is it?'

'I'm not a scientist, Kate. But from what I understand it's a new strain of Watoto.'

Kate's glass almost slipped from her grasp. 'Watoto? In America? Why haven't I heard about this?'

21

'Because the US authorities are keeping it quiet at the moment. They don't want to panic anyone. Anyway,' he lied, 'like I said, it's not too serious, because it's contained. Thank God it didn't break out in Manhattan . . . My brief is to help the World Health Organization put together a team to create a vaccine in case of future outbreaks.'

'Easier said than done. I've been trying to find a vaccine for Watoto for fifteen years.'

'But with very limited resources, am I right? Now Watoto is seen as a . . . potential threat to the West, things are different. We're assembling this team, to be based out in California at a state-of-the-art lab, the best equipment, money no object. All the top brass in your field. Well—not quite all of them. They want you to join them too.'

'What?'

Harley repeated it in a level voice. 'They—we—want you to fly out there and join the team. As soon as possible. They need you. You're one of the world's leading experts on Watoto. You had it. You survived. You've spent years researching it. The WHO contacted MI6 and asked us to recruit you.' Another lie. But he knew she would never agree if she knew the whole truth.

*       *       *

Kate felt numb. Twice in her life she had almost been killed by a virus—Watoto itself and, at the Cold Research Unit, a mutated version of it that Gaunt had created. Two years ago she had discovered the truth about that, almost died at the hands of a psychopath and, worse, almost lost Jack.

22

She was still recovering from the trauma, seeing a therapist, the weekly reassurance of steepled fingers across a coffee table and the soft pull of tissues from the box next to her when her emotions spilled out; trying to live a 'normal' village life, growing odd-shaped vegetables, three-legged races at Jack's school sports day, hay fever, nights out in the local pub with Isaac and Shelley and the local farmers. And now she was being asked to disrupt her life again and fly across the world.

She shook her head. 'I can't. What about Jack? He's finally settled in his new school in the village. He's made friends. So have we. And what about Paul? I can't leave them both here, there's no way—'

'It sounds to me like you're making excuses. If that's the real reason you don't want to do this then they can both come with you.'

Kate stared at him incredulously. 'An epidemic of a highly infectious deadly disease has broken out. Even if it's contained within this reservation, I wouldn't want Jack anywhere near there.'

'Like I said, it's contained. But if you're worried, Jack could stay in the UK, with your sister, perhaps?'

She shook her head. 'Out of the question. Miranda's husband's recently left her, and Jack managed to give both her kids his chickenpox. She can't cope as it is.'

'What about taking him to Boston? That's where his dad lives, isn't it? It's completely safe on the East Coast.'

'No, he's moved, he got a new job at the University of Dallas.'

'Dallas is fine. Besides it's not going to be for

23

ever, Kate, probably a few weeks at most. I'll be coming too—I can't give you all the details until you agree, but a number of agencies are working alongside the WHO to respond to outbreaks like this.'

Kate was puzzled. She knew that serious epidemics and pandemics came under the auspices of GOARN, the Global Outbreak Alert and Response Network, which was part of the World Health Organization. This unit was made up of various UN branches, the Red Cross and other non-government bodies. Why were MI6 involved?

'We need you, Kate.'

She shook her head. 'We've only just got back into a normal routine. No, I'm sorry, it's absolutely impossible. I'd love to go, and be part of the team that could finally crack Watoto—but I can't. Please don't ask me again. I'll do what I can to help—I can put my research on hold here and work with the team via Skype, or whatever—but I'm not going out there.'

Kate rubbed her finger and thumb into her eyes, squeezing so hard that she saw stars. Once the black spots had cleared, she saw Harley gazing at her, not in an antagonistic way, but thoughtfully, patiently, as if he was waiting for her to say, *'Oops, did I say no? I meant yes, of course. Let's go.'*

That chilled her, somehow more than if he'd insisted. She had a horrible feeling that saying no wasn't really an option.

## 3

### OXFORDSHIRE

*This* is normality, thought Kate the next day as she stood in the rain at the school gates. Her son was often the first one out, tumbling through the doors with his hair sticking up in a tuft at the front, knees grimy and shirt buttoned up the wrong way.

Since Harley's visit the night before, she hadn't been able to think about anything except his offer. Her gut instinct had been to say no. After everything she'd been through, she craved a settled life for her family. She didn't want to drag Jack halfway across the world, or leave him behind and make him feel as if she was abandoning him. But this was Watoto, which she saw as a personal enemy, and if she said yes, she would suddenly have unlimited research resources, and the chance of making the final breakthrough that she and Isaac had been working towards, on and off, for so many years. Then she tried to imagine how she would feel if the team of scientists managed to come up with an effective vaccine for the virus without her involvement—but equally quickly dismissed the thought as selfish.

Her thoughts were interrupted by a gentle poke in her side from the point of an umbrella. 'Hello, you,' said a voice.

'Shelley, hi!' Kate hugged her friend. 'How are you? How's Isaac getting on at the conference?'

'Good, I think. We Skyped last night. He claims that he misses me madly, but you know Isaac, he's

25

such a boffin. He can't get enough of research papers and keynote speeches and whatever else they do at these things. But he was so sweet, you know: before he left, he wrote "I love you" in jellybeans on my pillow. Good thing that Callum didn't spot it, otherwise all I'd have had left would have been an "o" or a "v"—if that!'

'Ah, that's really romantic. He should give Paul a few lessons. He's so unromantic it's not even funny.'

Shelley's blonde hair was all over her face, a shifting mass of curls. She pushed them back from cheeks reddened by the wind. 'Paul adores you.'

'I know,' said Kate. 'At least I think I do. He keeps proposing to me, so he must do—I wish he'd be a bit more demonstrative sometimes, that's all.'

Shelley put her head to one side. 'I'd say a proposal was a pretty demonstrative gesture, wouldn't you?'

Kate laughed, realising how contrary she sounded. 'It's hard to explain. Maybe I'm being paranoid, but it's like he proposes because he thinks he should, rather than because he desperately wants to marry me . . .'

'You're being paranoid, you daft cow,' Shelley said, smiling at her.

Kate thought she was probably right. She was looking forward to seeing Paul again, after the night away, but this was tempered by the prospect of his reaction when she told him about Harley's visit. What if Paul wanted them all to go? He'd probably give her a lecture about her duty to protect the public. And, thought Kate, he'd be right to. I *do* have a duty.

She must have looked worried again, because Shelley put a hand on her arm. 'Everything OK,

26

Kate?'

'Oh, I'm fine . . . It's nothing much. Just a boring work thing. Look, here comes trouble.' She raised her voice so that Jack could hear, as he came pelting through the puddles to fling himself into her arms. He still had a couple of chickenpox scabs but had quickly bounced back to his old self.

'Mummy!' he cried ecstatically, as though she'd been away for a month instead of one night. 'I missed you so much!'

She swung him around, laughing as she kissed his pink cheeks and felt the joy of his sturdy little eight-year-old body in her arms. Having a duty to protect the public was one thing—but what about her duty to protect her son? She'd already failed at that once, and vowed she'd never let him down again.

'Can Callum come round to play battles?' he asked, pretending to punch Callum in the stomach. Callum stood next to his own mother, holding her hand. He was shy, small and blond like Shelley, and so different from the stocky Jack. He giggled and feigned doubling up at Jack's swipe, then whispered in Shelley's ear.

'Callum wants Jack to come over to us instead,' Shelley said, straightening up. 'Is that OK with you, Kate? He can stay for tea.'

Jack and Callum both cheered.

Kate hesitated. She'd missed Jack and would have preferred him to be at home with her—but she also really needed to talk to Paul when he got home from work, and it would be difficult with two noisy boys charging around the place with wooden swords and shields. 'I'll pick him up about seven, then,' she said, hugging Jack. 'Be good, sweetheart.'

27

Kate walked back down the lane from the school, keeping an eye out for the water-filled potholes, her head down to shield her face from the brisk unseasonal wind. She unlatched and swung open the five-barred gate of their rented cottage. Paul's car wasn't there, and she cursed softly under her breath. He had been out all day at a client's office in Newbury, trying to help them identify the source of a computer virus that had wiped out half their data, and his phone was switched off. *Come home, Paul, I need to talk to you*, she implored the empty space on the gravel. Why did he switch off his phone when she had asked him so many times not to?

Leaving the gate open for him, she put down Jack's book bag and searched in her pockets for the house keys. She gazed up at the house as she rummaged. It was a beautiful, half-timbered, thatched country cottage. 'Looks like it should be on a jigsaw,' Paul had said when they first saw it. If it was a jigsaw though, she thought, it would have a few pieces missing—one of the thatch's eaves had a chewed sort of appearance, and one of the shutters at the front window was hanging off. Still, they loved it. It felt like home.

Kate let herself in to the living room. The huge stone fireplace that dominated the room looked cold and uninviting with the dead ashes of yesterday's fire still in the grate. *Ridiculous weather*, she thought, *lighting fires, in June?* Imagining with longing the sensation of hot sun on her skin, she went into the kitchen and flicked the kettle on, but even as she was reaching for the teabags, changed her mind and uncorked a half-drunk bottle of Merlot instead. Pouring herself a large glass, she went back into the living room and was sinking into a faded pink armchair when she heard Paul's car rolling onto the driveway.

A moment later he came in, ducking to avoid the low wooden doorframe. His face lit up when he saw her.

'Hi, angel,' he said, coming over to kiss her. He was stubbly, with the dark circles under his eyes that he always got after sitting in front of a computer screen all day. 'How did the lecture go?'

'Not bad,' she said. 'Bit of a tough gig. But there's something—'

'Where's Jack?' he interrupted, calling back over his shoulder as he went to pour himself a glass of wine. He took a deep gulp, then came up behind Kate and slid his arms round her neck, nuzzling her hair, the glass held precariously, its ruby contents tipping dangerously towards Kate's lap.

'Gone to play with Callum. Shelley's going to give them tea. Which is good, because I need—'

'*Me*. That's what you need. Because I need you, and—'

'Paul! Listen, please. Something's happened. Sit down.'

'What?' He sat down on the sofa next to her, scanning her face with alarm.

'That agent guy turned up at my lecture.'

Paul looked puzzled. 'The *lettings* agent? Short bloke with the hairdresser's car?'

'Oh, for heaven's sake. Not him. Harley, the MI6 guy. The one who was there when . . .' She couldn't say it. *When Jack nearly died. When I nearly died.*

29

'. . . you know . . .'

'Him? Thought we'd seen the last of him. What did he want?'

'Paul, he wants me to go to California. Now. There's a new virus, and they think it's a mutated strain of Watoto. People are already dying. But it's all been contained so far, on an Indian reservation, and they're keeping it quiet because they don't want to panic everybody. He said they need me to join a team working on it out there, that the lead scientist has asked for me.'

Paul was silent for a moment. Kate looked at his downcast eyes as he stared into the depths of his wineglass. She studied the contours of his face, the sharp planes of his cheek and jaw, so familiar to her years before they had even met. His twin, Stephen, had been the love of her life. For the hundredth time, she looked at Paul and couldn't prevent herself wondering: is it him I love, or still Stephen? She had long ago concluded that it was a question that she neither wanted nor needed to know the answer to. Not yet, anyway, not while things were going smoothly in their lives.

And things had indeed been going smoothly—until Harley showed up.

'If MI6 are involved, they must have formed an inter-agency operation. It must be serious. Have they asked Isaac too?'

'No. At least I don't think so. Perhaps they don't realise how knowledgeable Isaac is on Watoto. It makes sense for us both to go, as research partners.'

'But you're the primary expert. How long would it be for?'

Kate shrugged. 'As long as it takes to find a vaccine, I guess. Or until the powers that be decide it's not a priority any more and the funding runs out. Though Harley said they are throwing unlimited resources at it. Isaac and I are so nearly there—if we were working with other top virologists and had a state-of-the-art lab, maybe, together, we could finally crack it. You know what, I think that'll be my condition: that Harley lets Isaac come too. I might consider it then.'

'Would they let me come with you, do you think? You could be gone for months.'

'Yes, Harley said we could all go . . . if you wanted to come, that is. I'd hate to be out there without you.'

'And what about Jack?'

Kate shuddered. 'I don't know. Jack's been begging to go and stay with Vernon this summer—we could maybe extend his visit? He'd be OK with his dad.'

Paul drained his glass, put it on the coffee table in front of him, and sunk his head into his hands. 'This is a nightmare.'

Kate moved closer to Paul on the sofa, hugging his side and burying her face in his chest. He smelled of that morning's aftershave, and it reassured her. 'I swore to Harley that there's no way I would go, but part of me is saying I can't turn my back on this, not when my being on the team would give them a better shot at preventing a pandemic taking hold. I don't know what to do. But whatever happens, I promise I won't go without you.'

'Why don't you talk to Isaac, get his advice? Maybe they've already asked him, and he said no.'

'He's in San Diego at that conference, remember? He won't be back till Tuesday. But I'm

31

sure he'd have rung me if they'd asked him to go.'

Paul sat up, gently pushing her away so they could face one another, eye to eye. 'Let's be logical about it. Yes, you could make a difference. Yes, it's your field. But listen, they could've asked Isaac, couldn't they, and it sounds like they haven't. You're not the only virologist working in that field. There are others, maybe not as good as you—but others who haven't been through what you've already been through, and who don't have families to think about. It's not fair that they're putting it all on your shoulders. They've already got a team on it out there.'

They talked on, listing pros and cons, sometimes arguing, sometimes rationalising, swinging one way and then the other in the debate. Along the way, Paul lit the fire and Kate made toast and uncorked another bottle of Merlot. Finally Paul opened his laptop and googled 'new virus in California', 'death on Indian reservation', 'new strain of Watoto', and every other permutation he could think of, but nothing came up. Kate gazed into the fire, trying to allow herself to by hypnotised by the flames—anything for a respite from the dilemma whose ramifications were multiplying like a virus in her brain.

'I'd better get Jack,' she said, eventually, checking the time on her mobile. 'I told Shelley I'd pick him up at seven.'

'Want me to go?' asked Paul.

'No, it's OK, thanks. I could do with some air.' The heat from the fire had burned a flush in her cheeks, and Kate suddenly yearned for the cold wind to cool them down. Slipping on her coat and wellies, she set off along the lane into the village.

A weak evening sun briefly struggled through the clouds, gently highlighting hawthorn hedges and the swaying branches of trees overhead until the clouds once more overtook it. The thought of having to leave Jack with his dad for however long it took to develop the vaccine, knowing that could mean anything from six months to a year, was intolerable.

No. I can't do it, she thought. I won't.

But then she wavered, thinking of the thousands of lives that could be saved. Weighing up the opportunity to work in a state-of-the-art lab with resources second to none, money no object . . .

The image of Jack's face when she'd picked him up in the playground flashed into her mind. He was so happy here. A normal little boy again. Nothing, not fame nor fortune nor acclaim, could persuade her to jeopardise that for a second time.

Not even thousands of innocent lives?

Still deep in thought, she rounded the corner of the lane leading to Isaac and Shelley's small but beautiful Georgian manor house, bought as a wreck five years ago and lovingly restored. When she saw what was outside, she stopped in her tracks.

A police car was parked in the driveway. Suddenly, cutting through the evening silence of an English village came the ear-splitting sound of a scream, loud, high and panicked. A scream of primal pain—and it was coming from the house of her best friend.

Kate started to run.

## 4

### SAN DIEGO

Angelica stood in the shadows of an alleyway that ran alongside the Metropolitan Hotel, one of San Diego's finest, the kind of place where senators and rock stars stayed when they were in town. She reached down and patted a knee-high leather boot, just to double-check, touched her auburn wig to make sure it was still neatly in place, and carefully adjusted her designer backpack. She closed her eyes, briefly clasped the obsidian ankh that hung round her neck, and then she was ready.

She waited until the doorman was occupied with another guest, hailing them a taxi, then drifted in through the revolving doors.

It was cool inside the lobby, but busy, women in suits wheeling miniature cases behind them, businessmen barking into BlackBerrys. She stayed away from the front desk, keeping her eyes downcast whenever she passed someone. Angelica had practised this many times: the art of switching that inner light on and off. Revealing her beauty when she needed to dazzle a room or put somebody under a spell, then dimming it, rendering herself almost invisible. It was all about projection, confidence, attitude. Mousy little people naturally scurried through the world without being noticed. She was able to tap into her inner mouse, or reveal the lioness, at will. She avoided eye contact, wore no perfume, thought no sexual thoughts lest she give off pheromones that attracted attention. She was good at this. That was why she was doing this important job herself. Cindy had already played her part well. But this job was going to require far more skill.

Propped on an easel, a sign confirmed what she been looking for:

**INTERNATIONAL CONFERENCE OF
IMMUNOLOGY & VIROLOGY,
Main Ballroom**

A shot of adrenaline raced through her system, but she breathed deeply, staying calm. So many of them here: virologists, academics, doctors, biochemists, representatives of big pharma companies. Most of the top experts in immunology under one roof, from all over the world. She had studied the delegate list in detail and had been thrilled, though not surprised, as it was predestined, to see that her two main targets were here.

They would be in there now, enjoying post-conference drinks, chatting with their fellow academics, perhaps discussing a paper they had read, or where to go for dinner. None of them, yet, would have any inkling of what was to come. As she had foreseen, the authorities were keeping the outbreak under wraps. Part of her would love to stride into the room, get their attention by switching on her inner light and tell them what was on its way—not only today but in the future. She would love to witness the panic, the horror. Because, more than anyone else, the people in that room would understand the threat faced by the world.

And they wouldn't be able to do a thing about it.

35

But she couldn't draw attention to herself, couldn't risk leaving any witnesses who had seen her. She needed to be patient. She took a seat in the lobby, in the shadows near the elevators, and waited.

She only had to wait ten minutes before he appeared: Dr Isaac Larter. He was tall and gangly, balding, the remains of his hair sticking up at crazy angles, with large expressive hands and a grin on his face. He was talking to another man, Japanese perhaps, and they were both laughing as they exited the ballroom. No sign of Dr Maddox. She must be inside. The woman would love to lay eyes on her, see her in the flesh while her flesh was still intact. But she was pleased Larter had come out. It suited her plan perfectly.

For a moment she thought the two men might be heading out together, which would have made things tiresomely complicated, but then Dr Larter lifted a palm to say farewell to the Asian man.

Angelica rose from her seat and followed him towards the elevators, padding silently across the lobby. The elevator doors pinged open as she got there and she stepped in after him. It was just the two of them. More good luck. Not that she believed in luck—everything was going exactly as it was destined.

Larter pulled a BlackBerry from the pocket of his linen jacket and started tapping away on it with his thumb, smiling to himself. Now was the moment for her to step out of her self-imposed shadow and flick the switch that would illuminate this small space. She widened her eyes, licked her lips and pushed out her chest.

'Dr Larter? It is Dr Larter, isn't it?'

He looked up from his phone, curious. He swayed a little—he had clearly had a few glasses of something, which was more good news for her. 'Yes . . . that's me. I don't believe . . .?'

She stuck out her hand, ensuring she made eye contact as he took her hand in his and shook it. She let the handshake linger for a moment longer than was natural.

'Sonia Tyler,' she lied. 'I'm a huge fan . . . I mean admirer of your work.'

'Really?' Her words had the desired effect. Surprised, but flattered. And she was pleased to see him quickly look her up and down, taking in her beauty. He might be happily married, the thought of an affair or even a dalliance while away from his wife far from his mind, but he was not immune to her charms.

'Yes. I'm sorry, I hope I'm not embarrassing you.'

He smiled, showing her a mouthful of crooked teeth. Disgusting. 'Not at all.'

She smiled back, coyly. 'I'm studying immunology at the University of California and writing my thesis on the attempt to find a vaccine for the Watoto virus. Your work is so important and groundbreaking. Your new research paper has really inspired me. I was very excited when I saw your name on the delegate list, but I had no idea I would actually get to speak with you.'

'Well . . .'

She could see how happy the attention and praise made him, but he was lost for words. 'That's marvellous.' He eyed her backpack, no doubt thinking it was full of textbooks. If only he knew the truth.

'I'm so happy that you came all the way to America for this conference.' She meant it. This was destiny in action again.

The elevator glided to a halt and the doors opened. 'Er . . . this is my floor,' he said, clearly disappointed that the conversation was about to end.

'Mine too!' she exclaimed as if this was the most exciting coincidence of her life.

They walked down the corridor together, Dr Larter awkward, her gushing about how she had been reading about a breakthrough in the UK, where they had discovered that antibodies could pass into cells and fight viruses from within. 'It's so exciting. To think we might only be a few years away from cracking the code of how to defeat viruses.'

'Yes,' he agreed. 'It might take years of further research but . . .'

She flung herself forward, as if she had tripped over her own feet, making it look like she had gone down hard on her wrists. Letting out a girlish shriek, she sat up and clutched her left wrist, tears filling her eyes.

He crouched beside her. 'My goodness. Are you all right?'

She blinked up at him. 'My wrist . . . it really hurts. I think I might have broken it.'

'I'm sure . . .'

She interrupted him with a cry. 'Oh, Dr Larter, it really hurts. I need to put some ice on it immediately. I guess if I . . .' she moaned '. . . go downstairs they might be able to help me.'

Men were so predictable. The damsel in distress, the beautiful woman in need of help—especially

38

one who had pumped up his ego with praise—there was no way he would leave her to fend for herself.

'Let me call down for you, get someone to bring up some ice,' he said.

She nodded pathetically. 'That would be . . . so kind. I'll go into my room and wait.'

'No, no, come into my room. I'll call them from there and tell them how urgent it is. Look, here we are.'

He put his arm round her and helped her up, and she made sure to lean into him, to press her warm body against his, so he would feel the swell of her breasts. He produced his keycard and a moment later they were inside. He hurried over to the phone and she reached behind her and locked the door while he wasn't looking. Then pulled a small pistol from her boot.

As he picked up the phone to call the hotel desk, she said in an urgent tone, 'Dr Larter.'

He turned and his mouth fell open. She enjoyed seeing the expression on his face: the shock and confusion.

'Put down the phone,' she commanded, aiming the gun at his forehead.

'What are you doing?'

She stepped towards him. 'Get on the bed,' she said.

He froze. 'Miss Tyler,' he said with a shaking voice. 'I'm only a scientist . . . I don't have any money . . .'

'I said, get on the bed. I have no interest in your fucking money.'

He let out a weird noise, like a squeak, and half-turned. She moved quickly, aiming a kick at his back, sending him crashing into the bedside table, the phone and lamp tumbling to the floor. She grabbed him by his jacket and pushed him on to the bed, straddling him and holding the gun to his temple.

'What do you want?' he asked, trying to stay calm. But his terror and shock were making him shake.

'Take off your jacket and shirt,' she commanded.

'What?'

Confusion flitted across his face, but he obeyed, pulling off his jacket, then unbuttoning his shirt. It was almost funny. Did he think she wanted his body? He had no idea how much he disgusted her, how nauseous his pale, flabby body made her feel.

'Now lie on the bed, and don't move. If you do, I'll shoot you in the balls. Understand?'

He nodded. There were tears in his eyes. Pathetic, how some people crumbled at the first sign of pressure. It astounded her sometimes how weak most people were. If they had been through what she had experienced in her life, they would end up killing themselves or going insane.

She really hoped he didn't soil himself. That would be highly inconvenient. She decided she needed to calm him down.

'I'm not going to hurt you, Dr Larter. So try to relax. Close your eyes, OK?'

He did as she asked, his eyelids flickering like they were resisting his attempts to keep them shut.

She straddled him on the bed, ignoring the smell of alcohol that wafted off him—wondering if, despite his fear, he would grow hard from the feeling of her warm, leather-clad body against his crotch. It had been known to happen. Other men had died with an erection and a smile on their lips.

40

That wasn't going to be Larter's fate, though.

She reached behind her and pulled off her backpack, unzipping the front pocket and producing a syringe that she had already prepared with a colourless, odourless liquid. GHB. She took hold of Isaac's arm and slipped the needle in, injecting the drug directly into a vein before he could pull his arm away.

'What was that?' he asked, alarmed, opening his eyes.

She pointed the gun at his face. 'Close your eyes. It was just something to help you relax. Now, keep quiet.'

She checked her watch. The drug would take effect in fifteen to twenty minutes, leaving Dr Larter intensely drowsy and disorientated. The fact he had already consumed several glasses of alcohol helped. After a while, he stopped trying to open his eyes. He wasn't unconscious but was relaxed, probably feeling as if he was in a dream. His heart rate would have slowed, and beneath the drowsiness he would be experiencing a mild euphoria. He was in the perfect state for what she needed to do.

'Don't go to sleep, Dr Larter,' she whispered.

A smile appeared on his lips.

'I need you to sit up, OK?'

Again, he obeyed. 'Good boy,' she said. Then she unzipped the main compartment of her backpack.

*     *     *

A little while later, Angelica led Isaac out of the room. She had put his shirt and jacket back on,

41

buttoning the jacket across his belly. She held him by the crook of his arm, leading him slowly down the corridor towards the elevator. To anyone who might pass, he would look like a drunk being helped along by, well, she probably looked like a call girl.

They took the elevator back to the ground floor and she walked him over to the ballroom. Isaac barely seemed to register where he was or what was happening. But he was still smiling faintly.

She took him inside. The drinks reception was in full swing, lots of middle-aged men and women standing around in groups of three or four, chatting, pontificating, exchanging views and business cards. She looked around for Kate Maddox, whose photo she had found online, but there was no sign of her. No matter.

She sat Isaac down on a chair near the centre of the room.

A heavyset man standing nearby grinned at them.

'He's had too much to drink,' she said. 'But he insists he doesn't want to go to bed . . . again.'

The man guffawed at that and she winked at him. It didn't matter that he'd had a very good look at her face.

'Do you mind keeping an eye on him while I go to the ladies' room?' she asked. 'I won't be long.'

'No problem, sweetcheeks,' the man said, clearly wondering if he could take a turn at hiring her.

She walked out of the reception and all the way out of the hotel, back out through the revolving doors. Striding briskly away, she covered three blocks until she found her car, the sleek white Maserati, where she had parked it. She brushed aside the two Hispanic men who had stopped to admire it, whistling as they watched her climb inside.

She pulled the cellphone out of her pocket.

While Isaac had been in a semi-conscious state, she had taped three pounds of Semtex around his midriff, then covered it with a bandage. Three pounds of the plastic explosive was enough to destroy a two-storey building. Certainly sufficient to decimate the reception room at the hotel and kill everyone in it.

She thought of Dr Larter, sitting in his chair, the heavyset man probably wondering where she had got to. Larter, in his delirious state, would have no idea that beneath his shirt was the Semtex and a detonator that she could trigger by calling it from her cellphone.

She dialled the magic number now.

And heard the explosion from three blocks away, saw smoke shoot up above the rooftops. She closed her eyes and pictured the flying body parts, the carnage, the balls of flame. She could almost smell it. It made her feel hungry.

Angelica put the car into drive and headed out of the city, thinking about the end of the world.


5


Kate would never forget the sound of Shelley screaming, the sight of her sobbing in the kitchen, clinging to the worktop, her face scrunched up with shock and grief, a policewoman hovering awkwardly beside her. As Kate ran into the kitchen Shelley launched herself at her, pressing her wet face against Kate's neck.

'What is it? Tell me!'

'It's Isaac. There's been a huge terrorist attack, on the hotel he was in! Oh, Kate! My sweet, clever Isaac—he's dead. Oh, how am I going to tell Callum?'

Over the next five minutes, Kate learned that Isaac, her friend and colleague, the man she spent more time with than anyone else, had been blown to bits by an unknown assassin who'd planted Semtex in the hotel ballroom where the post-conference drinks party had been taking place. Thirty-two other eminent virologists and immunologists had also been killed, but further details were sketchy, and the death toll was still rising.

She joined Shelley in an outpouring of grief that made the policewoman and her colleagues step back as if they'd never seen such a raw display of emotion before. And when the boys came in from the field at the back of the house, still brandishing their toy swords, Kate had held Jack whilst Shelley sobbed out the news to Callum that his daddy had died. Shelley had tried so hard to regain her composure, but to no avail. Tears welled in Kate's eyes every time she thought of it.

A growing horror combined with her grief over Isaac: someone had targeted the immunology conference. They were trying to kill people like her. Had it not been for Jack's chickenpox, she would have been in that room with Isaac.

Kate offered to stay the night with Shelley and Callum, but Shelley refused. 'I just want to be alone with Callum,' she'd said, brokenly, hugging Kate as they both wept again. Kate tried to insist, but

Shelley was adamant.

'I'll be back tomorrow morning,' promised Kate, lifting her glasses to wipe her eyes.

As she and Jack hurried home down the lane, her BlackBerry kept bleeping. She disengaged her hand from Jack's, and glanced at the phone's display. Three missed calls from Harley; but the only person she wanted to speak to—apart from Isaac of course—was Paul. When she got back to the cottage, she told Jack he could watch TV for a while instead of having a bath, then went straight into the kitchen where Paul was making dinner.

'Hi, sweetheart, I thought we would have pasta to—' He turned and saw her face. 'Kate, what is it?'

She fell into his arms and sobbed against his chest. He stroked her hair and held her, waiting patiently for her to start breathing normally again so she could tell him what had happened.

He spent the next ten minutes fussing over her, telling her to sit down, asking her over and over if he could do anything, get her anything. She sat at the breakfast bar and stared at her hands. They were trembling. But mostly, she felt numb. Then she remembered.

'I need to call Harley. He's been trying to ring me. Can you see if Jack needs anything while I call him?'

'Sure.' He looked at her with wide eyes. Paul wasn't usually very good with big emotional scenes. He never knew what to say. Anything that didn't require fixing or have a solution flummoxed him. But he had been good friends with Isaac too. He shared her pain—and her fear.

She called the MI6 officer.

'Dr Maddox,' he said, as soon as he answered,

45

'I've been trying to get hold of you. Have you heard . . .?'

'About the bomb? Yes. It's . . . Do you have any idea who did it?'

He paused, as if he was wondering how much he could tell her. 'No, no, we don't. No one has claimed responsibility. None of the survivors saw anything, and the room in which the CCTV was recording was on the ground floor and was destroyed in the blast. I'm very sorry about your research partner.'

'I should have been there with him.'

'I know. But luckily for us—'

She interrupted him. 'What do you mean, "for us"?'

'Listen, a lot of top people in your field died in that attack. If you'd been killed too, when you're the leading expert in Watoto . . . It doesn't bear thinking about. Kate, Dr Maddox, we really need you to join this team to find a cure for the virus. Please reconsider.'

'Oh my God,' she said. 'Do you think they are connected? The outbreak and the bomb?' In all the grief and confusion, it hadn't struck her before.

Harley took a breath. 'We had a phone call. A message. An hour after the bomb went off.'

'What did it say?'

Harley recited the message. *'And She sent a plague upon the Earth, a plague born in the cradle of mankind, and those who would stand in Her way were consumed by the fire of Her wrath. None should dare stand in Her way.'*

'Is that it?'

'Yes.'

'And you think it's genuine?'

46

'We're taking it seriously, yes.'

'Can't you trace these things?'

'The call was made from a throwaway mobile phone. Impossible to trace.'

'The cradle of mankind,' Kate said, echoing the message. 'That's meant to be in Tanzania, where Watoto originates.'

'Yes.'

She took a sip of the sweet tea Paul had handed her. 'It's a warning, isn't it? Anyone who tries to stop the plague will be killed.' She felt a chill run down her spine.

Harley said, 'I realise that telling you this will probably make you more reluctant to help, but . . .'

'I have a responsibility.'

He made a noise as if he was waiting for her to continue.

'I do have a responsibility. Isaac's already been killed. I knew some of the other scientists at the conference, too. And these terrorists, whoever they are . . . we can't let them win. The virus is only on the Indian reservation at the moment, isn't it?'

Harley hesitated for a moment. 'Yes.'

'But surely the terrorists are going to try and spread it beyond there, if they're threatening a plague?'

'That's why it's even more vital that we find a vaccine as quickly as possible. And why we need you.'

Kate took another sip of tea. She could hear the TV in the other room, the high-pitched blare of a cartoon. She had almost made up her mind. She had to go. If the World Health Organization was now putting its resources into finding a cure, she owed it to Isaac to do everything she could to

47

contribute.

But what about Jack? Did she really want him to accompany her to America, a country that was under threat of a killer virus? Paul too. She herself was immune to the original Watoto virus, but not necessarily a mutated one. She knew Paul would insist on taking the risk, but Jack was a different matter. At least Vernon wasn't anywhere near California. She could give him strict instructions about safety precautions to follow. And at the first hint that the virus was anywhere approaching Texas she would make sure Jack was on the next plane back to the UK, to her sister's.

'Are you still there?' Harley asked.

'Yes. I'm thinking. Let me go and talk to Jack. I'll get back to you in the next hour.'

She terminated the call and walked into the living room, where Jack was sitting cross-legged on the floor, his head tilted backwards and mouth slightly open, far too close to the television. Tears had left pale tracks down his cheeks.

'Jack, I need to ask you something.'

He looked up, slightly annoyed at the interruption of his viewing. She muted the TV and sat down next to him, holding his sticky hand. 'We might have to change the plans for the summer holidays—'

He jumped up, an expression of panic on his face. 'You're not going to tell me I can't go and stay with Dad, are you?'

'No—probably not. In fact, the opposite. All I was going to say was, I've been offered a job in America and I don't know exactly how long it's going to last. It might be a month, which would be ideal because then I can pick you up from Dad's and we could fly home together—but it might be longer than that. Would you be OK with staying at Daddy's for longer, if that's how it works out? I don't want to take the job unless you would.'

'Would I have to go to school in Dallas?'

'I don't know. Unlikely—but it's a possibility. You'd be able to come back to your class here afterwards though.'

'I would miss you,' he said thoughtfully, still staring at the muted cartoon. 'But you know Charlie Freestone in Year 3? He lives half a year with his mum and half a year with his dad. So we could be like that. It's only fair that Daddy gets to see me half the time too. I miss him. And you remember that boy next door I played with last summer—Bradley? I could play with him every day when I'm over there, and go to school with him.' He hugged Kate round the neck. 'Yay! I'm gonna go and Skype Daddy!' His face fell. 'But what about Callum? I can't leave him, his dad's died . . .'

'Shelly just told me they're going to France to stay with his grandma, so he won't be here. You're a great friend for thinking of that.'

'You're a great mummy,' he said. 'Can I turn the volume back up again now?'

Ten minutes later, Kate sent a text to Harley: *OK. I'll do it.*

\*       \*       \*

Three days later, Kate welcomed the gin and tonic brought to her by the almost supernaturally attractive Asian flight attendant, pressing the glass against her forehead before taking a large

49

gulp, then another. She felt as though her alcohol consumption had tripled in the past few days.

Dreading the thought of handing Jack over to his father, she reached across and touched her son's hair. He looked up briefly from the film he was watching on the plane's entertainment system, earphones blocking out the adults' conversation, and smiled, showing the gap between his front teeth.

'I'm going to see Bradley again,' he informed her.

Kate took comfort in the fact that he was so excited about the trip, and about seeing his dad and his friend Bradley, but she felt sick at the thought of him being so far away. Vernon had promised to take some time off work but, while he adored Jack, he had never been the most attentive of fathers. And he had a new girlfriend now, Shirl, although Kate suspected she was hardly as new to the scene as Vernon claimed.

Paul sat beside Kate, looking pale. He had been anxious and restless ever since Harley turned up. The MI6 man's presence had brought back into vivid focus memories of that night two years ago when Paul had looked on helpless as his twin brother sacrificed his own life to stop Gaunt once and for all. As hard it was to believe, there were others, still at liberty, who had shared Gaunt's warped ambitions and engaged in a sick race— or, as Gaunt had called it, 'a delicious intellectual game'—with each other to create the world's deadliest virus. It was a secret competition, with little cells of scientists across the globe taking part.

Immediately after the events at Gaunt's lab, Kate and Paul had been interviewed by Harley, and Kate had told him that she remembered Gaunt talking about someone called Mangold. Harley had raised an eyebrow at that and told them that the name Charles Mangold had been found in papers in Gaunt's office; papers that showed a number of large deposits into Gaunt's bank account.

After that, Paul had spent hours scouring the internet, trying to find Charles Mangold, but there was only so much he could do online. To track down Mangold's current location, Paul would have needed to travel to America, but a criminal record, acquired during his days as a hacker, made this impossible. All he could do was pass on the information to the relevant law enforcement agencies and seethe with frustration when they failed to take it any further, and Harley and his employers appeared to have done nothing about Mangold either, much to Paul's consternation.

It had taken some major string-pulling by Harley to get Paul a visa for this trip, but Kate was glad she'd insisted on him coming too. She kissed Paul's stubbly cheek, drawing a smile.

Jason Harley slipped into the seat across the aisle from them. According to the map on the jumbo jet's TV screens, they were halfway across the Atlantic, the tiny cartoon plane on the monitor edging ever closer to Dallas. Harley had surprised them with seats in First Class, the first time Kate or Paul had ever turned left when getting on a plane.

Paul glanced at Jack to make sure he wasn't able to hear them, then leaned across and demanded: 'So, what do you know about the people who planted the bomb at the hotel? Has no one taken responsibility for it since you got the anonymous message?'

51

Harley winced. 'Please keep your voice down. But no, they haven't.'

Paul dropped his voice. 'Don't you think it's a coincidence that a good percentage of the world's top virologists were murdered shortly after a new killer virus breaks out in America?'

Harley didn't respond.

'What I don't understand is why you spooks were involved in this before the bomb went off, when it was "just" a viral outbreak. I thought that kind of thing was dealt with by the World Health Organization?'

Irritation flitted across Harley's face at the word 'spooks', but he kept his tone neutral. 'That's a fair question. But I can't divulge any more information to a civilian at this point.'

'A civilian? That's a hell of a nice way to put it. You're dragging our family across the globe. The least you can do is tell us what's going on.'

'Please don't raise your voice.'

'Why, because you don't want people to get scared? If some horrific African virus has broken out and someone is blowing up virologists, maybe they should be scared.'

'Paul.' Kate laid her hand on his arm. 'Come on, stay calm. You're going to scare Jack. You're scaring *me*.'

In truth, Jack was oblivious, still glued to a movie, the volume pumped up to block out the roar of the jets that filled the cabin. But she wished Paul wouldn't talk about virologists being blown up. Not when Isaac had been one of the victims, and when she was a virologist herself.

Paul hissed across the aisle to Harley, 'You must have suspected terrorists were involved before the bomb. Otherwise, why were *you* sent to recruit Kate?'

Harley blinked. 'Mr Wilson.'

Paul laughed sarcastically. '"Mr Wilson"? Please, I feel we're close enough for you to call me Paul.'

'Mr Wilson, we are in a public space. We agreed to allow you to come on this trip purely in order to make Ms Maddox happy. Other than the desire to keep Ms Maddox happy, there is nothing to stop me putting you on the first plane home.'

'It's *Doctor* Maddox, actually,' said Paul, with more than a hint of aggression in his voice.

'Oh, for heaven's sake. Call me Kate. But you're not sending Paul home, OK?' Kate interjected.

Harley put his hands up in an international peacekeeping gesture. 'Listen, I'll tell you more when we get to California. I promise. I will tell you everything you need to know.'

6

They landed at Dallas/Fort Worth International Airport in the late afternoon. Kate felt jittery from caffeine and jet lag, and Jack was clingy and grizzling. Probably as much from the back-to-back cartoons on the in-flight entertainment as the prospect of their parting, Kate thought. She hoped so, anyway. It had been a really tough time for Jack. He'd adored Isaac, and it had been confusing and painful for him to witness Callum's anguish. Kate had been proud of him, though, especially when he voluntarily gave Callum his prized Lego Transformer, 'to cheer him up'.

53

Thanks to Harley, they bypassed Customs and Immigration. Clearly there were some advantages to travelling on Agency business. Kate had refused to be parted from her son until she saw with her own eyes that his father was there to take safe delivery of him, so they all made their way to Arrivals. As they passed through the door, Harley fell back, not wanting Vernon to see him and start asking awkward questions.

Vernon was waiting on the other side of the barrier, talking to a skinny seen-better-days bottle blonde in a tight animal-print skirt and scuffed cork-soled wedge sandals. That must be Shirley, thought Kate. He was so engrossed that he failed to register Jack's arrival until his son was right in front of him, jumping up and down, his good mood temporarily restored, shouting 'Daddy!'

'Oh, hey, Jackie-boy, how'ya doing?' he said at last, pausing a second longer to finish his conversation with Shirley. Kate gritted her teeth. Was this how he was going to treat Jack for the whole summer?

'Good, Dad! Can we go and see Bradley later? I sent him an email to say I was coming to visit, and I typed it all by myself!'

Jack ducked under the rope and hugged his father round the waist, and Vernon hugged him back. Shirley ruffled Jack's hair awkwardly, and Jack bestowed on her one of his best fake smiles.

Kate felt mollified by the expression of genuine pleasure on Vernon's face. Then he saw her, and the smile faded considerably.

'Kate. How are you?' He completely ignored Paul, even though they had met on several previous occasions.

'OK, thanks.' Kate didn't know what else to say. She noticed that more hair had retreated from his head, though it seemed to have redistributed itself in his ears, nose and on his chest. He'd put on weight, too. Shirl must be spoiling him, she thought.

'Hi—you must be Shirley,' she said, holding out her hand to the other woman. 'I'm Kate, Jack's mum.'

'Hi, Kate, sure, I guessed,' Shirley said, politely but somewhat frostily, accepting the handshake but dropping Kate's hand as fast as humanly possible.

'So, you're off to save the world?' Vernon still had not made eye contact with Paul.

'Hardly the time to be flippant,' Paul interjected, riled at being so comprehensively blanked. Vernon continued to ignore him. Kate stepped between them.

'Thank you for taking Jack. You will look after him, won't you? Don't let him go near anyone who seems sick,' Kate blurted, earning herself a scornful look from Vernon. 'And if any cases of Watoto are reported in Texas . . .'

'Yes, yes, I'll put him straight on a plane to Miranda's. I got your email instructions, don't worry.'

Shirley suddenly winced and clutched her stomach. 'Excuse me, I have to go to the bathroom,' she blurted, and rushed off in the direction of the Ladies.

Vernon looked embarrassed. 'She's, ah, having a few health problems,' he said.

'Sorry to hear it. But I hope they won't interfere with your ability to do stuff with Jack,' Kate said, and Vernon gave her a scathing look.

'I just want a quick word with him. Privately,' she

said, drawing Jack aside and kneeling down beside him so that they were at eye level. She put her arms round him, breathing in his little-boy smell: shampoo and grime and sweet-sour breath.

'Almost time to go!' she said, injecting a brightness into her voice. 'You still excited about staying with Daddy for the summer?'

She felt him nod vigorously into her shoulder.

'Bradley will be so happy to see you again. I bet he's really missed you. You two will have lots of fun together. Daddy's going to take you to a baseball game, and swimming, and all sorts of great stuff. Oh, and here—I've got something for you.'

She unwrapped one arm and delved into her shoulder bag, bringing out a plastic bag with a box inside. Jack dived into it, and held up the box. 'A new Transformer! Thanks, Mum.' He hugged her again, but his voice sounded suddenly flat.

'I thought you and Bradley could put it together.'

He clung to her more tightly. 'Mum?'

'Yes?'

'You know how someone on purpose blew up Isaac with a bomb?'

Before she could think of something to say to put his mind at ease, Jack continued, his lower lip trembling: 'Don't let Dad see me crying, but I'm really scared, 'cos Callum said his dad was murdered by terrorists who want to kill scientists, and you're a scientist too. What if someone makes a bomb and puts it where you are, and kills you when I'm in Dallas?'

'Oh, Jack,' she said, rocking him gently in her arms. 'We don't know why those people put a bomb in Isaac's hotel. I'm sure it wasn't because he's a scientist. There are thousands and thousands of scientists in the world! It won't happen to me, I promise. Now, promise me you won't worry about it, because I'll be perfectly safe. I've got Paul to look after me.'

'*I* want to look after you,' said Jack sullenly.

'You can send me lots of pictures and things to show me what a good time you're having with Dad, OK? Because that'll cheer me up, and that's a great way to look after someone.'

'OK,' said Jack, wiping his nose on her shoulder. Kate straightened up and led him back to where Vernon and Paul were standing by the barrier, neither of them making the least attempt at conversation. Like bloody children! she thought, but the momentary flash of irritation immediately disappeared, to be replaced by a dull ache in her heart as she kissed her son's smooth cheek and handed him over to his father.

\*     \*     \*

From his vantage point beside the doorway to Arrivals, Harley watched the family saying their goodbyes. He couldn't understand what Kate had ever seen in Vernon Maddox. And he wasn't too impressed with Paul Wilson either. If it had been up to Harley, he would have left Wilson in the UK. The guy was a liability, and undeserving of such a lovely woman.

He had a word with himself. What was he doing, thinking of her as 'lovely' and forming opinions about her personal life? His job was to make sure Kate got to the lab and, unlike Wilson, he wasn't about to let emotion cloud his judgment. Harley prided himself on his rational,

57

professional approach, untainted by prejudice or feeling. Whatever was best for Britain: that was all that mattered. In the course of his career he had encountered things that had shocked him, and that most people would find horrifying or unethical. But if there was a rational case for it, Harley could assimilate anything.

It was what made him such a good MI6 officer. A safe pair of hands.

Without letting Kate and Paul out of his sight, he made for a nearby news kiosk and picked up a couple of packs of chewing gum. Glancing at the newspaper stand beside the cash register, the headline on the *Dallas Morning News* caught his attention. Momentarily forgetting about keeping an eye on Kate, he picked it up, swearing under his breath. The cat was out of the bag.

*OUTBREAK*, screamed the headline. *Killer virus on loose in Los Angeles. Authorities urge citizens 'Don't Panic!'*

Harley dropped a couple of dollars on the counter and exited the kiosk, absorbed by the story, which had pushed the news about the bombing off the front page. The newspaper reported that fifty-nine deaths had been confirmed, with many more cases in hospital. That meant it was spreading through the city even faster than they had feared. He scoured the paper, looking for any suggestion of a link between the bombing and this outbreak. Aside from a passing reference to the bombing now seeming even more unfortunate, 'just when we need virologists the most', no connection had been made. The media didn't know about the message that had been left—not yet anyway.

His cellphone rang.

58

'I take it you're in Dallas?' It was the voice of Nicholas Lepore, Harley's Director.

'Yes, we've—'

'Good, good. Listen. There's been a change of plan . . .'

When Lepore had finished his briefing and ended the call, Harley stood for a moment, wondering if the cold ripple of fear that crept up his back and prickled his armpits was a wholly rational response. He looked over at Kate and Paul. They weren't going to like this. Not one bit.

## 7

'Hey, I'm afraid we're going to have to get a move on. Kate and I have got a plane to catch,' said Paul. 'A private jet, apparently,' he added, unable to resist the chance to gloat. Sometimes Kate wished he and Vernon would just take their shirts off and wrestle, get it out of their systems.

Vernon whistled. 'Jeez, Kate. Since when did you become a VIP?' He turned to Jack: 'Hey, buddy, we should have a helicopter to whizz us back to my place, right?' He chucked Jack's cheek, but the boy looked pale and miserable now that the actual moment of parting was upon them.

Kate bent down to give Jack one final hug, and he clung tightly to her, making her neck wet with his tears.

'Be good, Jack, OK?' she whispered into his ear. 'Have an amazing summer. Do what Daddy tells you. I promise I'll email and call whenever I can.'

'Let's go, Jackie-boy,' Vernon said, as Shirley

returned. He peeled his son's hands off the back of Kate's neck and ruffled his hair. 'You and me and Shirley are gonna have an awesome time, right? I'll take you swimming tomorrow, and that's a promise.'

'Right,' Jack said, in a high quavery voice, unable to take his eyes off Kate. 'Bye, Mummy.'

'Bye, my darling.' She had to speak in a small, tight way to prevent the lump in her throat choking her. 'I love you.'

'Love you too, Mum.'

And he was gone, tears pouring down his face, looking back at her over his shoulder as Vernon and Shirley led him away, dragging his little wheeled suitcase behind him. Kate closed her eyes briefly, overwhelmed by the pain of not knowing when she would next see him. She swallowed, then straightened her back. Harley appeared next to them, looking stressed.

'Ready?'

Kate blew her nose on a tissue she found in her skirt pocket. 'Come on then,' she said. 'What are we waiting for?'

\*       \*       \*

There really was a private plane, a six-seater Hawker light jet normally used for whisking high-ranking government officials around the country. Harley sat on his own, up near the cockpit, leaving the rear of the cabin to Kate and Paul. Neither of them could sleep. Kate's brain was abuzz, wondering if she was doing the right thing leaving Jack with Vernon, worrying about what lay

60

ahead. She had no idea how quickly the virus was spreading or how long they had. Scientists don't like to work against the clock. Fighting viruses was a long, slow process, small step after small step, and Eureka moments were few and far between. She had so many questions and, like viruses, they multiplied until her head was bursting with them.

She watched Harley remove his shoes and recline in his vast leather seat, stretching out his legs. Tension had been coming off him in waves on the plane across the Atlantic, and now she saw his shoulders sink quickly into an enviable sleep. She realised that, despite everything, she liked him. He had an old-fashioned quality, a stoic, take-it-on-the-chin Britishness that made her think of army officers in black-and-white war films.

Her thoughts of Harley were interrupted by a hand squeezing her leg. She looked around, surprised to see Paul sitting there with the sort of naughty grin on his face she hadn't seen for quite some time.

He gestured towards Harley. 'He's asleep and the stewardess is nowhere to be seen . . .'

'Ye-es? And?' Although Kate suspected that she had already guessed.

Paul leaned in, whispered in her ear, then took her hand. They ran into the toilet together, giggling like newlyweds. Paul slammed the lock into place and pushed Kate up against the wall. She breathed in the familiar musky scent of his skin and they kissed deeply.

'What if he wakes up? It's a bit bloody obvious where we've gone!' she said, breaking off the kiss. She ran her hand down Paul's hard belly towards the bulge in his jeans. He shrugged. 'I'm sure we're not the first, and we won't be the last. Are you a member of the Mile High Club?'

'Not yet,' Kate said, unzipping him and sliding her hand inside his boxers. 'You?'

'Nope,' he replied, lifting up her skirt and pulling down her knickers. The beige moulded wall of the plane's small bathroom felt cool against Kate's hot flesh.

'Oh, darling,' Paul said, kissing her neck and slipping a finger inside her, groaning when he felt how wet she was.

Kate felt tears fill her eyes and she held Paul tightly as he pushed his hard cock into her. 'I love you,' she whispered, before losing herself in the sensation of his thrusts; gentle at first, then becoming faster and harder. He lifted her up so she was sitting on the edge of the basin, and she leaned back, putting a hand on either side of it to steady herself as the movement increased in speed and intensity. They were both panting.

Over the engine noise, Kate heard a sound right outside the bathroom. 'Stop!' she hissed, and they both froze, their eyes wide, like guilty schoolkids caught in the act. There was a soft knock and the sound of a woman clearing her throat.

'Everything all right in there?' the flight attendant enquired drily through the door. Paul gave another gentle teasing thrust and Kate had to press her lips together to stop herself from either giggling or moaning—or both.

'Just a minute,' Paul called, with as much dignity as he could muster. 'I think she's on to us,' he whispered to Kate, resuming his activity with renewed vigour.

'Yes, well, when there are only three passengers

on a plane, and two of them suddenly vanish, I think it's a fairly safe bet as to what they're up to,' Kate said, digging her fingernails into his back. 'We'd better get back to our seats . . .'

Paul groaned. 'Not yet.' He slid out of her. 'Turn round.' She did what he asked, bending over the sink, biting her lip as he pushed deep inside her. She could see his face in the mirror, his eyes screwed up tight, and she thought how beautiful he was, and how beautiful his cock felt, and then she closed her own eyes and threw back her head, spiralling with him into an ecstasy made all the more intense by the uncertainty of what lay ahead.

\* \* \*

By the time the plane landed, Kate was exhausted. But despite the doubts and the fears, her curiosity was burning, adrenaline still fizzing from the amazing sex. Fortunately Harley seemed to have remained asleep throughout. Kate squeezed Paul's hand. We've still got it, she thought. That chemistry.

As they walked down the plane steps, Kate saw that they had landed in a small airfield, half a dozen hangars dotted around a single runway. Beyond the airfield there was little to see—no signs of civilisation, just an arid ochre landscape populated with spiky trees and tumbleweed. In the near distance, rocky hills blocked the horizon. The sky was sheer blue, the sun a white ball of fire that hurt her eyes, even at six thirty in the evening. The heat swept over her and she had a moment of dizziness. Paul grabbed her arm as she swayed on the steps.

63

'Steady,' he said tenderly. 'Are you all right?'

'Yes, just about.' She turned to Harley as her feet touched solid ground. 'What is this place?'

Harley had taken off his jacket and sweat had already begun to darken his shirt beneath his armpits. 'Lone Pine Airport,' he replied. 'We're in north-east California, about a hundred miles from the state border.'

'The border with Nevada?' Paul asked.

'Yes. We're between Death Valley to the east, and the Sequoia National Park to the west. That's where the research lab is based.'

'In a national park? But I thought we were heading to LA.' Kate noticed a pair of black BMWs parked outside the closest hangar, three men standing beside them, one black, two white. They were wearing dark suits and inscrutable expressions.

Harley spotted them at the same moment and raised a hand in greeting. The men opened the doors of the two cars, got in and started to drive slowly towards them through the heat haze.

'FBI?' Paul asked.

Harley nodded, then cleared his throat. 'There have been some developments.'

'What do you mean?' Paul exchanged a worried look with Kate.

Harley didn't reply.

The two cars drew up beside them and the black agent got out, walked round the car and opened the back door. He had broad shoulders and a shaved head, and was carrying a little too much weight around the middle.

'Dr Maddox? Your carriage.' He gestured for Kate to get into the car. She ducked inside, glad to get out of the heat.

Paul made a move to follow her but the agent stepped into his path. 'Uh-uh. Not you. You're not coming. Just Dr Maddox.'

'What the hell?'

Harley said, 'Sorry, Paul—like I told you, there have been developments.'

Paul tried to push past the agent, who blocked his way, placing his hands on Paul's chest. At the same time, Kate got back out of the car. 'Hey, what's going on?'

'Get back in the car please, Dr Maddox,' the agent said. The other FBI agents had emerged from their car and were standing watching.

'Harley, can you please tell us what's going on?'

'OK, OK . . . Listen, there's no need for all this aggression. What's your name?'

The agent who had blocked Paul's way looked at Harley like he'd just broken wind. But he replied, 'McCarthy.'

'Good. Agent McCarthy. We're all on the same side, right? Let me talk to Dr Maddox and Mr Wilson for a couple of minutes, explain the situation, and then we can be on our way. OK?'

McCarthy folded his arms and made them wait for his reply. 'OK. You got five minutes.'

'I need ten. Come on, Kate, Paul, let's get back into the plane.'

\*       \*       \*

'So what the fuck is going on?' Paul asked.

Harley had the demeanour of a middle manager who has been told to make half his team redundant.

65

He rubbed his eyes, then reached under his seat and produced a newspaper. He handed it to Kate, who gasped at the headline then scanned the text. 'Fifty-nine dead already? The containment at the reservation failed?'

Harley avoided her eye.

She opened the paper. The headline across the inside spread read: KILLER FLU SWEEPS THROUGH LOS ANGELES. The first four pages were dominated by the story, accompanied by snapshots of a few of the victims: a young mother in her twenties, an elderly black man, a muscular guy in an Abercrombie & Fitch T-shirt and, worst of all, a seven-year-old boy.

Kate gazed with horror at the picture of the boy. It was the kind of school photograph kids across the world pose for once a year, the school sending home glossy prints to the parents. Kate had almost identical portraits of Jack in her suitcase. The caption read: *Tommy Walker, 7—the youngest victim of Indian Flu.*

Paul read aloud over her shoulder: '*A doctor at Los Angeles County Hospital, who did not want to be named, told us that none of the antiviral drugs that are normally effective have worked in combating what he believes is a new, deadly strain of flu. "This is far worse than swine flu or any of the other epidemics that have broken out in recent years. We are at a loss how to treat it and are desperately seeking advice from the World Health Organization and the Centers for Disease Control."*'

Paul read on. '*The number of people suffering from the disease is currently unknown, as few people report to hospital with flu, especially in poorer communities where people have no health insurance*

66

. . .' Paul skimmed to the final paragraph. '*If you develop flu symptoms, the advice is to stay at home, drink plenty of fluid, do not travel. Family members you have come into contact with should call the number below but should also stay at home, away from other people, even if they currently feel well*, blah blah blah . . . Oh *shit.*'

Kate couldn't tear her eyes away from the picture of seven-year-old Tommy Walker. It hit her like the wave of heat that had almost floored her on the steps of the plane. She tried to imagine how Tommy's mother must feel, if she was still alive. Suddenly, even more so than when she had learned of the bombing and Isaac's death, this whole thing, the outbreak of this new strain of Watoto, all felt very real.

'As I told you in London,' Harley said, 'the authorities here decided not to go public about the outbreak. They didn't want a repeat of the fallout that followed the swine flu pandemic, when the WHO were accused of exaggerating the dangers so the sale of vaccines would soar, boosting profits for the drug companies. The allegations were rubbish, but it's made some of the decision-makers cautious, if not paranoid. So they decided to keep it under wraps until they knew exactly what they were dealing with. They put together this team in secret, hoping some progress would be made before the situation escalated.'

'But you can't keep things like this quiet these days!' said Paul. 'Let me guess—it leaked online.'

'That's right. First of all, Twitter. A lot of people in LA tweeting about how sick they felt. Then a couple of days later, those people stop tweeting, and the friends and families start to leave messages

67

mourning the deaths of their loved ones, apparently from the flu. And then a doctor at a hospital in LA ripped the whole thing open with a blog post about how this super-flu had started filling up the hospital, how he'd never seen anything like it—not realising it's actually Watoto because no doctor in LA would ever have encountered Watoto. Of course that blog got picked up by people on Twitter and Facebook and it hit the national press. I only found out about it at the airport when you were saying goodbye to Jack. Fortunately, the message we received after the terrorist attack on the hotel has not been leaked.'

'Isn't the CDC supposed to be in charge in these situations?' Kate looked up from the paper. Her entire body felt cold.

Harley nodded. 'In the normal course of events, yes. But in this instance . . . well, I haven't been entirely . . . forthcoming with you about how this is all set up.'

'Why doesn't that shock me?' Paul said.

'All right, all right.' Harley glanced nervously out of the plane window. The three FBI agents were standing motionlessly by their cars. 'Look, I shouldn't really be telling you this, but we're in a need-to-know situation here. Under normal circumstances, the Centers for Disease Control would take the lead in the event of an epidemic or pandemic within the United States, while the WHO would have global responsibility. But in cases where terrorism is—'

'Terrorism? So you suspected terrorist involvement before the bombing?' said Paul.

Irritated by Paul's continued antagonism towards Harley, Kate flapped a hand at him to be quiet so they could hear what the MI6 man had to say.

Harley continued: 'After the anthrax attacks in America in 2001, the US Government set up an agency called the BIT—Bioterror Investigative Team. Initially it was a small unit, working out of FBI headquarters, monitoring and investigating suspected bioterrorist groups and individuals. Then, after Clive Gaunt's attempt to release the Pandora virus in London by infecting your son with it, the two governments decided it was time to join forces. The BIT became an international agency, charged with monitoring bioterrorism on a global basis. Whenever something out of the ordinary happens—like an exotic virus breaking out where it shouldn't—the BIT steps in. I joined them not long afterwards, and because of our previous . . . involvement, it fell to me to enlist your help and escort you over here. Usually I'm based in London, but I'll be staying on to help with intelligence.'

'So you *did* suspect terrorist involvement before the bomb went off?' Kate asked.

'Like I said, if something out of the ordinary occurs, we investigate. And this case was unusual from the start. It made no sense, Watoto showing up on the reservation. No one who worked there had been to Africa. And even though hundreds of people pass in and out of the casino every day—'

'Watoto has a short incubation period,' Kate interrupted. 'It's highly unlikely someone who'd contracted the disease in Africa would make it all the way to a casino outside LA. They'd be far too sick by that time to want to go gambling.'

'Exactly. Which made us suspect the source of the virus was closer to home. That's why BIT took the lead on this. Obviously we're working with the CDC, who will keep the public informed and try to contain the outbreak. But it was BIT who put together this team and set up the facilities where you'll be working. Previously, the team were going to be based in LA, but in light of the media coverage we've decided to move the whole operation out here. Also, it hasn't been announced yet but the airports in LA are going to be shut down tonight. No more domestic or international flights in or out of the city.'

'That makes sense.'

'And to prevent leaks to the media, only necessary personnel will be permitted anywhere near the lab. Which is why we can't allow you in there, Paul.'

Before Paul could respond, there was a loud knock on the door of the plane. It opened and Agent McCarthy stuck his head through. 'Time's up.'

'Give me one more minute,' Harley said.

'We've got to get moving.'

Kate stood up. 'Let's go. I've heard enough.'

Paul blinked up at her, surprised. 'Kate?'

She gestured to the pictures in the newspaper. 'I don't want to waste any more time sitting around here speculating about who, how or why this outbreak happened. Right now, I just want to get on with helping to find a cure.'

In the doorway, McCarthy applauded with slow handclaps. 'Finally, someone around here speaks sense.'

Paul got to his feet and Kate took both his hands in hers. 'I wish you could come with me, but it sounds as if I'm going to be working all hours. I won't get to see you anyway.'

'But I want to help.'

'There's nothing you can do,' Harley said firmly.

Paul opened his mouth to argue, but McCarthy stepped forward to usher her away: 'Let's get going. Dr Maddox, you're coming with me and Agent Thompson. Harley, you should wait for further instructions. Agent DiFranco will drive you and Mr Wilson.'

He smiled grimly at Paul's expression. 'Don't look so frightened, my friend. We're not taking you to Los Angeles.'

## 8

The old man knew death was coming. He felt it stirring deep within his bones, in the way they creaked when he heaved himself out of his bunk each morning. He heard it in the pleading of his heartbeat whenever he got excited or did anything strenuous. Sometimes, when he looked out at what all the guards told him was 'the best view in the prison'—over yonder at the bay, the flat horizon a taunt for the men held in this Federal Correctional Institute—he thought he could see death coming for him, a dark shape in the distance, creeping closer every day.

Well, screw death. He wasn't afraid. Just as long as he got to do one more thing—that thing he'd been waiting all these years to do—before he shuffled off this mortal coil.

He stood at the window now. For the last fifteen years, this room in the low-security wing of the prison had been his home. Once, before he was betrayed, before that *bastard* took a large sharp rod and fucked him with it, he had lived in a beautiful house, the kind of place his father could only have dreamed of. His brains had taken him a long way. He was a Mexican immigrant who'd been living the American Dream. He'd had a great job doing important work—OK, so some of it was illegal, but that did not make it any less vital. In his spare time there had been stunning women, luxury yachts, fine wines. The only ones who wanted his attention in this godforsaken shithole were a lot more hairy and a little less tender than the women who had never even written him in prison.

He clenched his teeth, waiting for the tremors of anger to subside, his hand resting on the cool surface of the microscope they allowed him to keep. It was not much better than a child's microscope, pitifully inadequate. Still, it was better than nothing. Beside it, he had placed his reading material, the *Journal of Virology* and *The Infectious Disease Review* at the top of the pile. He liked to keep up with what was happening. There had been so many advances, so many fascinating new diseases, since his incarceration.

He picked up a copy of *Immunology Today* and leafed through it, but couldn't concentrate. For weeks now he'd been on edge, more desperate than ever to get out of this shithole. Since he'd been here, both his parents had died; his sisters had married and remarried and spawned children he'd never seen. He'd missed the chance to become a father. And the men who put him here had made it clear there would be no parole, even though he had never murdered anyone with these hands, never robbed a bank or tried to blow anything up.

72

He was a sacrificial goat. The man who knew too much.

He switched on the TV and channel-hopped, a little flutter of anticipation in his belly. Prisoners were only allowed a few channels: ESPN, CNN and Fox News, the Weather Channel, and a handful of Christian channels on which preachers hectored and begged for money. He had pleaded for the Discovery Channel, for the occasional documentary about his favourite subject, but the bastards would not listen.

Now, he settled on Fox News, and the presenter's words immediately grabbed him.

'. . . *Indian Flu, a deadly new virus that is sweeping through Los Angeles . . .*'

The old man sat on his bunk and stared, rapt, at the TV.

'. . . *symptoms are similar to a bad case of flu: fever, head cold . . . Victims describe it as being like the worst case of flu you've ever had, multiplied by ten . . .*'

He leaned forward. It was happening.

'. . . *and then the victim is killed by what appears to be a seizure . . .*'

They showed footage of people waiting, shivering, in a hospital, dozens of them lined up. He could almost picture the virus particles swirling and leaping through the air around them.

'. . . *the CDC reports that this particular flu virus has not been seen before, but denies that it is a new strain of swine or bird flu. Sufferers are being advised to stay at home and drink plenty of fluids. Do not go to the hospital. A special helpline has been set up . . .*'

For the next two hours, the old man continued to stare at the TV.

This was it. The one. For many years, he and scientists like him had issued warnings that one day a mighty plague would sweep the earth. The authorities—the CDC and the WHO and all those other government motherfuckers—pretended they were prepared for it.

But he was the only man in America who knew what it was and how to stop it.

He called for the guard. After a few minutes, one of the older guards arrived. Officer Hillier. He looked tired.

'What's up, Doc?' he asked wearily.

In the prison, people always said this to him. It drove him nuts, but he ignored it.

'Is anyone in the prison sick?'

Hillier raised an eyebrow. 'What kinda question is that?'

'A perfectly reasonable question. I just want to know if anyone in the prison has contracted this virus they're talking about.'

Hillier looked over the old man's shoulder at the TV. 'Oh, that. Just a buncha people with a bad cold. Yeah, a few people here have got sick. Why you asking? Want to experiment on them, huh?'

The old man grinned at him. 'You're an asshole, Hillier.'

'And you just lost your privileges for a week, Doc. And that includes using the phone and the internet. And the TV.'

He hadn't expected that. 'No, please, Hillier, I need—'

The big guard stuck a broad finger in his face. 'Shut the fuck up. I'll send someone to take away your TV later. Enjoy it while you can.'

The old man watched the guard retreat from the

cell, banging the door shut behind him, and shook his head, the thinnest of smiles on his lips.

Let them take away his TV, his internet, his phone. They'd all be dead soon. If they knew what he knew, Hillier and the rest of them would be offering him all their money, their houses, their fucking *wives* in return for his help. Hillier was one of the people whose slow, hideous death he'd buy a ticket to watch.

He knew he wouldn't have to wait long.

## 9

'So, Dr Maddox,' said Agent McCarthy, leaning back in the seat and stretching his arms over his head, linking his fingers together, palms facing the car roof. The leather underneath his buttocks complained noisily. 'Been to Sequoia before?'

He was a big man, particularly when stretching, and his bulk seemed to fill the back of the car. His flesh had the compacted appearance of someone who works out a lot but who also loves his food a little too much.

'Sequoia?' Kate looked out of the window. All she could make out was the faint outline of bare rocky peaks rising against the deepening blue of the evening sky. 'The big tree?'

'The national park,' said McCarthy, making a face at her.

'Oh. Yeah. Sorry, I did know that. I blame the jet lag. No, I haven't been there before. But it is the home of those giant trees, right?'

'Right. We don't get to drive through it, though.'

'The park?' The conversation felt to Kate, through her jet lag, as though it was going in claustrophobic spirals of incomprehension.

'No, the real famous sequoia, the one everyone's heard of: it fell across the road in the thirties and the sucker was way too big to be moved, its trunk is, like, twenty foot wide, so they cut a hole in it and made it into a tunnel instead.' He made sawing gestures with his right hand, and then curved his palm in an arc, as if stroking an invisible cat's head, to indicate the tunnel.

'Redwoods are even bigger, though—they're over the other side of the park. Those puppies are so big you can drive right through the middle of 'em, even when they're still living.'

Jack would love that, Kate thought, driving right through a tree. She vaguely remembered seeing photographs of sequoias—or maybe redwoods—in an encyclopaedia. It was so surreal, she thought, to be in this car with two FBI agents, making small talk about big trees.

'Right,' she repeated dully, pulling out her BlackBerry to text Paul, but there was no signal. Being separated from both him and Jack within such a short space of time was making her feel irritable and lonely. And she felt nervous too. There were people out there who wanted to kill scientists. Still, this was probably the safest place she could be—in a car with two FBI agents.

'Shit signal in this whole area,' commented McCarthy, air-texting with his thumbs. Kate couldn't decide whether she liked him or whether he annoyed her. At least he had a bit of personality, she thought, unlike the silent Thompson behind the wheel, who hadn't said a single word the entire journey. Apart from his arms turning the steering wheel, he hadn't even moved. Kate had spent some time staring idly at the back of his neck, small tight rolls of flesh from his bald head descending like supersized wrinkles into the collar of his black jacket, and it had remained completely immobile.

'Are we nearly there?' she asked, and was immediately reminded of Jack again. 'Where exactly is this lab?'

'Can't tell you that, ma'am,' said McCarthy. 'Not its exact location, anyway. I can tell you it's just inside the park. Actually, it's only about an hour's drive cross-country from the airport, but unfortunately there ain't no roads through Sequoia that way, so we gotta go down and round and up again. Wouldn't want to drive through those mountains anyhow. The air gets pretty thin at twelve thousand feet.'

'What's the set-up at the lab?'

McCarthy swivelled a forefinger into his ear and jiggled it about a bit. 'I haven't been there myself, but I'm told it's a category four, state-of-the-art equipment, in a converted hunting lodge.'

'Will you be staying there with me?'

'For the foreseeable future, yes, ma'am. Plus we got Thompson here and some other security guards who'll be looking after the joint. Not that anyone knows this place even exists, so you don't have to worry.'

Kate nodded. That was a relief. 'What's your name?' she asked.

'McCarthy.'

'No—your first name. Or do I have to call you McCarthy?'

He looked at her, slightly sheepishly. 'Tosca.'

Kate laughed. She couldn't help it. The name was ridiculous, but simultaneously kind of cool, and suited him perfectly. She held out her hand.

'Call me Kate, then, Tosca, if we're going to be spending quite a bit of time together.'

'Nice to meet you, Kate,' he said, shaking her hand and inclining his head. Kate thought that, all things considered, he was probably a good one to have on side—presuming he could move fast enough to pull his gun if required. But at least he had a sense of humour—and, God knew, there wasn't a whole lot to laugh about in the state of California at the moment.

\*     \*     \*

They drove in silence for another hour or so, and Kate was almost falling asleep, with her cheek against the cool tinted glass, when the car abruptly pulled off the road and bounced along on uneven ground on the edge of a densely wooded area. The sun was long gone, and the car headlights made eerie shadows of the trees. Her head banged against the window and she sat up, rubbing her temple. 'What happened to the road?'

They were literally driving between trees now, with little other than tyre tracks in the soft undergrowth to indicate that any other vehicle had been here before. McCarthy pointed ahead. 'Starts again over there. This is the back way in. The official road in is about five miles thataways, blocked off so curious tourists can't drive up to take a look. Last thing they need is hikers banging on the door asking to use the bathroom, so they make

78

it look like it's deserted.'

'Is this the national park?' They were bumping along in dark forest now, and Thompson, behind the wheel, had an even more rigid set to his shoulders as he negotiated the BMW through the trees.

'Edge of it. It's right over there.'

'Are there bears in here?' Kate peered out at the foliage around her.

*'Lions and tigers and bears—oh my!'* sang McCarthy in a falsetto voice, and Kate rolled her eyes.

'Just asking.'

The road suddenly reappeared in the middle of a clearing—as if someone had merely forgotten a chunk of it—and the smooth tarmac felt like a return to civilisation. After another ten minutes the car pulled up at a huge iron gate manned by a guard with a machine gun. Behind the gate, Kate could just about make out the rear of a huge building, neo-Swiss in appearance with gables and wood cladding. To the right of the house was a helipad, and to the left, a large coop filled with squawking chickens. The whole compound was surrounded by razor wire, giving it the unfortunate look of a prison. Guantanamo Bay for hens, thought Kate.

'Here we are,' said McCarthy, gesturing towards it. 'Home sweet home. Plus chickens. What is this? Colonel Sanders' secret HQ? Oh, I know— laboratories do keep chickens, don't they, to culture flu vaccines in eggs?'

'Biochemistry labs often keep chickens, but not outside like this,' said Kate. 'They'd need to be SPF—specific pathogen free, kept in sterile conditions. I think these are more likely to be

79

providers of roast dinners.'

Thompson rolled down his window and exchanged some terse words with the guard, who said nothing in reply but opened the gate to allow them to drive in. Kate wondered if that was the first duty he'd had to perform all day. She couldn't imagine there was much else to do, other than watch the chickens scratch away in their pen, and scan the width of the skies for eagles high above the forest.

A tiny but rotund Hispanic woman, dwarfed by a large flowery apron, came to the back door to meet them. She looked at them through eyes so narrowed that they almost vanished into the wrinkles on her face. She nodded at McCarthy, unsmiling, as he removed Kate's suitcase from the trunk of the BMW and ushered them both into the lodge. Thompson stayed in the car.

'Friendly round here, aren't they?' she whispered to McCarthy, trying to disguise her nerves with flippancy.

'You are Dr Maddox,' stated the Hispanic lady, still nodding. 'We expected you.'

'Yes, hello, do call me Kate,' she said, holding out her hand. The woman stared at it with suspicion before giving Kate's fingers the briefest of tugs. 'I am Adoncia. Housekeeper.'

There was a considerable amount of luggage in the hallway, from designer suitcases to scruffy canvas rucksacks and, as McCarthy introduced himself to Adoncia ('I am McCarthy. FBI Agent'), Kate flipped over a luggage label on the nearest suitcase, a smart gold Louis Vuitton, and read in neat capitals a name she recognized: Junko Nishirin, with a Tokyo address. She felt inordinately

80

relieved—this confirmed that the team was only now being scrambled—so much easier to start when they were all on a level playing field, rather than having to catch up with an existing team's efforts, and fit in with their social structure.

She heard light footsteps on the bare wooden boards of the wide staircase, and turned to see a petite Japanese woman descending, her hair an immaculate sheet of ebony and her make-up looking as though it had been professionally applied.

Kate felt very conscious of the fact that her own hair was in limp clumps, and the same mascara she had applied in the cottage yesterday morning was now resting in creases under her eyes. The Japanese woman was wearing a tight black miniskirt and ballet flats, with a perfectly ironed Ralph Lauren cotton shirt. When she saw Kate, she beamed at her. 'Welcome!' she said, with only a trace of an accent, coming down the final few steps with a slim white hand outstretched.

'You must be Kate Maddox. We are so pleased to have you on board. I am Junko, one of the three other virologists here. I have been waiting for you. You're in the next bedroom to me—shall I show you up there? It is so nice to meet you.' Her face suddenly turned sombre and she cast down her eyes. 'I am so sorry to hear of Dr Isaac Larter's death. A terrible tragedy.'

Kate felt a little overwhelmed, and had to take a deep breath at the mention of Isaac's name. But Junko was so friendly, and she liked her immediately. 'Thank you,' she said. 'I still can't believe it. Yes, please do show me the room. It's great to meet you. I've read your paper on . . .'

She tailed off, her mind having gone completely blank as to the subject of Junko's paper, but the woman kindly pretended not to notice.

McCarthy, with Kate's rather battered old suitcase in one hand, moved across the lobby and picked up Junko's solid Louis Vuitton. 'Allow me, ladies,' he said.

'This is Tosca McCarthy,' Kate told Junko. 'He's an FBI agent. And a bit of a joker. But at least he's a gentleman.' Junko inclined her head towards him, and led them both up the stairs. Adoncia had vanished, with a loud 'tut'—presumably it had been her job to show Kate to her room.

Junko paused on the landing of the first floor. A thick steel door stood in front of them. 'The lab is through here—more secure on the first floor, and better light. It's a great facility. But we'll take a look at it later, after you have freshened up.'

She continued up another flight, and Kate sniffed discreetly at her own armpits, blushing at the thought of how obvious it might be that she needed a shower. McCarthy was puffing and panting behind them, sounding like a stressed buffalo. 'Jeez, ladies, you got rocks in here?'

'Who else is in the team?' Kate asked Junko, ignoring McCarthy's grumbles. 'Is everyone here? Have you started already?'

'We're starting tomorrow morning,' Junko said, smiling back at her over her shoulder. 'The Aeromedical Isolation team are bringing us in a patient at dawn, via army helicopter—assuming he lasts the night. It will be great to have some live tissue samples to work with so early on. Professor Kolosine from Yale is heading up the team. He got here two days ago. I met him when I arrived this morning.'

Kate stopped short on the stairs, causing McCarthy to bump into the back of her. '*The* Glenn Kolosine? Are you serious?'

She felt a frisson of excitement, as if Junko had told her she'd be working with Sir Isaac Newton. Kolosine was a legend among virologists, having made a number of important breakthroughs in the studies of some of the big hitters of the viral world: he had been instrumental in developing a vaccine for SARS; and led a team that mapped the DNA of Ebola and Marburg. She was surprised he hadn't been at the conference, though he had a reputation for being a lone wolf so presumably he avoided things like that. Luckily for him.

Junko rolled her eyes very slightly. 'Yes, I'm serious. And so is he . . . as you'll soon discover.'

Kate wondered what she meant by that, but felt too worn out to question her. She craved the welcome hot pinpricks of water from a long shower on her tired head and shoulders, and the sound of Paul's voice in her ear. She had already decided not to call Jack for a few days, as difficult as that would be—she knew from experience that it always tended to make him decide he was missing her, even if he'd been perfectly fine before she called. Vernon had promised that he would let Jack ring her if he wanted to.

They arrived on the second floor, and Junko led them down a dingy hallway decorated with self-conscious Americana: beribboned corncobs in shallow woven baskets on reproduction dressers, rag rugs on the dark wooden floors, a doleful-looking rocking horse. 'Hard to imagine there's a Cat 4 lab downstairs, isn't it?' she commented, opening a door at the end of the hall.

Kate's room was pleasant, a patchwork quilt on the double bed, calico curtains and a washstand with a large china bowl and jug on it. The sickly smell of potpourri permeated the air, and Kate flung open the nearest window as soon as she walked in.

'What's the plan for tomorrow?' she asked Junko, as McCarthy heaved her suitcase on to a luggage stand next to the bed.

'Breakfast at seven. Adoncia's cooking makes up for her lack of social skills, so don't miss it. You'll meet the others then: the other virologist, Chip Oakley, and the technicians—I haven't learned their names yet. Well, I'm going to bed now. Sleep well, see you in the morning.'

'Good night.' Kate sat down on the bed and watched as Junko and McCarthy retreated, closing the door behind them. The house felt utterly silent. She reached into her handbag and got out her mobile phone—but there was absolutely no signal, and no telephone in the room either. She sighed, flopped back on to the pillows, and was asleep within seconds.

*     *     *

She was awoken by a light knock at the door.

'Ready for breakfast?' called Junko, and Kate sat bolt upright. She felt a flutter in her belly. It was time to meet the rest of the team.

Paul watched the car containing Kate and Agent McCarthy retreat into the distance. He clenched his fists, kept his breathing slow and deliberate, and counted to ten in his head. The BMW he and Harley were in started its own slow crawl out of the airfield, and Paul thought he would snap if Harley tried to speak to him now.

The last couple of years, this anger was something he had to deal with whenever he was under pressure. His therapist, the same woman who talked to him about the bad dreams that soaked his sheets at night, had taught him a number of anger management techniques. Breathe deeply. Count. Remove yourself from the situation.

Paul exhaled through slightly parted lips, closed his eyes for a moment, and regained his composure. He did not like this new, bitter, person he seemed to have turned into. Often, he wished he could turn back the clock to become once again the man he was when he first met Kate, before the discovery of what had happened to Stephen had knocked his world off its axis. His faith in humanity had been badly damaged and he wanted to regain it, to see the good in people again.

He wanted to find peace—so he could move on, be the man he was meant to be, a supportive, dynamic partner, a great stepdad, and maybe a dad too, if Kate was up for it. But it was hard for him to get close to that peace when some of the men who were connected to Stephen's death were still free.

Finally, when his heartbeat had returned to a

steady pace, he turned to Harley. 'Where are we going?'

'First thing tomorrow we're heading to the field office in San Francisco,' Harley replied. 'Once we're there, we'll find somewhere to put you up while you wait for Kate. Or you can return to the UK, if you prefer.'

'No way. I'm staying right here till she's done.'

'OK. But you realise you could have a long wait?'

Paul felt the anger coming straight back again. Fucking Harley. He had never met anyone who was able to wind him up so easily. 'I'm not going anywhere.'

Harley shrugged. 'It's your choice. Anyway, it's been a long day. We're going to check in to a motel and rest up till the morning.'

'Whatever,' Paul replied, giving the floor once again to his inner teenager. Turning to the dusky landscape rolling by the window, he began counting to ten again.

\*     \*     \*

Agent DiFranco pulled up by a motel on the west side of Bakersfield. Despite the hour, it was still stiflingly hot. Paul was desperate for a shower, and his eyes burned from lack of sleep. Harley was right; it had been a long, long day.

The motel clerk, a skinny brunette with her hair piled up on her head and a tattoo of a panther on her upper arm, checked them in to three rooms.

'Y'all from England?' she asked on hearing Harley and Paul's accents. 'Do you know Radiohead?'

'Not personally,' Harley replied drily.

Paul caught her eye, shooting her a look that said, 'Yeah, this guy's a jerk,' and she smiled at him, revealing a gap in her teeth you could drive a motorbike through. She handed each of them a key and told them their room numbers. Paul and Harley were in adjacent rooms; DiFranco a few doors down.

'Cellphone reception is lousy in the rooms,' she said, 'but we got wi-fi if you need it.'

'Great,' said Paul, drawing another smile from the receptionist. She reminded him a little of poor Amy Winehouse.

'I don't think we'll be needing that,' Harley said. DiFranco snickered, for no good reason Paul could tell. When the receptionist turned to get their keys, Paul saw DiFranco take a good, long look at her behind, actually tilting his head to one side. Creep.

As Paul unlocked his room, he heard DiFranco say to Harley, 'Hey, we should have a talk.' He kept the door open a crack and listened, hoping he might catch something they said, but they had moved out of earshot.

He stripped and showered, then took a clean T-shirt and pair of boxers out of his suitcase. The room was like the inside of a car that had been parked in the sun all day; dog-killing weather. He examined the air-con unit and concluded that it was a piece of junk. A great weariness washed over him. He didn't have the energy to complain or ask for another room.

Instead, he opened the window, which gave a view of a row of cars and the freeway beyond, and lay down on the creaky bed. He picked up his iPhone, wanting to call or at least text Kate. The receptionist was right: he had half a bar of signal that flickered on and off; he sent a text telling Kate he loved her, was sorry about earlier and would call her in the morning. He added four kisses.

He closed his eyes. He'd slept in worse places—prison, for one.

When he next opened his eyes it was dark. It took him a few moments to remember where he was. A crap motel, a long way from home. Alone.

He could hear someone talking outside the window. He rolled on to his side and groped for his phone to check the time. Half past midnight. He crept to the window and stood behind the curtain. The voice outside belonged to Harley. After a moment, when he couldn't hear another voice, Paul realised Harley was on the phone, obviously forced outside by the poor mobile reception.

He pressed his face to the glass. Harley was standing by their car, his back to Paul, who could make out the odd word. 'Report . . . spreading fast . . . Bakersfield . . .'

Paul quickly pulled a chair across the room and stood on it so he could listen through the open window, his body concealed by the curtain and the darkness inside the room. If he really strained he found he could hear almost everything.

'So what do you want me to do?' Harley went on. 'No, I'm heading back to San Francisco in the morning. I've got Paul Wilson with me. Yeah, yeah . . . I know.' He laughed. Paul didn't think the person on the other end of the phone was praising his good qualities. What was that expression about people who eavesdrop never hearing good things about themselves? 'Thankfully, Kate Maddox is a lot more cooperative. Yeah, I know—I had to tell her a white lie to get her to agree.'

Paul got that feeling you get in your stomach when you go over a bump in the road. His suspicions were right: Harley couldn't be trusted.

The MI6 man went on: 'Yeah, Wilson is obsessed with what happened to his brother, Stephen. The guy that Gaunt was . . .'

To Paul's great frustration, Harley began to wander away, his voice growing quieter until he couldn't hear it any more. He slapped the wall with frustration.

Hearing Harley talk about Stephen in such a dismissive fashion enraged him, especially when Harley knew all too well what had happened, and why Paul found it hard to let go. There were still people out there who had been involved in Stephen's death. Or rather, one man. Charles Mangold.

And then it came to Paul what he should do.

He wasn't going to allow Harley to take him to San Francisco. Because now, for the first time, he had a chance to avenge his brother's death—and maybe find the inner peace he craved.


11


There were six people already round the long refectory-style table when Kate and Junko came down for breakfast, including McCarthy, who proceeded to introduce Kate to everybody as though he'd been there for weeks. He seemed perfectly at ease in the situation, laughing and gesticulating—Kate would have assumed he was

89

slightly drunk had it not been 6.30 a.m. It helped, though, having him there. He certainly broke the ice.

There was an epidemiologist, William, who was about her age with sandy thinning hair. His body was so slight that he looked as though a strong puff of mountain breeze would be enough to bear him away, but his features were strong, and he looked like a man on a mission. Then there were three lab technicians—two young men, one fat, and one very tall, whose names Kate instantly forgot, and one very pretty woman, small, busty and pouty, whose name was Annie. Kate and Junko were the only non-Americans.

The sixth person was the third virologist, Chip Oakley. He had the narrowest face Kate had ever seen, topped by an enormous pair of tortoiseshell-framed spectacles, and his welcome smile looked more like a frown. His eyes, magnified through the thick lenses of his glasses, seemed to pop out at her. He was wearing a knitted tanktop the likes of which Kate hadn't seen since about 1978. No wonder we need the FBI and all this security, she thought; this lot wouldn't have the strength to take the skin off a rice pudding. Although, even if they were all built like Marines, it wouldn't be much good if someone set off another bomb.

'He looks a bit weird,' Kate whispered to Junko, trying to distract herself from thoughts of bombs and Isaac, as they took two seats at the end of the table furthest from Chip.

Junko grinned. 'He's all right, actually. Bit of an uber-geek, but knows his stuff. I worked with him on H1N1 at Berkeley a few years ago.'

'Where's Kolosine?' She felt a slight flutter in

her ribcage at the mere thought of the man.

Junko rolled her eyes. 'He likes to make an entrance, if I remember rightly.' She poured them both a glass of water from the jug on the table.

'I'd kill for a cup of coffee,' Kate said. 'Is there any?'

Annie, who had been busily applying more lipgloss at the table, piped up: 'Plenty of coffee, day and night. Nothing stronger, though, so don't go expecting wine with your dinner tonight. This place is dry.'

'Are you serious?' Kate was aghast. Did they really expect her to be holed up here indefinitely, without even a relaxing glass of wine at the end of a long day? Outrageous!

''Fraid so. Prof. Kolosine's orders. No alcohol on the premises for the duration of the project.'

'That's tantamount to cruelty,' Kate said miserably, picking at a croissant from the basket on the table and suddenly missing Paul with a fierce longing.

'You tell him that, honey,' said Annie, snapping shut her compact. 'No cellphone reception here, either, and no landline 'cept the one in Professor Kolosine's locked office, which is for emergency use only, so we were told last night.'

'*What?*' Kate felt sick. How was she supposed to call Paul, or Jack?

'More incentive for us to develop a vaccine as soon as possible, I guess,' said Chip, in a surprisingly deep voice, completely at odds with his nerdy Junior High appearance. 'They want us to be as isolated as possible so we can really focus.'

Adoncia pushed open the door of the dining room with her rump, dragging in behind her a trolley containing a big pot of coffee and a platter of scrambled eggs and sausage links, which she dumped wordlessly on the table. Kate's stomach gurgled in anticipation.

There was silence for a few minutes while everyone helped themselves. 'So, folks,' McCarthy said. 'Let's hear it. What are we really up against here? And not too much of your scientific jargon, either—I am a simple man.' He made a silly face, but no one except Annie laughed.

Junko pushed away her unfinished eggs and leaned her elbows on the table. 'It appears to be an intense strain of Watoto, which is bad enough in its familiar state, but this one seems to kill people much more quickly—in four days, as opposed to the six or seven Watoto usually takes. The stats that William's been receiving indicate that we're dealing with a ninety-nine per cent mortality rate, which is one of the worst we've ever seen. It's a filovirus—not a flu virus at all, despite the media calling it Indian flu. Its closest relatives are Ebola and Marburg—but this strain of Watoto is even more deadly than those.'

There was a roar from the corridor, and everyone's heads jerked up. 'Kolosine,' mouthed Junko at Kate, and the door burst open. A huge, hirsute man stood framed in the doorway. He was wearing a checked plaid shirt, with a thatch of dark chest hair curling out of the top. He had longish brown hair, and the sort of beard that made Kate relieved that she hadn't seen him eat soup. His eyes were bright green and very clear, and his voice seemed to boom out from the bottom of his sneakers. He completely ignored Kate.

'Suits on, people—we've got a live one coming

in any moment. The Aeromedical Isolation Team are bringing him in a VATI. Police sergeant in the LAPD, thirty-two years old, in advanced stages of the disease. This is our best shot: fresh tissue samples, a chance to observe the effects of the virus first hand—don't fuck it up.'

'What's a VATI?' asked McCarthy, helping himself to another croissant as, all around him, chairs were being pushed back and people were rising to their feet.

'Vickers aircraft transport isolator—it's a way of transporting very infectious patients,' said Kate. 'Looks like a gurney with a plastic tent over it.'

'I knew that,' McCarthy said, buttering the croissant.

Kolosine was still standing in the doorway, urging his team out. He looked more like a lumberjack than a world-renowned scientist, Kate thought. She walked up to him and held out her hand. 'Hi, Professor Kolosine, I'm Kate Maddox. It's an honour to meet you, and I'm—'

'Yeah, yeah, hi, let's get going,' he said, ignoring her outstretched hand, and looking right over the top of her head. 'We got work to do here. I'll see you in the lab in twenty minutes.' With that, he turned on his heel and strode out, leaving Kate standing with her mouth hanging open in disbelief. Junko came up behind her and squeezed her elbow.

'Don't take it personally,' she said. 'The great Professor Kolosine doesn't have much time for mere mortals like us. Come on, I'll show you where the lab is.'

Kate clenched her teeth together and shut her eyes tightly for a moment to try and contain her anger. Kolosine had better be as brilliant as everyone said he was.

'Right,' she said. 'Bring it on.'

## 12

Paul waited for Harley to come back, hoping to eavesdrop further on his conversation, but when Harley returned he had put his phone away. Paul heard him go into his room and shut the door.

Charles Mangold. Since Stephen's death, finding Mangold had become an obsession for Paul. He felt like that Nazi hunter—what was his name?—who had sworn he wouldn't rest until they were all brought to justice. But Paul's efforts had been stymied because his criminal record meant he could only track Mangold online. But now he'd finally been allowed into the US he could pursue leads that would have been impossible over the internet.

He could almost feel Stephen watching him, urging him on, saying, *Do it, Paul. Find him. For me.*

He paced the room. First step would be to get online, look up Mangold and see if his name had appeared anywhere recently. That night at the lab, when Gaunt had been convinced he was invincible, and that Kate and Paul would never get out alive, Gaunt had let slip that Mangold lived in Utah. Yet Paul had never been able to find any online trace of an address in that state. His internet searches had established that Mangold had headed a company called Medi-Lab, which was based in a small city called Sagebrush, to the west of LA. There had been no fresh results in the last two years.

94

He grabbed his phone and turned on data roaming but, as he'd expected, there was no 3G connection here so he couldn't get online via the mobile network, nor any wi-fi. He pulled on his jeans, socks and shoes and exited the room as quietly as he could, creeping along the front of the building, gratefully breathing in the cooler air.

At reception, the skinny girl with the panther tattoo had been replaced by a considerably less skinny man with a grey beard and bags under his eyes. He turned his basset hound-like gaze on Paul.

'Hi. The girl on reception earlier said there was wi-fi available?' Paul realised that he was whispering. He cleared his throat and spoke up. 'Is that right?'

'Only in the lobby. Ten bucks an hour.'

Outrageous. But he had little choice. He took out his wallet, thankful that he'd got some money changed at Heathrow, and handed over a ten-dollar bill. Armed with the password, he sneaked back to his room, noting that the light inside Harley's room was off. It was 1 a.m. now and only the occasional car glided past on the freeway. He grabbed his MacBook Air and headed back down to reception. There, perched in an uncomfortably shiny plastic armchair in the corner, he connected to the wi-fi. The first thing he did was Google Charles Mangold and filter the results to the most recent.

Nothing he hadn't seen before.

To refresh his memory, he went into a folder he had set up to save the scant details he had previously discovered about Mangold when searching at home.

The most useful item came from the online archive of the Ventura County Star. Paul read it over now, probably for the tenth time since he had first found it. The words never failed to make the hairs stand up on the back of his neck.

Charles Mangold was the founder and president of Medi-Lab Research, a company based in Sagebrush that specialised in research into, and manufacture of, antiviral drugs. The company was heavily involved in research into HIV, as well as research into the common cold and flu viruses. Medi-Lab Research was one of Ventura County's largest employers until a significant health scandal in 1991, when it was accused of endangering the lives of its employees and the wider community due to 'safety violations' and, more seriously, 'misuse of biological agents'. The company's headquarters and laboratories were shut down by the Department of Health. Two employees were taken seriously ill and diagnosed as suffering from a hemorrhagic virus, although precise details are not available. Both of the affected workers died.

Several key members of staff were arrested, but Mangold went to ground and has not been seen since. The company's reputation was ruined and it ceased trading shortly afterwards.

Where was Mangold now? At the time of the scandal, in 1991, Mangold had been fifty-three. So, assuming he hadn't died in the last couple of years, he would now be seventy-four. What would he be doing?

He read the line about the haemorrhagic virus again. Could it have been Watoto? Officially, there had never been an outbreak of Watoto in the US, but maybe there had, and the authorities had kept it under wraps.

He closed the laptop lid. Perhaps this was a foolish plan. But what was the alternative? Tomorrow, Harley and DiFranco would drive him to San Francisco and dump him in some cheap motel. He would go mad, sitting around with nothing to do, no way of contributing or helping.

Well, screw Harley and the BIT and MI6 and the FB sodding I. He wasn't going to sit around on his arse, not when there was a man out there who needed to pay for what had happened to Stephen. This was his chance, and he wasn't about to let it slip away.

He quickly packed again, and as he wound up all the chargers and leads, he noticed that Kate's BlackBerry charger was among them. Shit. He remembered packing it, and he had forgotten all about it when they separated at the airfield. He hoped they would have a spare charger at the lab so he could contact her.

Dragging his duffelbag behind him, he slipped out of the door and walked down towards the freeway, heart pounding with the anger that propelled him onwards. He didn't know how he was going to get there, or how long it would take, but Mangold's trail would start in Sagebrush.

Paul was going to track him down, whatever it took.

97

# 13

Midday, on the San Bernardino Freeway. The sky was a sheer, metallic blue, the sun burning through the ozone, baking the earth, the air outside the vehicle lethally hot. Two women sat inside the car, protected from the scorching sun by the air-con that ruffled the golden hair of the woman in the passenger seat. She sat upright, sunglasses on, her beautiful face serene, while the driver thumped the radio with the palm of her hand.

'Goddamn piece of junk.' The driver stabbed buttons on the radio, eliciting one hiss of static after another, before punching it again, using the same move she would use to break a man's nose. She switched it off, silence filling the car. She was solid and muscled, with a neck that bordered on bullish and a high colour in her wide cheeks, cropped curly dark hair and biceps like a Marine.

Without moving her head, Angelica said, 'Keep calm, Sister.'

Heather made a low sound under her breath, putting both hands on the wheel and concentrating on the road. She was rarely calm. Sometimes, in the moments after orgasm, or after she'd killed someone, when their blood was still fresh on her hands, a stillness would come over her, like light filling her body, taking away the pain. But it never lasted long. She ran on rage. It was the fuel that powered her.

The traffic was crawling in and out of the city, stretching across every lane. Horns sounded out like seabirds calling to one another.

'Don't see why I can't get a decent car like Cindy's, instead of this heap of shit,' Heather complained. Angelica ignored her. She had heard it all before.

Eventually, when she realised Angelica wasn't going to say anything to mollify her, Heather said, in a quieter voice, 'I'm sorry.'

The corners of Angelica's mouth lifted a millimetre. 'No need to apologise, Sister.' She reached across and stroked Heather's hair with a crooked index finger. 'We all feel anger. We just have to point it in the right direction.'

Heather pressed her head against Angelica's finger, but it was withdrawn quickly, and she snatched a glance at the woman beside her, looking for the same sign she'd been seeking for years. But Angelica had slipped back into neutral, and was gazing straight ahead at the backs of other cars.

They drove in silence for a while. Heather gestured at the line of cars crawling out of the city, the faces of their occupants etched with stress visible even from the other side of the freeway. 'Wonder how many of them are already infected?' she asked.

Angelica merely smiled enigmatically. 'They have no idea what's coming, do they? They're worried now—but imagine the chaos in a month's time . . .'

Heather paused. 'Dadi . . . *we're* ready, you and I—we've been ready for years . . . but the other Sisters—are they?'

Heather liked to do this; to elevate herself to the unofficial position of Angelica's second-in-command by slyly casting doubt on the commitment of the others. Angelica knew it, but indulged it nonetheless.

Angelica pretended to consider. 'Sister, you know how hard we've trained to prepare for this. I believe we've all followed our instructions to the letter. Peak fitness, unquestioning dedication, limitless thanksgiving . . .'

'Even Sister Preeti?'

'Preeti isn't a warrior. She has other skills we need. I will keep her at the ranch when the time comes. Simone, Cindy, you and I will handle the business. Brandi will drive.'

'Good plan,' said Heather, accelerating towards a stray dog that wandered dangerously across the freeway. 'As always.' The car hit the dog and Heather smiled as its mangy body somersaulted in the air beside them.

They entered the city. The streets were bustling, life going on as normal, the beautiful people of LA shopping, scurrying between offices and lunch places, cruising along with their tops down, despite media reports of a killer virus ravaging their city.

Angelica checked her phone. 'We're early. Let's drive around for a while.'

They cruised the coastline: Malibu, Santa Monica, Venice, down to Redondo Beach. Finally, when they had seen enough, Heather turned the SUV round and they headed towards South Central, checking the coordinates on the satnav.

\*      \*      \*

The two men were waiting in their own vehicle, a black Jeep only marginally smaller than Heather's SUV. Lil Wayne pumped from the stereo, the two men nodding along almost imperceptibly. Heather drove past them once, taking a good look, then circled the block and pulled up behind them.

The two women got out, momentarily stunned by the unseasonable heat. They waited for the doors of the Jeep to open. There was no one else around.

This was South Central, the part of LA that tourists are warned, in block capitals, with exclamation marks, to avoid. It was Simone's home turf, and Angelica had originally intended to bring her along. But Simone had started to tremble at the mention of it—something about some unfinished business, the reason that Simone had joined the Sisters in the first place—and Angelica needed someone with earthquake-proof nerves, someone who would be ice-cool anywhere.

The men were younger than Angelica had expected. Barely nineteen, by the look of them, but tough, cooked hard by years on these streets. She looked them over, in their brand-new sportswear with diamonds in their ears. It didn't matter how tough or rich they were. Neither of those things would offer protection from what was coming. What was already here.

She spoke quietly and calmly, ignoring the wide eyes of the two men, the brute, lustful looks they gave her—and the sneer as their gaze turned to Heather. One of them, who stepped a pace further forward than his colleague, was way over six foot, wore a white-and-grey basketball top and had his hair in dreads. The other, half a foot shorter, was wearing a black jacket buttoned up against the heat and had a shaven head.

'We all set?' Angelica asked.

'If you police, this is entrapment. My lawyer's just waitin' for my call.'

'We're not police.'

This meeting had been set up through a chain of contacts. The two men should have felt one hundred per cent confident that they were not undercover cops. The question irritated Angelica. Made her want to put a bullet in this punk's head.

Basketball Top looked her up and down. 'You sure don't *look* like police. All right. You got the money?'

Angelica nodded. 'Let me see the merchandise.'

The men—boys—exchanged a look of amusement before Black Jacket popped the rear door of the Jeep and unlocked a security trunk, then watched Angelica and Heather's reactions, like two boys showing off their first car, expecting the women to be impressed.

The guns were covered with a sheet, which Black Jacket pulled back. Angelica scanned the weapons, checking them against the inventory in her head. Half a dozen Glocks, a pair of Sig Sauers, two AK-47s, an Uzi, black and dull and deadly, plus enough ammunition to keep a National Rifle Association convention happy for a weekend.

'Check it,' Angelica said, and Heather—who had stayed silent so far, watching the two men like a cat keeping an eye on two mice—snapped into action, lifting the weapons and looking them over, running a hand over each of them, inspecting the ammo. The boys watched her. They appeared to be growing increasingly amused. Black Jacket kept staring at Angelica. She sensed he was the more dangerous of this pair.

Eventually, Heather nodded. 'It's good.'

'Sure it's fuckin' good,' said Basketball Top. 'Now—payment please, ladies.'

Heather went to the SUV, reached inside and took an envelope of cash from the glovebox. She handed it to Angelica, who passed it on.

Basketball Top thumbed through it and, taking a look around to double-check there was no one watching, gestured for Heather to take the guns. She set about transferring them from the Jeep to the SUV. Sweat soaked through the back of her T-shirt. When she was done, she came back and stood beside Angelica.

'Thank you, gentlemen,' Angelica said. 'Have a good day.'

Black Jacket couldn't keep his mouth shut any longer. The words he had been longing to say erupted from his mouth. 'You are one fine bitch.'

Heather immediately stepped forward. 'You apologise.'

Basketball Top laughed. Black Jacket said, 'What?'

Heather took another step closer. 'Apologise for calling her a bitch.'

'Fuck you, dyke,' said Black Jacket.

Basketball Top stopped smiling. 'Yeah, fuck you. Bitch.'

'Matter of fact,' Black Jacket continued, pulling a Glock from the waistband of his pants, 'maybe I will. Fuck you both, even the ugly—'

Before he could finish the sentence, Heather launched herself at him, surprising him with a punch to the throat. He gasped, his gun clattering to the ground, and she grabbed him and thrust him into his friend, who was scrambling to get his own gun out. Heather used Black Jacket as a shield and aimed a kick at Basketball Top's hand, connecting with the gun and sending it flying in a low arc until it crashed against the side of the Jeep.

Angelica scooped it up and trained it on the taller man.

Heather aimed another quick punch at the other one, breaking his nose and sending him to the ground. He reached for the Glock and she stamped on his hand, the finger bones crunching beneath her boots. He tried to push himself up and she stamped on his face. Then again. And again, until she was panting with exertion and Black Jacket's face was a pulp of blood and bone.

'Who's ugly now?' she said, spitting into the red mess.

Basketball Top put up his hands up. 'Hey,' he said.

Heather walked up to him, picking up the dead man's gun and pointing it at the remaining man's face.

'Hey, come on . . .' he started.

Heather shot him through the forehead.

Angelica laid a hand on Heather's shoulder. 'Thank you,' she said. 'Though you didn't need to kill the tall one. He was about to run home to his mom.'

Heather's breathing changed from sharp and shallow to slow and deep. Her pupils dilated. There was blood on the front of her T-shirt, darker than the sweat on her back.

'He called you a bitch,' she said. 'Nobody is allowed to do that, not ever.'

Angelica regarded her. She was so loyal. Always had been. Like a dog—a faithful, dangerous attack dog. She might have been ugly on the outside— the dead boy had been right about that—but on the inside she was beautiful. And she would be rewarded. They would all be rewarded.

In the distance, she could hear a siren, growing gradually louder.

'Come on, we'd better go.'

They got back into the SUV. As they drove off, Heather couldn't resist reversing over Black Jacket's body. The way the SUV bumped over him made her smile. Angelica smiled too. Another beautiful day in sunny California.

After a little while, she said, 'Take a left here.'

'Huh? Where to?'

'You'll see.'

She directed Heather until they reached Hollywood. Eventually, they pulled up outside a bar called the Rattlesnake. There were trucks parked out front, a few Harleys and a big neon Coors sign. She would definitely be able to find what she was looking for here.

The last few days, she'd been fighting off a rising feeling inside her, a familiar urge that took hold of her every couple of weeks. Usually, she could ward it off with cold showers or ten minutes beneath the sheets on her own, but sometimes that wasn't good enough. The craving was for something very specific. The closer they came to the Great Day, the more urgent became the desire; filling her, spreading outwards from her belly to her loins. The killing of the two gun dealers had brought the longing to fever pitch.

She couldn't hold off any more.

'Wait here,' she told Heather. She smiled and leaned closer to her right-hand woman. 'I'm going to bring you a present.'

Heather frowned. As Angelica sashayed into the bar and half of the men drinking there looked up as if they could smell the heat coming off her, she remembered why she never brought Heather along on these outings. Fuck it. Today Heather was going to join in. Angelica had a role for her to play.

*       *       *

Ten minutes later, Angelica walked out of the bar with a twenty-year-old construction worker in tow. Patrick was a thing of beauty, with sandy hair, a light tan and a lean, ripped body. Plus he had a boyish smile and, from the bulge in his jeans, a big cock. Angelica swallowed hard and said a little thank you to the Goddess.

Heather looked Patrick up and down and wrinkled her nose. 'Who's this?'

Angelica slid onto the back seat and gestured for Patrick to join her. 'This is Patrick. Be nice.'

'Hi, Sweet Lips,' Patrick said.

Heather looked at him with disgust and Angelica laughed and ruffled his hair. Then she leaned over between the seats and kissed Heather on the lips, before jumping back and putting her arm round Patrick. In the rear-view mirror, Heather displayed a look of confusion and excitement.

'Woo hoo!' exclaimed Patrick. 'Time to party.'

Angelica told Heather to drive them to a motel. She sent Heather to check them in to a room and while they waited, she climbed onto Patrick's lap and took hold of his face, kissing his soft lips, slipping her tongue into his mouth. He tasted of beer and peanuts. She felt her breath quicken as his penis pressed against her through his jeans. Oh yes, it was big.

He tried to grab her, to pull her closer, but she pushed herself off him and opened the door, exiting the SUV just as Heather returned. Angelica stroked Heather's short hair and leaned forward to whisper in her ear. 'Bring the guns. And your knife.'

She reached round and playfully patted Heather's ass.

Heather's eyes glinted with excitement. Patrick got out of the vehicle, grinning and walking awkwardly, and Angelica gestured for Heather to toss her the keys, leading the young man up to the motel room while her sidekick fetched the holdall from the trunk.

Once they were all inside the dingy room, Angelica shut and locked the door, then pulled the drapes closed. She turned to Patrick, a hand on her hip. Heather stood slightly behind her, the holdall containing the guns at her feet.

'Take your clothes off,' Angelica said.

He stripped as eagerly as a virgin in a teen movie, down to his shorts, which bulged comically.

'Those too.'

He pushed them to the floor and stood naked before them, proud and erect. 'So, what, are we going to, like, all get it on?'

'Shut up and lay on the bed,' Angelica commanded.

His eyes widened but then he smiled again. 'Sure.'

He lay back. Angelica walked along the side of the bed, looking him up and down. He had the body of a Greek god, a marble statue in a museum. But real, hot flesh. She took his penis in her hand and squeezed it lightly, enjoying the feel of the thick, veiny shaft, running her thumb lightly over its circumcised head. Predictably, he tried to pull her down on to the bed but she put her free hand on his chest, pressing into the smooth flesh with her long fingernails and pushing him back down. She traced her nails down across his six pack until one hand held his cock and the other cradled his balls. She bent over and took the tip of his penis into her mouth, tasting him, running her tongue over his most sensitive spot and making him moan and reach out to touch her hair.

She stood up, wiping her mouth with the back of her hand. Heather was standing by the door, staring. It was a little irritating. Angelica said, 'Bring me my bag.'

'The holdall?'

'No,' Angelica snapped. 'My tote bag.'

Heather obeyed, and Angelica snapped it open.

'Whoah,' Patrick said from the bed. Angelica had produced two sets of handcuffs.

'If you won't stop being a naughty boy and trying to grab me,' Angelica said, 'you'll have to be cuffed. I'm in charge here.'

There was a flicker of doubt on his face, like he wasn't sure how much of this was role playing, but then he smiled and nodded. 'Cool.'

Angelica held out the cuffs to Heather. 'Cuff him to the bed.'

Heather did as she was told, so the man's arms were stretched behind him, bound to the metal headboard. He grinned up at them. 'So are you going to fuck me now?'

Angelica didn't reply verbally. She gestured for Heather to approach her, simultaneously removing her own clothes, pulling her T-shirt over her head, unzipping her boots and pushing down her leather trousers. She stood in her white underwear and shook down her hair. She felt the power of the Goddess coursing through her. Her skin, as she touched it, felt ultrasensitive, all her nerve endings tingling.

'Go on, strip,' she said to Heather, noticing that her Sister was standing there, gawping. Over the years, Heather had watched Angelica undress many times, and Angelica had become increasingly aware of the way that Heather looked at her body, sneaking peeks when she thought Angelica wasn't looking. Angelica had always thought it was because Heather was envious of her taut, toned stomach, her long limbs, her small-but-perfectly-shaped breasts. Heather was all lumps and bumps, with biceps a Marine would be proud of, broad shoulders and a flat chest. Her strength was admirable but she was far from sexy. In fact, Angelica suspected Heather was asexual. She had never shown any real interest in men or women. She was purely dedicated to Angelica's cause.

Heather removed her clothes clumsily, the guy on the bed barely paying her any attention, his eyes focused purely on the taller, slimmer woman who now removed her bra, climbed onto the bed and straddled him, pressing her crotch against his through her underwear, leaning forward so her long hair swept across his chest. He pulled against the handcuffs, his desperation to touch her clear in the flex of his muscles. He had beautiful arms.

A beautiful chest too. She kissed him there, flicking her tongue across his nipples in turn, which made him groan. She took one nipple lightly between her teeth and applied pressure. He gasped. She trailed kisses down from his pecs to his abs,

109

that strong, toned stomach. He bucked beneath her, his cock so hard against her underwear. She moved her face down to his groin and gently ran her tongue from the base of his cock to the tip, making him thrust against her face. That annoyed her, but it was okay, she understood his eagerness.

She took him into her mouth again, as deep as she could, reaching up to his chest as she sucked him, digging her nails into his chest, raking them down to his stomach, then up again. The sounds he made were half-pleasure, half-pain.

His quickening breath made her worry that he might come too quickly so she removed her mouth, causing a groan of disappointment, and she sat back on his strong thighs, touching her own breasts, stroking them while she looked into his eyes, taunting him, making him pull as hard as he could against the handcuffs.

'I want to lick you,' he said. 'Come up here.'

Angelica looked at Heather, who was standing beside the bed, still staring at Angelica—staring at her breasts.

'Why don't you join us?' Angelica said, and Heather crawled on to the bed. She reached out and cupped one of Angelica's breasts.

Angelica took hold of Heather's wrist and removed her hand, surprised by the flash of disappointment on Heather's face. Before she could speak, Heather leaned forward and kissed her, sticking her tongue in Angelica's mouth. She heard Patrick say, 'Whoah,' and for a moment Angelica let Heather kiss her, even kissed her back, as Heather's hand returned to her breast. It felt exciting, even though the other woman was a clumsy kisser, her mouth too wet. Heather's free

110

hand was suddenly inside Angelica's underwear, her middle finger probing and slipping inside her.

Angelica pulled away. 'No.'

Heather looked shocked. 'I'm sorry.'

She tried to kiss Angelica again, but the blonde woman turned her head so Heather's lips connected with her chin.

'Fuck him,' Angelica commanded.

'What?'

'I said, fuck him. I want to see you do it.'

'Hey,' Patrick said. 'I don't want her to fuck me—I want you.'

'Shut up,' Angelica said, slapping his face hard. He looked stunned. She turned back to Heather. 'Get on top of him.'

Heather hesitated, then manoeuvred herself so she was straddling Patrick. She took his cock in her hand, but it had wilted.

'For fuck's sake,' Angelica said, pushing Heather aside and taking hold of the soft penis. To Patrick, she said, 'Close your eyes and keep them shut. In fact . . .' She whipped a pillowcase off one of the pillows and fashioned it into a blindfold, tying it around his eyes.

She returned to his cock, which was recovering already. Good boy. She worked it gently with her hand, until it was fully hard, then facing the foot of the bed, in the reverse cowgirl position, pushed herself onto him, his cock filling her, the angle meaning he pressed against her G-spot. She fingered her own clitoris as she rocked slowly against him.

'Don't come,' she ordered, as her own orgasm approached. She was dimly aware of Heather kneeling on the bed watching her, and she tried to

111

push the memory of Heather grabbing her from her mind. She didn't want to think about it. Had she been blind all these years? Yes, if she was honest with herself she had been deliberately blind. She had always known Heather had feelings for her, it was why she did everything Angelica asked, without question. And she had used that. But admitting to herself that Heather liked her in a sexual way was too uncomfortable. She loved Heather as a sister. That was all. Her presence now, staring at Angelica with sad eyes, was grating. But feeling sorry for her, and deciding to be charitable, she gestured for Heather to come closer.

As she rocked with increasing pace on Patrick's cock, she pulled Heather towards her and put her hand between the other woman's legs, stroking her with two fingers. Tears trickled from the corners of Heather's eyes as Angelica brought her closer to orgasm, her fingers now deep inside her, her other hand pinching Heather's nipple. Her own orgasm approached and she rocked faster and moved her fingers inside Heather at the same pace. Heather's breathing got faster and faster, and Angelica felt the waves of bliss crash over her as—oh, here it was—she came hard, and Heather came too, at the same moment.

The two women were drenched in sweat, and Angelica shuddered as she moved off Patrick.

'Don't stop,' he pleaded.

'Don't worry, I'm going to suck you again,' she said.

Angelica pointed at his penis and gestured for Heather to take him in her mouth. Heather obeyed, and Angelica wondered if Heather enjoyed tasting her juices on the boy's cock. She pulled on her

112

discarded underwear and unzipped the holdall, the sounds of slurping and groaning from the bed making her feel nauseous.

She pulled out a Sig Sauer and found the bullets, loading it, then moved to the head of the bed, pointing it at Patrick's face.

His breathing got faster and deeper as Heather's head bobbed faster. He started saying, 'Oh baby, oh baby,' and Angelica positioned her free hand on the back of the blindfold.

As he came in Heather's mouth, Angelica whipped off the blindfold, allowing him a moment to realize it had been Heather who was going down on him. Then she shot him in the face.

\*       \*       \*

They drove home in near silence.

At one point, after looking like she had been desperate to speak for an hour, Heather said, 'Have I displeased you?'

Angelica shook her head. 'No, Sister. You did well. But . . . let's not tell the other Sisters about this.'

'OK.'

Angelica turned to look out the window. It was of no import, of course. It made no difference to their great plans. But right now she wanted Heather away from her. Miles away. Just until the memory had time to go cold.

# 14

'Everyone in the lab in twenty minutes.'

Nobody was going to disobey the famous Glenn Kolosine. Kate and the rest of the team rose as one from their seats at the breakfast table, leaving their food half-eaten, taking a final gulp of their coffees. Annie led them all up to the first floor of the building, where Kolosine was waiting in front of a steel door.

He produced a swipe card, opened the door with it, and ushered them through into a changing room.

Kate was relieved to find individual cubicles. She stripped, stowed her civilian clothes in a locker and emerged into a small antechamber where a biosafety suit was waiting for her. The suit was state-of-the-art: lightweight, with a large, clear visor, and in-built radio so the scientists could communicate with each other, pressing a numbered button on a pad to control which other team member they wanted to talk to. By the time she had suited up and emerged into a short corridor that led to the lab, all the irritation that crawled beneath her skin had vanished, leaving behind a calm determination and a different kind of itch: the need to know, to solve the problem, that burning curiosity that all good scientists feel.

Junko emerged from her changing cubicle and smiled at Kate from behind the mask of her helmet, which was stamped with the number 6. Kate was number 3.

Junko's voice emerged through a speaker beside Kate's left ear. 'Are you OK?'

Kate found number 6 on her communication pad and pressed it.

'Yes, I'm—' she began, but her words were drowned out by a roar of noise, the *whomp-whomp* of a helicopter descending on the building, so close by that it sounded as if it was going to land in the room with them. The others—Annie, Chip and the two lab technicians whose names Kate couldn't remember—emerged from the cubicles and stood beside them, waiting for Kolosine. Kate recognised the light in their eyes, the suppressed excitement. The rush of noise from outside dropped away and before anyone could speak, Kolosine emerged, his hairy face inside the mask reminding Kate of a hamster in a ball, minus the cuteness. His voice blasted into the helmets of every team member.

'OK—you three, come with me.' He pointed at the men. 'Ladies, you wait here.'

To get to the lab, they had to pass through an airlock. Kate and the other women stood back while the men entered the airlock and closed the door behind them, leaving them in silence.

Kate realised her mouth was hanging open. 'Did he just call us "ladies"?' she broadcasted to Junko and Annie simultaneously.

Junko pulled a face. 'I think he is a brilliant man. But he is also—what is the English?—a sexist asshole.'

'You got that right, sister,' said Annie.

The next ten minutes crawled by, Kate and the other two remaining mostly silent while they waited to be let into the lab. It was sweltering in the suit and a bead of sweat rolled into Kate's eye. She breathed deeply and thought about Paul, wondered what he was doing. Probably waking up in some

115

nice comfortable hotel room, enjoying a full breakfast on government expenses. She hoped he was all right and not still fighting with Harley.

Finally, Kolosine re-emerged and gestured impatiently to them.

'Never meet your heroes,' Kate muttered to herself, but she felt another surge of adrenaline as they passed through the airlock and entered the dazzling white space of the lab. She looked around. It was the kind of lab every scientist dreamed of working in: spacious, state-of-the-art equipment, everything shining with the gleam of newness. The air pressure in the lab was kept low so that no stray virus particles could be sucked out of the room. And lining the walls were biological safety cabinets in which, Kate knew, the virus samples would be kept locked away. CCTV cameras recorded their every move from each corner of the lab. Kate knew that cameras would be set up all around the exterior of the building too. All category four labs had these, as well as alarms, to detect intruders. And, according to McCarthy, this place had extra security because of the bombing. It was more secure than any bank vault.

A Trexler isolator—a kind of plastic tent used to quarantine patients, larger than the VATI—had been set up in a small room behind another metal door, a window giving a good view of the patient beneath the plastic sheeting. This room had its own exit that led outside through another airlock. Kate approached the glass and peered in, standing shoulder to shoulder with the other scientists, only Junko holding back.

The patient lying on his back inside the isolator was in his mid-to-late twenties, dark hair, broad-shouldered and probably handsome, though his good looks were masked by a grey pallor and a layer of sweat. In the silence of the lab, Kate could sense that, like her, everyone was holding their breath. Then the patient turned his head and looked at them with pink eyes. His lips moved but his words were inaudible. Kate didn't know if it was her imagination, but she thought he'd said, 'Please. Please help.'

She moved away from the glass, catching her own reflection as she turned. But in her reflection she was a child, a child watching her own parents writhe and burn with fever, a nurse wringing water from a cloth on to her mother's forehead. Kate could still feel the urge to comfort her mother, the need to hold her and make her better, even though she had been forbidden from going near either of them.

'Kate?' Junko's voice came over the speaker in her helmet. 'Are you OK? You bumped into me. I think you are shaking.'

Kate unthinkingly tried to touch her own face then shook her head. 'Damn suit. I'm . . . I'm fine, Junko. I just . . . it took me back to my childhood.'

The Japanese woman looked at her with surprise.

'Both my parents were killed by Watoto. I was told to stay away from them, but I ran up to my mother's bed as she was dying and hugged her.'

'Oh my God. What happened?'

'I caught it. I was taken to a hospital in Nairobi where they kept me in an isolator very similar to that one. It took me back, that's all.'

Before she could say anything else, Kolosine gestured for attention. 'OK, people, listen. This is LAPD Officer Marshall Buckley. First started showing signs of Watoto-X2, which is now the official name of this new strain, or Indian flu as the fucking media insist on calling it, three days ago. That means he would have contracted it a day or two before that. It has a very short incubation period, as with the original strain. This man has volunteered to help us in this urgent situation. To donate his body to science.'

'He's not dead, Kolosine,' Annie protested.

'Not yet. Anyone else want to say anything smart? Anyone else want to get the fuck out of my lab?' His eyes bulged. 'Thought not. I need a volunteer, somebody to go in there and talk to him and get a blood sample.'

'I'll do it,' Kate heard herself say.

Kolosine's attention snapped to her. 'Ah. Kate Maddox. The great Watoto expert. I guess this is a familiar scene to you, huh?'

'I wouldn't say that.' She was aware that the other scientists and lab technicians were staring at her. 'But I had Watoto as a child. I'm more likely to be immune than anyone else.'

'Not necessarily—and you're the only one who hasn't had their own blood sampled yet, so some might say you're the last person that ought to go in. But go ahead if you want, Miss Gung-Ho. The suit will protect you.'

A minute later, after Kolosine let her through the door, Kate sat down on a chair beside Officer Buckley. Shrouded by the isolator, he turned his head slowly, like a turtle, to look into her eyes. It reminded her so much of seeing her father with Watoto. His hair was stuck to his scalp with sweat and he breathed rasping, shallow breaths

118

through his mouth. A microphone and speaker had been fed into the isolator so the scientists could communicate with the sufferer inside. It made it difficult to interact with the patient and that frustrated Kate, but even though the suit protected her from the virus they couldn't risk particles being released into the lab and beyond.

'Hi,' she said softly, making sure to keep eye contact with him through the plastic. 'My name's Kate.'

'I'm Marshall,' he said. His voice was weak and muffled further by the plastic isolator.

'How bad are you feeling?' she asked.

'Like I'm on fire,' he said. 'My whole body hurts. My skin . . . it's like somebody scrubbed me with freaking sandpaper or something, then poured gasoline on me and lit it.'

He coughed, spasms that sent deadly sprays of spittle into the air inside the isolator.

'Go on,' she said.

'And my head . . . It's like I got the worst hangover I ever . . . had.' He tried to smile but it flickered and died on his lips.

'How long have you felt like this?' Kate asked.

'I only felt this bad since yesterday. Two days ago I thought it was just a cold, you know. I went into work, took some cold medicine, sucked a freaking lozenge, like that helped any. Went to bed that night thinking I probably got flu, going to have to take a day off. Then I woke up feeling like this, called the station to tell them. Next thing I know there are guys in bio suits like you're wearing asking me if I wanted to help out, would I sign some papers.'

He coughed again. 'You a doctor?'

119

Kate replied, 'Not that kind of doctor. I'm a scientist, a virologist. We're trying to find a cure for what you've got.'

'And what have I got?'

'Hasn't anyone told you?'

'Nobody's told me squat.'

Kate felt a prickle of anger beneath her skin. 'It's called Watoto,' she said. 'Or to be precise, Watoto-X2. It comes from Africa.'

'Africa? What in hell is it doing in LA?'

'That's one of the things we're trying to find out. But Watoto . . . I've had it.'

His eyes widened. 'And you got better.'

'Yes.' She felt tears sting her eyes. Despite many years of research, Kate had seldom had an opportunity to become acquainted with the patients from whom her live tissue samples came. But what was wrong with giving him a little hope?

He was quiet for a minute, closing his eyes, and Kate thought he might have drifted off. She was about to start the process of taking the blood sample when Buckley's eyes opened again.

'I want to see my kids,' he said.

Kate swallowed. She wanted to tell him he would see them soon, that everything would be fine. But she couldn't go that far. Instead, she simply nodded. She wished she could reach inside and squeeze his hand.

'Tell me about your children,' she said.

He told her. He had two daughters, aged five and three. Millie and Harper. Millie was at elementary school and loved Barbie and argued about everything. She had a real strong personality, like her mom. Harper, the three-year-old, was into *Sesame Street* and looked like her dad, everyone

120

said, and she shared his calm character too. On his second day of feeling sick, the girls had made him a get well soon card, with a smiling family of stick men and a shining sun.

Last time he saw them, when he said goodbye, they and their mother were all complaining of feeling a cold coming on.

Kate couldn't stop thinking about Jack, and how she would feel if it was him lying there close to death—as no doubt many parents in Los Angeles were doing right at that moment, with their own precious children. Or worse, the children who were having to watch, helpless, as their parents writhed and gasped in agony, the way she had watched in that Tanzanian village . . . All her working life had been dedicated to eradicating Watoto so that nobody else would ever have to go through that anguish—and yet here they were, in the grip of a potentially unstoppable pandemic of this new, supercharged Watoto.

Except there was no point thinking like that. Anything could be stopped. It was almost certainly too late to save Officer Buckley, but there were many millions of parents and children out there who were, unwittingly, relying on her and Kolosine and the rest of them. Now, more than ever, it was time to face and beat her nemesis.

Kate stood up. Built into the side of the isolator were two glove units to allow samples to be taken without physical contact with the patient. She slipped her hands into the slots, so she could now touch him with her gloves, and picked up a syringe and tube. 'Officer Buckley, you're not afraid of needles, are you?'

He shook his head, wincing at the effort. 'That's

121

one thing I ain't afraid of.' He rolled his head to one side and looked into Kate's eyes. 'I just want to see my daughters again,' he said. 'You will be able to help me, won't you? My little girls . . .' He fell silent.

Kate couldn't respond, did not know what to say. How could she tell him that it was highly unlikely he would ever see his children again? That within a couple of days, his daughters would be as sick as he was now? There was nothing she could say that wasn't a lie.

When she looked up from preparing the syringe, she saw that the big, tough LA police officer was crying.

## 15

'We're going to the pool today, right, Daddy?'

Jack hovered outside Vernon and Shirley's bedroom, dressed only in his stripy trunks and un-inflated orange armbands, wearing swimming goggles. There was no answer from the other side of the closed door, only the swell of what sounded to Jack like some really boring music.

'Right, Daddy?' Jack raised the pitch of his voice a little higher to make sure he was heard over the violins. ''Cos you promised we could today. You said you'd teach me to do diving. You said so, on the way back yesterday.'

He pressed his ear against the door, and heard Shirley crying quietly. She'd been in bed with a really bad tummy-ache ever since they'd got home from the airport.

'Daddy, you're definitely in there, aren't you?' he persisted, hopping from foot to foot on the wooden landing floor. The door opened suddenly, and Jack looked up into his father's face. Through the plastic lenses of his goggles, Vernon appeared slightly blurry and distorted. There was no mistaking the barely concealed irritation and stress on his face, though.

'Jack,' he began, leaning an arm against the doorframe as though the effort of even speaking was too much. With a sinking feeling, Jack knew what was coming. He ripped off his goggles and flung them down the landing, where they spun along the wooden boards and skidded into a vase full of pampas grass taller than Jack himself.

'You're gonna tell me we can't go, aren't you! It's NOT FAIR!'

Vernon picked up his small son and hugged him, but Jack squirmed and kicked out in fury and disappointment.

'I'm real sorry, Jackie, but Auntie Shirley is really sick. I can't leave her. She's in too much pain.'

Jack paused for a moment. 'Are you sure she doesn't have the Indian flu?' he asked quietly. 'Are we all gonna get it?'

Vernon shook his head. 'It's definitely not flu. It's her diverticulitis. It's flared up again.'

Jack neither knew nor cared what divert-whatever was, as long as it wasn't the deadly flu. 'But you promised you'd take me swimming today.'

Vernon moved Jack's chin so that he was forced to look at him. 'Now, Jackie, I didn't actually promise—I said I'd take you if I could. And I can't, not today. You're going to have to be real grown-up and try and understand.'

'You *did* promise! And, I'm not a grown-up, I'm EIGHT,' yelled Jack, and wriggled so hard that Vernon had to put him down.

'Well, if you're going to be this naughty, I couldn't take you anyway,' Vernon said, looking disapprovingly at him over his half-moon reading glasses.

'Oh, so what? I'm going over to Bradley's. I bet his mom will take us because she's nice, not like you.'

Vernon snorted. 'I doubt that Gina Morton's been straight long enough to take her kids swimming since they were born.'

Jack put his hands on his hips and glared at his father. 'Gina Morton ALWAYS stands up straight, so THERE.' And with this devastating parting shot, he marched straight down the stairs, out the back door and through the gap in the hedge into Bradley's backyard.

\*       \*       \*

'Going swimming, honey?' Gina said when Jack appeared in her kitchen, bright red with anger, still barefoot and in armbands.

He climbed up on his favourite bar stool and accepted the carton of chocolate milk that Gina automatically removed from the refrigerator and slid in front of him, taking a long slurp through the straw.

'No. Daddy said he'd take me and now he's not going to 'cos Auntie Shirley is ill. It's not fair. I only got here yesterday!'

He put his elbows on the breakfast bar and sunk

his chin in his hands.

Gina breezed around the counter and gave him a hug. She smelled funny, but not in a bad way. Her skirt was all floaty like the Dementors in Harry Potter, and on her ankle she had a bracelet thing with shells and little bells on it, so she tinkled when she walked. Her skin was very brown and wrinkly, and she always looked like she'd been crying, even though she didn't sound like it.

'So you have plenty of time left to go swimming with your dad. I know it's tough, honey, but let's look at the positive—if he wasn't so busy taking care of Shirley then we wouldn't be seeing so much of you, would we? And that would be real sad for Bradley, and for me. It was awesome that you came for pizza last night, and now you're here today too! Besides, Bradley and Riley's daddy works so hard making movies that he hardly EVER sees them. He lives in California, which is real far away?'

'My mum's gone to California,' Jack said glumly. 'She's working too hard to see me too.'

'Ah, you poor thing.' Gina gave him another squeeze, and he noticed the faded tattoo on her wrist. The sharp edge of the deflated armband scratched the side of his chest. 'But your mom is doing real important work, your daddy says, trying to find a cure for this horrible flu. And she'll be back before you know it. Now, what are you boys going to do today? Seeing as you're in your swimsuit, what do you say we get the water slide out? You go find Bradley—he's in his room watching TV last I saw of him—and I'll go hook up the hose, OK?'

Jack brightened. The water slide was awesome. 'OK!' he said, slipping off the stool and running

125

upstairs calling his friend's name.

When he and Bradley came back downstairs half an hour later, Bradley too dressed in his swimming trunks, they burst into the garden—to find Gina asleep on a sun lounger, with a small squashed homemade cigarette on the patio beneath her spread-out fingers.

'Your mum sleeps a lot, doesn't she?' Jack said, squinting at Gina's prone form. Her skirt had ridden up to reveal legs hairier than Vernon's, and she was snoring gently.

'Yeah,' Bradley said. 'And she'll get mad at me if I wake her up. I'll go get Riley, he knows how to fix the slide. Riley!' he yelled, almost in Gina's ear, in the direction of the battered old silver Airstream trailer parked at the back of the yard. Gina stirred and mumbled, but didn't wake up.

Jack looked around him anxiously. He was slightly scared of Bradley's older brother, who smoked the funny cigarettes too, and had a whole ton of dark swirly tattoos across his arms, back and chest. He had a moustache and slicked-back hair, and mostly talked in swearwords and grunts.

The side door of the Airstream slid open and Riley's greasy dark head appeared. He looked as sleepy as Gina, even though it was almost lunchtime. 'What is it, short-ass?' he mumbled, as Bradley ran forward and grabbed his brother by the hand, pulling him down the three metal steps. Riley was wearing a grubby white vest and a pair of boxer shorts.

'Come help us set up the water slide, please? Mom's taking a nap. Pleeeeease?'

Riley scratched his head violently, but allowed himself to be dragged over to the garden hose and the rolled-up plastic slide that Gina had managed to remove from the garage before she fell asleep. With bad grace, he rammed the hose into the garden tap and set the water flowing down the long narrow plastic sheet. 'There you go, now leave me the fuck alone, OK?'

'Thanks Riley!' chirped Bradley, hugging his brother round the waist. 'Come play if you want, it's so fun.'

The midday sun was blazing hot, and Jack could feel the burn already on his narrow shoulder blades. Even the heat of the rubber armbands was beginning to sting the delicate flesh of his inner arms, so he ripped them off. He noticed that neither Gina nor his daddy had been out brandishing the Factor 50 like his mum would have done, and he missed her with a pang so deep that tears filled his eyes. But then Bradley grabbed his hand. 'Come on, let's do the first one together!'

Holding hands, the two boys took a running jump at the slide, and skidded down its length, the cold water a shock to their hot bodies, colliding at the end in a heap of limbs, both giggling uncontrollably. Jack forgot about his mum, and his burning shoulders. 'Again!' he cried, running back to the start. 'On our tummies this time!'

Some time later, when they were both soaked, scraped and exhausted, they decided to stop for a lemonade break. Bradley went into the kitchen to grab a couple of Snapples, and Jack lay down in the shade of the Airstream to wait for him, panting like a dog. Gina was still snoring on the deck.

Riley was talking on his mobile phone inside the Airstream, and Jack listened, awed by the language he was hearing. 'Yeah, dude. I'm fucking freakin'

127

out here. He's not answering my calls. I mean, I know he's a loser, but he's my dad, right? And he's a rich loser, too, har har. What would you do? That shit is getting outta hand . . . Dad ain't got no one to take care of him out there. What if, man, I dunno, what if he's like lying in his house, sick? Or worse?'

There was a pause. 'I'd drive, of course. I'll hook the trailer up to the Lincoln. Sweet.'

Another pause. 'Nah, man, I never get the flu and shit like that. Strong as a horse and hung like one too, har har!'

Jack did not understand what that meant. But then he found it hard to understand quite a bit of what Riley said.

'Why not? Boring as fuck around here. Besides, if I go see the old man, he'll front me a few hundred bucks to get home again—he'll freak 'cos of this flu epidemic, and want me to get home safe—and I'll be in the money. We could drive up to Seattle or somewhere. Wanna come?'

There was an even longer silence, and then: 'Well, screw you, I'll go by myself.' Jack heard the phone clatter down. 'Fucking pussy,' said Riley.

Jack stood up when he saw Bradley carefully carrying the two bottles of Snapple towards him. 'Let's go inside,' he hissed. 'I need to tell you something important!'

Once in Bradley's room, they sat on the bed, leaving two soaking imprints of their wet trunks on his Transformers duvet cover. The air con was on full blast, and they both shivered.

'Your brother's going to hook up the trailer and drive to California to see your dad so he can give him some money,' said Jack, feeling very important

128

at being the bearer of such big news. 'You won't tell him I told you, will you?' he added nervously.

To Jack's surprise, Bradley's eyes brimmed over with tears. Bradley scrubbed them away with the back of his hand, and climbed under his duvet. 'I'm cold,' he said in a muffled voice, but Jack could hear him sniffing under there.

'Why are you crying?' he ventured. He felt bad that his news had been taken that way—he hadn't realised it would upset his friend.

''Cos that means Riley's going away again, and the bad flu is in California, and Mom thinks that Dad's probably got it 'cos I heard her talking to Riley about it, and if Riley goes, he might get it too and what if they both die?'

'They won't,' Jack said with confidence. 'Riley never gets the flu and shit, and besides my mummy is going to make an injection that cures it. I know she can, because she gave me one once when a bad man gave me a nasty sort of flu. It was in my bum— *butt*—and it hurt. But it stopped me getting sick.'

'We should go find your mom, and get her to make sure my dad is OK,' said Bradley, emerging red-faced from under his duvet. 'She's in California too, right?'

'Right,' said Jack, staring at his friend. He thought how much he already missed his mother, and how pleased she would be to see him. It had been great to visit his dad, but he was so busy looking after Shirley . . . 'Will Riley let us come with him?'

Bradley looked doubtful. 'I dunno. Would your dad let you go?'

Jack thought of Vernon, and the closed bedroom door. 'I don't think he'd mind. I could just leave him a note.'

'Cool. Let's go ask Riley!'

* * *

'You must be fucking joking,' said Riley, when the two boys appeared at the door of the Airstream. 'How did you know that's where I'm going?' He glared at Jack, who quaked.

Bradley ignored the question. He reached out his skinny arm and leaned nonchalantly on the doorframe of the Airstream, and then jumped back like a scalded cat as the hot metal pressed into his palm. 'Does Mom know?' he asked, slyly.

'No, she doesn't, and if you tell her, you are one dead boy. Got it?' Riley narrowed his eyes and loomed menacingly into his brother's face. Bradley was unperturbed.

'I won't tell her—if you let me come with you.'

He ducked out of reach as Riley tried to slap his head. 'You little fucker! That's blackmail.'

'She'll take the keys away if she knows. Or let your tires down like she did that one time before . . . Aw, come on, Riley, he's my daddy too. I'm worried about him as well.' Jack watched in admiration as Bradley changed tack and went for the sympathy vote. Fat tears dropped down his cheeks. 'Pleeeeease, Riley? I'll be good, I swear. I'll sit in back and play my DS, I won't bug you while you're driving . . . And, remember, you *did* say you'd take me on a trip in the Airstream. You promised!'

Riley shook his head incredulously and scratched at the mass of black hair in his armpit. 'Shit.'

130

'Please?' Bradley reached out and took his brother's hand, sensing capitulation.

Riley wavered for a moment, then shook his head. 'No way. If you wanna be a snitch, that'll just show what a baby you are. Now get outta my way.'

He retreated into the Airstream, and Bradley looked crestfallen. But only for a few seconds. Bouncing back, he whispered in Jack's ear. 'Don't worry, I've got a plan!'

## 16

It was mid-afternoon when the truck rumbled into Sagebrush and pulled to a halt. Paul hopped down from the cab into a cauldron of heat. Looking around him, at the cars and trucks spitting up dust on the freeway, at the desert landscape and the vast, forbidding sky, he felt a long, long way from home.

'Downtown is that way,' the driver said, pointing up the road. 'Gonna be a long walk. Maybe the folks over at that gas station could call you a cab.'

'That's OK. I'll walk. Thank you so much for the lift. Ride, I mean.'

The truck driver looked Paul up and down. He'd been quiet the whole journey. 'Whatever you're searching for, I hope you find it.'

The truck pulled away. Through force of habit, Paul took out his phone. He had sent Kate a couple of texts asking if her phone was still alive and, if it was, to call him. No response yet. Frustrating—but she must either be busy or her BlackBerry was dead and she had no way of charging it. He yawned so hard he thought it might dislocate his jaw. Part of him wanted to lie down here in the long, dry grass by the side of the road. But he needed to get into town.

Put one foot in front of the other and keep going, he told himself.

After leaving the motel early in the morning, he had walked into Bakersfield, found a small park and laid down in the shade of some trees, where, clutching his duffel bag, he had slept like a baby for several hours. He figured that Harley would assume he'd left town immediately, and if he was going to chase after him, would have done so first thing.

Later, waiting by the side of I-5, thumb uplifted, he had wondered if he was making a stupid mistake. But then he reminded himself that he was doing this for Stephen, and for Kate. And because he didn't trust Harley and his government chums.

What would they do if they caught up with him? Lock him up? Deport him? Before that happened, he needed to find Mangold and figure out what to do with whatever information he unearthed. He had around four hundred dollars in cash and he knew that as soon as he used his Visa card to withdraw more he would be tracked down. That money wouldn't stretch far, though. He couldn't waste it on cabs.

After a long wait by the side of the road in Bakersfield a chain-smoking salesman had picked him up, dropping him an hour or so later in the middle of nowhere, a little place called Lebec. From there he'd endured another long wait before hitching a ride with the silent truck driver.

The road he was walking on seemed to go on for ever, and he began to wish he'd taken the truck driver's advice and found a cab. There was no shade, and the only sound was the wheels on his duffel bag bumping along behind him. His bottle of water had long since run dry. Lurching with dizziness, sweat pouring into his eyes, he walked on, lizards skittering out of his path. He thought of his brother, and felt a sudden fierce longing to have him by his side. The next moment he was on his knees in the dust, throwing up the remains of the club sandwich he'd eaten that morning.

He waited for five minutes before hauling himself back on to his feet and pressing on. Eventually, just as he was about to collapse with fatigue and heat exhaustion, the city thickened, the spaces between the buildings contracting. He found a 7-Eleven and bought a bottle of water, some breath mints and a couple of energy bars. He also picked up a newspaper.

'Wouldn't wanna be in LA right now,' the cashier said as he handed Paul his change. The cover of the paper showed a woman roller-skating while wearing a flu mask. Paul walked out of the shop with his nose buried in the news. The official death toll had ticked up since the previous day. On page 9, beyond the pictures of hospital corridors crowded with sick people, it was reported that the veteran actor Josh Sparks had died of Indian flu, his cleaner finding the body in his Hollywood mansion after he had taken to his bed with 'a cold' a couple of days before. The first famous casualty. Paul had no doubt that this news would help spread knowledge of the virus worldwide.

A little way up the road from the 7-Eleven, he came across a small business hotel. Hundred dollars a night, wi-fi in every room. That was a big

133

chunk of his cash, but, right now, he didn't care. He barely made it into his room and to the bed before he collapsed.

*       *       *

It was dark when he woke up, his mouth as dry as the desert he'd travelled through. He drank copiously from the tap in the bathroom and felt a little better. It was 9 p.m.—he'd been asleep again for hours—and more than anything he wanted to talk to Kate, but his iPhone was dead. After plugging it in and finding that she hadn't texted or attempted to call him, he opened his laptop and checked his email in case she had sent him a message—nothing.

He spent a while running searches for 'Charles Mangold Sagebrush address' but again drew a blank. Next, he searched for the address of Medi-Lab, but it had shut down so long ago the location wasn't showing up in current records.

Kate often teased him for being a geek—'the best-looking geek in Oxfordshire' she would laugh—but the work he did in computer security was challenging and important. Six months before, his team had helped break an international paedophile ring that had been operating a trade in vile videos. Paul's combination of instinct and intellectual ability helped him crack layer upon layer of secrecy, and the head of the CEOP, the Child Exploitation and Online Protection Centre, had praised his work highly.

Somewhere in the vast depths of the internet would be the answers he sought. Mangold's records, his address, everything he'd done online, should be out there.

If anyone in the world could find him, it was Paul.

He was about to start a new search when hunger drove him to abandon his laptop and head out for a bite to eat. There was an old-fashioned American diner across the street from the hotel, the kind of place he loved. He ordered a cheeseburger with fries and onion rings plus a bottle of beer. The waitress, a pretty teenager with auburn curls, giggled as Paul's stomach rumbled audibly throughout his order.

'Guess I'd better tell the chef to make it snappy,' she smiled.

'Like a crocodile sandwich.'

She laughed politely before disappearing, and Paul leaned back in his booth and tried to unknot the tension from his shoulders. He had a cold bubble of anxiety inside him. He wished he could get in touch with Kate—he was worried about her.

When the waitress returned with his beer, he asked her if she had heard of Medi-Lab.

'Medi-Lab? It sounds familiar . . .'

'It was a pharma company. Actually, it probably closed before you were born.'

'Oh yeah. But my mom would know more—she's lived here her whole life. That's her behind the register,' she said, gesturing towards the till.

A minute later a smiling woman came over. She looked barely older than the waitress, but Paul supposed she must be in her late thirties or early forties, with the same auburn hair as her daughter, but cut shorter, and cornflower-blue eyes. She was wearing the same figure-hugging blue-and-white uniform too. It suited her.

135

'Lucy here tells me you're asking about an old business in Sagebrush? I'm Rosie.' She had that wary look in her eyes that many beautiful older women carry, made suspicious by a lifetime of men pursuing them, promising them the earth and letting them down.

'I'm Paul.' He had considered giving a false name but didn't think it was worth it. He adopted his best charming English gentleman expression, friendly and guileless, aiming for Hugh Grant in the *Bridget Jones* films.

'He looks a little like Daniel Craig, doesn't he, Mom?' Lucy said, nudging her mother with her elbow.

Paul smiled. He had always wanted to be compared to James Bond.

'Now,' Rosie said, ignoring her daughter. 'What business did you want to know about?'

'It was called Medi-Lab,' he said, and the way her face changed was as if he'd told her he had just been let out of prison—a look he remembered well.

'Jeez. I haven't heard anyone mention Medi-Lab for years now. It's practically a cuss word round these parts.'

'You've heard of it?'

'Sure. Everybody above a certain age around here has heard of Medi-Lab.'

'You mean, like, really old?' Lucy interrupted.

Rosie gave her daughter an affectionate smile. 'I think table seven are ready to order.'

'Aw, Mom, I wanted to listen.'

'Go on, scoot.'

Lucy sashayed across the diner to table seven and Rosie turned back to Paul. 'Sorry about that. What was I saying? Oh yeah—Medi-Lab was one of the biggest employers in the city. Pretty much everyone in Sagebrush either worked there or knew someone who did. But it's ancient history now. What do you want to know about that old place for?'

He had his answer prepared. 'I'm a writer. I'm researching a book about big business in Ventura County and the Medi-Lab story seemed like an interesting tale.'

'Hmm. Well, "interesting" would be one word for it. You could also try shocking or downright shameful. I don't even know if I want to talk about it, if I'm honest.'

'It would be an enormous help to me if you could. It's that shocking element to the story that I want to get across. I heard that the top man walked away scot-free.'

'Charles Mangold.' She stared into the middle distance, clearly remembering something that disturbed or upset her.

'Did you know him?'

But Rosie had slipped into a reverie, nervously chewing a thumbnail until Paul said, 'Are you OK?'

'Huh? Yeah, yeah. Just remembering something . . .' Paul waited, trying to contain his growing excitement. 'But like I said, I don't know if I want to dredge it all up.' Lines had appeared on her forehead from where she was frowning so deeply and Paul felt a twinge of guilt. But if this woman could assist him, he had to press her.

'It really would be an immense help,' he said softly.

Rosie sighed and was on the verge of replying when the manager gestured to her from the counter.

'Wait here,' she said. 'I'll think about it.'

'Please,' he said, looking straight into her eyes.

She frowned again and he watched her return to the cash register to serve a customer, his mind racing. This was the best lead he had so far. If she said no, he would be back to square one. She *couldn't* say no.

He stared into his beer, tapping his foot impatiently, thinking about what he could offer this woman in return for help. He would pay her every penny in his savings account if it led to finding Mangold.

A shadow fell over his table. When he looked up, the waitress, Rosie, was standing there. And from the way her gaze shifted when he tried to catch her eye, he had a horrible feeling she was going to say no.

## 17

Kate sat on her bed, wearing a pair of cotton shorts and a plain white T-shirt. The encounter with Officer Buckley had left her feeling shattered, but more determined than ever. She'd just given a blood sample that Chip was now testing. As she rubbed the sore spot on her inner elbow, she thought what a shock it would be if it turned out she *wasn't* immune to Watoto-X2—she had been taking it for granted that she would be. She had asked McCarthy, who she found twiddling his over-sized thumbs in the breakfast room, to let her know when Kolosine emerged so she could talk to him and find out—or at least try.

The wait dragged on for an hour, and Kate filled the time pacing the room and going over what she had learned about the virus, trying to figure out why it was so lethal, what had caused the mutation. She felt Isaac's loss more than ever; she had grown accustomed to bouncing ideas around with him, and she missed his insight and those penetrating questions, testing her theories, suggesting avenues for further exploration. She didn't know if BIT had got anywhere with the investigation into the bombing—she would ask McCarthy later.

Why had the terrorists done it? Presumably their aim was to take out the people who might potentially find a vaccine. But if the terrorists knew anything about what they had unleashed, they ought to have been aware that virus research was a painstakingly slow affair. Clearly, these weren't rational people. Kate shuddered to think who was behind it. Was this the work of a rogue individual like Gaunt, or some kind of group? Either way, the bomb seemed a huge risk to take for something that was likely to have little effect. After all, there were many more virologists out there who *hadn't* been in that reception room.

Unless the terrorists had been masking the true target behind a massacre. Had they been after someone in particular? Someone who had been at the conference . . .

A sudden chill rippled across her skin and her stomach lurched. Was it egotistical to think—to fear—that the targets had been Isaac and herself? After all, they were the leading experts in Watoto, and had recently published a paper on it. Kate's name was on the delegate list. They might not have known she had cancelled.

139

She sat down, took deep breaths, trying to control her growing sense of dread. Could the terrorists really have been after her and Isaac? Was she just being paranoid? What if the attack had been prompted by their research paper, which detailed their latest findings into Watoto? If the bioterrorists considered them a threat that had to be neutralised at all costs, perhaps she and Isaac had come closer than they realised to making that final breakthrough.

Kate put her hand to her forehead, tried to concentrate. She could remember almost every word of the paper—nothing jumped out at her. But maybe if she showed it to the rest of the team, one of them might spot something. She was just reaching for her laptop when there was a knock at the door and Kolosine walked in, not waiting for an invitation.

'Couldn't you wait? I might have been getting dressed,' she said, sounding more outraged than she really felt.

'Want me to come back in a few minutes, give you a chance to get your clothes off?'

For the second time that morning, her jaw dropped.

'I need to talk to you,' Kolosine said, unashamedly scanning her bare legs beneath the brief shorts.

'Oh, good because I want to—'

'My office.'

He hurtled out of the room, leaving Kate no option but to follow, having to break into a jog to catch up with him.

Downstairs in his office, a spare space with a desk, computer, printer and a scattering of thick books, Kolosine threw himself into an office chair and gestured for Kate to sit too.

'Tell me, Dr Maddox, how long have you been working towards a vaccine for Watoto?'

Kate put her hands on her hips. 'All my adult life, pretty much.'

'All your adult life, huh? Well, you know how long we've got to find a vaccine now? Let me tell you. We got a couple of weeks before it kills pretty much every man, woman and child in LA. A month before it wipes out the West Coast. Even though the LA airports have been shut down, it won't be much longer than that before it reaches the walls of Buckingham Palace. This thing spreads fast. It's ultracontagious and the incubation period is four days, a good amount of time for the carrier to infect a ton of other people.' He leaned back in his chair and put his hands behind his head. 'If you've been working on Watoto for twenty goddamn years, how the fuck are we gonna find a cure in two weeks?'

Kate kept her voice level. 'It's your team, you tell *me*. And I'm well aware of all that. I believe that we were—are—so close. The people who unleashed this virus must have thought we—'

'The people who unleashed it? What are you talking about?'

She blinked at him. Hadn't Kolosine been told about the message BIT had received after the bombing? Did he not know that someone had deliberately started the outbreak? She decided not to confuse matters right now. 'Kolosine, I know this virus better than anyone.'

'Yeah, it killed your folks, huh?'

'And I survived it.'

He scratched his beard and rubbed his eyes in

141

a blur of motion. 'Clearly. Listen, Kate, I'm not saying you're not useful to us. I was thrilled when I heard you'd be joining the team.'

'Really?'

'Yeah. I would have asked for you if it hadn't already been arranged.'

'Thank you.'

'Not because of your "skills"'—he waggled two fingers in the air—'but because I want your antibodies. I want your blood. The test results are in, and yes, you are immune. You're one of the lucky ones.'

*　　　*　　　*

Kate needed some air. She strode through the building and out into the sunshine, walking past the chicken enclosure to the edge of the clearing in the forest. Beyond the gate, the road stretched into the trees. Out there, bad things were happening. But here, it was peaceful, silent apart from a gentle chorus of birdsong.

'Hey, Kate.'

She jumped, holding her palm to her chest. It was McCarthy, walking down the path towards her, a pair of sunglasses concealing his eyes. He'd startled her, but it was nice to see a friendly face.

'Tosca. Did you follow me?'

'Came out for a smoke.' He produced a pack of Marlboro from his jacket pocket, lighting up in one fluid motion. 'And you can save the lecture for a man who gives a shit.'

'Let me have one.'

He looked surprised but offered her the pack

then lit the cigarette for her. 'Didn't take you for a smoker.'

'I haven't had a cigarette since I was at university.' She inhaled, felt the soft smoke fill her lungs. 'Whoa. Head rush. But I needed one.'

'Rough morning, huh?'

'Rougher than a cat's tongue.' It was an expression of Paul's.

'I hear you. That poor mother . . . That poor sucker—ah, you know what I'm trying to say.'

She took another drag on her cigarette. It tasted bad but she was going to smoke it all the way down. 'It's that dick, Kolosine. He told me the only reason they asked me out here was because I survived Watoto. That meant I was likely to be immune to the new strain. I was tested today and I *am* immune. Kolosine thinks he can use my blood cells to create an antivirus.'

'Well . . . that's a good thing, right?'

'In theory. I mean, of course, if he's right and my blood can help stop this outbreak, I'll be ecstatic. I won't care that they didn't actually want me for my expertise. My priority is to find a cure, whatever it takes. But the thing is, I've been working with my own blood for years. I've spent two decades trying to do what he's suggesting for the original strain of Watoto, and it doesn't work. I can't identify the right peptide. Not to mention that this is a whole new strain.'

'You're gonna have to break this one down for me. I'm not a scientist, remember.'

She stared into the trees, thought she saw something move there. An animal, probably. She hoped it wasn't a mountain lion. 'OK. When you catch a virus, your body tries to fight it. It creates

143

antibodies. With something like regular flu, your body usually wins. The period when you're sick is when the antibodies are battling with the virus. But you know all that, right?'

'Uh-huh.'

'So when you fight a virus and win, your body never forgets. It knows which antibodies to create to kill the virus. That's why you never get the same virus twice. Like with the flu—if you encounter a strain of flu you've had before, you might feel the first stirrings of symptoms but it never develops into the full-blown illness. It's how a lot of vaccines work. You give somebody a weaker version of the virus, their body fights it off, and after that the antibodies remain to stand guard against the full version of the vaccine.'

'But it doesn't work with all viruses?'

'No—if it did it would be easy. We would create a weak, non-fatal version of Watoto and use it to inoculate everyone.' She took a final drag of the cigarette. 'Kolosine's going to take another blood sample and run my antibodies over a peptide library.'

'What's that?'

'A peptide library? Well, in my body there will be huge numbers of antibodies that respond to every virus I've ever had. Among them, like a needle in a haystack, is the particular antibody that we need to fight Watoto. The peptide library should help us find that needle.'

McCarthy made a confused face.

'Come on, it's not that hard. The antibody is a key, but I have thousands of keys in my blood, and we have no idea which key we need. The only way to find it is to work out which lock it fits. The peptide library contains a massive number of locks, including the Watoto lock. We pass all the keys over all the locks until bingo, one key fits the Watoto lock and lights up. And that's it—you have found the Watoto key, which you can then use to make a vaccine.'

'If I'd had you as a teacher at high school, maybe I wouldn't have flunked science.'

'Thanks.' Her smile turned into a frown. 'But the thing is, I've tried it dozens of times myself and the key will never show itself. The antibody must be really scarce in my blood. But Kolosine says he's developed a turbo-charged process that he reckons will work.'

'Which would be awesome, right?'

'Yes, but . . . I don't know, maybe it's because I've taken a dislike to him.' She threw down the cigarette and ground it into the dirt with her heel. 'I will go along with it, and of course I hope he turns out to be right. Because if he is, this whole thing could be over already.'

'But you don't believe it?'

'Nothing's that easy, Tosca,' she said. 'Come on, we'd better get back.'


18


As Kate trudged back up the stairs and along the hallway to her room, a door opened.

'Kate!' It was Annie, peering exaggeratedly up and down the hall to check that nobody was looking. She jerked her head to indicate that Kate should come in.

'Check out what I've got,' she said in a stage whisper.

Kate smiled, and then laughed out loud when she saw what Annie had been concealing behind her back—a small half-full bottle of Jack Daniel's.

'Excellent!' Kate said, feeling like a schoolgirl rebel; first the cigarette, now an illicit drink.

'When's your next shift?' Annie asked, closing the door behind them and gesturing for Kate to sit down on her bed.

'Not till eight thirty,' Kate said, checking her watch. Annie was rinsing out another tooth mug in the en-suite, and Kate lay back on the bed, feeling herself unwind a little in anticipation of a drink and some female company.

'Here you go,' Annie said, unscrewing the bottle and pouring a generous measure into the mug. The sharp sweet smell of the liquor in Kate's nostrils took her back to her student days. She laughed again.

'I haven't drunk JD out of a mug in the middle of the afternoon since I was at university,' she said, accepting it.

'Desperate times . . .' said Annie cheerfully. They clinked mugs, and Kate took a sip.

'Ah, that's better. Thanks.'

'You're welcome. I could see the terror in your eyes when I said this place was dry.'

'Ha, you're making me sound like an alcoholic. I'm not—but it's a bit of a stressful situation, wouldn't you say?'

Annie's expression turned serious. 'Just a bit. So, how are you finding it here?'

Kate shrugged, not sure how much to admit to. She was glad Annie had asked her the question

146

before she'd finished her drink. 'Great facilities,' she said neutrally. 'Fantastic to be able to work with an unlimited research budget, too—I'm not used to that.'

'I bet you miss your partner, though,' Annie fished.

'Work partner or home partner?' Kate asked, visualising Paul and Isaac with a pang of longing for each so strong that she almost downed a huge gulp of the JD before thinking better of it. Kolosine would skin her alive if she went drunk to her next shift. This didn't seem to concern Annie; she was guzzling her liquor as though it was apple juice.

'Well, both, I guess—but I was thinking of your research partner. I was so sorry to hear about that.' Annie put a hand on Kate's forearm and squeezed. 'You had a lucky escape, didn't you? How come you weren't at that conference too?'

Kate frowned. 'How do you know I was meant to go?'

Annie looked momentarily flustered. 'Oh, sorry, Kate, I didn't mean to pry. I just assumed you were meant to be going if Isaac Larter was. Weren't you?'

'Yeah, I was, as it happens. My son had chickenpox so I cancelled last minute. Anyway, can we change the subject? How did you end up in this team?'

Annie opened her mouth to speak, and then froze, pushing her blonde curls behind one ear as though this would help her hear better. 'Wait— what was that?'

'What?' Kate hadn't heard anything.

Annie put her fingers to her lips, placed her mug on the floor, and tiptoed towards the bedroom

147

door. She slowly turned the door handle—and then wrenched the door wide open, dashing out into the hallway. 'Can I help you?' she shouted after someone.

Kate got up and followed her out, still clutching her mug. She saw a flash of meaty calf vanish around the corner towards the staircase, and a brief swish and crackle of nylon overalls.

'It was Adoncia,' said Annie in disgust. 'That woman creeps me out. I swear she had her ear pressed against the door. What the hell was she hoping to hear?'

Kate looked down at her drink. 'Maybe she suspected we had illicit alcohol in here,' she said.

Annie giggled. 'Maybe. Quick, let's go get rid of the rest of the evidence.'

But Kate put her hand over the top of her mug when Annie tried to give her a refill. She'd only had half of the first one, and was already feeling woozy. *At this rate I'll need a nap before my shift*, she was thinking, when there was a loud rap at the door.

'Now what?' Annie said, hastily concealing her cup again.

Junko stuck her head into the room. 'Hurry, both of you, we've all got to get into the lab—now. Kolosine's orders. It's an emergency.'

'What's happened?' Kate jumped to her feet, unspeakably relieved that she hadn't had another drink. Annie stood up too, and visibly swayed.

'You'll see,' Junko said grimly. 'Just hurry.'

## 19

'Thank you so much for agreeing to talk to me,' Paul said to Rosie.

'That's OK. It was a shock to hear Mangold's name again—I hadn't thought about Medi-Lab in an awful long time.'

Paul had met her back outside the diner at eleven, having first returned to his hotel room for a shower and a shave. It was still warm despite the late hour and he put on a polo shirt and a clean pair of jeans, wanting to look respectable and trustworthy. He was wide awake now, his body clock so out of kilter it didn't know what time zone it was in. He still hadn't heard anything from Kate, so while he waited he'd emailed her, cryptically, saying he was safe but couldn't tell her where he was, and asking her to reply and let him know she was OK.

He checked the news while he was online: the first cases of Indian flu had been reported beyond LA, in parts of Los Angeles County. A woman had died in Pasadena, another in Malibu. Twitter was full of LA residents tweeting about how they felt sick, and scared.

Back at the diner, he had been starting to worry Rosie had changed her mind and sneaked out the back door, but she came out at 11.30 and suggested they head to a nearby bar. She had changed out of her waitress's uniform into a white blouse and denim skirt. The bar was quiet, but airless and sweaty. As he sat down opposite her at a table in the back, it struck him again how attractive she was.

Attractive but haunted, the fine lines of her face mapping a history of adversity. Like Kate.

'So what do you know about Medi-Lab?' he asked, after they had exchanged a little small talk.

'My father used to work there. Not in the lab or anything like that. He was a salesman—selling Medi-Lab's drugs to doctors and whatnot. He wasn't at home much when I was a teenager, on account of him always being out on the road. He'd come home, what, once a month? He called home a lot, though—every night before I went to bed.' She rested her chin on her palm, her eyes misting. 'Every night without fail.'

'Do you know what kind of drugs he was selling?'

'I'm not one hundred per cent sure. Antibiotics, mostly, I think.'

'Not antivirals? Antibiotics treat bacteria. I thought Medi-Lab predominantly worked on virus research?'

'Hmm . . . well, like I said, I'm not totally sure. Drugs. That was all the detail I knew. Daddy helped doctors cure sick people. Some months, he'd help a lot of doctors and I'd get presents and my mom would get a lot of new clothes and everyone would be smiling. But most months, things would be tight, the refrigerator would be half-empty and my mom would sit around looking sick with worry . . .'

Paul waited for her to continue.

'Then, when the big scandal happened with the virus and the company went bust, my father lost his job. After that, the refrigerator was pretty much always half-empty.' She smiled suddenly. 'Listen to me. What a drama queen. Talking like some character from a Charles Dickens novel. But it was shitty—excuse my French—back then. Daddy was always raging about Mangold, about how it was all his fault the company had gone under, and how he'd gotten away with it, was still living in his big old house with plenty of money.'

'Do you think I could talk to your father?'

Her voice was quiet. 'He died.'

'Oh. I'm sorry. How, er . . . what happened?'

'He died of pneumonia. It was a long time ago now—a couple of years after he lost his job. He was only forty-three. But he got sick a lot in that couple of years, I think because he was so depressed, drinking a lot.'

'That's really sad. I'm sorry to dredge all this up. It must have been hard for you.' He knew these were platitudes, but he didn't know what else to say. And while the sympathy he felt for Rosie and her late father was genuine, he couldn't help wondering how useful this information might be in locating Mangold.

'How much do you know about the big health scare that led to Medi-Lab being closed down?'

'Only what Daddy told me and what was on TV at the time. They were working on a cure for some nasty African virus when there was a breakout. It was contained, but a couple of people died.'

'Was it the Watoto virus?'

'I don't know . . . The name kind of sounds familiar.'

From living with Kate, Paul had a good knowledge of nasty viruses. 'Or could it have been Ebola, or Marburg?'

Rosie shook her head. 'I don't know. Maybe the second one you mentioned. Anyway, whatever it was, a couple of the scientists who worked in the lab there caught it and died. I remember there were

151

journalists all over the place. Daddy said the place was crawling with secret agents.'

'FBI? I thought the Department of Health were responsible for closing it down?'

'Hmm. He definitely said secret agents. But maybe he was mistaken.'

'And do you know what happened to Mangold? Apart from continuing to live in his big house?'

'No, not really. Except Daddy . . . I just realised I keep calling him Daddy. Huh. How about that? My *father* used to cuss him so much I started to hate him myself. I know he lived out of town. Still does, for all I know.'

Paul took his iPhone out of his pocket, ready to type in a note. 'Do you know where?'

Disappointingly, she said she didn't. 'Are you trying to find him?'

'Yes, I want to try to interview him.' He hated being disingenuous, especially when Rosie was being so open.

'Can't you just look him up on the internet or something?'

'I've tried—believe me, I've *really* tried. He seems to be completely off the radar. Any idea how I can find out where he lives? I *need to know*.'

He had raised his voice and her body language changed in an instant. Where previously she had been leaning forward, now she sat upright in her chair, shoulders back, her eyes narrowing. 'OK— what's really going on here?' she demanded.

'What do you mean?'

'Well, you seem pretty worked up about finding Mangold. Beyond the call of journalistic duty, I'd say. Are you really writing a book about him?'

Paul exhaled. What was the point in lying?

152

'Actually—no . . . Sorry. It's a long story.'

'I think I'd better go.' She stood, briskly gathering up her purse.

'No, please!'

Paul didn't know how much Rosie could really help him, but he didn't want her to leave. He was enjoying her company, more than he'd enjoyed anyone's company for a long time. With the exception of Kate and Jack, of course. The thought of her running out alarmed him, and he fleetingly regretted telling the truth.

'Please,' he said. 'Sit down and I'll tell you everything.'

She hesitated, then sat back in her seat, tracing with her fingertip the edges of a stain on the table in front of her. 'Sweet Home Alabama' came on the jukebox, and Paul noticed her finger tapping in time to the intro. He was surprised that she'd stayed. She didn't know him, had no idea if she could trust him. But there was something about her that made him think she was lonely, that maybe she didn't have anyone to talk to apart from her grown-up daughter and her customers. And that maybe she was enjoying his company too.

'Thank you. OK . . .' He paused, aware that the story he was about to tell would sound far-fetched, even though it was true. He had to be careful how he told it. 'A couple of years ago my twin brother, Stephen, was killed by a virus—a man-made virus.'

'Man-made? Do things like that really exist?'

Paul nodded. 'I used to be sceptical about that kind of thing too. But it does happen. And Mangold was involved. He was funding the guy who made this virus. Because of that, he was partly responsible for my brother's death, so I need to find him.'

153

'This is crazy,' Rosie said.

'I knew you'd think it sounded crazy.'

'No, I meant, a few hours ago, this was just a normal, boring day. Then this Englishman walks into my diner and cracks open the past, then starts telling tales about searching for the man who helped kill his brother with a deadly virus.'

'Yeah. It's insane. But believe me, I've seen crazier things.'

'I bet you have.'

The air between them was thick with tension. Rosie was looking straight into his eyes, trying, it seemed, to read him.

'Excuse me,' she said, standing up again, once more hooking her bag strap over her shoulder.

'Are you leaving?'

'Don't look so worried. I'm only going to the bathroom.'

He sat and waited for a few minutes, convinced she had left the bar and that, unless he went back to the diner and begged her to reconsider, he would never see her again.

But then her reflection appeared in the mirror on the wall, holding two more bottles of beer.

'Mangold,' she said, sitting down and pushing one of the bottles across to him, 'ruined my father's life. You know, I met him a couple of times, when I was a kid. They used to hold an open day for all the staff and their families every summer.' She sipped her beer. 'I gotta admit, I'd sure like to find Charles Mangold too. There are a few things I'd be keen to say to him.'

Paul nodded. There was a fire in her eyes now. It made her even more beautiful, especially when she leaned towards him across the table and he could

154

see the swell of her breasts, her skin aglow with perspiration, a pink flush around her collarbone. He couldn't help it: he was aroused. He made himself think about Kate, feeling horribly guilty, but telling himself at the same time that it was OK to find another woman attractive, so long as you didn't do anything about it.

She looked right into his eyes, holding his gaze for a few seconds longer than necessary. 'I think I know just the person who could help.'

## 20

Kate and Annie followed Junko towards the lab, walking briskly to keep up with her. Annie was surreptitiously huffing into her cupped hand, and Kate slipped her a stick of gum.

'Is it Buckley?' Kate asked as they entered the changing room and, for the second time that day, began slipping into their safety suits.

Junko nodded. Within minutes, they were suited up and in the lab. Kolosine and the rest of the team were gathered around the windows of the small room in which Kate had sat with Officer Buckley earlier that morning.

Kate edged her way to the front, and gasped with shock. Buckley, who had been lying as still as a corpse earlier, was having a fit. He thrashed about on his cot, limbs shaking violently. His eyes bulged and his tongue protruded from his mouth.

'He's having a seizure,' Kolosine commented, as if he were describing a dance move.

'But Watoto doesn't cause seizures!'

155

'Could it be a fever seizure?' Annie asked.

Kolosine looked at her scornfully. 'No. If this was a small child we might suspect that, but not in an adult. This is something new. This, it seems, is how victims of Watoto-X2 die—the seizure usually finishes them off before the haemorrhaging starts. Less messy, at least. It's fascinating. I've never known a virus cause this kind of violent seizure in an adult before.'

'Why isn't somebody in there helping him?' demanded Kate. 'Didn't they send a nurse with him?'

'He's beyond help. There was a nurse, but she got sick and had to go back,' Kolosine said flatly.

Kate moved towards the door. 'We can at least comfort him. He needs to be turned on to his side, so he doesn't swallow his tongue. Come on, let me in.'

Kolosine sighed. 'A proper Florence Nightingale, aren't you?'

'Fuck you, Kolosine.'

Though she couldn't hear anything over the speaker in her helmet, Kate sensed the collective gasp from the other scientists. Kolosine glared at her from behind his visor. She couldn't remember ever receiving a look of such naked hatred before.

'Fine,' he said. 'Be a heroine.'

Once inside the room, Kate hesitated. Buckley was writhing and crying out, shaking like someone was sending two thousand volts through his body.

'Sod this,' Kate muttered, and she ripped aside the plastic sheet that sealed the cop inside the isolator, bending to manoeuvre him on to his side.

'It's OK, it's OK,' she whispered as his terrified eyes met hers. She held on to him, shocked by

156

the violence of the tremors, wishing she could do something, anything, to stop his suffering.

She clutched him for a long time, her eyes squeezed shut. Eventually, he went still. She opened her eyes and looked into his face. She wouldn't be able to feel his pulse with her thick gloves on, so she put her visor close to his face, as if they were kissing. There was no mist on the visor. No breath.

She looked up as she became aware that Kolosine was tapping furiously on the glass. He spoke to her—shouted at her—through the radiocom, filling her helmet with fury.

'You're contaminated, so we are leaving the lab. Wait for us to exit then come through. Make sure you put your suit into the disposal bin and scrub your whole body.'

God, she wished she could mute him. She watched as Kolosine led the others out of the lab, Junko and Annie both looking back at her, frowning behind their visors. A great wave of exhaustion crashed over her.

She forced herself to look down at Officer Buckley before exiting the lab. *You need to freeze this image in your mind*, she told herself. *Because this is it. This is the reality of what's out there.*

*This is what you have to beat.*

\*       \*       \*

Dawn broke, and Kate had barely slept. This was only her second full day at the lab and already the pressure to find the vaccine was becoming unbearable. For a while she lay fretting under

157

her incongruously twee patchwork quilt, reliving Buckley's dreadful last moments, feeling physically sick with the responsibility resting on her shoulders, and the shoulders of the rest of the team. Bright morning sun streamed through the thin calico curtains, and Kate put the pillow over her head to block it out.

When she had emerged from the lab after decontaminating herself, Kolosine had sent her to her room, like a naughty child. She had spent the time poring over her research paper, hoping it might reveal to her some elusive detail that could help solve this puzzle.

Finally giving up on sleep, she got up and set off for the breakfast room, taking her laptop with her. She was re-reading her research paper for the tenth time when the epidemiologist walked in, a huge mug of coffee in one hand and a large laptop in the other. He looked utterly haunted.

'Hi . . .' she said. 'How are you getting on?'

William shook his head and took a big swig of the coffee. 'Got a minute? I'll show you.'

He pulled out the chair next to her and sat down, pointing at his computer screen. His hair was sticking up in all directions, as though he'd just got out of his bed—although Kate suspected he hadn't been near it all night.

'This is my first graph, the epidemic curve so far,' he said, indicating a steeply inclined green line. 'Number of cases—y-axis; date and time of onset—x-axis. Look at that rate of infectivity—have you ever seen anything this bad?'

Her jaw dropped at the evidence.

'I had active surveillance here, here, and all over this region, up till last night,' he said, rubbing his eyes. 'The internet went down at about eleven p.m., and hasn't come up again since. No ethernet, certainly no wi-fi. Nothing. But you can bet your bottom dollar that this data hasn't got any more positive overnight . . . Anyway, see you later. I need to get on. Let's hope that your antibodies live up to their hype, eh?'

Kate couldn't even raise a smile as William left the room. She had never felt such a panicky, desperate anticipation.

Junko came in and sat down opposite her, looking tired, but serene and still immaculate.

'How are you?' Junko asked.

'Worried.'

'You look it. Me too. We have so little time. I have been in the lab all night, examining the blood samples from Officer Buckley.' She shook her head to indicate the apparent futility of her night at the microscope.

'I'm so worried about my son,' Kate said. 'He's in Dallas—it's not going to be long before the virus spreads from coast to coast . . . I can't believe I was gullible enough to allow him into the country. I believed them when they told me it was contained on the reservation.' Junko was quiet, and Kate imagined she was thinking about her family in Japan. She envied Junko the knowledge they were so far away—but how long would even they be safe?

'The cause of death . . . the seizure—you haven't seen that before with Watoto?' Junko asked eventually.

'No. Normally, the victim dies after they start to bleed. They don't bleed to death, but their organs fail. So this deviation in the virus is very strange.'

159

Kate spoke quietly, as if to herself. 'Very strange. We need to take a closer look, see how this virus compares to the known Watoto strain.'

Junko sipped her coffee. 'I'm already running comparisons—that's one of the things I did last night. We've already sequenced the DNA, and Watoto and Watoto-X2 appear to be exactly the same. There is nothing I can see that would indicate why this new strain is more fatal. And why it kills through a seizure rather than bleeding.'

'Maybe it doesn't matter,' Kate said. 'The vaccine—if we manage to develop one—will work on both.'

'Yes. In theory. Unless there is something else . . .'

She trailed off, deep in thought. Kate waited for her to emerge from her trance, but before she did, Kolosine burst into the room and headed straight over to them.

'Maddox, upstairs, now.'

Kate pushed herself to her feet, explaining to Junko, 'He needs another sample of my blood to create a phage display. I'll catch you later, Junko, I'm going to stay in the lab after I've had the test.'

Twenty minutes later, blood taken, Kate peered into the electron microscope, examining the familiar form of the Watoto virus. It was like looking at her own face in a mirror, she knew it so well. Except the virus didn't change, didn't get older, didn't frown or get tired. Today, it felt as if her nemesis was stronger than her. It was winning.

Junko was right. The new strain appeared identical to the common strain that Kate had caught in Africa, the one that had killed her parents. So why was it even more deadly and why did it act so fast? If Kate had caught this strain of Watoto all those years ago, she wouldn't be sitting here now.

Staring at the virus's worm-like shape, she had a niggling feeling that the answer was right in front of her if she could only see it. She had told Junko that perhaps the new qualities of the virus didn't matter, that essentially they still had to create a vaccine for the same organism. All the same, if they could crack the puzzle of why the two strains appeared to be identical yet killed their victims in different ways, they would be able to solve the whole thing. Then again, if Kolosine's tests were successful maybe she wouldn't have to worry about it. There was no reason why her antibodies wouldn't work against this new strain as well as the old.

He was at the other side of the lab, pacing back and forth beside the machine that, he hoped, would give him the answer. Kate's blood sample, which had been left on a chip for an hour so that the antisera could incubate, was now being subjected to a barrage of tests inside the machine. If all went well, the peptide—the correct lock they needed to create a vaccine, as she had explained to McCarthy—would light up and they would be able to take the relevant antibody and use it to create more antibodies—enough to vaccinate everybody.

The air in the lab crackled with tension. Kolosine wouldn't allow anyone else near him or his precious machine. Inside his suit, she could see beads of sweat rolling off his forehead. She exchanged a worried look with Chip, who was seated at one of the computers.

'How are you getting on over there?' she asked.

He shrugged. 'I've never tested so many samples

161

in such a short space of time. I'm pretty much seeing double—but nothing useful is showing up. Nothing. Every time I manage to think of a new hypothesis, it comes to nothing. I feel like banging my head against the wall.'

'Know the feeling,' said Kate glumly.

## 21

Paul rapped twice on Rosie's front door and waited, looking around at the neighbourhood, his eyes shielded from the sun by a pair of sunglasses he'd picked up at a drugstore on the way over. It was a neat, pretty block mostly comprised of white clapboard houses with apple trees in their front yards and swings on their porches. It was one in the afternoon, the precise time she'd told him to come over, as she needed to get to her shift at the diner, but his knocking went unanswered.

Paul checked his watch. He became aware that he was being scrutinised by a snowy-haired man in the front yard of the house next door, which was considerably larger than Rosie's, though identical in every other way. The man was tinkering with a sprinkler system that sat at the centre of his immaculate lawn.

'Afternoon,' Paul called, raising his hand and wondering at the same time if Rosie had changed her mind and was hiding inside, waiting for him to go away.

The man nodded coolly and turned back to his sprinkler.

Paul was about to knock again when the door

162

opened and Rosie beckoned him inside. Her hair was damp and a towel was draped haphazardly over the back of a nearby chair.

'I'm sorry. I just got out the shower.'

Paul stamped on an involuntary image of Rosie naked. Since meeting Kate, he'd never entertained even a fleeting fantasy about any other woman. It's fine, he reassured himself. A natural chemical reaction. One that you are not going to act on.

'That's OK,' he said. 'I was busy making friends with your neighbour. Friendly guy.'

Rosie motioned for him to follow her into the kitchen at the back of the house. A jug of lemonade sweated on the worktop and she poured him a glass. She was wearing a red-and-black-check flannel shirt and shorts and her feet were bare. She had, Paul noticed, a small tattoo of a flower on her ankle.

'Lived here long?' he enquired, looking around at the scruffy but homely kitchen.

'This house, ten years. This neighbourhood, my whole life. I like it here. It's safe. A good place to raise a daughter. Not too much crime, and the local kids are polite and pretty well-behaved.'

Right on cue, Paul heard Lucy exclaim 'Holy fucking shit!' from the living room.

'Most of 'em, anyway.' Rosie grinned. 'Guess we'd better see what she's cussing about, huh?'

Paul set down his glass and followed her into the living room. He had wanted to ask her about Lucy's dad, but reminded himself that it wasn't his place. He was only here because Rosie had promised to help him find out what had happened to Mangold.

Lucy was in a big, tatty armchair, wearing a pink T-shirt and a pair of denim shorts, her long bare

163

legs curled beneath her, gesticulating at the TV.

'This is so messed up,' she said, thumbing her phone and exchanging messages with her friends as she simultaneously hopped between news channels: Fox, CNN, CBS. 'Afternoon, Mr Craig.'

Paul smiled. 'Hi, Lucy.'

'What's messed up?' asked Rosie.

Lucy shot her mother a look, as if it were the dumbest question she'd ever heard. 'This,' she replied. 'This freaking virus. It's getting, like, really really scary.'

On CBS News, a map of Los Angeles County filled the screen. The map was coloured according to the number of Indian flu cases reported in each area; the darker the hue, the higher the number. Los Angeles was spattered with patches the colour of blood. The outskirts of the city, along with a number of surrounding communities, were coloured orange, indicating that the virus was taking a vicious hold: Santa Monica, Pasadena, Huntingdon Beach . . .

The shot on screen returned to a pair of presenters seated at a desk. One of them was saying that there had also been isolated cases reported in Portland, Seattle and Las Vegas, all of them people who had visited LA in the last week.

'The Department of Health have acted swiftly and those people have been quarantined, along with their families,' said the presenter.

'That won't stop it for long,' Paul muttered. He turned to Lucy. 'Have they said how many people are dead?'

Lucy stopped texting and looked up at him solemnly. 'Five thousand.'

'That can't be right,' said Rosie.

164

'It is. I swear. And they said they think that, like, up to a hundred thousand people have already got it.'

'Sweet Jesus,' Rosie breathed, clutching the back of the armchair her daughter was in.

Paul went cold. The numbers had exploded since yesterday—but this was what happened when epidemics of highly virulent diseases broke out. And tomorrow it would be ten thousand. It would multiply fast from now on. 'What's the fatality rate? Have they said?'

Lucy looked up at him with damp eyes. 'Ninety-nine per cent.'

She tilted her face towards Rosie, who was staring with horror at the TV screen, now showing a helicopter view of Los Angeles.

Across the bottom of the screen ran a ticker-tape with the words: BREAKING NEWS: LOS ANGELES COUNTY QUARANTINED. CENTERS FOR DISEASE CONTROL ACT TO PREVENT DEATH TOLL RISING.

The camera zoomed in on soldiers constructing a roadblock on the outskirts of the city. In an agitated voice the news anchor informed viewers that the National Guard had been called in to 'police' Los Angeles, that the city's hospitals had ceased accepting new patients, that following the closure of the airports earlier in the week, all roads in and out of the city were closed. People were only being let out of the county after being screened at the border for the Indian flu, and already the queue of cars and trucks was a mile long as panicked drivers waited to be given the all-clear. The broadcast cut to footage of a burning building, a reporter's voice informing viewers that a clinic had been set on fire in South LA as desperate victims of the virus had learned that stocks of antiviral medicines were stored there. A mini-riot had broken out. There were reports that a doctor had been shot.

Lucy shuddered. 'Mom, Jamie and Martina are in LA at the moment. I'm really scared.'

Rosie's voice was quiet. 'Maybe they managed to get out in time.'

'They're not answering their phones.'

'Who are Jamie and Martina?' Paul asked gently.

Lucy was too upset to speak, so Rosie answered for her: 'School friends of Lucy's. They had summer jobs in Jamie's aunt's restaurant in Santa Monica.'

They all looked at the TV again. A public health official was talking about how people in the city should stay home, keep doors and windows shut; how there was an emergency health line in operation plus another number for concerned friends and relatives. The official looked grey. He said that the President would give a live TV address later, that health professionals were doing everything they could to keep the situation under control and were working around the clock to find a vaccine.

'What advice would you give to anyone watching this in the city of Los Angeles now?' asked the presenter.

The grey health official stared at the desk in front of him and said, 'Pray.'

Rosie walked over to the TV and switched it off.

'Have there been any cases reported in Sagebrush?' she asked her daughter.

'I don't know. They didn't say.'

Rosie knelt beside her daughter and they hugged. Paul turned away, allowing them a moment

166

of privacy. He felt sick. And he desperately wanted to talk to Kate.

'Let's go,' Rosie said. She turned to Lucy. 'I'll see you at the diner later. Wear your face mask, OK?'

'OK, Mom.'

Paul followed Rosie outside into the sunshine that bathed this peaceful neighbourhood, arcs of water from next door's sprinkler glinting in the light. Kate was out there. Safe for now, he was sure, in her secluded lab. But for how long?

How long did they have?

\*     \*     \*

They set off in Rosie's car, a Nissan that had seen better days, driving in silence for the first few minutes. Paul watched the quiet suburban streets roll by. 'Who are we going to see?' he asked eventually.

Rosie kept her eyes on the road. 'His name's Jon Watton. He worked at Medi-Lab with my father. He was one of the sales managers there. We've kind of kept in touch over the years. He watched out for me. He's a good guy.'

She paused, then added: 'I never thought it would be possible for a virus to be ninety-nine per cent fatal.'

'Oh, it's possible. Rabies was one hundred per cent before a vaccine was developed. Ebola is around ninety—and there's no vaccine for that one. Luckily, it's not airborne so it's reasonably easy to contain.'

'How do you know all this?'

'My girlfriend is a virologist.'

167

'Your girlfriend?'

'Yes. Well, partner. Maybe I'm too old to say girlfriend. Didn't I mention her last night?'

'I don't think so.'

'Oh. I'm sorry . . .'

She didn't look at him, but her grip on the wheel appeared to tighten. 'Hey, Paul, look—why would it bother me if you have a girlfriend? Just seems odd you didn't mention her, that's all.'

'I'm sure I did.' But the truth was, he knew he hadn't. He remembered a point in the conversation where it could have come up, but he had deliberately swerved around the subject. Guilt stabbed at him again. He forced himself to keep his tone even. 'She's in California at the moment, working on finding a vaccine for Indian flu.'

Rosie braked harshly at a red light, making him jerk forward in his seat. 'Let's hope she finds one, huh?'

## 22

After looking at William's depressing statistics Kate returned to the lab, where the scene was equally grim. She and Chip waited, exchanging nervous looks, while Kolosine paced back and forth. The waves of tension coming off the head scientist could have been used to power a small town. Kate tried to focus on studying more samples of Watoto-X2, but the stress was contagious and it was impossible to concentrate.

Eventually, after thirty minutes of alternately pacing and staring into his machine, hoping to see the luminescence that never came, Kolosine stormed out of the lab.

'Looks like it didn't work,' Chip said evenly as the door slammed shut.

Kate sighed. So it wasn't going to be that easy. She had tried to warn Kolosine that her blood hadn't yielded an antivirus in all the years she and Isaac had been working on the project. Just because he had new technology, there was no reason to expect a different result. She only hoped Kolosine had some other ideas up his sleeve.

\*       \*       \*

Kate stood beneath the shower, closing her eyes as the hot jets of water cleansed her body of any nasty microbes that might have clung to her. Drying herself afterwards, she felt a rush of blood to the head and had to take a seat on the wooden bench. Since coming to the lab she hadn't spoken to Paul once, and the pressure was beginning to get to her. She felt guilty that he wasn't there with her, and furious that Harley had brought him out to the US and then not allowed them to stay together. If they'd known what was going to happen, Jack could have remained at home in Oxfordshire with Paul for the summer.

She went down to the communal area and found the rest of the team gathered around the TV watching news reports. There was no sign of Kolosine. A collective gasp went up when they heard that LA was now under quarantine. Kate listened intently for news of other locations where outbreaks had been reported. No mention of Dallas. But an air passenger could easily have carried it there already, which would mean Jack was in danger too. She needed to get Jack out of the country before they closed all the airports.

Later, she decided, she would demand to go into Kolosine's office and use the telephone to speak to Paul, emergency or no emergency. A landline seemed to be the only option—even after borrowing Junko's charger and powering up her BlackBerry, she still hadn't got a signal.

On her way back to her room, she bumped into McCarthy and followed him outside into the open air. They wandered down towards the woods.

'Want a smoke?' he asked.

She shook her head. 'No, that was a one-off. But ask me again later, when Kolosine has his next screaming fit. I don't suppose you have a phone I can use?'

'I got no signal either.' He pointed at his phone screen. 'It's a fifteen-mile drive to the nearest place in range, so you're not gonna get there on foot. The internet's down—guess the folks at the internet service provider HQ are all sick, or worse . . .'

A Cat 4 lab with no means of communication with the outside world—it was unsettling beyond belief, especially knowing the people who had planted the bomb at the hotel were out there somewhere. 'Yeah, I know. William is freaking out—he can't collect any more data. And if we don't have data, we've got to rely on the TV for our facts, which isn't exactly scientific . . . But all that aside, I have to get to a phone.'

'I ain't got no car, before you ask,' McCarthy said. 'Not an emergency, is it?'

'Pretty much.' Kate's tone was sombre. 'I need to get my boy out of the country. Do you know when

170

they're going to shut the airports?'

McCarthy hesitated. 'No,' he said. 'Not exactly. Soon, though.'

'I've got to get Jack out on a flight before they do.' Kate clutched at McCarthy's arm. 'Tosca, can you arrange it? Send him back to stay with my sister in Oxfordshire? If Vernon will fly with him, all the better, but if not, Paul can take him home. Please, just get him out. Even if he has to fly on his own.'

The sun filtered through the branches and dappled the soft ground around them, and the only sound was birdsong from somewhere high above them. It was hard to imagine the pain and chaos taking hold not so far away from there.

McCarthy sat down in the crook of a low tree branch and stared reflectively at Kate. He took out a large white handkerchief from the pocket of his black jacket, and wiped the sweat off his forehead.

'OK,' he said. 'Give me the details. I got a call scheduled with my boss tomorrow—assuming Kolosine lets me use the landline, which he'd better. We'll sort something out.'

Kate paused. 'Not till tomorrow?' she asked in a small voice.

McCarthy shrugged. 'Sorry, Kate. There are chains of command. I can't just call him up unless it's a national emergency. Tomorrow will be fine, you wait and see.'

Kate reached down and hugged McCarthy round his neck. 'Thank you,' she said, sighing with relief. McCarthy laughed, embarrassed. '*De nada*, sweetpea,' he said. 'Anything for you.'

They sat for a while and watched an eagle wheel a lazy arc above their heads.

'So what's happening,' Kate asked, 'with

171

attempts to find the terrorists who planted the bomb?'

'We've got everybody looking for them.'

'But no progress?'

He stared into the woods. His silence spoke volumes.

*      *      *

With a heavy heart, Kate returned to her room and lay down on the bed, sheer exhaustion sending her almost immediately into an unsettled doze. What seemed like mere minutes later there was a heavy knock at her door, and the sound of a man's voice calling her name. Kate awoke, thinking for a second it was Paul, before realising where she was.

'Just a minute,' she said, jumping out of bed and wrapping her bathrobe securely around her naked body. She glanced at her reflection in the dressing-table mirror and noted the huge crease down the right side of her face. 'Who is it?'

'Harley. Jason,' said the voice, and Kate wondered why he'd given his names in that order.

'Maddox. Kate,' she retorted as she opened the door, but Harley wasn't smiling.

'Sorry,' he said when he saw that she wasn't dressed. 'McCarthy said you were up here. Are you sick? You don't look too well.' He backed away slightly.

'I'm tired, that's all. I've been sleeping—I'm on the night shift at the moment.'

'Ah, sorry,' he repeated, looking down at the wooden floorboards. 'I didn't mean you don't look good, I just meant—'

172

Kate held up her hand. 'Stop, please, it's OK. You've caught me at a bad moment. It's been a tough week. Is everything all right—apart from the virus spreading, of course? McCarthy told me . . .' She trailed off, remembering he had asked her not to tell anyone what he'd told her. 'Why are you here?'

Harley scratched his head. He didn't look too good himself, Kate noticed, with big grey bags under his eyes and unruly stubble peppering his chin. 'There are a couple of things I need to talk to you about. Urgently.'

## 23

Jon Watton lived in a condo on the edge of Sagebrush. He was in his late sixties, Paul estimated, with a bald head and a nose that looked like it had been broken in a fight. He fixed them drinks before heading for an old rattan armchair, wincing with pain as he lowered himself into it.

'Are you all right, Jon?' Rosie asked, sitting down opposite him. Paul perched on the end of a sofa, next to a sleeping tabby cat. The room was sweltering and smelled of tinned meat, and the sofa had so much cat fur on it that it had taken on the colour of the cat.

'It's just this arthritis,' he said. 'It's my knees, mostly. Doctors can't do a damn thing.'

'I'm sorry to hear that,' Rosie said.

Jon waved a hand dismissively and said, 'Never mind me. It's lovely to see you, Rosie.' He coughed, and the cat opened an eye, looking at him disdainfully before closing it again. 'How's that daughter of yours?'

'Oh, she's good, good. Freaked out by everything that's going on in LA right now.'

'Aren't we all. Freaked out. I love the way you young people talk.'

'Young people? Can you say that again. A few times, please.'

They laughed and Paul tried to join in, but he couldn't hide his impatience. Jon Watton noticed and looked over at him. 'So, you want to talk to me about Medi-Lab?'

'If you're sure you don't mind,' Rosie said.

'Anything for you. Though I'm not sure exactly what help you think I can be.'

Paul had persuaded a reluctant Rosie that it would be best for them to use his cover story, so as not to risk scaring Watton off.

'Mr Watton,' Paul started, 'I'm writing a book about Medi-Lab and Charles Mangold. I wanted to find out more about what went on there.'

'What went on?'

'The scandal that closed it down, but also . . . well, anything else you might remember about the place that seemed unusual or wrong. And we're trying to find Charles Mangold too. I want to interview him.'

'OK, let me think.' The older man coughed again.

'Are you sick?' Rosie asked.

'Oh, don't worry, it's a cold—I haven't got the Indian flu. I haven't been out of the house to catch it.' He laughed hoarsely, setting off another coughing fit. 'So, where do you want me to start?'

'Rosie tells me you were a sales manager,' Paul

said.

'Yup. That's right. I spent most of my time out on the road. Rosie's father was one of my sales guys. We'd visit surgeries, try to get them to prescribe our drugs. Spent a lot of time sleeping in motel rooms.'

'And were you around when the scandal hit and the company closed down?'

'I was. We all got called back from the field, which kind of pissed me off as I was about to close a big deal I'd been chasing for a long time.'

Paul felt itchy and frustrated. He wasn't sure what information he was trying to pry out of Watton and consequently didn't know exactly what to ask. He decided to be as direct as possible.

'Were you ever suspicious of anything untoward going on in the labs?'

Watton hesitated. 'When the secret service turned up and closed us down, I was as shocked as everyone else.'

Paul leaned forward. 'So it was the secret service, not the Department of Health, who closed the company down?'

'My father said the same thing,' Rosie reminded him.

Paul nodded and waited for the man to continue.

'Well, the Health people were there, but there were definitely secret service agents around too. I assumed FBI . . . They had the whole place shut down. They put up tape around the whole building—no one was allowed near it, including the staff. To be honest, I watched most of it on TV. I remember seeing footage of them arresting Mangold, leading him out to a car, driving away with him.'

'What was Mangold like?' Paul asked. Never having come across a single photograph, he imagined him as some kind of monster: leathery, evil, a megalomaniac in a lab coat.

Jon Watton coughed again and Paul watched droplets scatter across the space between them. 'He always seemed like a decent guy. Serious but friendly, kind of like a science teacher I had in high school. But then I only met Mangold once or twice. First time was when I started at the company and I got the big "welcome aboard" speech, and then . . . Well, only one other time after that.'

Paul had been trying to interrupt Watton's flow for the last few seconds. 'The closure—the agents showing up—that was because of a rare virus that broke out?'

'Yep. Apparently they weren't observing the correct protocols, so the lab bosses took the rap.' Watton shot a glance at Rosie. He was acting shiftily, Paul thought, like he wanted to say more but was afraid to. 'Mangold was crushed. He moved outta town, I heard, became a recluse. Disappeared right off the map.'

Paul was about to ask something else when Watton was seized by another coughing fit, doubling over, his face turning purple. Rosie grabbed a glass of water and handed it to him, her eyes full of concern.

'I think we oughta go,' she said to Paul. 'Besides, I need to get to work. My shift starts in an hour.'

He nodded. Jon Watton was clearly more ill than he'd let on. Paul rose from his chair and waited for the older man's coughing jag to end. His mind was racing, questions tumbling over one another. He would have liked to continue the interview, but

176

Rosie needed to work, and he had no car.

'Damn,' he said to Rosie, suddenly remembering: 'My phone's out of juice. Can I charge it up in your car? I've got a cigarette-lighter charger—I completely forgot to ask you on the way over.' Then he turned to Jon and shook his hand. 'Thank you so much for your time.'

'You're welcome, son. Let me know if there's anything else I can do.'

'I wouldn't mind using your bathroom before we go, if that's OK.'

'I'll wait in the car—give me your phone and charger, I'll get it plugged in now,' said Rosie as Jon directed him through a bead curtain dividing the room from the hallway. She gave Jon a hug and a kiss on the cheek.

'Look after yourself, you hear?'

When Paul came out of the bathroom, Watton was waiting for him. He grabbed Paul by the arm.

'Listen,' he hissed. 'There's more. Stuff I didn't want to say in front of Rosie.'

Paul looked out through the window, where he could see Rosie in her car. She appeared to be holding Paul's iPhone to her ear. 'What is it?'

Watton started to cough again, his frail body folding over. Paul tried to lead him over to a chair but Watton swatted him away with kitten-like swipes.

'I can't . . . talk . . . right now,' he wheezed. 'But come back later. On your own.'

## 24

Oh hell, Kate thought. Now what's happened? 'Give me a couple of minutes to get dressed,' she said. 'Then we can talk.'

'I'll wait out here,' Harley said sheepishly, moving into the hallway and scrutinising the rocking horse. Kate closed the door behind him and tore around the room trying to find some clothes that weren't scrubs. She dressed quickly in jeans and an old pink Killers T-shirt, and dragged a wide-toothed comb through her hair. She would have liked to put on some make-up, not because she wanted to impress him, but to make herself feel like a functioning human being again, rather than a drone chained to a laboratory bench. A visitor was a visitor, she concluded. Their mountaintop hideaway was already starting to feel as confined as the Big Brother house. She decided against the make-up though, and instead smoothed the quilt flat over her unmade bed. She realised she was procrastinating, in case he was bringing her more bad news.

'Come in, I'm decent now,' she said, opening the door again. Harley smiled at her and suddenly traced his forefinger down her face. 'You've got a crease,' he blurted, and for a moment it was hard to tell which of them was more embarrassed.

'Er, yes,' said Kate, blushing furiously. She was angry with Harley for lying to her, even if he had been following orders. The knowledge that he'd let her bring Jack to the States when there was a killer virus that was not contained, as he'd claimed, sickened her. Still, there was something so solid and well-meaning about Harley that she couldn't help but like him, despite his duplicity.

'Have a seat.' She pointed to the wing armchair by the window, drawing back the curtains to let in the daylight, and went to sit on her bed. 'So, what's going on?'

'When did you last talk to Paul?'

'I haven't been able to speak to him at all since I got here. There's no mobile signal, and the only landline is locked in Mein Führer Kolosine's office. Apparently it has to be a case of life and death before he lets you use it.'

She smiled as she said it so that Harley would know she wasn't having a go at him—but when he remained grave, her face fell. 'What? Has something happened to Paul?'

'I don't know where he is, Kate. He did a runner from the motel on the first night and nobody's seen him since. I thought you might have spoken to him.'

Kate jumped off the bed and rushed over to the window, her hand to her mouth, as if she was expecting to see Paul outside in the chicken coop. 'What?'

'So you haven't heard anything from him at all?'

She shook her head. 'Why did he go?'

'I don't know,' said Harley. 'He was pissed off that we wouldn't let him go with you. And I think it's possible he may try to find you. I have to stress the importance of you not telling him where you are, if you do speak to him—although I'm sure you know that. We need to keep the location of this lab secret. And if we find him, we're going to have to send him straight back to England.'

'Good,' said Kate vehemently. 'He can take

179

Jack with him. Seriously, Jason, I want them both out of the country as soon as possible. It's not safe. I've asked McCarthy to organise a flight out for Jack. He's going to let me know tomorrow. But, bloody Paul, what's he thinking?' She walked in agitated circles, one hand against her forehead, and then sat down heavily on the bed again. 'Don't worry. I wouldn't have the first clue how to direct him to where we are. "On top of a mountain in the Sequoia National Park"—not a lot to go on, really, is it?'

They sat in silence for a moment or two, Kate trying to process this new piece of information.

'This is all . . . too much,' she said at last. 'What makes it worse is that we're really struggling here. Kolosine had this big idea about using my blood, but that didn't work and . . . For a long time I've felt like I was on the verge of finding a vaccine for Watoto, but having to achieve it in a few days, and with this new strain . . .'

'Don't you think you'll be able to do it?' Harley asked in a quiet voice.

'Given the team we've got, and the resources . . . if anyone can, we can. But we could carry on working day and night and equally not get anywhere. Or at least, not in time to do any good.'

Harley slumped down in his chair, stretching his long legs out in front of him. 'Not to put more pressure on you, Kate, I know how hard you're working but—shit—this is . . .' His voice faded out for a moment and he seemed to be struggling for composure. 'It's . . . everyone's worst nightmare, like something out of a disaster movie. Did you hear we've had to quarantine LA County? Martial law, total curfew. A zero tolerance, shoot-to-kill

180

policy on looters and curfew-breakers. If things continue this way there'll be people dying so fast that the hospitals and mortuaries won't cope. Bodies piling up all over the place. They're looking for mass grave sites already. And the worst thing is, no one can see how to avoid the same thing being repeated all over the States within a matter of weeks if we don't find a vaccine. Even with no flights going in or out of the country, the odds of someone having got on a plane with it before the shut-down—well, they're pretty short, despite the precautions the airports have been taking and the fact that the LA airports closed earlier in the week.'

'I know. I've been trying not to think about it, to stay focused and not panic.' And not think about it reaching Dallas. Or London, Kate thought. 'There haven't been any more terrorist attacks, have there?' she asked, chewing the skin around her thumbnail.

'No. And no more messages. But we haven't got any closer to finding the people responsible.' He sighed. 'Anyway, sorry to have to give you something else to worry about. But we need to try and find out where Paul's got to. Can you call him? I'll get you on to the landline downstairs,' Harley said.

'With pleasure,' Kate replied grimly.

Harley stood up and rolled his head around, an audible cracking sound coming from the back of his neck. 'Ow,' he said, rubbing it. 'I need some sleep.'

'Sleep here for a bit if you want, after we've got this call done,' Kate offered, gesturing towards her bed. 'I can hang out with Junko next door—and I'm back on shift in an hour, anyway.'

Harley looked longingly at her bed, then shook

181

his head. 'Thanks, I'd absolutely love to, but I've got way too much to do. We're still trying to find out who planted the bomb at the hotel . . . I've got to go straight to the BIT office in San Francisco after this. Come on then, let's try and call Paul.'

When Kate and Harley knocked on Kolosine's office door, he flung it open and stood glowering in the doorway, his arms crossed.

Harley stepped forward and held out his hand. 'Jason Harley,' he said. 'I don't believe we've met.'

'I know who you are,' said Kolosine, looking disdainfully at Harley's outstretched arm. 'I won't shake your hand, thanks—best to maintain a minimum of contact in the current situation.'

'Right. So—can I ask how your work is going here?'

Kolosine rolled his eyes. 'I'm sure Kate's already told you. We've got nowhere. Her blood was useless. Next question?'

'We need to use the phone,' Harley said firmly.

Kolosine huffed but stood aside to let Kate into the office. She felt his eyes on her as she grabbed the receiver of the old-fashioned office telephone on the desk and began to dial Paul's number. She turned her back on Kolosine and held the receiver tightly to her ear. As she waited for Paul to pick up she heard Harley say from the doorway, 'I apologise for the situation with the phones, but I've arranged for an engineer to come out tomorrow to install some new lines and sort out the internet access.'

She tuned out Kolosine's grumbling reply. After what seemed like whole minutes of silence, Paul's automatic answerphone message clicked in without the phone having rung first. 'It's switched off,' she called to Harley, who was hovering outside.

Kolosine, to her relief, had now disappeared off somewhere. It felt wonderful just to hear Paul's voice, but her pleasure was tinged with anxiety—Paul *never* turned off his phone.

The beep signalled for her to leave a message. 'Hey, darling, it's me. Been dying to speak to you all week—there's no signal here, internet's down, but I've finally got to use a landline—and you're not picking up! Please call me straight back on this number, Paul, please, I'm really worried about you.' She squinted at the number handwritten on the telephone's label and read it out. 'I'll be waiting for your call for the next half hour, then I've got to get back into the lab. If it's busy, try again—I need to hear your voice, OK?'

When she hung up, she realised that she had tears in her eyes, and Harley had moved away discreetly. She sat down in Kolosine's chair and rang again and again, in case Paul had been on the phone, causing it to go to voicemail, but the same thing happened every time.

She dialled Vernon's number instead—might as well make use of unfettered access to a phone—and had a perfunctory conversation with him about Jack and then insisted that Vernon fetch Jack from next door, where he was playing with Bradley. When she heard Jack's voice, she thought he sounded a little shifty, as though he was about to do something naughty. He asked for the address of the lab so he could send her a postcard.

'On top of a mountain, darling,' she said. 'But don't worry about the postcard. Write me an email instead. And Jack—you will be a good boy for Dad, won't you?'

When they eventually said their goodbyes, it took

Kate some time to compose herself, during which she continued to try Paul's number, automatically redialling over and over. She looked around Kolosine's office—anything to take her mind off Jack. It was very obviously a temporary base, with no personal effects whatsoever, just a packet of Lucky Strikes, a pen, a calculator and a Wildlife of Sequoia calendar from 2007 on the desktop.

She was doodling on the corner of the calendar with the pen, when suddenly, on about the thirtieth redial, she heard the soft burr of an international ringtone instead of the click straight to voicemail. She jumped, and held her breath, twirling her finger through the old-fashioned telephone cord. The ringtone ceased, and a woman's voice, American and husky, said 'Hello? Paul's phone.'

Kate was too shocked to speak. She held the receiver away from her ear as the voice repeated, 'Who's there? Hello? *Hello?*'

## 25

After promising Watton he would return later, Paul joined Rosie in her car to find her looking sombre.

'You've just missed a phone call,' she said, handing him the plugged-in iPhone. 'This second. I said hello and they hung up on me.'

He checked his call log—an unfamiliar number, dialled from within the US. He hesitated. Could it be Harley?

'Did they hang up as soon as they heard your voice?'

'Uh-huh.'

If it was Harley, trying to trace him, he would surely have tried to keep Rosie on the phone, probably asked some questions about where she was. So who would hang up upon hearing a female voice on the end of his phone?

Shit.

He pressed the number on the screen to return the call. It rang a few times, then the voice he knew better than any other said, 'Hello?'

'Kate?'

There was a long pause, during which he wondered if he had misrecognised her. Then she said, 'Who was that woman?'

He ignored the question. 'Oh, Kate, it's so good to hear your voice. I've been trying to get hold of you.'

There were waves of annoyance coming through the phone. 'Who was that who answered your phone?'

He glanced up at Rosie, who was looking in the other direction, making a show of not listening.

'Someone who's trying to help me,' he said.

'Help you with what, exactly? And where are you? Harley says you've done a runner. Nobody knows where you are or who you're with. What the hell are you playing at?'

'I'm trying to find Charles Mangold.'

'*What?*'

'It's my only chance to hunt him down, I've got to . . . Hang on, is Harley there now?'

'Yes, he's waiting outside.'

'You mustn't tell him what I've just said.'

'What do you mean? You've hardly told me anything.'

'I don't want him to know I'm looking for

185

Mangold. He'll only try to stop me.'

'Or maybe he'll want to help.'

'No, Kate, I don't trust him. He'll haul me back to San Francisco and lock me in a hotel room until the virus reaches my door.' He took a few steps away from Rosie. 'Listen, I'm starting to make progress—I've met a guy who used to work for Mangold, name of Jon Watton . . . But I don't want to say any more until you promise me you won't tell Harley anything.'

He heard her sigh. 'OK, OK . . . I promise.'

'Thank you. Listen. I'm in a place called Sagebrush in Ventura County, west of LA. Mangold used to run a company here called Medi-Lab. It got shut down in the early nineties after a big health scandal—a couple of people died in an outbreak of some unnamed virus they were working on. A virus that sounds very like Watoto.'

Kate was quiet for a moment. 'That doesn't mean he's behind this outbreak too.'

'I know. But think about it—we know he was paying Gaunt and his cronies to create deadly superviruses. And now it seems he was working on Watoto back in 1991. That's some coincidence. Even if he's not behind this outbreak, the fact he was funding Gaunt makes him responsible for what happened to Stephen. I have to find him, Kate. It kills me to think that anyone who had a hand in my brother's death is still walking free. I would have thought you'd feel the same.'

'Of course I do. You *know* I do. But you need to be careful. I'd rather you were home in England. I've already arranged to send Jack back. I don't like the thought of anyone I love being in America while this virus is spreading.'

'I'm not leaving without you, Kate. And not until I've found Mangold. How is the research going?'

'Not brilliantly.'

They were both quiet for a second until Paul said, 'And how are you?'

'I'm worried, Paul. Worried to death. This strain of Watoto—it's so much worse than the one I had.'

'But if anyone can find a vaccine, you can.'

'Maybe. But what if *no one* can?'

'That doesn't sound like you, Kate . . . Kate?'

'Sorry . . . I thought I could hear a strange noise—like there was someone else on the line.'

Paul said, 'Hello? Hello?' There was a distinctive click.

'Someone was listening to us. But I didn't think there was another phone here.'

Paul snorted. 'You're in a government facility surrounded by FBI agents. It's hardly a shock. Probably Harley himself. Shit.'

'No,' she said in a whisper. 'Harley is right outside the door. I can hear him talking to one of the other agents. Hang on—he's coming in—I have to go, OK? I love you. Please take care. I'll call you again as soon as I can.'

'OK, but what—'

She had hung up.

Fucking Harley. Paul thumped the top of Rosie's car.

'Hey, steady,' she said.

'Sorry.'

'Everything OK?'

He shook his head and pulled open the car door. *Not brilliantly*, Kate had said. He knew that meant they were getting nowhere. He watched a young family pass by on the other side of the

187

street: a healthy young couple with three kids and a dog. The boys were playing with the dog, laughing uproariously as it bounded along; the dad stroked his daughter's hair and held his wife's hand. They had probably seen the news, knew about the virus that was cutting a swathe through the population of Los Angeles. Did they have any idea how far and fast viruses like this could spread? That if a hidden team of scientists didn't start to make progress, fast, the life of this family, and millions like them, would be devastated. Wiped out.

Paul clenched his fists. 'Hey,' he called out. The dad turned around, polite caution on his face. 'You should keep your kids indoors,' Paul said brusquely, crossing the street to talk to them. The little girl looked up at him, startled. 'The virus is only fifty miles away. It won't take long to get here.'

The husband and wife exchanged glances, then the man shrugged. 'It'll be a storm in a teacup, I'll bet,' he said. 'Like swine flu and avian flu—all over-hyped to sell newspapers and give anchormen something to talk about.'

'It's not,' said Paul, urgently. 'Trust me. It's not.'

The parents stared at him as though he was a raving lunatic. 'Well, thank you for your concern. Come along, kids, let's go get ice cream.' They rounded up their small charges and hurried away as fast as they could, as if Paul had threatened them with a pitchfork.

Paul slumped back against the window of a sports equipment store, watching them go, and wondering if they'd still be alive in three weeks' time. Whether *he* would be. He liked this world. He didn't want it to end.

## 26

Angelica awoke from her siesta and sat up in bed, feeling the welcome whisper of the cool silk sheet as it brushed over her perspiring body. She had been suffering a nightmare in which she was in a cheap diner surrounded by grimy, brick-dusty construction workers with crewcuts and crude tattoos who all ignored her. In the dream she had felt a growing sense of outrage at this. How dare they ignore her? There were dozens of them, all of them shovelling in All Day Breakfasts or scraping their chairs across the dirty tiled floor, and generally being the type of trash that the Goddess couldn't wait to see wiped off the face of the planet. She got out of bed and went straight to her shower.

'End Times,' she said to herself. 'It's all starting.' No wonder her nerves were on edge. She towelled herself dry with the vast soft bath sheets that the other Sisters replaced twice a day, regardless of whether Angelica had used them or not, and thought about her dream. Now that she was wide awake, it took on a different hue; the idea of all those nasty brutish men dying in agony; workers, captors, bankers, soldiers, scientists—it gave her a thrill that was sexual in its depth and intensity. Most of all, she thought about the teacher who had assaulted her as a child; the man who had made her hate all other men. Imagining *his* death throes made her shudder with pleasure. This was no dream, either—it was really happening, and she had made it happen. She prostrated herself on the carpet, her arms spread wide and an ecstatic smile on her face.

'Thank you Sekhmet, thank you for choosing me, thank you for making me the instrument of transformation in this world. Thank you for your power, and your love, and your vengeance on my behalf . . .'

The Goddess had come to her years ago, when she'd been a broken, hurt child, picked her up in Her beautiful arms, and saved her—not just saved her, but chose her as the instrument of the world's transformation. Then, in turn, she had led Angelica to her Sisters: Heather, angel of vengeance; devoted Preeti; beautiful Cindy; Simone the warrior, and practical Brandi. Bitter, resentful, hopeless lives, all transformed by the Goddess.

'Thank you, Sekhmet,' she repeated. 'Make us worthy of your trust.'

Angelica dressed, crept out of the mansion and got into the fastest of her cars, the white Maserati, and drove slowly out of the compound, keeping the engine noise down to a soft purr so as not to alert the other Sisters to her absence. It was only once she was out in the desert that she retracted the roof, put her foot on the gas, and roared off down the open road, the dusty early evening air whipping her long hair around her face. She laughed with exhilaration, feeling the breath of Sekhmet in the heat of the desert wind. It already felt as though she, her Sisters and the High Priest were the only ones left on the planet. That she was driving over the diseased dead bodies of the unworthy, the oppressors, the unenlightened.

It would be a brutal period of cleansing, no doubt about it, and she'd found it hard at first to believe what the High Priest had told her: that the entire population of the world would have to be purged for the rebirth to take place. But Sekhmet, Goddess of Pestilence, Lady of Flame, had waited five thousand years for this. There had been a few dry runs in the meantime: indigenous Indians wiped out by viruses brought to the Americas by white men. The Incas, too. But what was coming would be on a far greater scale. Destruction and death were balm to Sekhmet's proud and vengeful heart as she watched the cycle of time go round and round . . .

Few people understood that time was repeated in five-thousand-year cycles. The Mayans had known it, and some minor Indian cults, but that was before the rise of modern science. This blind faith in carbon dating was laughable—could they not see how unreliable a tool it really was? Yes, dinosaurs had existed, but not millions of years ago; they had emerged, far more briefly than commonly perceived, at the very end of each Cycle, to roam a world lying in ruins, with only the Sisters left unscathed to usher in the Golden Age.

Those who somehow avoided the virus would die in the riots and violence. In Los Angeles the descent into anarchy was already underway. With the complete breakdown of society would come starvation, fights to the death over food and resources; all those diseases that medicine had kept in check would overrun the world like the plagues sent to ravage Egypt.

The world was full of people. Too full. The planet needed purging. It was a shame that the female as well as the male population had to die, but there was nothing Angelica could do to prevent that, if the Goddess so decreed it. And she would still have her Sisters—they were all immune. A good number had been lost to the virus, but that had been necessary to ensure the final selection would stay healthy when the time came. Seven Sisters, the Prophecy foretold, though Angelica was still awaiting clarification of this. There were only six at the moment: her, Heather, Cindy, Simone, Brandi and Preeti.

*Where is the seventh?* she wondered. There was a possible candidate, but Angelica had doubts about that one. She needed her for now, for the information she supplied—but that was a means to an end.

Angelica drove as fast as she could down the arrow-straight road, between dark rocky canyons and vast flat desert, a hundred, a hundred and thirty—forty—fifty—miles an hour, the energy of the Goddess coursing through her veins, feeling utterly unstoppable. And the Goddess sent her an immediate and crystal-clear message:

*The name of the seventh Sister is Kate Maddox, not the other one you are considering. Maddox too understands the power of the Plague. And you and she are similar in many ways—ways that she will come to understand.*

Yes, Angelica thought. Dr Maddox, you are perfect for us. Thank you, Sekhmet. So that's why you saved Maddox from the blast. It makes sense now.

As she thought about Kate, Angelica's cell phone rang.

'I'm listening. Yes. Tell me.' She bit down on her irritation. The person on the other end of the line was always in a hurry, always worried that someone was going to walk in and catch them.

She listened, becoming increasingly concerned as

192

her contact talked.

'Dadi Angelica, they're closer than they think . . . Kolosine hasn't a clue; from what I can tell, he's exhausted his only idea . . . But Dr Maddox . . .' She told Angelica the worrying news. 'There's something else . . .'

Angelica ended the call and immediately called Heather.

'Sister Heather.'

Things had been stilted between them since the scene in the motel. Neither of them had mentioned it, but they had stayed away from each other, only communicating when it was essential. Perhaps this was the bright side of what Angelica had just learned: it gave Angelica a good reason to put distance between them, even if it meant a change to the plan, a change that involved sending her most reliable Sister miles away.

'Dadi.'

'I have a mission for you.'

'Yes?'

'I need you to go to Sagebrush.'


27


Paul perched on the edge of the armchair, holding a glass of flat Coke that Watton had given him and trying to ignore the cat rubbing round his ankles. Outside, the night throbbed with the sound of crickets.

After Rosie had dropped him off, Paul had gone up to his room intending to lie down for a moment while he thought over the questions he wanted to ask Watton. The next thing he knew he was waking up with a furry mouth and it was dark outside. He'd raced downstairs and got the front desk to call him a cab.

The older man adjusted his glasses. 'I didn't want to tell you this while Rosie was around because she's such a sweetheart . . . I don't want to upset her.'

Paul leaned forward, eager to hear more but mindful that he needed to let Watton tell the tale in his own time.

'I understand.'

'OK, so . . . A while before Medi-Lab got shut down, I volunteered for something . . .' He started coughing and Paul gritted his teeth. But then the cat jumped on to Watton's lap and he scratched it behind the ears. This seemed to calm him, and he continued:

'A memo went round asking for volunteers who wanted to earn a little extra. They wanted healthy men and women who were willing to give up some of their spare time. I was always up for earning more, especially with sales being slow. So I put my name down.'

Paul waited for him to continue.

'It seemed like easy money. Heck, it was easy money. And damn good money, too. All we had to do was go to the lab a few times, let them prod and poke us and take a blood sample. Then they gave us a cold.'

'A cold?'

'Yep. A mild dose of flu. They gave us that, we got sick—but nothing too bad, just the usual, you know? Blocked nose, sore throat, high temperature . . . Actually, I did feel pretty rough for a couple of

194

days and they said that it was fine to take the time off work, stay in bed. I was worried I'd lose the extra money, but they told me it was all good. Then Dr Diaz came round and gave me another shot. He said it would make me feel better. And it did.'

'Who was Dr Diaz?'

'Oh, he was the head of research at Medi-Lab. Dr Camilo Diaz.'

'He came to your house? The head of research?'

'That's what I said.'

'Was he alone?'

'Yep. Which was unusual, 'cos you hardly ever saw him outside of his lab. He was Mangold's right-hand man. Real clever guy, though he had a bit of a rep as a ladies' man. Always had a younger woman on the go.'

'Did Diaz tell you what was in the shot he gave you?'

'He just said it was some kind of new vitamin shot they were testing.'

Paul mulled over what Watton had told him so far. He wasn't sure why the old man hadn't wanted Rosie to hear this. Unless . . . 'Let me guess, Rosie's dad was one of the other volunteers.'

'You guessed it. And he had the same experience as me.' Watton leaned forward. 'A few months later, all that business with the virus happened and we got shut down. We were unemployed. I suddenly had a lot of spare time. And I spent a lot of that time thinking on what had happened.'

'Go on.'

'Well . . . before we did the trials, Dr Diaz got us to sign a whole sheaf of legal papers saying in a very long-winded way that we accepted full responsibility, understood the risks, yada yada yada.

195

That if anything happened to us as a result of the trials, the company could not be held responsible. He tried to rush us into signing it, saying it was just a formality, but I read through the whole thing. By the time I got to the end, I was about ready to back out.'

'Because you realised it was dangerous.'

'Uh-huh. Well, risky at any rate. I talked about it with Owen—Rosie's dad. I said to him that I didn't think he should do it. I was a single guy, and I really needed the money. I had some pretty big credit card debts, you see. But Owen had a family. He had Rosie.'

'But he needed the money too?'

'I reckon I wasn't the only one with debts. You see now why I didn't want to talk about this in front of Rosie. He must have needed the money bad, 'cos it was like he didn't give a shit about the risk. I don't think he even read through the waiver.' Watton sighed. 'So, anyway—that's what I wanted you to know. Mangold was testing something potentially dangerous on his employees. If you're writing a book about the son of a bitch, maybe that oughta go in it. It wasn't right that Diaz took all the blame for what went down. Wound up in jail while Mangold walked away a free man.'

'Diaz was put on trial?'

'Yeah.' He coughed, wincing and rubbing his chest. 'He got twenty-five years.'

'That's a hell of a long sentence.'

'They threw the book at the poor bastard.'

'Diaz—D-I-A-Z?' Paul asked, getting out his phone so he could type it in to his Notes app.

'Yup. Camilo Diaz.'

'Do you know anything else? Like what prison he

196

got sent to? Or whether he's still in? He might have got out for good behaviour by now.'

Watton laughed, the laughter quickly turning into a wheeze and then a coughing jag. When he'd recovered, he shrugged. 'I don't know.'

'Do you have the internet here?'

Watton just laughed again.

Paul stared at his phone screen. He could turn on data roaming to access the internet, but it would immediately make his phone traceable. Still, he had already used it once, to phone Kate back. Sod it. He slid a switch on the screen and waited while the phone connected to a 3G network. Then he ran a search for 'Camilo Diaz Medi-Lab prison'.

The results included a news article about the doctor dated a couple of years ago. It described how he had continued his work even in prison, publishing papers and helping to educate some of the other prisoners, teaching classes in biology and science. A model prisoner, by all accounts. Most importantly, it included the information that Diaz was in Glencarson Prison.

Unfortunately for Paul, Glencarson Prison was in Los Angeles.

## 28

'Kate, Kate . . . Please, wake up.'

She opened her eyes, unsure of where she was. In her dream, she had been back at home in Oxford and she instinctively looked to her left to see if Paul was there. But the side of the bed on which he always slept was empty. The reality of where

197

she was and everything that had happened recently came rushing back to her, making her want to pull the quilt over her head.

'I'm so sorry, but I need you to help. I think I've made a breakthrough.'

The room was dim and there was a female form standing over her, silhouetted in black against the grey. It was Junko.

'Very sorry to wake you . . .'

'Junko. What . . . what time is it?'

'About midnight, I think.' She checked her watch. 'Yes, one minute past twelve. I'm sorry, Kate, but I've been working, and I think I've found something very important. I need to show you. I'm—'

'Please don't say sorry again.'

Kate reached over and switched on her bedside lamp, in time to see Junko bite her lip to stop herself from apologising.

'Please, will you come with me to the lab?' she said instead. 'I would have woken Kolosine or Chip, but . . . well, I will explain when we get there.'

Kate rubbed her eyes. Her head felt like it was stuffed full of overcooked pasta. 'OK, of course. Just let me go to the loo.'

Junko stared at her blankly.

'The bathroom. I need to pee really badly. And, um, I'm not wearing any clothes.'

The Japanese woman looked embarrassed and Kate couldn't help but laugh. She really liked Junko—her dedication to the cause, her quiet determination. Beneath her rather neat and prim exterior, Kate could sense a rebel trying to get out.

'I'll meet you in there. Please come quick!' Junko pleaded.

198

Kate studied her. She was jiggling from foot to foot, completely unable to stand still. 'You're really excited, aren't you?'

'Yes, yes. I think this could be it, Kate. How do you say it? I think I've cracked it, already!'

*       *       *

Brandi gently applied the brakes, bringing the black Ford Expedition to a halt before reversing into a space between the trees. She killed the engine, leaving them in pitch darkness. It was 00.10 a.m. and the forest was as silent as a cemetery.

Brandi was an expert mechanic and driver, ex-army, left for dead after an explosion in Iraq. Three years ago she had crawled from the wreckage of a bombed truck, barely aware of who she was, and kept going, hitching rides and stealing cars and bikes, heading east until she reached China. Angelica had found her in Shanghai and brought her back to the States, made her part of her plans. All Brandi wanted was a home. Somewhere to belong. She would kill for Angelica. The bomb that had almost killed her had left her with screaming tinnitus, and the only time the ringing in her ears ceased was when Angelica whispered to her.

Angelica, who sat in the passenger seat beside Brandi, was whispering now. 'We know our mission.'

The other three, Brandi, Cindy and Simone, replied in one voice: 'We know.'

'We know who we are,' intoned Angelica, looking intently at them all. Cindy was her first and favourite Sister. Angelica had found her in a bar in a one-horse town in Nebraska, passed out through drink, a group of local men circling her, gazing at her with lust and violent intent, and Angelica had rescued her, nursed her through her withdrawal from the alcohol, whispered to her and held her as she shook with the DTs, telling her of the great plan the Goddess had for all of them.

'We know.'

'We love our Sisters and the Goddess.'

They reached out and squeezed each other's hands. 'We love.'

'We hate those who would stand against the prophecy.'

Their united voices dropped an octave. 'We hate.'

Angelica was quiet for a moment and Brandi knew she would be communing with the Goddess. Even though it was dark in the car and all she could see were the black shapes of the trees through the windshield, she closed her eyes and dipped her chin, saying her own silent prayer.

'Sisters,' Angelica said when the prayer was done, 'does everybody understand absolutely and without hesitation what they have to do?'

They murmured assent.

'Sister Brandi, keep the headlights turned off and drive to the gate. If you don't receive a message by one fifteen, we will have failed. You are to head back to the ranch immediately, contact Sister Heather and burn everything. The Goddess will give you further instructions.'

Brandi blanched. 'But Dadi Angelica . . .'

Angelica leaned over and kissed her on the cheek. Her lips were like ice. 'Don't be alarmed, Sister. It's a precaution, that's all. We won't fail.'

200

Kate checked her watch. It was ten past midnight, and Junko was waiting for her outside the door to the lab. She was still bouncing from foot to foot, impatient for Kate to join her. There was nobody else around; Junko had been working on her own, although Kate noticed a light burning in the breakfast room as she passed it.

'So what have you found?' Kate asked. Her heart was beating hard now, infected by Junko's enthusiasm. Could she really have figured out how to create a vaccine for Watoto? Surely that was too much to hope for.

'I need to show you.'

Junko opened the thick steel security door and they stepped inside, finding their biosafety suits and stripping off, Kate wondering why she had bothered to get dressed in the first place.

Before they put on their helmets, Junko said, 'It was all thanks to you, Kate.'

'What do you mean?'

'Your research paper. You left your laptop on the table earlier and, I'm sorry, but I couldn't help but read it. I've read it before, of course, but not recently. I don't understand why Kolosine didn't circulate copies for all of us to read as soon as we got here.'

'Of course I don't mind—it's public property. As for Kolosine, I don't think he knows what he's doing, Junko. His ego is so big it blots out every idea but his own.'

Kate had seen their head scientist only once since the failure to reveal the antibodies in her blood. He had called a team meeting in which he expressed his frustration in four-letter words, yelled at full volume, as he told them how useless and worthless they were. Kate and Junko had developed quite an extensive private language of facial gestures to indicate to each other exactly what they thought of him, as he ranted and swore and slammed his hand on the table. The rest of the team just put their heads down and stared at the floor, and William the epidemiologist looked as though he wanted to punch someone.

They donned their helmets and pushed through into the lab. Kate followed Junko across to the electron microscope that was kept in a darkened corner. Junko had already processed the samples of Watoto-X2 and prepared them for viewing.

'Take a look,' Junko said, 'and I'll explain.'

\*       \*       \*

Angelica stopped and caught her breath, checking her watch—00:15—as she clung to the blue oak she was scaling. She had a slim but powerful Maglite attached to her belt, which illuminated the thick canopy of branches around her, the ground far below shrouded in darkness. Just below her, she could see Cindy's head; Simone was parallel with her in the next tree and Angelica could hear them both panting with the exertion of climbing so high. They had been practising night-climbing for days now, back at the ranch. It was exhilarating, being so far from the man-made world. Up here, in the silence, the cool breeze caressing her skin, her heart thumping in her chest, she felt closer than ever to the Goddess.

She waited a moment for Cindy to catch her up, drawing level and perching on a thick branch beside her.

'Are you OK, Sister?' Angelica asked.

Cindy nodded, but Angelica could see a flash of fear on her face, which was shiny in the torchlight.

'Don't be afraid,' Angelica coaxed. 'Sekhmet is watching over us.'

'I know, I . . . Jesus!' The branch on which Cindy was resting shuddered violently and she grabbed at Angelica, her fingers skidding across the soft, black leather of her leader's outfit. They were all wearing black leather from head to toe. Earlier, Cindy had giggled as she'd dusted her legs with talcum powder and pulled on the skin-tight trousers.

'Do not say that,' Angelica hissed.

'I'm sorry, Dadi. I—'

'What's going on?' asked Simone from her position a few feet away.

'Quiet, you two.' Angelica felt the anger bubble up from within. She shone her torch into Simone's face, and the other woman coolly shaded her eyes with her free hand. With her smooth ebony skin, and black outfit, she was almost invisible. Simone the Warrior. Simone had been living with a drug dealer in LA, a man who beat her daily and pimped her out to his clients, until one day Simone snapped and fixed him up with a lethal dose of heroin. Angelica had found her wandering the projects, penniless, shivering with fear and hunger. She had bought her a hot meal and as she ate Simone told her about her upbringing, about the men her mother brought home and what they did to her. Angelica hugged her and promised her a new,

203

better life, and a way of getting back at those men and the world they had created.

Behind her, Cindy sat on a branch, her fear forgotten, seemingly as at home as a squirrel in the treetops. Not for the first time, Angelica was struck by how beautiful Cindy was. But now was not the time to be thinking of such things.

Angelica shone her torch in the direction of the fence. 'Follow me. We're losing precious minutes here. Go swiftly. And be careful.'

The fence was a distance of three trees, and Angelica moved across the branches, knowing that one false move would send her hurtling down into the darkness. They were already fifty feet up, level with the top of the fence, and the fall would mean death or paralysis. The others stuck close behind her.

Minutes later, Angelica reached the fence. Now was the moment of truth. If their helper on the inside had done their job properly, the electrified fence would be disabled, along with the CCTV. She checked her watch. The insider had been instructed to switch everything off at 00:20 and turn it back on ten minutes later. It was now 00.21.

Cindy touched her on the shoulder and whispered in her ear, 'Let me test it. If the power is still on, it's better that I die than you.'

She reached out and stroked Cindy's hair. 'No. It is my destiny,' she told her.

Straddling a thick branch that almost reached the fence, Angelica shuffled along as gracefully as she could, then, trying not to let the others see that her hand was trembling, stretched out her hand to touch the metal, aware that if the power was still on, the shock would char her flesh, send thousands of volts through her body and blow her out of the tree—she would be dead before she hit the ground. Intoning a silent prayer, she touched the metal.

Nothing. Just cool metal. The power was off.

She closed her eyes and exhaled, then snapped back into action. Gripping the top of the mesh fence, she launched herself off the branch and flung her body against the fifty-foot-high fence. It swayed for a moment, but she held tight and waited. Years before, she had helped break a political prisoner out of jail. That had been much harder, having to time her and the prisoner's ascent to avoid sweeping searchlights. This was easier. She pulled herself to the top, swung herself over so she was on the other side, then stopped, removing the Maglite from her belt and pointing it at Simone, who was next in line. Cindy brought up the rear.

Angelica descended the fence as swiftly and easily as a spider traversing a web. When she was ten feet from the ground she paused and listened, to make sure there were no guards waiting at the bottom. She heard no signs of life. The insider had, again, done a good job. An hour before, Angelica's new would-be disciple had gone out to chat with the guards, offered them a drink of coffee which they'd gladly accepted, not knowing it contained a strong dose of rohypnol along with the sugar and cream.

She dropped the last few feet and reached the ground, landing like a cat and crouching in the darkness, waiting for the other two. They jogged as a group towards the building. It was so easy. A fire escape led up to the roof and they ascended it slowly, careful not to make any noise. They passed a lit window and Angelica peeped inside to ensure no one was looking out before they crept on by.

205

Now, on the rooftop, she would see if their helper on the inside had done everything she asked. She crossed the roof to a fire door and tested it.

It opened. Moments later, the three of them were inside. It was 00.39.

Angelica stopped and pulled off her miniature backpack. She produced a small roll of paper and smoothed it flat against the wall, shining her torch on it. It showed a floorplan of the building. The other women gathered around as she pointed out where each of them was to go, giving them a final reminder of what they had rehearsed at the ranch.

Finally, she pulled her gun from the holster on her outer thigh. It was a Sig Sauer P220, her favourite pistol, the first one she had ever been trained to use. A suppressor had already been screwed in place. Cindy carried the same gun, but Simone preferred a Glock 17.

Angelica spread out her arms and the Sisters drew close, putting their arms round each other's shoulders and touching foreheads. She kissed their cheeks, lingering for a moment longer on Cindy's soft face.

Then, without a word, they scattered, each with their own target; their personal mission in which they could not fail.

\*       \*       \*

Kate peered into the microscope, staring for what felt like the millionth time at the Watoto virus. This new strain was so similar to the old that its morphology—its shape and size—was as familiar to her as the smell of Jack's skin. Watoto was shaped almost like a seahorse, setting it apart from its haemorrhagic cousins—the worm-like shape of Ebola, and the cigarette-like form of Marburg.

'What am I looking for?' she asked Junko.

'Something you have seen many times, I think,' the Japanese woman replied. 'But it was a mystery to you. Or a ghost. You mentioned it in your paper.'

'The ghost?'

'Yes. Remember, in your paper, you said that sometimes when studying the virus you thought you could see a trace of something that didn't belong, like a ghost flickering in and out of sight. You thought perhaps it was a contamination.'

Kate stared back into the microscope: the virus was so tiny that a million of them could fit on the head of a pin. But it taunted her. Had done for years. She hardly dared to feel excited or optimistic. Could Junko have really found the key to beating this killer?

'Go on,' she said.

'I—' She stopped. 'What was that?'

They both stared towards the door.

'I don't know,' said Kate. 'But it sounded like a gunshot.'

29

Angelica turned the door handle and slipped silently into the room. The virologist called Chip lay in the bed, his mouth open. He was snoring. Angelica looked at the picture of the rather ugly woman on the bedside cabinet, wiry hair and a weak chin. She was probably relieved to be enjoying some peaceful nights.

She held the barrel of her gun an inch from Chip's forehead and fired, the suppressor rendering the shot silent as his brains and fragments of skull splattered the headboard. Chip was one of the lucky ones. Didn't most people want to die peacefully in their sleep?

*       *       *

Simone entered William's room. Dadi Angelica had explained at some length what this guy did—he was an epidemiologist, whatever the hell that was—but Simone hadn't really been listening.

All she knew and cared about was that it was her mission to end him.

He was curled up in a foetal position, his face scrunched up with anxiety. Bad dream.

She folded a stick of chewing gum into her mouth. She felt like an angel of mercy, come to rid him of his nightmares.

She tapped him on the forehead with the tip of her gun, just hard enough to wake him, to bring him out of his bad dream. The moment he opened his eyes, she shot him in the face.

*       *       *

Kolosine was awake in his room. He had been in the lab until late, working in solitude in his own workspace in the corner, slamming freezer doors, rattling tubes and cursing loudly, partly out of sheer

208

frustration, but also because he didn't want anyone near him. He lay on his bed and chewed the inside of his cheek, tasting the coppery blood and trying to force his brain to work, to make connections, to do its goddamn job.

He had been so sure Maddox's blood held the answer. So confident that, unknown to everyone else, it was his only shot. Once that had failed he'd felt like a rock singer who, when facing a difficult crowd, pulls out his greatest hit, his sure-fire crowd-pleaser . . . only for it to be greeted with silence.

Now what were they going to do? None of the other halfwits in this place had a snowball's chance of finding a cure—not that loser Chip, not the Japanese chick, whose chance of success was nearly as small as her tits, and certainly not that waste-of-space Kate Maddox, who had been pursuing a cure for Watoto longer than the Redskins had been trying to win another Superbowl.

He pulled the quilt up over his head, wishing he'd brought Jenny with him. Her warm twenty-three-year-old body and mouth would have provided some comfort in these dark days. Suddenly, an image of his mom flashed into his head, washing away the naked postgrad. He hadn't seen his mom since last Thanksgiving, when they'd quarrelled as usual about the grandchildren he had yet to produce.

Well, guess what, Mom? The way things are going, nobody is gonna have any freaking grandchildren to look forward to.

His eyes filled with sudden, unexpected tears. What the hell was wrong with him? He was

209

debating whether to reach for his secret stash of whisky when he heard a click. It sounded like someone coming into his room.

He stuck his head above the quilt, realising as he did so that he was hoping to see Dr Maddox slipping into his room, maybe in a lab coat with nothing underneath, and she would let the lab coat slide off her shoulders before climbing on top of him.

But it was a different woman, dressed in black leather, gorgeous but terrifying. She was pointing a gun in his direction, hesitating just long enough for him to scream before she shot him in the head and his brain switched off for ever.

*        *        *

Agent McCarthy's eyes snapped open. He had heard a scream. It sounded like it had come from a nearby room. The bedside clock told him it was 0.43.

As he flicked on the lamp and swung his legs out of bed, he caught a glimpse of himself in the mirror, undershirt and shorts straining to contain his bulk. Damn, he was out of shape. When all this was over, he was going on a diet.

His holster was hanging from the back of a chair. He grabbed his gun and stuck his head out of the door just in time to see a figure coming out of the room two doors down—Kolosine's room. It was a woman with long black hair, clad head to toe in leather. She had her back to him, but he could see she was carrying a gun. Before she could turn, he ducked back into his room, suddenly aware of his heart pounding in his chest.

Grabbing the pillow from his bed, he pushed the door open swiftly with his foot and stuck the pillow out into the corridor, knowing that if the woman was there she would fire at the sudden movement. But no shot came.

He peered out. The hallway was empty.

Closing the door quietly behind him, gun down by his side, McCarthy tiptoed along the landing, wishing he was lighter on his feet and wondering what the fuck was going on. He peered into Kolosine's room.

'Holy—'

He didn't care for the head scientist. But seeing him with a bullet hole in his forehead made his insides flip. He pressed his back against the open door, concealing himself inside Kolosine's room. He looked out. No movement; no noise either. As quietly as he could, McCarthy exited the room and moved along the hall. He passed another door and looked in. One of the scientists—Chip—with his face obliterated. And in the room next to his, the housekeeper, Adoncia, also dead. He paused at the corner that led to the stairs: one flight up were the other bedrooms; the labs were one flight below. Where was Thompson? He was supposed to be on night duty, keeping an eye on the CCTV, but the lazy bastard had probably fallen asleep. And what about the other guards?

Holding his gun against his chest, he stepped out from the corner wall.

Nothing.

He tried to process what he knew. A black-clad woman. Who the hell was she? So far, they had got nowhere in their attempts to find out who had

211

blown the hotel to shit. Now it looked like the hunt was over. The terrorists had come to them.

But he had no idea how many of them there were in the building. If it was one woman, he could handle that. More, and his priority should be to raise the alarm. Kolosine's office, with the only goddamn phone in this freaking place, and the only means of contacting the outside world since the internet went down, was on the floor below. That's where he needed to head.

Except Kate was upstairs.

He paused. Kate's bedroom was on the floor above. Plus Junko. Were they already dead? The possibility made him feel sick. Over the last few days he had bonded with both of them, especially Dr Maddox. Should he go up first, check they were OK and, if so, get them into a safe place?

The dilemma paralysed him for a moment, then he made his decision. The priority had to be to raise the alarm. As he crept towards the stairwell, his eye fell upon the fire alarm on the wall. He could set it off, alert anyone who was in the building—but it would alert the intruder or intruders too; better to maintain the element of surprise. He didn't get why the assassin hadn't come to his room. But he wasn't going to bitch about it.

He dashed down the first flight of stairs, then crouched and pointed his gun down the second flight. Still no sign of anybody. He descended the remaining stairs and walked as quietly as he could along the hallway, passing the security room. He went inside. Slumped over the desk, beneath a bank of blank CCTV screens, was Agent Thompson.

'Nick?'

McCarthy tugged on his colleague's shoulder,

and Thompson's head rolled back. His throat had been slashed. Blood pooled on the floor around him, dripping from the chair, oozing into the instrument panel on which the dead agent rested.

McCarthy gagged. An image flashed through his mind of Thompson with his wife and kids, laughing together at a fundraising event last Christmas. Shock and sadness were quickly replaced by fury, a quiet anger that rose up through his body, made him want revenge, caused him to picture himself putting a bullet into the motherfucker who had done this.

He pressed a button on the control panel, switching the CCTV back on. The screens lit up, and he leaned forward, barely breathing, for a better look.

There were two people in the lab, standing over a microscope, apparently oblivious to what else was happening in the building. They were wearing bio-suits, so he struggled at first to make out who it was. But then one of them turned to face the camera and he saw that it was Kate. He needed to get out of here, raise the alarm, then get straight to the lab.

As he turned to go, his eye fell upon the next screen. It showed a woman walking cautiously along a hallway.

Shit, it was *this* hallway.

As he reacted, instinctively raising his gun, the woman stepped into the doorway. Her eyes widened when she saw him and he fired first, hitting her square in the chest, waiting for the blood to bloom and fountain around him. But there was no blood. She must be wearing a Kevlar vest. She began to fall, winded, pulling the trigger of her own gun on her way down, a fluke shot that entered McCarthy's right ear and exited the back of his head. The world folded in on him in a nanosecond.

\*      \*      \*

'That sounded like a gunshot,' Kate said.

Junko's face, behind the plastic screen of her helmet, had gone pale. 'Are you . . . sure?'

Kate nodded. 'Definitely.'

'What shall we do?' Junko asked nervously.

'There's a back exit, isn't there? The one they brought Officer Buckley through.'

Junko nodded eagerly. 'Yes. Of course.'

'Let's go out, wait, see if we can find McCarthy or Thompson . . . find out what the hell is going on.'

To reach the exit, they had to go through the small room in which Officer Marshall Buckley had died. The room had been cleaned out now, the body sealed and shipped out by air to be added to the piles of corpses awaiting cremation.

She could almost feel Buckley's presence as they hurried to the door. She pushed down the metal handle.

'Oh, shit.' Of course, it was locked. Why had she been expecting anything different? She looked for a set of keys, but they were nowhere to be found.

'I'm scared, Kate. What if it's the terrorists—the people who bombed the hotel?'

'It's OK.' She might have given Junko a hug had they not been wearing these stupid suits. 'Look, maybe it's nothing to worry about.' She forced a laugh. 'Might have been McCarthy dropping his gun or something. I wouldn't put it past him.'

214

Junko didn't look convinced.

'Listen, Kate, I need to tell you about what I found, with the virus, just in case . . . in case I die and you survive.'

'Junko, don't be—'

They both turned at the same time. They had heard another bang. Not a gunshot this time, but a door slamming, metal on metal. And the faint sound of voices, getting closer. Somebody was coming.

## 30

Paul rented a car from a place on the edge of town and drove it to the diner where Rosie worked. He parked up and went to sit on a wooden bench outside, waiting for Rosie to finish her late shift. Through the window he could see that Lucy was with her, and he smiled as he watched them working together. Rosie must have sensed someone watching her, because she looked up. Maybe it was a trick of the light through the glass, but he could have sworn she blushed, before tucking a few loose strands of hair behind her ear and attending to a customer.

He was hit by a vision of Rosie naked, her limbs entwined with his, her soft breasts pressed against his chest, her thighs parting as she looked into his eyes and gasped his name as he pushed into her . . .

Kate's face swam into his vision and he felt a stab of guilt. But surely it was natural to find other women attractive. Humans were not meant to be monogamous . . . He shook his head, disgusted with

215

himself. It was Kate he wanted. Kate he loved.

Like he'd told her, Rosie was helping him with the search for Mangold, that was all.

Half an hour later, at midnight, Rosie and Lucy emerged into the balmy night air.

'Evening, Mr Craig,' smiled Lucy, though some of her usual sparkle was missing. Worried about her friends in LA, Paul guessed.

'What's up?' Rosie asked. 'Something happened?'

Paul looked at Lucy, who put her hands up. 'OK, I get the hint. I'll wait in the car.' She held her palm out for the keys.

When she'd gone, Rosie sat down on the bench next to Paul. 'I went back to see Jon,' he said. He had decided not to tell her that Watton had asked him to return. 'I had some more questions I needed to ask him.'

'Oh, Paul, I hope you haven't made him more sick.'

'He was fine. Keen to talk, in fact. And I found out some interesting stuff.'

He recounted most of what Watton had told him, omitting any mention of her dad.

'So what now?' Rosie asked, when he'd finished.

'I've rented a car and I'm going to head to LA, to talk to this Dr Diaz. Want to come?' He looked right at her, a laugh in his voice to let her know that he was joking, much as he would have liked to have her company for a while longer.

She grinned back at him. 'Sure, nothing I'd like better than to hang out with a bunch of cons.' The grin died and she looked towards the car where her daughter was waiting for her. 'No, Paul, I need to be around for Lucy. She's freaking out about this virus. Anyway, you'll never get permission to visit a prison that close to LA, not with the outbreak! They'll be desperate to keep everybody out, stop it getting in and infecting the inmates. If I were you I'd call them up before you drive all the way over there to be told "no visitors".'

'Good idea,' he said. 'What will I do without you?'

She inclined her head, and he noticed the precise angle her lips curled upwards when she was flattered. 'Come back soon and tell me how you got on?' she suggested, looking at him hopefully.

'You bet.'

'Do you need to go right away? Why not come over and have lunch with us tomorrow? Or stay over tonight, if you like. It's late. Our sofabed is real comfortable.' The words came out in a rush and she couldn't meet his eye.

'I . . . I'd love to, but I need to drop by the hotel to pick up my stuff. I want to get going.'

'OK. If you're sure. But . . .' She looked into his eyes and he felt warm and cold at the same time. 'You'd be welcome to stay.'

There was a long, long pause. Paul reached out and touched Rosie's cheek.

'Thank you,' he said. 'I would really love to . . . but I'd better not. Thanks again, for everything.'

## 31

As arranged, the women briefly regrouped after the first killing spree.

'Are you hurt, Sister Cindy?' Angelica asked, concerned. Cindy was clutching her side and gasping.

'Took a hit,' she said. 'But when I was in the security room I got a good look at the screen. There are two women in the lab. A white woman and what looked like an Asian.'

Angelica smiled. 'Perfect.'

Simone rolled her shoulders and snapped her gum.

The heels of their leather boots clacked on the floor as all three strode towards the lab.

Angelica raised a hand to halt them. She readied her gun and prepared to open the door. At last, she was going to come face to face with the famous Dr Maddox.

\*           \*           \*

Throughout the agonising wait for the door to open, Kate's mind had been running through all the possibilities as to who might be out there. Three leather-clad women did not feature on her list.

She reached out and took Junko's gloved hand as the women approached. All three were beautiful. One was black, the other two white: a blonde and a brunette. The blonde one walked slightly ahead of the others; the body language and the way the other

218

two looked at her told Kate this was the leader. The brunette appeared to be in pain, walking unsteadily and pressing her hand against her ribcage.

The three came to a halt in front of the antechamber, then the blonde nodded to the black woman, who tried the door. But Kate had locked it. The black woman rolled her eyes, then pulled a gun from a holster on her thigh and shot the glass panel in the door. Fragments of glass bounced off Kate and Junko's suits.

The blonde gestured for them to exit the room.

Kate hesitated, and the blonde said to the black woman, 'Sister Simone . . .'

Simone—*Sister* Simone?—reached through the broken window, undid the lock and entered, pointing her gun at Junko's face. She grabbed hold of her arm and pulled her towards the door. Kate had no choice but to follow.

The blonde mimed removing their helmets, then sighed impatiently as they both hesitated again, Junko eyeing the microscopes, beneath which the virus waited to be studied.

'Take them off,' she shouted.

Their helmets hit the floor. 'That's better,' said the blonde. 'Now take the suits off. Quickly.'

Both scientists obeyed, though Kate didn't understand why they were being asked to do this. Did these women think the suits would slow down a bullet? Or were they planning to take them somewhere and didn't want them to be impeded by the suits?

The blonde addressed Kate coolly: 'Dr Maddox.'

Kate shivered. This woman knew her name. That couldn't be good news.

She faced the outer door of the lab and shouted,

219

as loudly as she could, 'Help!'

Simone laughed. 'No use shouting for help. They're all dead.'

'No,' Kate breathed, shaking her head. 'Please . . . no . . .'

'Shut up,' snapped the blonde. 'Tell me, how are your efforts to create a vaccine coming along?'

Kate was confused. Maybe these women weren't the terrorists after all. Maybe they were trying to get hold of a vaccine. 'We don't have a cure to the virus,' she said. 'You're wasting your time.'

Simone and the brunette laughed.

'D'you hear that, Sister Cindy?' said Simone. 'The doctor thinks we need some of her medicine.'

Cindy laughed, then winced with pain. The blonde was scrutinising Kate, tilting her head to one side as if she were studying a museum exhibit. It made Kate feel even more uncomfortable. But the fact that they weren't looking for a cure confirmed her original fear. These must be the same people who had bombed the hotel. Who had killed Isaac. Hatred stirred in her chest.

Simone, who was energetically chewing gum, said, 'Dadi Angelica, shall I kill the Japanese chick now?'

Junko whimpered and Kate grabbed hold of her. Daddy Angelica? What was that all about?

'No!' she addressed Angelica. 'Who are you and what do you want?'

'We want to save the world from itself, Dr Maddox. It's sick, diseased. It's been ill for a long time. But we have the antidote to this sickness. It's out there now, purging the planet, making it clean.'

Simone, who was still pointing her gun at Junko, said, 'Dadi, we should hurry. Brandi will be waiting

220

for us.'

Kate remembered the words of the sinister message Harley had told her about: *'And she sent a plague upon the Earth, a plague born in the cradle of mankind, and those who would stand in her way were consumed by the fire of her wrath. None should dare stand in her way.'* Hearing the way these women addressed each other, like members of a religious cult, it suddenly made a lot more sense.

At that moment, the door to the lab opened and Kate looked up with desperate hope, thinking that it might be McCarthy, or Agent Thompson, come to save them. But it was Annie.

'Careful!' Kate yelled. 'Go get help.'

Annie ignored her. Smiling like a soldier reunited with comrades, she walked calmly across the lab floor and, to Kate's astonishment, knelt on the floor before Angelica, smiling up at her. She wore the kind of expression a devout Catholic might wear before the Pope.

'I hope I have pleased you this time,' Annie said. 'It is such an honour to serve you. To be in the presence of your radiance again.'

Angelica inclined her head. 'Thank you for your telephone communications. Most helpful.'

Kate put her hands on her hips. 'I thought you said there were no phones here, apart from the one in Kolosine's office?'

'I lied. Adoncia had one in her room.' Annie looked irritated.

Kate almost laughed, it was so ludicrous. But Junko was sobbing beside her, and Simone's gun was still trained on them, though she was distracted by Annie. Angelica was gazing down at the lab technician; in a manner befitting a pope

221

she stretched out her hand and Annie kissed it. The other two women were staring at Annie too; the brunette, Cindy, smiling as if the scene were charming.

While the women were temporarily distracted, Kate looked around for a weapon. Could she grab the virus, threaten them with it? No, that would endanger Junko. Contracting the virus would simply be a much slower way of dying than catching a bullet. There were pipettes in racks, but though their tips were sharp, their plastic shafts were too soft. There would be bottles of sulphuric acid in the cupboard across the room, but there was no way she could get there, unlock the cupboard, locate the acid and open the bottle in time.

Then her eye fell upon something behind Angelica. If she was fast enough . . . These bitches had unleashed Watoto upon the world. They had killed Isaac. They deserved everything they got.

Like a sprinter coming out of the blocks, fuelled by anger and determination, she dashed past Angelica, knocking her off balance with her shoulder, reaching the Dewar tank of liquid nitrogen within seconds. She grabbed the handle, flipped open the lid and snatched up a polystyrene container, a piece of packaging that had once contained test tubes. White smoke billowed from the tank. The liquid nitrogen was kept at minus 350 degrees Fahrenheit; it looked like boiling water beneath a cloud of steam, but was far more dangerous.

Two of the women dashed across the room towards her: Cindy and Simone, raising their guns. Cindy was slower, pulling to a halt and grabbing her ribs, holding her gun with one hand.

222

'Don't kill her,' shouted Angelica, and they both paused for a second, long enough for Kate to dip the container into the tank and scoop up a generous measure. Angelica had ordered them not to kill her: feeling emboldened, she brandished the container.

'Get back,' she ordered.

The two women hesitated. Simone looked towards Angelica, as if awaiting an order, but Cindy made a lunge for Kate.

If the woman had been at full strength, she would have been able to snatch the container from Kate's hand. But her injury slowed her down just enough for Kate to take a half-step back—and throw the liquid into Cindy's face.

Cindy let out an agonised scream.

Kate turned to grab another scoop, but Simone was upon her. She shoved Kate to the ground, taking her legs out from under her with a swift kick, and jumped on to her back, twisting her arm and pushing her against the floor.

Cindy was still screaming. The liquid nitrogen had frozen her face, burning away the skin. Kate, with her cheekbone pressed against the ground, felt excruciating pain as her arm was wrenched almost out of its socket. She looked up, past Cindy, at Angelica, who was frozen to the spot, staring with horror at the shrieking brunette. Cindy dropped to her knees, hands in her hair, face ruined, eyes blind, lips and nose melting away, raw flesh peeling from her cheekbones. Kate couldn't have done more damage if she'd doused the woman with petrol and set her alight.

At the same moment Cindy hit the floor, Junko broke into a run towards the exit. Simone

223

immediately sprang up from where she held Kate against the floor and launched herself in pursuit.

Junko was inches from the door when Simone tackled her from behind at high speed. With a sickening crack, Junko's head smashed into the metal door. She slumped to the ground and lay there unmoving, Simone panting on top of her.

Angelica, who had remained frozen as a statue, finally came to life.

'Sister Simone, watch Dr Maddox,' she commanded, and the black woman obeyed, jumping up from the prone Junko and training her pistol on Kate. Meanwhile Angelica sank to her knees before Cindy and pulled her into an embrace.

'My face,' Cindy said, her voice distorted as if her mouth were full of thick liquid. It sounded like, 'Gy 'ace'. As well as burning off her lips—those pouting, bee-stung lips—some of the chemical had entered her mouth and blistered her tongue.

She fell to the ground, kicking her legs in agony, and Angelica squatted beside her, stroking her arm. Cindy was trying to say something to Angelica, who leaned closer to that ruined mouth. Kate couldn't hear what the burned woman said, but the blonde shook her head.

Cindy made a noise that sounded like *please*.

Angelica nodded. Then, looking over at Kate, she raised her gun and pointed it at Kate's face.

## 32

Rosie pulled into the drive and killed the engine. Later, she would remember seeing the monstrous SUV that lurked in the shadows on the other side of the road, but at the time she didn't pay it any attention. It was late, she was tired—and in her mind she kept replaying her parting with Paul, and the way she'd made a fool of herself asking him to come back and stay, like some desperate old woman. Of course he wasn't going to sleep with her. He had a girlfriend, a family. He was a good man. She laughed. Yup, that was the problem. Maybe she should go back to wanting bad guys.

'Mom, what are you doing?' Lucy asked.

'Huh?'

'We've been sat here for, like, ever. I need to get to bed.'

'Have we? I'm sorry, sweetie. I'm—not feeling too good.'

It was true, she had a splitting headache, and a sore throat.

She felt Lucy scrutinising her. 'Oh my God,' she said, panic in her voice. 'Tell me you're not getting the flu, Mom, please!'

Rosie forced a laugh. 'Of course I'm not! I always have a sore throat after my shift. Anyhow, the flu's nowhere near here.'

'Then what is it? Oh, wait—I know. It's Daniel Craig. You've totally got the hots for him.'

'Don't be ridiculous.' The last word cracked in her throat and she gulped. 'And his name isn't Daniel Craig.'

Lucy surprised her by taking hold of her hand. 'Aw, Mom, I'm sorry. Maybe he'll come back after doing whatever it is he needs to do.'

'He won't.'

Lucy unbuckled her seat belt and leaned over, giving Rosie a hug that she accepted with gratitude, clenching her teeth hard to stop the tears from coming.

'Daniel Craig's too old anyway. You need someone young, like Justin Bieber.'

Rosie pulled a face. 'Bieber's a baby. Maybe Zac Efron?'

'Mmmm . . . Maybe we could share him.'

Rosie shook her head. 'Lucy!' But her daughter had momentarily soothed the ache.

They got out of the car and went into the house, Lucy switching on the light and heading straight for the kitchen, calling back, 'Mom, you wanna glass of—' while Rosie checked through the mail.

She didn't finish the sentence.

Rosie looked up from the overdue bill she'd been ripping open.

'Lucy? You OK?'

There was no reply. Rosie dropped the bill and walked into the kitchen.

'Scream or run, and I'll slit her like a pig.'

There was a chunky short-haired woman crouched on the kitchen floor. Lucy was on her back in front of her, the woman holding her down by her hair. She had a knife pressed against her slender throat.

'OK, good, I got your attention. Pull that stool over here and sit down. That's it. I already took the liberty of removing all the knives, so don't even think about it.'

The woman spoke in a matter-of-fact, almost bored tone, but beneath the surface Rosie could sense rage and darkness of a kind she hadn't encountered since she'd finally left Lucy's dad. And even his rage—the madness that had finally compelled him to walk into a bar and start a fight he could never win—had been like a forty-watt bulb compared to the burning sun of this woman's anger.

On the floor, Lucy was sobbing, looking up at Rosie with terrified eyes.

'If you hurt my little girl . . .'

'Yeah, yeah. And she isn't so little. Nice and big, actually.' The woman stretched out the hand that wasn't holding the knife and, to Rosie's shock, squeezed one of Lucy's breasts. Lucy squealed and the woman pinched her nipple hard, making her cry out.

'Shut up.' She lifted the knife so Lucy could see it. 'I've got a headache. Keep being a noisy bitch and I'll slice those lovely perky nipples of yours right off.'

'Who are you?' Rosie asked, her own head pounding. Her mind was racing, visiting every corner of the kitchen, trying to identify weapons, ways out. Her cell was in her back pocket. If she could get to the emergency call button . . .

'Sister Heather.'

'Sister? What are you—some kind of nun?'

Heather roared with laughter. 'That's a good one.' Her face darkened. 'But nuns worship a man, don't they? You'd never catch me praying to *no* man. Stop struggling, bitch.'

She roughly jerked Lucy's hair, banging the back of her head on the floor. Instinctively, Rosie moved forward to help her daughter but Heather raised the knife. It looked like a hunting knife, the kind that could slice through flesh like it was butter.

'Sit down,' she ordered. 'Now, I want you to tell me where the doctor's boyfriend is.'

'What doctor? Who?'

'Dr Kate Maddox. His name is Wilson. Paul Wilson. A little birdy has told us he's sticking his nose into affairs that really don't concern him. Where is he?'

'I don't know what you're talking about.'

Heather sighed and, using the knife, slit open the front of Lucy's T-shirt, revealing her bra and midriff. Her belly bar glinted beneath the kitchen striplight. Heather pressed the point of the knife against the soft white flesh of Lucy's stomach, while Lucy cried and shook.

'Stop lying to me. The old man told me . . .'

'What old man?'

'Um . . . Watton. Jon Watton. Yeah, he told me, right before he told me where you lived and just before I put the old fucker out of his misery—' she mimed a hacking cough, grinning broadly—'that the doctor's boyfriend had been to see him with you earlier, then went back on his own. But where is he now, huh?'

Oh God—poor Jon, thought Rosie. 'I don't know.'

Heather sighed again. 'Do you really want to see your daughter's guts all over your lovely clean kitchen floor? It'll take ages to clean up. And getting the smell out . . . Not fun.'

Rosie was shaking so much she could barely breathe. If she told this crazy woman where Paul was, no doubt she would go after him, try to kill him. But she knew the woman would probably

228

kill her and Lucy first. Her knowledge of Paul's whereabouts was her only leverage. Give that up, and she might as well stick the knife in Lucy's belly herself.

'Come on, I'm getting bored.'

'Listen, I don't care what you want with that bastard. The truth is, I don't know where he's gone. We had a fight and he took off. Told me he was heading out of town and never coming back.'

From her position on the floor, Lucy looked at Rosie as if to ask her what she was playing at. Luckily, Heather was too busy staring at Rosie to notice.

'What was the fight about?'

'He wanted to sleep with me. I said no.'

Heather smiled. 'Men, huh? Probably wanted to fuck your daughter too.'

'That's what I thought. That he was using me because he wanted to get close to Lucy.'

'Mom . . .' Lucy spoke up for the first time.

'Sweetheart, shush.'

'Yeah, listen to your mother.'

Heather ruminated for a minute. Then she took a cell phone from her pocket. 'I want you to call him and talk to him. Tell him you changed your mind, that you want him to come back here, that your pussy is aching for him . . . Whatever it takes.'

She held out the phone.

Reluctantly, Rosie took it. She had no idea what to do next.

## 33

Kate pressed her hands against her face as if they would form a shield against a bullet. But the shot never came. She lowered her fingers.

Angelica had turned her gaze, and the gun, towards Cindy, who knelt on the floor, screaming with pain.

As Kate looked on, Angelica closed her eyes and her lips began to move. It looked like she was praying. Finally, she nodded.

'The Goddess is waiting for you, Sister Cindy,' she said, her voice choked. 'Know that you will be restored in glory, very soon.' She leaned over and kissed her on the head.

Then with one swift move she stuck the barrel of her pistol beneath Cindy's chin and pulled the trigger. Fragments of brain and skull scattered across the lab floor. Angelica got to her feet and stared straight at Kate.

'You bitch,' Simone snarled to Kate. 'You did that. Dadi, let me kill her.'

Kate's heart was hammering in her chest. She looked over at the tank of liquid nitrogen but Annie was blocking the way. Over by the door, Junko was either dead or unconscious, blood flowing like lava from her scalp and pooling on the floor.

'We need another two Sisters,' Angelica said. 'The Goddess said seven, and without Cindy we are down to five.'

Throughout the entire episode, which felt to Kate as if it had lasted hours but had only been a few minutes, Annie had stood passively watching from the sidelines. Now she stepped forward, her eyes shining.

'Take me. I will be your Sister. I know I wasn't ready before, but I am now—my life is yours—I beg you—take me!'

Her words provoked a sneer of disgust from Angelica. 'Why would I take you?' she said. 'You've already shown you can't be trusted.'

'But I did everything you asked . . . I listened in to Maddox's calls, I told you what you needed to know.'

'Shut up.'

Angelica raised her gun slowly, and Kate saw Annie's expression change from supplication to shock, then horror. Angelica squeezed the trigger, and Annie crumpled silently to the floor, her blood mingling with Junko's.

Even though Annie had betrayed them, Kate couldn't help shouting in protest. So much death. She imagined all the others must be dead too. Poor William and quiet Chip. Kolosine. And Tosca . . . The big man's smiling face flashed before her as she recalled him cracking one of his terrible jokes. She swallowed hard and tears sprang up in her eyes. She felt defeated, exhausted, but relieved in a purely instinctive, animal way that they weren't— for whatever insane reason—going to kill her. Not yet anyway. She might still see Jack again. And Paul.

Angelica checked her watch. 'It's twelve fifty. We need to leave. Now.'

She unclipped a pair of handcuffs from her belt, snapped one cuff onto her own wrist, the other onto Kate's. She seemed weary, Kate thought, and as though she was trying hard not to look at Cindy's body where it lay on the floor.

'You'll have to drag me out of here,' Kate said.

Angelica stuck her gun in Kate's face. 'You're going to walk. If you don't, after I've killed you, I'll drive to Dallas as fast as I can and shoot your brat in the face.'

Kate shuddered. OK, she would go along with them. She had no choice. The mere fact that this crazy woman knew of Jack's existence was too much of a threat.

'What about her?' Simone asked, gesturing towards Junko. 'She's still breathing.'

'Bring her along,' Angelica ordered. 'If she lives, it will be a sign that she is our Number Seven. Sister Preeti can minister to her.'

Simone stooped and lifted the tiny Junko easily over her shoulder, showing no sign of exertion as she carried her floppy body towards the door. Angelica pushed Kate ahead of her, her gun poking the back of her neck.


34


One of them had put a sack over her head and tied it loosely around her neck as soon as they got into the car, so Kate saw nothing for the duration of the ninety-minute journey. Her hands were cuffed tightly behind her back, with her right arm still shooting pain up to her shoulder, and her mouth had been gagged with thick gaffer tape.

She could tell that there was another woman driving, one who hadn't been present during the raid, as the others were in turn relaying to her what had happened. Someone seemed to be attending to Junko, for Kate smelled the sudden acidic tang of antiseptic, and Junko's moans grew louder. One of the voices said, 'Pass me that bandage, Sister.'

The mood in the vehicle was odd. When they spoke of 'Sister Cindy', their voices grew sombre, tearful even, but any bitterness or anger towards Kate seemed to have vanished. In its place was a calm resignation, and much talk of accepting 'the will of the Goddess'. When the topic of conversation moved on to the success of their mission, there was such elation in their voices that Kate felt an icy chill run through her. How could these insane women murder all those people in cold blood—she made a grim tally in her head: Kolosine, Annie, McCarthy (oh, poor Tosca!), Thompson, William, Adoncia, Chip, the lab tech guys, the security guards . . . not to mention their own 'sister'—and then talk about it with a barely suppressed jubilation? Kate had no doubt that these women were also responsible for the bomb that killed Isaac.

'I am proud of you, Sisters,' said the voice of the one Kate now recognised as the leader, the Daddy one. Angelica. 'Sekhmet is proud of you too.'

Sekhmet? Kate thought. Perhaps that was Daddy's boss. She leaned back on the headrest of her seat, trying to ignore the pins and needles in her arms. Oh shit, she thought. Shit, shit, shit.

\*     \*     \*

Kate realised they had reached their destination when the vehicle finally stopped and all the doors

233

slid open. She felt bright sunlight on her face, but beneath the blindfold she had no clue where she was—perhaps they had changed their minds about keeping them alive and were taking her to some deserted canyon, to shoot her and Junko, and dump their bodies for the mountain lions and coyotes to breakfast on?

But no, they were led up some steps and suddenly the atmosphere changed as they entered a cool, calm space, where their footsteps echoed off a hard slippery floor. Junko was still moaning, and had started to babble in Japanese, a terrible refrain of physical pain and confusion. It sounded as though she were in a wheelchair, or being carried on a stretcher, as her voice was coming from about Kate's waist level.

Kate was worried that her colleague had sustained a brain injury, but forced herself to stay positive: it was probably trauma and concussion. Surely if it was really bad, Junko would be completely unconscious? The scent of frangipani and furniture polish filled her nostrils, and she felt her legs tremble beneath her as a firm hand in the small of her back propelled her along a lengthy corridor. Then she heard the sound of a door opening, and the atmosphere altered again as she was pushed into a room.

There was a sudden cold rush of air conditioning on her hot damp cheeks as the thick hessian sack was torn off her head. Pain distorted the skin of her lips and mouth as the tape was ripped away, and light flooded her pupils, making her blink in the glare. As her wrists were released from the cuffs, she took in her new surroundings: a small, plain, whitewashed room containing two single beds with white pillows and duvets. Nothing else. Bars on the window, a heavy door like a prison cell's, with a grate at eye-level. From some distant part of her brain, the word 'wicket' came to her. That's what they were called, those grates: wickets. It made her think of English summers—cricket greens and cream teas . . . She almost wanted to laugh at the incongruity of the thought.

Junko had been placed on one of the beds, a large white bandage wrapped around the wound on her forehead, through which blood was seeping. Her skin was a terrible yellowy-white, and Kate saw her eyeballs moving beneath the veiled lids.

'Get a doctor for her,' she commanded, turning to see her captors' faces properly for the first time since the raid.

Two women were standing in the room, both wearing long white robes. They stared at her, impassive, arms folded. One had been in the lab—the very tall one with burnished ebony skin, huge eyes and shaved head. Her baldness only served to emphasise the beauty of her face, now that Kate could see it clearly. Sister Simone. The second was shorter, merely pretty where her companion was beautiful; auburn hair and a smattering of freckles across the bridge of her snub nose. She looked as though she ought to be wearing the tiniest of denim shorts and a tied-waisted plaid shirt, posing for a Pirelli calendar, rather than clad in what looked like a druid's clothing.

Kate blinked. Whatever else she had expected, it wasn't this. 'What is this place?' she demanded. 'Who are you people?'

Simone spoke first. She was much calmer now than she had been in the lab. 'We are the Sisters of

235

Sekhmet. I am Simone, and this is Brandi.'

'Are you a cult? What's with the robes?'

Brandi smiled, and when she spoke, Kate recognised the voice of the driver. 'We wouldn't describe it as a cult, no. We are a sacred organisation established to usher in the new Golden Age. As you can tell, it's already well underway. Within two years the world's population will shrink to one hundred thousand. These survivors will be the most enlightened souls . . . We wouldn't normally talk about it to lay people, but there's hardly any time left in this Cycle, and you have a really important job to do for us.'

'Right,' Kate said carefully, trying to take it in. 'And what exactly is it that you think I can do for you, assuming I would agree to do anything, after you've murdered most of my colleagues?'

'Dadi Angelica will come speak with you about that.'

'I can tell you this right now: I will not be helping you in any way whatsoever unless you get my friend to a hospital.'

Simone and Brandi exchanged looks. 'That won't be possible. But our own doctor is on her way,' said Brandi with a shrug, and left the room. Simone paused for a moment, then followed her. There was the sound of a key turning in the lock outside.

Kate sank back on to the bed, numb with shock and disbelief. Poor Junko was deathly silent now, and so still that Kate immediately jumped up to make sure she was still breathing.

'Junko,' she said, slapping her gently on the back of her hand. 'Wake up, please.'

Junko stirred and moaned faintly, but didn't open her eyes. With far more conviction than she

236

felt, Kate promised her, 'It's OK, I'll get us out of here. Don't worry.' She lifted up first one of Junko's eyelids with her thumb, and then the other. Her left iris seemed considerably larger than her right. Kate didn't know what this meant, other than that it was a very bad sign. She swallowed down the despair that was rising inside her as the door opened again, and Brandi returned, this time with a petite Asian-Indian woman carrying a medical bag.

'How is our patient doing?' the woman asked Kate, picking up Junko's wrist and taking her pulse. 'She is in a stable condition, so once I've stitched up the cut, she will need to rest. I'm Sister Preeti, by the way. I am a fully qualified MD, so please rest assured that your friend is in safe hands here.'

She gently unpeeled Junko's bandage, and Kate winced at the sight of the deep jagged wound and flaps of flesh that marred Junko's previously flawless skin. Preeti administered a local anaesthetic, and Junko groaned again, clutching at the air with her fists. Kate reached for her nearer hand and held it, stroking it as though it was Jack's.

'She is not in a stable condition!' Kate said, trying to keep her voice low for Junko's sake. 'One of her irises is enlarged, her breathing is irregular and shallow, and she's only semi-conscious! How can you possibly say that she's stable?'

As Preeti expertly swabbed and stitched the wound, Kate remembered holding Jack's hand like this, through so many childhood illnesses and playground accidents. Something twisted in her heart at the thought of the thousands of parents having to hold their children's hands and watch them slip away in a torment of fever and convulsion. Still, she thought bitterly, at least they were with their children. What if Jack died before she ever saw him again?

Missing him more than ever, she closed her eyes and tried to imagine that Junko's small hand was Jack's, telling herself that when she opened her eyes, she would be back in the cottage with him and Paul, with homework to do and spaghetti bolognese to make for supper . . . 'How are you doing?' the doctor asked.

Kate opened her eyes. The doctor was looking at her, the hand with the needle and suture thread hovering over the line of neat stitches in Junko's head.

Kate snorted. 'Oh, terrific, thanks for asking. How do you think I'm doing?'

'I meant, physically,' Preeti replied calmly, turning back to Junko and resuming her stitching. 'I appreciate this will have come as something of a shock, but please try to stay calm. We won't hurt you if you cooperate.'

'And if I don't?'

'I suggest that you do.'

Kate considered punching her. 'Threatening me isn't going to help. What would help is if I knew exactly what it is that you want me to do.'

'Dadi Angelica will talk to you about that.'

'Who is this person, and why do you call her Daddy?'

'Be patient. She will explain it all. And it's D-A-D-I, not the paternal proper noun you are doubtless imagining.' Preeti cut the end of the suture thread and taped a clean square dressing onto Junko's head.

'Junko needs an X-ray. She might have a skull fracture,' Kate said. 'She's far less conscious than she was when we arrived. She could be sinking into a deep coma. If she dies, you women will be guilty of another murder, you know that? Not that the numerous previous ones seem to have bothered you all that much, not to mention all the people who died in the San Diego hotel bombing. I assume that was you?'

Preeti merely looked at her serenely, her lack of denial confirming it.

'Time is too short for all that. Normal laws no longer apply—only the will of the Goddess shall be done now. Unless she is to be our seventh Sister, your friend will die. Most of Earth's population will die. It is decreed.'

Kate opened her mouth to protest, and then closed it again as the horrible truth struck her afresh, like a physical blow: yes, most of Earth's population would die soon if the virus wasn't stopped. And one of the few people who might be able to prevent Watoto-X2 raging like bush fire through all five continents was lying unconscious next to her—assuming Junko's breakthrough would make it possible to identify the antibody.

Preeti packed up her medical bag and got to her feet, then the door opened again and yet another astonishingly beautiful woman appeared, carrying a tray with a bowl of something steaming, and a hunk of bread, so fresh that the scent of it filled the room. It was the one who had been in charge at the lab; the one they called Dadi Angelica. She smiled at Preeti, who instantly inclined her head and gave a small bow of deference. 'Sister Preeti,' the woman said, 'how are our guests?'

'The patient is in recovery,' Preeti said. 'I've stitched her wound and checked her vital signs.'

Kate stood up, furious. 'No, as I keep saying, she is not "in recovery". She's probably suffered severe brain damage, and all you can talk about is the fact that you've given her a few stitches? Why won't you people listen? She needs to be in a hospital.'

'That isn't an option, I'm afraid,' said Angelica. With her hair down, and dressed in pale gold robes rather than the black leather she'd worn in the lab, she looked more like a Hollywood actress than a spiritual guru. And she was younger than Kate had first thought, somewhere in her mid-to-late twenties.

'Welcome to my house,' Angelica said to Kate. 'I trust the Sisters have been looking after you. I've brought you some food—miso soup. You should drink it while it's hot, you must be hungry.'

She offered the tray to Kate, meeting and holding her eyes. Her beauty was unreal; flawless golden skin, high cheekbones, enormous indigo eyes and thick blonde hair loose down her back. For a second Kate paused, held in thrall by the depths of those eyes. Then she reached out a clenched fist and, as if the tray was a volleyball, punched it out of Angelica's hands and high into the air. The tray spun and arced across the room before clattering loudly to the tiled floor. Hot soup splattered both Angelica and Preeti, marring their pristine robes and dulling their shiny hair into seaweedy clumps. Kate rushed for the door but Angelica was faster—before Kate had even got out into the hallway, she had caught up with her and was marching her back inside, her injured arm bent painfully up behind her back. The floor was littered with bits of broken bowl, sticky with soup.

'Oh, Kate,' Angelica whispered in her ear,

240

pushing her back on to her bed, 'I'm disappointed in you; we need you to cooperate, and this is not a good start. Now, we are going to leave you here while we perform a special ceremony to mourn our fallen Sister. When we are done, you and I will have a talk. First, though, we will bring you some cleaning equipment—I would appreciate you cleaning up this mess by the time I return.'

'Fuck off,' muttered Kate, rubbing her sore biceps, unable to stop herself feeling like a told-off child. Angelica smiled beatifically, standing over her with her arms folded.

'*Om Shanti*, Sister.'

Angelica left the room and, as the door shut behind her, a horrible thought struck Kate: McCarthy had agreed to talk to his superior tomorrow—today, now—to arrange for Jack to be taken out of the country. But McCarthy was dead.

Jack would still be out there. And, like everyone else in the US, he was in terrible danger.


## 35


Heather held out the phone to Rosie and said, 'Call him.'

'But I don't have his number.'

Heather made a hissing noise, like a cat whose tail has been trodden on, and swiftly brought the point of the hunting knife up beneath Lucy's chin. She held Lucy's hair in her other hand, balled up in her fist.

'I'm not lying!' Rosie blurted. 'Please. We never exchanged numbers.'

It was true. There had been an unspoken agreement between them, as if they knew that swapping numbers would make their temporary relationship more significant. This way, there was no chance of them contacting each other again. Temptation would be starved of oxygen and opportunity.

Heather pulled Lucy's hair tighter and pressed the tip of the knife higher, so that Rosie could see that with the slightest added pressure the blade would puncture the skin beneath her daughter's jaw. One quick movement and the knife would slash Lucy's throat.

'Thinking that I'm going to cut her throat?' the woman said. Her mouth smiled, but her eyes were like windows into hell. 'Don't worry, I'm not going to do that. Far too quick. First, like I said, I'm going to slice off those perky nipples. I quite fancy her belly bar—it's pretty—so I'm going to cut that out too. Her skin is so soft, I want to slice some of it off, take it home. And once I've finished playing with her, I'm going to ram this knife up her lovely tight—'

'No!' Rosie yelled, launching herself at Heather. But the woman swatted her aside with a muscular arm. Rosie fell hard on her side, smacking her head against a kitchen cupboard.

Heather sat perfectly still, unbothered by the sound of Lucy weeping. Rosie lay panting on the floor, dazed.

'I'm getting tired of this now. Tell me where the doctor's boyfriend is right this second.' She pulled Lucy's head back harder and made a jabbing motion towards her throat with the knife.

'He's at the Coopers Hotel in town.'

Rosie felt all the fight go out of her. Her skull throbbed, her shoulder screamed at her. But she didn't care about that, she just wanted this fucking psycho-bitch gone, she never wanted to hear Paul's name again, and she wanted to put her arms around her daughter and to hold her and hope that one day they could forget this ever happened.

'Good,' Heather said, the smile returning. 'Let's go.'

Rosie looked up at her through tear-blurred eyes. 'What?'

'You're coming with me. Both of you. I might need . . . what do you call it?—collateral.'

\*          \*          \*

Paul sat in his hotel room, staring at his phone. He couldn't stop thinking of Rosie, the way she had looked at him as they'd said goodbye. It would have been so easy to go home with her. To let her take him to bed. A double dose of guilt twisted his insides: guilt towards Rosie—had he led her on, unwittingly?—and towards Kate, because he'd been tempted, he couldn't deny it. But he hadn't acted on it. And he would never see Rosie again. The way that realisation made him feel brought a fresh twinge of guilt.

He tried to call Kate on the number she had phoned him from earlier that day, but it rang and rang. No doubt they were all asleep, her and the other scientists. Or in the lab, working through the night. He tapped out a text and sent it, even though she had told him she had no signal.

*I miss you, sweetheart. xxxx*

243

He couldn't think what else to say.

His rental car was parked downstairs. In the morning, he would head off to LA to try to find Camilo Diaz. He had no idea how he was going to get into the quarantined city. Maybe they were only stopping people getting out. Whatever, he would think of a plan on the way.

He lay down on the bed, hoping to feel the gentle tug of sleep. But he felt like he'd drunk twenty cups of strong coffee. A parade of faces flickered in his head: Kate, Rosie, Stephen, Jack, Jon Watton . . .

Morning seemed a very long way off.

\*        \*        \*

Heather marched Rosie and Lucy through the house at knifepoint, into the garage where she found a roll of parcel tape that she used to secure their hands behind their backs.

'No screaming when we get outside,' she warned. She had allowed Lucy to pull on a wrinkled sweatshirt over her sliced shirt. Rosie tried to catch her daughter's eye, to let her know that everything was going to be OK, but Lucy appeared to be in shock; she had no more awareness of what was going on around her than a sleepwalker.

Back through the house and out the front door. Heather hissed, 'Walk towards the SUV.' There was no one around. It was gone midnight; any nosy neighbours would be in bed.

Rosie considered screaming. But she knew that by the time anyone roused themselves to investigate, the psycho-bitch would have slit their throats and driven away.

244

Heather opened the back door of the SUV and shoved them into the cavernous interior. She sat in the driver's seat, placed the knife on the dashboard and pressed a button to lock the doors. The roads were quiet, just a few cabs cruising around looking for business.

Rosie tried to speak to Lucy, to ask her if she was all right, but Heather snapped, 'No talking in the back. And if either of you kids says "Are we there yet?" I'll cut your tits off.' She rocked with laughter.

Ten minutes later, they arrived at the Coopers Hotel, Heather pulling into a quiet space in the corner of the parking lot. She got out and locked the doors, then started to walk away. She'd gone a few paces when she stopped and slowly turned to face them, drawing a forefinger across her windpipe and showing them her teeth.

*The moment we get out of this*, Rosie thought, turning to press herself against her daughter, whispering to her that everything would be OK, *the moment we escape, you're a dead woman.*

'Talk to me, Lucy, please,' she implored. But Lucy remained silent, staring into space. Her eyes were glazed, her jaw slack. Rosie felt a new wave of panic rise through her. She had to get Lucy out of this, get her to a hospital.

She wriggled back towards the window, pressing her forehead against the glass, straining to see through the darkness. What was going on in the hotel? Would Paul be murdered while he slept, or would he put up a fight? And what did this woman want with them anyway? It had to have something to do with Mangold, with the questions Paul had been asking. Oh God, why had Paul walked into her diner? And why had she allowed herself to develop

245

feelings for him? She cursed herself.

She had one priority now. Getting Lucy out of this.

A man walked across the parking lot, close to the hotel.

'Hey!' Rosie yelled. 'Help! Help us!'

But the man couldn't hear her. The glass must be soundproofed. She couldn't manoeuvre her arms to bang on it. Maybe if she could get to the horn . . . She struggled to get through between the front seats, surprised that Heather hadn't thought of this—all she needed to do was press her head against the horn at the centre of the steering wheel.

Getting through the gap between the seats without use of her arms wasn't easy, but she scrambled through and managed to right herself so she was kneeling on the driver's seat. She leaned forward and pressed her head against the horn.

The door yanked open.

She heard Heather say, 'Nothing to see here,' then a strong hand grabbed her beneath the chin and thrust her into the passenger seat. The door slammed. Rosie looked up to see Heather staring at the horn, like she knew she'd fucked up.

'Goddamn bitch,' she said. She was panting with rage.

'Where's Paul?' Rosie asked. 'Have you killed him? Please God—'

Heather slapped her. 'Shut up. Just fucking shut up,' she screamed, and her loss of control was far more frightening than her earlier contained rage.

Rosie instinctively knew that to disobey would mean certain death. Heather was shaking with fury, her knuckles white where she clutched the steering wheel, sweat dripping into her eyes. A rank smell

246

filled the car.

It took a minute or two for Heather's breathing to return to normal.

'The bastard's already checked out.'

Rosie felt relief flood through her.

'Checked out thirty minutes ago.' She banged the steering wheel with the flat of her hand. Then she pushed open the door and dragged Rosie out into the parking lot. Rosie struggled, but Heather had a firm grip on her, and she opened the back door and shoved her in. Rosie landed with her head on Lucy's lap.

'Please, let us go,' she pleaded.

Heather was back in the driver's seat, turning the key in the ignition. 'Uh-uh. No way. You're coming with me. Wilson told the hotel clerk he was heading to LA. That's where we're going.' She banged the steering wheel again. 'Shit, man. Angelica's going to be *pissed*.'

## 36

Glencarson Prison, where Camilo Diaz had been living in minimum security exile for the last twenty-three years, was in south-east Los Angeles—within the quarantine zone. Paul tapped the address into the satnav. It was a ninety-minute drive; if he didn't get turned back at the roadblock, he would arrive at the prison around 2 a.m.—not exactly visiting hours. But he couldn't stay here a minute longer. He felt an urgent need to get going. By leaving now he'd ensure that, in the event they did try to turn him away at the roadblock, he'd have other options. Under cover of darkness, he might be able to sneak along the perimeter of the quarantine zone until he found somewhere to break through. Daylight would leave him too exposed to try it.

Setting off, he made a vow to himself. If Camilo Diaz couldn't help him, if this turned out to be a dead end, he would abandon the hunt for Mangold and go find Kate. Maybe that's what Stephen would have wanted: not for him go in search of vengeance but to be there for Kate, get her and Jack out of the country, away from all this madness.

Logically, he knew that was probably right.

But the hunger for retribution still burned inside him.

*       *       *

When he was younger, Paul had dreamed of visiting LA, picturing himself cruising wide open highways against a backdrop of palm trees, hot winds and endless blue sky. Now, driving through the night towards that city of dreams, he wished he was back in grey, homely England with Kate.

He wanted to put his arms around her, to feel the warmth of her body against his, the soft tickle of her hair on his face. He craved the sound of her voice, that mid-Atlantic accent that he found so sexy. More than anything, he longed just to have her there. She made him feel calm, centred. Until he met her, he'd been going through the motions: working, spending money, watching himself get older, trying not to think about any of it. All that had changed when he met Kate.

248

In a way, it was Stephen who had brought them together. Desperate to find out what had happened to him, they'd raced around the country, chasing down clues, facing danger . . . falling in love. It would have been easy for the passion to burn out, extinguished by the daily routine of work and child-rearing. Instead, he discovered that sharing a normal existence with Kate—and Jack, whom he adored as if he were his own son—made him love her even more.

The coast road was eerily deserted. Beyond the cliffs, the sea was a black mass. He made a silent vow to return here one day, with Kate and Jack, to see it when the sun was shining, when things were better. If things ever got better.

Just east of Malibu, as the highway passed through Topanga State Park, he heard a rumbling ahead of him. His first thought was *earthquake*, but a minute later he came upon a great convoy of army trucks, eighteen or twenty of them, heading towards the city. This was followed by a roar from above as a helicopter's navigation lights appeared above him, first one then another, following the line of the highway. A few minutes later he saw the first sign: QUARANTINED AREA. TURN BACK NOW, with the universal biohazard sign illuminated in neon. A glow on the horizon materialised into the distant lights of Los Angeles.

Guts twisting, Paul kept driving. Within minutes he came upon a wall of trucks. Striped barriers manned by National Guard troops blocked the road. He slowed down, passing yet more TURN BACK and biohazard signs. Overhead, a helicopter circled, its searchlight pinpointing his car. Two soldiers, guns slung across their chests, began to walk out towards him.

Paul hesitated, unsure what to do. Would they arrest him? Shoot at him? As the soldiers came closer, he saw they were wearing protective masks. Panicking, he threw the car into reverse and swung the car in a 180-degree arc, the soldiers shouting and breaking into a run behind him. In his confusion, he fumbled the gearstick into Drive and put his foot down—and almost drove straight into another car.

He stamped on the brake, jolting forward in his seat. The car—a large black Mercedes—had pulled up sideways across the road. Paul sounded the horn but the car didn't move. In the rear-view mirror he could see the soldiers getting closer.

The door of the Mercedes opened and someone got out. They walked towards him. There wasn't enough light to make out a face—not until they reached him and bent down, beckoning for him to open the window.

'Hello, Paul.'

\*        \*        \*

Heather turned up the radio with a gloved hand as she left Sagebrush's city limits and pointed the SUV towards the highway. The guy on KHTB, panic obvious in his voice, was informing listeners:

'. . . *cases have now been reported all around the surrounding area. We're getting reports of deaths in San Diego, Fresno, Bakersfield, Las Vegas . . .*'

Heather smacked the steering wheel and yelped with glee. 'You hear that? It's spreading. *And the benighted and the sinful shall be powerless to prevent the tide of change.* You said it, baby. Hell, yeah!'

250

Her words were lost on Rosie. She was still reeling from the shock of hearing places so near to Sagebrush listed among the towns affected. Beside her, Lucy was still in a catatonic state, staring blankly at nothing. She longed to reach out to her, but her hands were still tied.

The man on the radio was urging people to stay calm, stay indoors. Anyone who had come in contact with people who might be sick should stay at home. The government was refusing to confirm the death toll.

'They don't want people to be scared,' Heather said. 'But they oughta be terrified. You know what's gonna happen, huh? It's gotten out of LA. Pandora's box has opened. The Goddess has breathed her holy, cleansing breath all over this . . . devil's playground and . . .' She trailed off. She's quoting someone, Rosie realised, and she's forgotten the script. 'Whatever. It's gonna spread quickly now. This is when it really takes hold. In a few days, everyone round here will be sick. Then it'll be the whole state. Then the whole country. And then the whole world!'

It sounded as if she was building up to an evil cackle, but instead Heather swore loudly as something ran out on to the road.

'Freaking coyote.' She stamped on the brake and, to Rosie's amazement, wound down the window, pointing the gun into the woods beside the road. She fired off a couple of shots into the trees, then calmly wound up the window and drove on.

*     *     *

251

'Harley.'

'So nice to see you again,' the agent said. 'Mind stepping out of the car?'

The two soldiers arrived at that moment. 'Don't even try it, or I'll order these fine American soldiers to shoot.' He had produced his agency card, which he displayed for the guards.

Paul sighed, pushed open the door and stepped out into the warm night air.

'How did you find me?'

'We've been tracking your phone.'

Paul nodded. 'How's Kate? You were with her earlier?'

'Yes. She's all right. Working hard to find a cure. She could do without the distraction of worrying about you. What exactly are you trying to achieve, anyway?'

Paul hesitated and looked over at the roadblock. Maybe Harley turning up now wasn't such a bad thing, as long as he played this right.

'I've been trying to find Charles Mangold.'

'Mangold? Why?'

'You were there, Harley. You saw what happened to Stephen. Mangold was part of that.'

'So you've been on a wild-goose chase looking for some old man . . .' Harley lowered his voice. 'Why don't you just let it go, Paul?'

'Because Stephen deserves justice, that's why. As long as the people responsible for what happened to him are walking around free, I won't let go. Besides, it isn't a wild-goose chase.'

'Don't tell me you've tracked him down!'

Paul knew he had to tread carefully if he was going to enlist Harley's help in entering LA.

'Have Kate and her team made any progress

252

yet?' he asked.

Harley looked pained. 'Give them a chance, they've barely been at it two days.'

'Yeah, well, it's not as if time is on their side, is it? Anyway, the reason I ask is that while I was looking for Mangold I came across someone who I think can help.'

Harley raised a sceptical eyebrow. 'Who?'

'Mangold's former head of research, Camilo Diaz, is in Glencarson Prison. I think he could help, and I need to go and talk to him.'

Harley mulled this over. Paul got the impression that he was desperate enough to try anything, so he pushed it: 'We don't have time to stand around thinking about this. Any chance at all that we can find a cure—we have to take it.' He didn't feel guilty about leading Harley on. All he cared about was getting to Diaz.

'Have you tried calling the prison?'

'Yes. The line just rings out. A bit like the lab in Sequoia.'

'Really?'

'Come on, we need to get to the prison. You can get me into the city, can't you, with your ID?'

Harley hesitated.

'Come *on*.'

Finally, Harley nodded. He gestured for Paul to get into his car and they drove down the road towards the roadblock, where dozens of armed guards with dogs were patrolling the road, the military helicopter endlessly circling overhead. On the other side of the roadblock, a queue of cars stretched back as far as the horizon, people, many of them in family groups, standing by their cars, the tense threat of a violent eruption rippling through the night air. A mobile field testing unit had been set up on the other side of the checkpoint and medical personnel in full biohazard suits were calling people in one by one to test them for Indian flu. If any member of a family was found to be positive, the whole group was told to return home immediately. Nobody seemed to be getting through—the barrier hadn't lifted once in the whole time Paul had been standing there.

In one of the cars at the front of the line he could see a red-haired woman holding a toddler with identical colouring. The little boy squirmed on her lap then jerked as he sneezed: one, two, three times. Paul didn't rate their chances of getting out. The woman looked haunted, clinging to the last thread of hope, even though she knew that she and her son—her whole family—weren't going to make it out. Weren't going to make it full stop.

Paul swallowed. Thank God Jack was a long way from all this.

Harley stopped the car beside a soldier and rolled the window down.

The soldier was wearing a surgical mask and carrying a machine gun. He stooped to look into the car. 'Border's closed,' he said. 'You'll need to turn back.'

Another guard came over, pulling down his mask to spit on the ground. 'Why in hell do you want to get *into* the city? Every other fucker's trying to get out.'

Harley produced his badge and showed it to the guards. 'We're heading to Glencarson Federal Institute of Correction.'

The first patrolman scrutinised the badge. 'BIT? Never heard of ya.'

254

'You should have received a memo when the outbreak started,' said Harley.

The guard turned to his colleague. 'Did you see any memo?'

'Nuh-uh.'

Harley added, as patiently as he could, 'We're a federal team set up to prevent biological outbreaks.'

The border guards loved that. After they'd finished laughing, the first one said, 'Well, you ain't done a very good job, have you, buddy?'

'Just let us through.'

'You won't be able to get back out. We got strict instructions. No one gets out. But if you really want to go into the D-zone, then it's your funeral. Literally.'

'The D-zone?' Paul asked, leaning across.

'Yeah. The dead zone.'

The guard gestured to the men further ahead and the barrier was lifted. Harley drove through. As he accelerated along the empty right-hand side of the highway, Paul saw the incredulous look on the faces of those trying desperately to get out.

But no matter how great the danger, if it got him one step closer to Mangold, he would take the risk.

\*     \*     \*

Rosie stared out at the lights strung along Route 101. She felt sick and feverish and, as she watched the lights blur and dance in and out of focus, an icy sensation spread up her body from her feet. Could this be the Indian flu? She leaned over and kissed Lucy's head, praying that it wasn't, that her feverishness and Lucy's catatonia had been brought on by the trauma they were enduring. She'd had a sore throat for a couple of days now, but the virus hadn't reached Sagebrush—had it?

She cast the thought from her mind and tried to focus on the immediate problem of what this madwoman was planning to do when they got to LA. One thing was certain: if they pulled up at a roadblock, Rosie was determined to make her throat even more sore by screaming her head off.

But shortly after passing a sign warning them to TURN BACK, Heather stopped the car and sat in silence for a moment. Then she jumped out and wrenched open the rear door. Rosie's throat clenched with fear and she shrank back in her seat as Heather reached towards her. But, to Rosie's astonishment, Heather merely grabbed her seat belt and clicked it across her body. Then she ran around the other side and repeated the action with the unresponsive Lucy. What was she doing?

As if she'd heard Rosie's unspoken words, Heather looked right at her. 'I ain't doing this for your benefit, bitch,' she said. 'I just don't need you two crashing in on top of me when we get going.'

With that, she climbed back into the driver's seat, put on her own seat belt and re-started the vehicle, taking a right turn. They must be so close to the city, thought Rosie, but in the dark she was unsure exactly where they were. Somewhere close to Mulholland and Topanga Canyon. Heather turned on to another, quieter, road. In the near distance, Rosie could hear helicopters. She thought she could smell burning too, very faintly.

Yes, Rosie realised, this was Topanga Canyon. From here, steep hills sloped down towards the city, the lights of which stretched out beneath them. They were driving along a curving ridge. Rosie expected them to turn the corner around the great rock-face.

But instead, Heather turned the wheel right again and Rosie let out a shriek. 'Whoo-hah!' whooped Heather as the SUV dipped over the edge of the road and began to plummet down the slope. The vehicle bounced and shook as Heather continued to yell. Rosie was certain this was the end, with the SUV rushing towards the bottom of the slope, levelling out for a moment, then shooting down another steep hill, picking up speed as the engine roared. Their seat belts held them, but at that moment Rosie wished Heather hadn't bothered. They were going to die anyway, so wouldn't it have been quicker to crash through the windshield?

37

Morning light penetrated the small, barred window. Kate lay on her bed rubbing her sore arm and noting the progress of the large purple bruise slowly blooming across the skin above her elbow, like mould growing in a Petri dish.

She had cleared up the soup, with a squeegee mop and a bucket of soapy water one of the women had left, but only because the smell of it was making her feel sick. Having something to do, however menial and short-lived, had helped her collect her thoughts, too, distracting her from the fear that squeezed her insides.

The fear was back again now. She wrapped her arms round herself to try and stop the trembling, and cast her eyes over the small room. The two single beds and stark white walls gave her a sense of *déjà vu*. Somewhere she'd stayed in her early twenties, and there had been a room-mate there too . . . Of course: the Cold Research Unit. The place where she had first met Paul's twin, Stephen. The two rooms weren't that dissimilar. The main difference was that, even though she had been in isolation back then too, there hadn't been a lock on the door. And her last room-mate had ended up dead.

She looked across at Junko, praying that history wasn't about to repeat itself.

'Right, Junko,' she said, rolling on to her side, propping herself up on her good arm. 'Let's figure this out, you and me. What did you read in my notes that could possibly be the inspiration for your discovery—and how come I missed it? I wrote the damn paper!'

Junko didn't stir. Kate started to mentally review her entire thesis, chapter by chapter. She knew it so well, it had taken five years of her life to complete, and she had since, along with her co-author Isaac, lectured on it, lived, breathed, eaten and slept it. How could Junko have found something that Kate hadn't already thought of?

'Fair play to you, if you have,' she commented, aware that her voice sounded strained. 'I think you should wake up, so we can get cracking, don't you? We would make the most fantastic team. Imagine, if you're right about whatever it was you found— and I'm sure you were, because nobody's ever looked as excited as you did when you were about

258

to tell me—we could get a vaccine prototyped in days. Some of the FDA testing process would have to be bypassed because of the urgency—so we'd need to be pretty certain that it would be safe—but what alternative do we have, unless someone over at Harvard or the CDC has managed to crack it already? God, if we can't, I hope they have . . .'

Junko slept on, and Kate felt her throat constrict with frustration and worry. She had to get them out of here! There was one small window in the room, too high to see out of, so Kate dragged her bed across to the wall and climbed on it. If she stood on tiptoe she could just about look out, but there was not much to see. The room was clearly at the rear of the property, because all that was visible was an enormous field of what looked like the same variety of wild flower—something with a tangle of low branches and star-shaped red and white flowers. It looked vaguely familiar to Kate but she couldn't identify it, not being au fait with the flora and fauna of the American west coast. There were no roads or paths in sight, and the bare peaks and crops of mountains loomed on the horizon. From the position of the sun, Kate calculated that she was facing east. The thought that she was looking in Jack's direction was a tiny bit comforting.

There was no way out of that window. Even if by some miracle she managed to remove the bars and get the thick glass out of the frame, it would be too small for her to squeeze through. Kate turned and surveyed the room from her vantage point. Just the bathroom off to the right, no lock on the door, and no window in there. Nothing she could use as a weapon . . . Wait—the mop and bucket! Kate jumped off the bed and moved them out of sight behind the bathroom door. Perhaps the women would forget she had them. Perhaps she could fill the bucket with hot water and throw it in one of their faces, then poke the end of the mop in their eyes? She shook her head. It would hardly be as effective as the liquid nitrogen.

A key turned in the lock, and Angelica re-entered the room. Kate flushed the toilet and walked casually back to the bed, automatically checking to see if Angelica was holding a gun, feeling the same frisson of fear in the pit of her stomach that she did every time the door opened.

But all Angelica brought with her was a waft of the sort of perfume that cost a small fortune, and two cups of steaming green tea. Kate caught a very brief glimpse of the corridor outside, decorated in shades of terracotta and burnt orange, as tasteful and opulent as a five-star hotel in contrast to their simple room.

'Not a lot to see out back, is there?' Angelica commented, taking in the bed under the window. She handed Kate one of the cups.

'I wanted to look at something beyond these walls. See the sun,' Kate said. 'I get claustrophobic.'

'I want to talk to you,' Angelica continued, her voice soft and dreamy, as if Kate hadn't spoken. She pulled the bed back into place and sat down on the edge of it.

Kate decided to go along with her, clutching at the straw of hope that she was worth more to them alive than dead, if Angelica had somehow become convinced that she was 'one of them'. She sat down obediently next to her.

'Do you believe in God?' Angelica asked, seemingly apropos nothing.

'Kind of, I suppose,' said Kate. 'I don't belong to any specific religion though. Do you? Believe in God?'

Without a beat, Angelica said, 'It's true that there is a design to the universe, and an omnipotent ruler, but it's not Jesus, or a prophet like Mohammed, as many think. Because of the ridiculous myths surrounding these deities and notions of heaven and hell perpetuated throughout history by the ruling classes to suppress the workers, few have ever come close to the truth. The Ancient Egyptians did, at the start of the Cycle, as did the Mayans. A few groups in India understood elements of the truth. But most of Earth's population were not privy to the real facts.'

Kate was taken aback by Angelica's answer. 'Cycle?'

'The Golden Age. The entire history of the world is contained within a five-thousand-year cycle, that goes around and around for eternity. You and I have had this conversation innumerable times, in this room, using these words, with these events unfolding around us like the endless reflections in a room of mirrors. We are at the very close of this particular cycle. Time is almost up.'

'Yes.' Kate decided it was probably best to humour her. 'I remember hearing that the Mayan calendar ended in 2012. Funny how we're still here.'

Angelica smiled. 'A very minor miscalculation; a few months, that's all.'

Kate had to stop herself from rolling her eyes. 'But one of your colleagues mentioned Sekhmet earlier—wasn't she an Egyptian deity, one of many? If you don't mind my saying, your philosophies seem a bit . . . pick'n'mix. What makes you think

261

this Sekhmet is so important?'

Anger flashed on Angelica's face. 'You speak as though this is some kind of fantasy. This is not a trivial whim, an embroidered story like those in your Bible, evolving over the years from what their authors wanted them to be until they became little more than Chinese whispers . . . This is the truth, and I know it because I am the one Sekhmet chose to tell.'

Kate glanced over at Junko, who now seemed to be sleeping more peacefully. 'How could a mythical being from thousands of years ago tell you anything?'

Angelica smiled. 'She is not mythical. She exists, but in a different sphere to this earthly one. She came to me in a vision. I will explain more, but first I want you to understand how it feels. I have a gift to give you. Would you do me the courtesy of meditating with me?'

Kate almost laughed. 'You want courtesy, after you've killed all my colleagues and taken us prisoner?'

'It's the only way you can begin to receive a taste of what is to come.'

Kate thought she had better go along with it, considering the alternative might well be a bullet through her forehead. This 'peace and love' philosophy was at complete odds with the women's behaviour so far—but she needed to try and understand what was going on here, and what they thought their mission was . . .

She shrugged. 'OK then.'

Angelica pointed to a framed picture on the wall, the only decoration in the room. Kate had noticed it earlier; an abstract painting of a white

262

dot surrounded by red and white light rays fanning out around it.

'Don't close your eyes. You need to stay alert to the world around you, whilst losing yourself in the power of the Goddess . . . Look at the picture, focus on the pure light, the energy of Sekhmet condensed into something stronger than anything in the universe . . . pure energy, pure goodness and justice, pure creation and destruction, pure Knowledge . . . *Om Shanti*, Sister Kate, *Om Shanti*.'

*Om Shanti*, thought Kate, remembering hearing those words once in a yoga class. They meant 'Peace be with you', or 'I am a peaceful soul'— something like that. She almost laughed. 'Peaceful' was the last word she would ever use to describe Angelica's actions . . .

Angelica's voice dropped to a low, comforting hum. Kate turned her body on the bed so that she was facing the picture too, and copied Angelica by sitting cross-legged. She stared at the dot. After a few moments she found herself mesmerised by it— it was beautiful. But she couldn't still her mind, nor rise above the stress of the situation. Plus she had no desire to lose her wits in the presence of this woman. Above the sound of Angelica's voice, Kate could still hear Junko's laboured breathing. She sat completely still, trying to ignore the pain in her arm, and pretended that she was as lost in the meditation as Angelica was.

After what seemed like an interminable amount of time, Angelica stopped speaking, shook herself slightly, and turned to Kate, a beatific smile on her face.

'Well?'

Kate cleared her throat. 'Well. Yes, um, very

263

restful.'

The smile vanished in an instant. 'You think I am insane, don't you?'

Kate kept her face blank as Angelica continued.

'What you need to . . . assimilate, is that I am speaking the truth. There is no debate. And you, Dr Maddox, do not have a choice. Sekhmet told me you can be one of the chosen ones. If you accept this, and pass the trial, you will take your place alongside us.'

Kate absorbed this. A trial? What did that mean? 'And if I don't . . .?'

'The Prophecy foretells a great cleansing of the earth: plague, pestilence, fires, war . . . scorching the planet, razing civilisation in one hundred and one days. And from the smoking wreckage of the world seven women will arise who will rebuild civilisation, sculpting a new world in the image of the Goddess, Sekhmet. If you choose not to join us, then so be it. You will join Dr Larter in Hell.'

## 38

Jack almost immediately began to feel queasy in their hiding place—the built-in closet in the Airstream's bedroom. It was really bumpy on the road, and every time Riley drove round a corner, Jack felt as if the Airstream was about to detach from its hook-up and swing loose, and he'd be left behind. Having nothing to hold on to except Bradley didn't help either as, with each turn, he got bashed by his hard-sided suitcase, which was in there with him. Plus, the closet was baking hot, and

264

smelled of Riley's armpits. The boys had giggled a lot at first, but after about half an hour Jack could bear it no longer.

'Brad,' he said, in a needless whisper, 'Riley's driving, which means he can't see us. We don't have to stay in here the whole time, only when he stops.'

'Oh yeah,' Bradley replied, giggling again. 'I didn't think of that. Let's get out of here.'

They emerged gratefully from the closet and flopped down on the bed, breathing in the very slightly fresher air. There was an odd, stale, sweet smell to Riley's grimy bedclothes, but Jack didn't care—he was just happy to be out of the cupboard.

As he lay spread-eagled on the bed, partly to keep his balance in the rocking motion of the trailer and partly to stretch out his cramped limbs, Jack wondered when his dad would get back and find the note. Shirley had got so sick the night before that his daddy had taken her to the emergency room. It was great though, that Gina had invited him for a sleepover—it had made stowing away so much easier. Bradley had woken them up at five a.m., leaving pillows humped under the duvet on his bed and on the blow-up mattress on the floor Jack had slept on. Then they had hidden in the garage until they saw Riley emerge to get supplies from Gina's kitchen, which had been their cue to sneak themselves and their suitcases into the Airstream.

Jack had left a note in his dad's mailbox:

DEaR DAD, I'M GOING TO ~~KALLY KAFIL~~ CALLIFHORNiA TO SEE MUMMY. SORY THAT ARNTIE SHIRLEY IS SO ILL bUT NOW YOU WILL HAVE MoRE TIME TO LooK AFTER HER. DON'T WORY IM SAFE WITH

RILEY AND Bradley—THEY ARe GOING TO SEE THERE DADDY SO IF I CAN'T FIND MUM ILL GO WITH THEM TOO. LOVE YOU, JACK XXXX

That should be OK, Jack thought. He did feel nervous, though. This had to be by far the naughtiest thing he had ever done. He wondered if his mum would send him back to Dad's straight away when he got there, or if she would let him (and Bradley of course) stay for a few days? Riley would most likely go off on another trip—he'd probably be fed up with them by then.

Jack had already told Bradley that his mum would let them come in and look around the lab, like she had done one day in Oxford. He'd examined a drop of his blood through a microscope; it had been really cool. He had tried to get the address out of her on the phone yesterday evening, but all she had said was that it was on top of a mountain. Never mind, he could call her . . .

The rocking motion of the trailer began to make him woozy, and after a while both boys turned on to their sides, curled their knees up to their chests and fell asleep.

Jack awoke some time later, and noticed that something felt different. At first he couldn't figure out what, but then he realised: the trailer had stopped moving.

'Brad, quick, hide!'

He shook Bradley awake, jumped off the bed and bolted back into his hiding place, followed closely by a wide-eyed Bradley, sliding the door closed just as the main trailer door opened. Bradley had told him that Riley said it took a whole day to drive five hundred miles, so they shouldn't come out of the wardrobe till it was dark, by which time Riley would have gone too far to turn round and take them home.

'Is California *more* than five hundred miles away?' Jack had asked incredulously.

Bradley nodded. 'It's, like, maybe seven or ten hundred miles?'

Jack felt absolutely terrified about what Riley would say when he saw him, but Bradley had been confident it wouldn't be a problem. 'We'll say your mom has the injection to fix my dad's flu, then Riley will be, like, totally happy we're there,' he'd said. 'We just got to make sure he don't see us too soon, otherwise he prob'ly will take us home—and he'll be pissed about it.'

Jack crouched in the closet with his arms wrapped round his knees, trying to make himself as small as possible. He didn't want to go back to his dad's.

'Be totally quiet—Riley's in the bathroom,' hissed Bradley.

\*       \*       \*

The toilet flushed and the boys sat as still as rocks. Jack heard Riley come out, then the sharp crack of a ring-pull, some gulping, and a very loud belch, but he was too scared to giggle.

Once the car started, with the Airstream juddering away behind it, the boys emerged again. Bradley went straight for the refrigerator and helped himself to a dewy-cold can of Coke, handing Jack one of his very own (he wasn't allowed Coke

267

at home)—and three slices of processed cheese, which he peeled out of their clear plastic sleeves and wrapped into cigar-shapes before eating them. They demolished a Twinkie bar Bradley found in the cupboard, and half a packet of cookies.

'Let's watch TV,' Bradley said, clicking on a small wall-mounted television in the living area. There was some boring news programme on, everyone wearing white masks like Michael Jackson in the YouTube videos that Paul had once showed Jack. Even the man on the screen was talking into his microphone through a mask. Then the picture changed to a huge building full of rows and rows of beds with sick people in them. Weird, Jack thought. It looked like a basketball stadium—but how could there be beds in there?

'Aren't there any cartoons on?' he asked, and Bradley flicked the channel button until he found some. The boys settled down on the cushioned shelf that passed for a sofa, Jack's finger working into a small brown cigarette burn in the dirty flowered fabric.

\*       \*       \*

Three hours later when Riley next came back to use the toilet, he found them in the same spot, both curled up like commas on the cushions, fast asleep. 'WHAT THE HELL ARE YOU DOING HERE, ASSWIPES?' he roared.

They woke up and both burst into tears.

268

## 39

The sound of Isaac's name from Angelica's mouth made Kate go cold. Anger bubbled up inside her. She became aware of her own breath changing rhythm, becoming steadier, deeper. Involuntarily, she clenched her fists. The anger felt good. She needed to hold on to it, use it.

'Don't say his name,' she said.

Angelica raised a perfectly plucked eyebrow. 'He was a weak man. You should have seen him, how desperate he was to be praised, taking me into his room. The way his eyes ran up and down my body. So weak. Like all men.'

'He was a good man,' Kate retorted, furious that Angelica found this amusing. She tried not to let Angelica see that she was trembling. 'Worth a million of you. You think you're so beautiful, don't you? But I've got news for you, sister. You're ugly. It pours out of you, the ugliness. From your soul.'

The amusement on Angelica's face vanished and she raised the gun that Kate hadn't spotted, squeezing it, her knuckles whitening. 'Shut your mouth and listen to me. Or shall I just kill you?'

Kate bit her lip. She so wanted to scream at this woman, try to yell some sense into her. The two of them stared at each other, both refusing to look away. The room was silent.

But one of them was holding a gun. For now, Kate knew, Angelica held all the power.

'I'll listen,' she said.

Angelica relaxed and the atmosphere in the room changed in an instant. She folded her knees up under her chin and wrapped her arms round them, rocking gently on the bed. Then she stopped, and fiddled with her immaculate gold toenails. All of a sudden she looked like a little girl, frowny with concentration.

'Kate Maddox, it's your destiny to join us in ushering in the Golden Age. That won't happen until the earth is cleansed of all the sinful beings that currently inhabit it, except us, the Chosen Ones.'

It was on the tip of Kate's tongue to ask how Angelica, the murderer, thought she could possibly qualify as being without sin, but she took a deep breath.

'How do you know that this household won't succumb to the virus too? You're as likely to die as anyone else.'

Angelica shook her head, smug now. 'We're all immune.'

Kate stared at her. 'What? How?'

'The Goddess protects us.'

Kate couldn't help but roll her eyes. 'And you really believe that every single person on the planet will be killed off,' she said, 'except you women, here in this house?'

She tried to imagine the levels of delusion in their minds. She saw it like the spiral on a snail's shell, delicately twisting on itself; something beautiful and immutable, but far more fragile than they realised. She had read enough about post-apocalyptic cults to understand that their philosophical tenets, however implausible, would be completely incontrovertible to them.

Angelica's lips parted and an expression of ecstasy crossed her face. 'Not quite just us,' she

270

said. 'It is decreed. It has been so since the start of this Cycle and every previous one. A hundred thousand of the purest female souls will remain, but we are the rulers, the Chosen Ones—and so, the Goddess tells me, are you, Kate. You and Junko are both Sisters. The message comes through to me more and more strongly with each meditation.'

'Bit of a late addition, aren't we?' Kate asked, trying not to sound flippant. 'And poor old Junko isn't up to much at the moment.' She looked across at her motionless friend, her black lashes fanned out on her pale cheeks.

She felt very alone. What if she never saw Jack or Paul again? What if Junko didn't wake up?

Angelica seemed to read her mind. 'Nothing is late, or unplanned, Sister Kate. Sekhmet's divine plan is perfection itself. She knew, where I didn't, that we would lose one of our number. Junko will replace Sister Cindy, so that the prophecy of Seven Sisters will be fulfilled. That is how we know that Junko will recover.'

She leaned forward and grasped Kate's knee. 'You, Sister Kate, will sit with us on the jewelled thrones at the start of the Golden Age—isn't that the most glorious gift? To rule, knowing that you've been chosen? To wipe clean the slate of this corrupt and finished Earth, burn the pestilence out of it, and start again with your Sisters, worshipping and communing with Sekhmet herself, once more in human form, in a new world with no pain or death, just harmony and beauty for a thousand years, re-populating and fashioning the planet in our own images . . .'

Her eyes were shining with an excitement so genuine that, for a moment, Kate wondered

271

if it could be true—that the Apocalypse really was playing out at the whim of some channelled Egyptian deity keen to usher in a new world . . .

'Hang on a minute,' Kate interrupted, pulling herself together. 'Basic question I know—but if Sekhmet's a woman—you're all women—how exactly is that going to kick-start the human race, if everyone else has been wiped out?'

'We've made provisions for that, of course,' Angelica said, smiling beatifically at her, as though she was a kindly teacher and Kate a particularly daft schoolchild. 'We've had some extremely accommodating—if unwittingly so—male guests here at the ranch for short periods of time. Just long enough, in fact, for us to take what we require from them. Then we send them out again, if they're lucky. We sent our last guest out with a little extra something; a gift of our own. Something that he would pass on to everyone else on earth. He's done a very good job of it so far.'

'Can't you stop talking in riddles? That's how you spread the virus? You gave it to someone and sent them out into the world to spread it? Somebody on the Indian reservation?'

'No . . . our carrier must have taken it there. I can't remember his name, Cindy dealt with him. He was merely another weak man, like Dr Lart—'

Kate jumped off the bed, tuning Angelica out, unable to listen to any more of her shit. She clenched her fists and leaned her forehead against the wall, closing her gritty eyes and feeling the cold whitewash against her skin like a flannel, wishing she could wake up from this nightmare.

'It won't kill everybody, you know,' she said to Angelica over her shoulder. 'No virus has ever yet

272

been one hundred per cent fatal. At least one per cent of those who catch it will survive. There will be islands and communities it won't reach. Lots of people who've survived the original Watoto will be immune, as I am. And it's a matter of days, if not hours, before someone in the scientific community finds the cure. You can't assume we were the only scientists working on it. And it's not as if you can murder all virologists, can you?'

Angelica laughed softly.

'I told you, a hundred thousand women will survive. As I said before, don't underestimate us, Sister. Remember, we are the most evolved of any human beings on the planet at this particular time, in preparation for the change that has already started. We are chrysalises, weaving our—'

Kate held up her hand like a traffic cop. 'Oh please. Don't start that again. Can we just cut to the chase here? Are you going to kill me and Junko if we don't agree to join your twisted little cult, or what?'

Angelica shrugged. A muscle twitched in her jaw, and she instantly lost her serene expression. 'We are not a cult. But if you choose not to take advantage of the most incredible offer you will ever be made—well, then that's your funeral. Literally.'

## 40

Los Angeles was burning.

To the south, ribbons of black smoke rose to the sky in four separate locations, forming dark stains against the velvet blue of the night. A cacophony of sirens filled the air, even at 3 a.m. Rather than risk getting caught up in the mayhem in the centre of the city, Heather headed west, then south to Long Beach. She'd tuned the car radio to KNX, where a frantic newscaster was summarising the latest developments in an increasingly desperate tone.

In South Central, where the virus had taken the strongest hold, drugstores and clinics were being ransacked, then set ablaze by furious mobs. A pharmacist in Compton had been shot dead, not far from the spot where Heather had stamped the gun dealer to death. Witnesses said he had been trying to persuade the crowd that the anti-flu drugs they stocked would have zero effect, that they should go home, shut their doors, rest, pray. The mob didn't believe him. Somebody shot him, then another man pulled a gun and did the same to the gunman, whose twelve-year-old daughter stood crying beside him, a scarf wrapped round her face.

At the same time, The Bloods were convinced that the Crips had a huge stash of Tamiflu, and vice versa, and young men who usually fought on corners over narcotics were now slaughtering one another for a different kind of drug, one they believed would cure their dying mothers and siblings who lay in their beds, shivering and sweating their way towards death.

Heather had to swerve suddenly to avoid a group of looters, many of them wearing surgical masks and with hoods pulled up over their heads, who had smashed in the storefront of an electrical store and were running across the street lugging HD TVs and laptops. One of them had stayed behind to set the store alight.

There was no sign of the LAPD or National Guard. Radio reports said that they were trying in vain to keep the situation under control but had effectively ceded control of the streets to the mob. They were now concentrating their efforts on keeping people inside the quarantine zone.

A great metal band of cars ringed the outskirts of the city, choking the highways, filling the bridges, and people thronged on the beaches, where Coastguard patrols had orders to fire on any one who tried escaping by sea. At the road checkpoints, water cannons had been set up to blast anyone foolhardy enough to try to storm the barriers. But there were a lot of guns in LA and, the newsreader reported, a group calling themselves the Angeles Army had declared war on the government.

'People,' the newscaster urged, his voice trembling, 'stay home. Have faith in God.'

Heather laughed and said, 'It's exactly as the Prophecy foretells: *In the first days of the Plague, brother shall turn upon brother, sister upon sister, and flames will lick the sky, burning like their anger and their fear.*'

Rosie gave no sign that she'd heard. The woman and her daughter had not said a word since they entered the city.

Unperturbed, Heather continued along the Ventura Highway. Helicopters swooped overhead, flying towards the source of the smoke. A fire truck shot past, filling the air with its urgent wail.

'It's unstoppable,' she whispered happily to herself, picturing a million souls taking their last shuddering breath. Bodies being carted across front lawns, the streets of suburbia filling with the dead, warning crosses painted on white picket fences, crows descending from the skies to feast on cooling flesh.

She saw sandstorms whipping across the desert homeland of the Goddess, the sky turning black, lightning flashing in the spaces between the stars.

And when it was done she would walk the streets of the world with Dadi and her Sisters, and they would survey the silent avenues and shanty towns, the empty shopping malls and hushed bazaars, from Los Angeles to London, Cairo to Delhi, Tokyo to Cape Town.

She saw the end of days and the beginning of a new world, the prophecies staining the world red as they became real.

*　　　　*　　　　*

On the outskirts of Pasadena, Heather pulled into a deserted gas station.

'Just going for a leak,' she informed the silent Rosie and Lucy in the back. 'Don't try anything. I've disabled the horn, so that little stunt won't work. I'll be watching you.' She climbed out, yawned and stretched, looking up at the sky as she felt her vertebrae pop and release. It would be a beautiful night were it not for the smoke rising in the distance, obliterating the twinkling stars.

She took out her phone and called Angelica's voicemail. Angelica would be sleeping now, and hated to be disturbed, but Heather knew her phone would be on silent. 'All going to plan,' she said cheerily. She felt a twinge of guilt at lying to Angelica, but it was only a little white lie. Things would indeed be going to plan as soon as she caught up with Paul. 'I just need another day—he's in LA and I'm on his tail.' She glanced at her watch. Three a.m. 'By the time you wake up for morning prayers, I'll be on my way back, and the meddler will be dead. *Om Shanti*, Dadi.'

She hesitated, wanting to say something else. Ever since that incident in the motel room with that guy, she had wanted to speak to Angelica about what had happened. Actually, not so much to talk about it—she just wanted some sign from Angelica that everything was still the same between them. She hung up without saying any more.

The restroom door was locked, so she went to the side of the gas station, undid her combat pants, squatted and took a quick piss, keeping her eyes fixed on the SUV the whole time.

A rustle in the bushes behind her made her stiffen, and her hand automatically shot towards the curved hunting knife in the pocket of her combats. But fast as she was, it wasn't fast enough. A huge muscled arm, twice the size of Heather's own, had snaked round her neck and jerked her backwards into what felt like a brick wall, but was a man's chest.

'Nice car, lady,' said a voice in her ear, and Heather felt the blunt muzzle of a pistol pressing into her temple and smelled a rank mix of marijuana, body odour and alcohol.

'Yeah, nice. Shame it all bashed up.' Another voice. 'We still take it though. Hand over the keys.' This man was big too, and mean looking. What was visible of his face over the top of the flu mask was a mass of mahogany-brown fissures and sharp angles. The mask seemed to glow luminous white under the sodium haze of the streetlights.

'Well, shame you can't have it, assholes,' she retorted, staring down the man in the mask. The one holding her tightened his grip, cutting off her airway. Heather didn't panic—she never panicked—but as she tried to figure out how to break free, more men appeared from behind the gas station. They surrounded her, five or six of them, and Heather's heart sank. The irony—she'd taken a detour to avoid the centre of the city, and now this shit was happening in fucking Pasadena?

There was no way she was going to let some bunch of men defeat her. She *would not* fail in this mission. Thinking fast, she changed her tone:

'Take it, then, if you want it. People in there got the flu, though. I was just driving them to the hospital.' The pressure on her windpipe reduced her voice to a squeak, making her sound like a scared, vulnerable girl. That, and the thought that they'd probably been watching from the bushes while she was peeing, made her want to rip their hearts out with her bare hands.

The men looked at one another, and then over at the car. But it was dark, and the windows tinted. 'You ain't wearing a mask,' said the leathery one.

Heather tried to shrug, although it was hard, immobilised as she was by the enormous forearm.

'Your call,' she said, resisting the temptation to add 'loser'. 'I'm immune. Are you?'

'We'll risk it. We need wheels,' said the ringleader. 'Give us the fuckin' keys, lady.'

'Let go of me and I'll get them.'

The men all laughed.

'You ain't going nowhere. You one mean lookin' bitch,' said her captor, his voice so low in her ear that she felt the inside of her head vibrate. He leaned to one side, not letting up the pressure on her throat, and slid a meaty hand down her hip into the side pocket of her combats where her favourite hunting knife was kept. She tried to squirm away but he was far too strong. He removed the knife and tossed it to the leather-faced one. Then his hand delved into her front pocket for the car keys—but not before he'd snaked his fingers across to give a hard squeeze between her legs.

Heather sank her teeth into his massive forearm and bit it with all her strength. He bellowed with pain, and released the pressure on her for just a moment. She twisted out of his grasp—but turned right into the full force of a punch from one of the other men, rendering her immediately unconscious. She landed face-first, her broken nose grinding into the cracked asphalt.

*       *       *

Rosie and Lucy, their hands still taped behind their backs, lay silently in a bush next to where the SUV had been parked, not twenty feet from where Heather was out cold. Rosie watched the huge man kick Heather's prone form, and gave a very small mental cheer. When the seven men piled into the SUV, Rosie hoped they would drive over Heather

279

on their way out, crunching her bones like roadkill. But it seemed they had finished with her.

'Ain't no one in here. She was bullshittin' us, man,' she heard one of them say as they reversed at speed and then skidded on to the highway.

Everything seemed eerily silent once the gang had left, aside from the faint never-ending chorus of sirens in the distance.

'Luce, honey? Sorry I had to push you out. Are you OK?'

The moment she saw the men emerge from the bushes, Rosie had begun writhing around in the back seat until her fingers grasped the metal of the door handle behind her. She'd hung on, praying that the men would stop looking at the car, that an opportunity would come for them to slip out without being heard. When a cry of pain rang out as Heather bit her assailant, Rosie had shoulder-barged her daughter out of the vehicle and into the shadows.

Lucy didn't reply, but leaned her body into her mother's. Rosie would have given a month's salary to be able to put her arms round her, but she couldn't. Hell, a year's salary. She felt sick and shaky, but at least they were free.

'Come on, hon, we've gotta get out of here before she wakes up,' she whispered, staggering to her feet. 'Upsy daisy,' she said, trying and failing to smile. 'Sweetheart, let's go. *Oh hell*, I wish our hands weren't tied.'

Lucy grunted and rolled over on to her side, and then on to her front, her face pressing into the prickly earth around the bushes. Using her forehead as leverage, she managed to push herself to her knees, and then, wobbling dangerously, to a standing position. In the moonlight Rosie thought her daughter's skin was the colour of milk. 'Good girl, that's great, well done, honey. Come on.'

Lucy stopped and looked across at Heather's prone figure. Then she spoke the first words she had said since Heather had attacked her in the house:

'Where are we going?'

Rosie looked up at the smoking sky, at the fires burning in the near distance, trying to think straight while sirens shrieked and wails of grief and suffering came from a building nearby.

'We're going to find . . . a hospital . . . Or a police station. Somewhere . . .'

She jumped as something exploded in the distance. A gunshot. A scream. Her head hurt.

'Maybe just somewhere we can rest a while. Somewhere safe.'


41


Kate sat on the uncomfortable chair in the corner of her room, staring at Preeti's back as she tended to the still-unconscious Junko. If I had a knife, she thought, I could jump up and stick it between her shoulder blades before she had a chance to react. She'd never have thought herself capable of killing someone in cold blood, but then she'd never have dreamt of throwing liquid nitrogen in someone's face, yet she'd done it without a moment's hesitation.

It struck her that this doctor was the weak link among the Sisters. She had a slightly nervous air, and her medical background suggested that she possessed morals or ethics that might make her susceptible to reason. Kate decided it was worth a shot.

'Don't you feel ashamed?' she said in a low voice. 'You were trained to heal people, to help them. And here you are, trying to bring about the biggest act of genocide since the Holocaust. You unleashed the pandemic the whole scientific community has been dreading for years. Do you know how many people will die?'

Without turning to look at her, Preeti said, 'It is destiny. The will of the Goddess.'

'Hah, you should hear yourself!' She dropped her voice to a near whisper. 'You're brainwashed. Is that what's happened here? You were weak for some reason—something bad happened to you, like your husband left you or somebody close to you died—and you were looking to belong to something, looking for leadership. And Angelica came along and made you feel special, important. Filled your head with all this crap about the Goddess and the plague.'

Preeti didn't respond. She continued to examine Junko, lifting one eyelid then the other. The Japanese woman remained locked in her own world, not responding.

'I've got news for you, Preeti.' Keep using her name, Kate thought. Make it personal. 'There is no such thing as the Goddess. It's all make-believe. I don't blame you for being taken in by it—God knows, we all need something to believe in—but this virus is very real, and you are betraying thousands of years of medical progress and the oaths you made when you became a doctor.

282

Assuming you are a real doctor and not just some quack who bought her diploma online.'

Preeti's shoulders tensed. She still didn't look back but she replied with a shaky voice, 'I am a real doctor. I studied in Paris and Boston.'

'Then you should be ashamed of yourself. Surely you can see how wrong this is? Think of the millions of children who will die or be orphaned as a result of your actions. The suffering, the pain, the devastation? It's not too late, though, Preeti. You can—'

The door opened and the soldier came in. Kate had labelled each of the women in order to tell them apart. The soldier was called Simone. There was also the driver, Brandi, and of course the leader, Angelica. Apparently there was another woman she hadn't seen yet, for she'd heard the others mention a Sister Heather. So, five of them. If Junko woke up before Heather returned, that would be four against two. Not too bad. Even if Junko didn't wake up—and it seemed unlikely that she would—Kate only needed to get past four so-called Sisters.

Or she could try befriending one of them, sowing seeds of doubt, appealing to the human being beneath the brainwashed robot. Preeti was the obvious target. Perhaps instead of trying to shame her she should try a different strategy. But not while the soldier was in the room.

Simone cut an imposing figure as she stood over them, watching Preeti examine her patient. The role of prison guard suited her.

'Any progress?'

Preeti stood up. 'No. She is stable but there are no signs of her regaining consciousness.'

283

'She needs to be in a hospital,' said Kate.

Simone popped a stick of chewing gum into her mouth and grinned. While the other Sisters were as po-faced as bank employees, Kate had learned that the soldier was quick to smile—and equally quick to lose her temper. 'Hospital is the last place anyone would want to be right now.'

'Why?' Kate asked, knowing what the answer would be.

'Because if you're not infected when you walk in, you sure as hell will be when you walk out. In fact, last I heard all the hospitals in this part of California have shut their doors.' She laughed. 'Right now, being a medic is the most dangerous job in America. All those sick people, asking you to cure them but killing you with the very breath they use to ask. Your Chinese friend here is in the best possible hands.'

'She's Japanese.'

'Yeah, whatever.'

Preeti placed a hand on Simone's shoulder, caressing it. 'Dr Maddox was accusing me of being brainwashed,' she said, turning to look at Kate.

Simone smirked. 'Was she? Nobody's washed my brain, Sister. I woke up, is all. I ain't brainwashed— I'm enlightened.'

'You're sheep,' Kate said, trying to keep her voice steady, refusing to let them see her fear. 'Don't you have family out there? I take it none of you have children, but surely some of you have nieces, nephews, siblings . . .? And parents—what about them? You don't care about them dying? You think this will be some kind of paradise when they're all dead? Think again. It'll be a rat's paradise, that's all.'

284

'Rats?' Simone asked, seemingly shaken more by this than by the mention of her family.

Kate looked at her. 'Well, there will be a lot more rats around after the virus.'

'Huh?'

'They'll thrive in these conditions. All those bodies, all that food going to waste, nobody around to lay down poison or traps? The rat population will explode. They're going to have the time of their lives. Didn't any of you think of that?'

Simone gaped at her with barely disguised horror. 'Uh-uh. Angelica never said nothing about no motherfucking rats.'

'Perhaps the Goddess forgot to mention it. Cockroaches too. Every kind of pest and vermin you can think of. It won't only be you and your sisters who inherit the earth. Some Golden Age, huh?'

She folded her arms, enjoying Simone's discomfort.

'This is why you are so vulnerable to brainwashing. You've got no connection to the real world. You're looking for family. Angelica is like a mother or big sister figure to you, telling you what to do, persuading you that you finally belong. But your families are still out there. And they are going to suffer and die. You will have murdered them.'

'Don't listen to her,' said Preeti, tight-lipped, as she changed Junko's dressing.

'It's meant to be,' said Simone.

'Don't tell me,' said Kate. 'It is decreed? The will of the Goddess?'

Simone appeared impervious to Kate's withering sarcasm. 'Yup.'

'The Goddess is a story. Angelica made it up.

285

She's brainwash—'

Simone's hand was around Kate's throat before she even saw the woman move towards her, knocking the glasses from her face. Gasping for air, she tried to dislodge the woman's grip as she pushed her against the wall. The woman brought her face within inches of Kate's. Her breath was sweet, minty.

'If you try to tell me I've been brainwashed, or mention those fucking rats one more fucking time . . .'

Unable to reply because of the hand that was crushing her throat, Kate could only stare helpless into the woman's eyes. There was no anger, just irritation, as though Kate had wrecked her buzz. Her jaw continued to move up and down, working on the gum.

'We're not allowed to kill her,' Preeti said from over Simone's shoulder.

Tutting, Simone let go, and Kate gulped down a lungful of air as she retrieved her glasses from the floor and put them back on. She wouldn't let these women break her. She pulled herself up to her full height, all five foot seven, and said, 'It's not too late to stop this, you know. Junko and I can find the vaccine if you let us go, if Junko gets proper medical care and wakes up, we can stop the virus, I know we can.'

The women just laughed at her over their shoulders as they left the room, their only response the clunk of the key turning in the lock behind them.

\*       \*       \*

It was silent in the house when Kate awoke from a woozy, dreamless sleep. Immediately she registered that something had changed, but it took her a moment to work out what it was.

The silence. Normally, she could hear Junko breathing.

She got up and ran to Junko's bed, taking hold of her wrist and feeling for a pulse. With growing panic, she put her ear to Junko's chest, then crossed the room and flicked on the light. Junko lay motionless, her face waxy and her eyes closed.

'Help!' Kate banged on the door. 'Quick!' She shouted and banged as loudly as she could.

Within a minute or so Angelica pulled open the door. Simone and Brandi were behind her. All three were wearing white towelling dressing gowns and were flushed, as if they'd just got out of a hot tub.

'She's stopped breathing.'

'Fetch Sister Preeti,' Angelica barked at Brandi.

Kate tilted Junko's head back, held her nose and opened her mouth. Remembering her first-aid training, she blew three slow breaths into Junko's mouth. She stripped back the sheet, put the heel of her hands between Junko's ribs and pressed down as hard as she could, five quick compressions. Tears splashed her hands and she realised she was crying.

'Come on, Junko,' she whispered. Angelica and Simone were staring at her from the doorway, Angelica impassive, Simone with her mouth open, looking fretful.

Kate repeated the breathing and compression again. Junko's body didn't react.

'Please,' Kate implored. 'Don't, Junko, please

287

don't. We need you.'

She moved to breathe into Junko's mouth again, but Preeti appeared and grabbed her by the shoulder, pulling her away. Kate watched helplessly as Preeti tried the same resuscitation attempts that had already failed.

After a minute, Preeti looked up and shook her head.

'I'm sorry, Dadi Angelica. We're going to need another Sister.'

Kate launched herself at Angelica, aiming a punch at her cheekbone. Angelica blocked her easily, and Simone grabbed her arms from behind. Kate screamed in Angelica's face, 'You murdering bitch.'

'Sedate her,' Angelica said to Preeti, and the next thing Kate knew—the last thing she knew before darkness enveloped her—Preeti had grabbed her arm and a needle was sliding into her flesh.


42


Paul and Harley had barely spoken on their drive through the city, aside from a brief argument over whether to have the radio on or not. Paul fiddled with his phone all the way, as if it might magic up a call from Kate, until Harley snapped at him to put it away. There was sporadic network coverage, but no calls flashed up on his screen.

The rest of the time he stared out of the window, transfixed by the horrifying and surreal sight of buildings burning, people lining up outside smashed store windows, waiting for their turn to ransack the stock. Cops stood by watching. It reminded Paul of the riots in London in the summer of 2011, but on a much bigger scale.

Harley kept the windows rolled up. He looked very pale.

'It will be like this everywhere,' Paul said, 'if we don't find a vaccine.'

As they were nearing the prison, Harley's phone sprang into life.

'Oh my God,' Harley said, the colour draining from his face. 'All of them . . .? What about Kate Maddox?'

'What?' Paul interjected. 'What's going on?'

Harley waved him away irritatedly. 'We're in LA. OK . . . let me just do this and then we'll be head back.'

'What's happened?'

'The lab's been attacked. They're all dead.'

'No!' Paul cried out.

'Sorry, sorry—that's not definite, they may not all be dead. Kate's missing. Along with one of the other scientists, a Japanese virologist called Junko Nishirin. We think someone's taken them.'

'Or maybe they escaped,' Paul said, clinging to hope. 'We need to go and look for her. Now. Let's abandon—'

'No!' Harley snapped. 'We're almost there. The prison is ten minutes away. We've driven all the way through this hellhole of a city to get here and I am not turning back now. Besides, there will be very little we can do to help. Everything that can be done to find Kate is already being done.'

Paul had never felt so helpless, so desperate. Suddenly, making Mangold pay for Stephen's death ceased to matter. Everything else paled into insignificance compared with finding Kate. As if reading his mind, Harley barked, 'Paul, get a grip. Let's go see Diaz, find out what he knows about Mangold and this virus, then we'll head back north, OK?'

Paul's mouth was dry. He thought about coming clean, telling Harley that he'd exaggerated Diaz's role in developing the virus, that he'd said all that purely to enlist Harley's help. But he suspected that if he told the truth now, Harley would turn him out of the car and head back to Sequoia alone. Instead he gave Harley a nod and said, 'All right.'

\*          \*          \*

Glencarson Prison was almost exactly as Paul had imagined it: an imposing cluster of white buildings on the outskirts of Long Beach, the ocean calm and still beyond—apart from the constant buzz of helicopters that roamed the coastline.

Harley parked the car outside the prison. At the gate, he flashed his badge and explained that he urgently needed to talk to a prisoner.

The prison officer, who wore a name tag identifying him as M. Johnston, had a bald head and the bushiest moustache Paul had ever seen, looked them over and said, 'Did you call ahead?'

'I tried,' Paul replied. 'But no one answered. Why?'

'Because we don't have many prisoners left, that's why. Had an outbreak of the Indian flu. Half the inmates are in the medical block; a further quarter are in body bags already. Only a few COs left standing. We're supposed to be getting reinforcements, but it hardly seems worth the effort now.'

'What about Camilo Diaz?' said Harley. 'He's the man we've come to see.'

The officer caressed his moustache. 'Doc? Yeah, he's still alive. He's in minimum security.'

'Can you take us to him now?' Harley asked.

The officer scanned the deserted road that led to the prison, judged that there wasn't much risk in leaving his post. 'I guess. Come on, follow me. I reckon if you're carrying the Indian flu you'll have already given it to me.'

'Ditto,' said Paul.

'Nah, I reckon I'm gonna be OK. I never catch a cold. My wife always said I got the constitution of a bear.'

'Is that right?'

'Yup. A big ole grizzly. God rest her soul.' Paul and Harley exchanged a shocked look as Johnston muttered, 'Goddamn Indian flu.'

Paul blurted, 'Your wife died of Indian flu?'

'Yup. Day before yesterday.'

'I'm so sorry. What . . . what are you doing here, at work?'

Johnston shrugged, the shrug of a man who is lost but desperately trying to cling to something to keep himself from falling apart. 'Somebody needs to look after the inmates we got left.'

The three men fell silent as they passed through a second gate and walked across a dusty courtyard towards the minimum security wing. Johnston swiped a card at the door and they entered a cool, quiet building that housed the non-dangerous prisoners. Entering a prison for the first time since his own stint behind bars made Paul's skin crawl.

291

But this place had a very different atmosphere from the cramped, noisy jail in which he'd done his time. It felt almost civilised—or would do, were it not for the air of death that hung over the place.

Johnston led them into the visitors' room. 'Wait here and I'll fetch Doc to you.'

Harley and Paul sat down at one side of a rectangular table and watched as Johnston let himself through another locked door. He slammed it behind him, the sound echoing through the silent building.

'Poor guy,' Paul said.

Harley rubbed his face with his palms then stared at them as if he'd made a terrible mistake. 'This place is swarming with the virus. Johnston's almost certainly carrying it. If we get out of here without catching it, it will be a miracle.'

Paul felt a chill run through him. Up until now, he hadn't allowed himself to entertain the thought that he could get the virus. Before he had a chance to formulate a response, the door reopened and Johnston appeared. With him was an old man in an orange prison-issue jumpsuit. Camilo Diaz. He had a thatch of hair the colour of vanilla yoghurt: off-white flecked with specks of black. He stood straight and tall and appeared healthier than anyone Paul had seen for days.

Johnston led Diaz over to the table and they sat opposite Paul and Harley.

'Who are you?' Diaz asked in a strong voice.

Harley placed his badge face-up on the table. 'Jason Harley. I'm with the Bioterror Intelligence Team.'

'Bioterror?' Diaz had a slight accent—South American or possibly Mexican. 'So you're here

292

about this so-called Indian flu? Don't tell me that asshole CO actually got a message out for me.'

Harley blinked. 'What message?'

'I told one of the guards here—Hillier—that I needed to talk to someone about the outbreak. You aren't here because of that?'

'Hillier's dead,' said Johnston. 'Flu took him yesterday.'

'We're here because we want to talk to you about Charles Mangold,' said Harley.

Diaz shot Harley a look. 'Well, that's a stroke of luck because I want to talk to *you* about Charles Mangold.'

Paul leaned forward. 'What was the message you tried to get through, Mr Diaz?'

'*Doctor* Diaz. This virus, it's not a flu but a new variation of a virulent African virus called Watoto. As soon as I heard the first news reports and learned about the symptoms, I suspected Watoto. And then the guards and the other prisoners here started to get sick and I carried out some tests.'

'Tests?'

'I have certain privileges here. A colour TV. A supply of books and journals. And a good microscope and some basic lab equipment in my room. One of the sick COs let me take a blood sample from him. There's no question: it's Watoto. We called it Watoto MR. Today they're calling it Watoto-X2.'

'And this is the virus you were testing on employees at Medi-Lab?' Paul asked.

'Yes . . . well, it's more complicated than that. But essentially, yes. It was one of the viruses we tested. I tried to alert the authorities days ago. And now here you are, finally!' His bitter laugh echoed

293

round the room. 'Over two decades I've been in this goddamn place, with the most pathetic equipment, when I could have achieved so much. All I can do now is play with common cold samples, if I am lucky enough to catch one, and read research papers. It's funny, for years I tried not to think about Medi-Lab—it made me too angry, after the way Mangold betrayed me. It seemed our research was doomed to remain in the dark, forgotten. Then a few months ago I read a fascinating paper by an Englishwoman about Watoto. I thought, at last, somebody else is going to discover the cure. She's going to find the satellite.'

Paul sat up straight. 'You mean Kate Maddox?'

'Yes. Do you know of her?'

'She's my girlfriend.'

Diaz clapped his hands together. 'My, my. The plot thickens, no? And where is your brilliant ladyfriend now?'

'We don't know,' said Harley quietly.

Paul felt fear and nausea fill his body again. 'Hold on, did you say somebody else is about to discover the cure? You mean, somebody as well as you?'

Diaz stared at them impassively, as if challenging them to disbelieve him.

Paul and Harley both leaned across the table. Paul said, 'And does anyone else know it? Does Mangold know?'

Diaz pulled a disgusted face. 'Yes. He does. But it was me who discovered the cure. I was the first one to test it—on myself. Years ago.'

'And do you remember how to create it?'

'Of course I do! I am not senile.'

'This is incredible,' Paul said. 'You need to tell

294

us. We need to get something into production straight away.'

Diaz sat back and laced his fingers. 'I can do that, certainly. But I have two conditions. First, I must be released from this place. I want my freedom.'

'That's impossible,' Johnston said.

Diaz shot him a look of contempt. 'Maybe I should wait until you're all dead, then I can take the keys from your body and let myself out. I'm immune. Watoto could wipe out half the world, but I will survive. I don't have many years left and I want to spend them as a free man.'

'OK,' said Paul. 'Let's go.'

'Hang on,' Harley protested. 'We can't—'

'What choice have we got?'

Johnston, sitting quietly beside Diaz, nodded in agreement.

'What's the second condition?' Harley asked.

'I want you to take me to Charles Mangold. Now.'

## 43

Rosie and Lucy trudged in silence along the side of the Ventura Highway. They had been walking all day, and the sun was setting. Nobody had stopped for them, and no police cars had passed by. Rosie's mind raced constantly; should they stay out of sight or keep going? They were targets for muggers and looters, their hands already conveniently bound behind their backs—or would it be better to try and attract attention, to get help? They had nothing worth stealing, no money, jewellery, phones;

nothing. She kept glancing at Lucy, her heart bursting at the shock and trauma etched on her daughter's features.

'At least we're together, baby,' she said. 'I couldn't bear it if you were going through this without me.'

At that moment, Rosie sneezed, and it was as if the sneeze short-circuited her brain, scrambling all the signals as though her thoughts were a mass of tangled wires. For a second the ground tilted beneath her and a flood of nausea washed over her. Unable to steady herself, she stumbled and fell to her knees.

'Mom? Are you OK?'

Confused, Rosie nodded and staggered back up, waiting for her head to clear. She swallowed bile; cold sweat drenching her. 'I'm fine. But we have to get this damn tape off our wrists.'

'I bet people would stop if we could wave at them. But we can't,' said Lucy in a small voice as they made their way right to the edge of the freeway for the twentieth time that day. There was very little traffic, just the occasional laden-down car heading out of town to join the queues of people trying to get out of the city.

'There's a ramp over there,' Rosie said, dipping her chin in the direction of the interchange ahead. 'Let's head for that and pray that someone will stop for us when they come off the freeway.'

'Nobody has yet,' said Lucy miserably. As they staggered along, shoulder to shoulder as it was the only way they could touch, she kept looking across at her mother.

'Mom . . . are you sick?'

Lucy's voice seemed to come from the end of a

long tunnel. Rosie opened her mouth to reply, and found she couldn't speak for a few moments.

'I don't feel too good,' she confessed, and Lucy stopped in horror, tears jumping to her eyes.

'You have the virus!'

'No, baby, I'm sure it's just stress,' Rosie mumbled. 'Or hay fever . . . You know I always get hay fever around now.' But her legs were so weak and unsteady it was as if her kneecaps had been removed. 'I'm so tired. I need to lie down for a while,' she admitted.

Lucy looked around for somewhere to rest, her shoulders shaking with sobs. 'Don't you dare die on me,' she howled suddenly. 'I don't have anyone else!'

Men's voices rang out from the nearby slip road. 'Oh, thank God,' Rosie said, 'Come on, we can get help.'

They forged forward, one last push, thought Rosie—but then stopped short. There was indeed a group of men, seven or eight of them, all white, in their thirties, incongruously dressed in smart business suits. Or at least the suits would have been smart when they'd first donned them—well over a day ago, by the looks of them. Now they were ripped and dirty, and Rosie saw a patina of vomit all down one man's tailored jacket. They weaved up the ramp, in the middle of the street, singing angrily, several of them swigging openly from bottles of what looked like bourbon. They were all very drunk—but they were the first people Rosie had seen all day.

'Excuse me,' called Lucy, a moment before Rosie, who was beginning to have a bad feeling about this group of men, could stop her. 'Please

297

could you help us?'

They all stopped as one at the sound of her voice, and turned to look. There was a mixture of expressions on their faces: rage, bewilderment, hopelessness, inebriation. Rosie's knees were trembling so badly she could barely stand, and it wasn't just the onset of her fever.

'Help you?' The first man squinted at her. 'Why should we help you? Maybe you can help *us*, though . . .' He turned and made a lewd gesture to the others, and they all laughed—the sort of futile laughter that was closest to tears.

'See, the thing is,' he said, coming closer, 'we got nobody we have to be good for, not anymore. Wives, girlfriends—they're gone. Our kids too. Most of the other guys in the neighbourhood. Even my fucking boss is dead.'

Lucy backed away. 'Have you got the flu?'

'Not yet we don't. But we will. We all will. So we thought we'd have ourselves one final party, didn't we, boys?'

The 'boys' cheered weakly.

'And what do we need at a party, besides booze—which we already got?' He appealed once more to his friends.

'GIRLS!' they roared, pressing in closer to Rosie and Lucy, close enough that they could smell the alcohol on their breath and the bitterness in their hearts.

'Hey, boys,' said Rosie, putting on her brightest smile although her head was pounding and her throat felt as though she had gargled razorblades. 'We'll party with you, won't we, honey?' She raised her eyebrows at Lucy, widening her eyes to implore her daughter to go along with it. 'But first we need you to cut this tape off our wrists. And if any of you has any Advil, I'd sure appreciate it. We can't party with our hands tied, and we got mugged back there. I got a headache. So, do us a favour, eh, and maybe we'll see our way to getting into the party spirit for you?'

The men, swaying, looked at one another. Rosie swallowed hard. She had just invited a group of eight drunk, desperate men to produce a knife and approach them with it. Men with a death wish, who wanted sex. But what choice did she have? They were unlikely to run into anyone better. Besides, thought Rosie grimly, if she really did have the flu, then meeting her end at the sharp point of a drunken banker's knife was probably a less painful way to die.

'Cool,' said the man with vomit on his jacket. He walked up to Lucy and stroked her face, then the breast that Heather had threatened to cut off. 'You're pretty,' he said. He was bald on top, and the jacket seemed too big for him.

'She's sixteen years old.' Rosie had to grit her teeth to stop herself spitting at him. She wished with all her heart that she had never set eyes on Paul. If she hadn't, then she and Lucy would be holed up in their house, doors and windows locked, eating canned tuna and waiting for it all to go away. Not out here by the side of a freeway, about to be raped. Lucy's eyes were like saucers and she was shaking all over. Rosie almost wished they were still with Heather. At least there was only one of her.

Rosie sneezed, once, twice, three times and then, to her horror, vomited a stream of pale bile at the man's feet. He recoiled in disgust, despite the fact that he'd already thrown up over himself.

299

'Oh my God,' said one of the others. 'Look at her. She got the flu!'

'Fuck! She got the flu!' they chorused, backing away immediately.

'Wait,' called Rosie, a dribble of vomit running down her chin. She wiped it on her shoulder. 'Please, wait!'

But they had all run away, their silence more chilling than their shouting had been.

'We're going to die,' said Lucy. 'We're actually going to die.'

Rosie mustered up her last reserves of strength to reply firmly: 'No, we are not. We are going to find somewhere we can rest. We've been walking for hours and I need to sleep a while. I don't have the flu, I'm just tired and my head hurts from when that insane woman hit me.'

They turned and walked at a right angle to the freeway until they came to a residential street, low shabby houses with junk-strewn front yards and beaten-up cars on blocks outside. 'Over there,' Rosie said, gesturing to a For Sale sign. 'God, who would buy that dump? But it looks empty. Come on.'

There was not a soul in sight as Rosie and Lucy went round to the rear of the boarded-up house. 'Can you kick this door in, Luce? I don't have the energy.'

Lucy narrowed her eyes at the flimsy back door. Her first kick bounced off it, and she growled in frustration.

'Imagine it's Sister Heather,' Rosie said, managing a faint smile. Lucy tried again, three times harder, and the door splintered and swung open.

300

'Good girl.' Rosie kissed her daughter's cheek, and they stepped into a dingy, damp-smelling kitchen. Rosie closed the back door by reaching behind her with her tied hands. She opened the kitchen drawers the same way, but they were all empty, as was the whole house. 'Damn. I thought there might be a knife or some scissors. Looks like we're stuck with this tape. Let's go lie down a while, OK, honey? We'll have a sleep and then decide what to do.'

'I have to pee,' said Lucy miserably. 'Will you help me?'

With difficulty, they both used the bathroom, and then curled up on the dusty carpet of one of the empty bedrooms, falling into a restless sleep almost immediately.

## 44

Riley had been really, really angry, and Jack and Bradley had both cried till snot ran out of their noses. When Riley had finally stopped yelling at them, Bradley had explained about Jack's mom being a doctor working in a lab in California, and that she had a cure for the flu so, even if their dad had caught it, she could give him a shot and make him better. But it didn't make Riley any less mad.

'For fuck's sake, you little twats,' Riley said, lighting a cigarette and blowing smoke in their faces. 'Don't you have any idea how big California is? Plus, no one has found a cure for Indian flu, so if Dad *has* got it, he's basically screwed. You two have totally messed up this trip, you realise? If I take you home, I've wasted two days gas money and travel time. But getting you to this lab could add two days on the other side! Jeez. Whereabouts is it, anyways? I guess I'll have to take you there, and then your mom can look after you—if she doesn't have me arrested for child abduction or some shit like that.'

Jack and Bradley, heads hung low, were still snivelling. 'California,' said Bradley.

'Duh—I got that. Whereabouts?'

'I don't know, 'zactly,' Jack confessed. 'On top of a mountain, she said.'

Riley laughed mirthlessly. 'Why does that not surprise me?'

'California didn't look that big on the map,' Bradley protested, hiccupping.

'Well, it is, shit-for-brains. It's huge. What's the name of the lab? I could Google it.'

The boys looked at one another.

'Um,' Jack said. 'My dad said it's a secret lab.'

Riley rolled his eyes and took a savage drag of his cigarette. 'Right. Great. Fan-fucking-tastic. So how did you think you'd find it?'

'I was going to ring Mummy to tell her we're coming. I know her number.' Jack had rallied slightly, and adopted an *I'm not completely stupid, you know* expression. But Riley seemed to think otherwise.

'And speaking of your dad, what in hell have you told him about where you are?'

Jack puffed out his chest. 'I left him a note telling him that I'd gone to visit Mummy, with you and Bradley.'

'Ri-ight. Sheesh. This gets better and better. Your dad will tear my balls off and feed them to the

302

dogs if he ever sees me again.'

'He doesn't have any dogs,' Bradley pointed out helpfully, as Riley took out his cellphone and rang his mother. He told her that he was coming back with the boys, and they both started to cry again.

'Don't take us back, Riley,' Bradley begged, once Riley had terminated the call.

Riley narrowed his eyes at his little brother. 'I haven't decided what to do with you yet,' he said darkly. 'Just gettin' the old girl off our backs for now. Chill the fuck out.'

\*     \*     \*

'I need to go next door and get Jack,' Vernon said, once he had put the weak and traumatised Shirley straight to bed. They had spent an uncomfortable two days in the hospital, Shirley hooked up to an IV drip. Sedated and miserable, she gave no reply but simply turned her head to the wall and fell asleep.

Vernon stopped in the driveway and picked up his mail, with Jack's note on top of the pile. He read it incredulously, the blood draining from his face as he saw the words 'going to California'. He gave a great bellow of anxiety and charged up to Gina's front door, pounding hard on it.

'Gina! GINA! Why didn't you tell me! Where are they? Have you called the police? Gina!'

Gina answered the door and Vernon pushed past her into the hall. She looked tiny and shrunken, like a raisin, even more red-eyed and vague than usual. He wanted to slap her. While she'd sat here getting stoned, her kids—and his—had hared off across the country into the heart of a killer epidemic. He grabbed her by the shoulders and shouted into her face.

'HAVE YOU CALLED THE POLICE?'

'Hey, Vernon, it's OK,' she said, startled out of her torpor. 'Relax, they're fine. Really. I just talked to Riley, he's on his way back.'

Vernon sank down on to the bottom stair, his head in his hands.

'Why didn't you tell me?'

Gina sat down next to him, her wide hips touching his, which immediately made him leap up again like a scalded cat. He remembered, too late, how she had always had a problem with over-familiarity.

'Honey,' she said, standing too and rubbing the side of his arm in a way that made him twitch with discomfort, 'You were in the hospital with Shirley. You had enough on your plate. The kids will be fine with Riley, I swear.'

'How old is he again? Twenty?'

'Seventeen. But, like, a totally mature seventeen.'

'I want to speak to him,' he said belligerently.

'Sure.' Gina floated across to the telephone. 'Go easy, though, Vernon—he didn't know that the boys had come with him. He found them hiding in the Airstream when he took a comfort break.' She dialled a number and handed the receiver to Vernon.

Vernon clamped the phone against his ear, fuming as the ringtone turned into a voice message. The fact that the receiver smelled of patchouli enraged him further. *'Hey, losers, it's Riley. Leave me a motherfuckin' message and I might get back to you. Or maybe I got better things to do . . .'*

'Riley? This is Jack's father, Vernon. I do not

304

appreciate you taking my eight-year-old son on an insane road trip into the heart of an epidemic that is probably killing thousands of people a day.' He tried to rein in his anger and frustration, but failed miserably. 'Now you listen to me, and listen to me good: Jack had better be back here by tonight, or you will be in serious trouble, do you understand? So you turn that heap of metal crap right around and get back here NOW.'

He slammed down the phone and clenched his fists.

Gina shook her head slowly. 'Not cool, Vernon. I told you: Riley didn't know Jack had stowed away.'

Vernon put his face very close to hers. 'Well, in that case, if anything happens to those kids, I am holding *you* personally responsible,' he hissed through clenched teeth, before turning and barging his way out of the house.

A feeble voice called down the stairs to him the moment he set foot inside his own place:

'Vern, angelpops, please could you bring me some camomile tea? With half a teaspoon of honey, not too hot . . .? And I could do with a foot rub too, if you have a minute . . .'

Vernon marched into the kitchen, flicked on the kettle, and slowly and repeatedly banged his head against a cupboard door.

\*     \*     \*

Riley listened to the message that Vernon had left on his cellphone.

'Who does that asshole think he is?' he said scornfully. 'Right, kids, that's decided. We're going to California. Nobody tells me what to do.'

305

He switched off his cellphone, threw it into the footwell of the car with the Twinkies wrappers, and headed west on the open road.

## 45

When Kate was a child, her Aunt Lil had kept a canary in a cage. Bertie, that was its name. The poor thing used to sit there all day, on its perch, tweeting absent-mindedly. It was bad enough, the young Kate had thought, keeping a winged creature locked in a cage, unable to fly. But Aunt Lil also had two cats, a pair of neutered toms, and they would prowl around the bird's cage, occasionally licking their lips, waiting for the day Aunt Lil accidentally left the cage door open. Kate felt very much like that canary now. Caged, frightened. Waiting for the cats to get her.

Earlier, after the women had carried Junko's body from the room, with Angelica issuing orders to take her into the woods and bury her 'with the others', Kate had lain on her bed and wept. It had all come out: the grief and shock and fear, the days of intense anxiety, all the death she'd seen. She wanted Paul, she wanted Jack. She wanted to go home. But it seemed likely that she was going to die in this place. She would never see her son again, she wouldn't find a cure for Watoto. Instead the insane women who were keeping her prisoner would triumph.

Evil would win.

But when it seemed she had cried all she could, when it felt like she had no more tears, she found something flexing inside her: the strength at her core, the kernel of hope and determination that had seen her through so much in her life. All of her experiences—from watching her parents die in Africa, through surviving the fire at the Cold Research Unit, to thwarting Gaunt's attempt to unleash his deadly virus—had combined to create something tough at her centre, something tougher than she realised.

And the anger was there too, a fire that kept on burning low, only requiring her to think about Isaac, or Officer Buckley, or the photo of the seven-year-old boy from the newspaper—or Jack's fate, if these women weren't stopped—for it to roar up and fill her with the need to keep going, keep trying. To never give up.

Because even when all hope is gone, you can still win the game.

She thought of Isaac and Junko and the people at the research lab, the virologists who'd attended the conference in San Diego—none of their deaths should be in vain. They had devoted their lives to trying to eradicate disease. And now that she was the only one left, it was up to her.

To get out of here. To find the vaccine.

She thought back to what Junko had said in the lab, just before Angelica and the others had burst in. She had been talking about something Kate and Isaac had written in their research paper. What was it she'd said?

*'Remember, in your paper, you said that sometimes when studying the virus you thought you could see a trace of something that didn't belong, like a ghost flickering in and out of sight. You thought perhaps it was a contamination.'*

The ghost. It was something she and Isaac had debated for ages. He thought it was trivial, a mistake, and that it shouldn't be included in the paper. But Kate had always felt it was important somehow, that she just needed to find out what it was. And Junko had obviously thought so too.

But what had Junko discovered?

Kate got off the bed and paced around the room, the kinetic energy helping her to think. What was it that made Watoto-X2 different from the original strain? They appeared to be identical. But this new strain was deadlier. It was the *way* in which it killed—suddenly, rather than dragging its victims towards a slow, gradual death—the kind of death her parents had suffered. Officer Buckley had died from a seizure at the end, sudden and unexpected. What could have caused that?

She stopped pacing. She could feel the knowledge there, so close to the surface of her brain yet tantalisingly out of reach. She wished she was in the lab right now, able to examine the virus, to hunt for the ghost.

Eventually, her brain aching with frustration, she lay down on the bed and closed her eyes. Junko's face swam into her vision and she managed a brief smile, remembering how sweet she had been. And how intelligent.

What secret did you take with you, Junko? she thought. And how can I unlock it?

Worn out, she fell into a shallow sleep.

\*        \*        \*

The sound of women shouting woke her up. It was

pitch black in the room, but she knew this room almost as well as her own bedroom by now and she found the door easily, pressing her ear against it.

The voices of the Sisters, raised in anger, some distance away but coming closer, and audible in fragments: '. . . hasn't jeopardised us . . .' '. . . I won't have you making her angry . . .' Something inaudible, then '. . . the Goddess is demanding blood . . .'

The last one sounded like Angelica. The fact that they were fighting gave Kate hope. Maybe they would all shoot each other—although that wouldn't do her much good, locked in this room.

The shouting stopped and she could hear footsteps coming towards her room. She stepped back from the door, but the urge to hear what was happening was too strong and she pressed her ear against it again. She could hear two voices: Angelica's and, she was sure, Preeti's. It sounded as if they had stopped a metre or two from her room.

And when she heard what they said, she had to clasp her hand over her mouth to stop herself from crying out.

## 46

Angelica drained the last drops of her breakfast protein shake. It usually energised and invigorated her, but today it sat heavily at the bottom of her stomach like cement. She replaced the jug on the refrigerator shelf for the others to take their share—it was one of the ranch rules that it must be consumed daily, so potent were the health and spiritual benefits of this particular drink. Angelica had first come across its secret ingredient in an Alexandrian street market, and had subsequently imported several years' supply of the grey powder.

Still unsure as to why she felt so out of sorts, she decided to go for a run. She changed into a tight singlet and brief Lycra shorts, laced up her running shoes, and set off down the drive of the ranch. The sun blazed down onto her bare head and, as always, she thought of Sekhmet, the Eye of Ra, the destructive Sun Goddess. The Egyptians had been so fortunate, she thought, picking up her pace as she struck out down the deserted road at the end of the drive. They too must have been visited by Sekhmet, communed with Her. There were so many images of Her. Angelica felt privileged that, to her knowledge, she and her sisters were the only ones since Egyptian times that the Goddess had spoken directly with—what an incredible gift!

And yet . . . why had it been so long since she had felt Sekhmet's presence? It had been days now, and the closest she had come to it was the burning of the sun rays on her head. Had She deserted them? Had Angelica misunderstood Her command? After all, if they sacrificed Kate Maddox, they would only be five, and the prophecy of Sekhmet's Seven Angels wouldn't be fulfilled. Perhaps Sekhmet was angry at her, perhaps she had screwed the whole thing up and the Golden Age would never happen . . .

It was getting hotter and hotter. Angelica wiped away the sweat that dripped down her face, and changed her high ponytail into a makeshift bun, to keep the hair off her neck. She was panting hard as she turned a corner and then—

310

'*Oh!*'

She was there! Sekhmet herself!

Angelica immediately prostrated herself, face down in the dirt of the road, dazzled by the Goddess's radiance.

'*Om Shanti*, Sekhmet, sweet Sekhmet, I am your faithful servant, speak to me,' she gabbled, fear and awe swirling and eddying through her in waves of heat and dust and delight.

She risked a glance. The Goddess herself, majestic and splendid, huge on her throne, her lion's head and grave eyes, the Ankh of Life in her hand. The rising morning sun was directly behind her head, forming the crown she always wore, dazzling Angelica, but she could just make out the silhouette of the serpent in front of the sun, and the vulture-headed sceptre in her left hand.

Joy sprang in Angelica's breast—this was a sign! Everything was on track, she'd done the right thing by sending Heather; the Goddess had chosen to come down and manifest herself, and the fact that Sekhmet was on the throne meant that she had come to receive supplicants who would seek her counsel. She had come to talk to Angelica! It was incredible. Angelica usually only saw her in dreams or visions.

'Yes, Lady Sekhmet, I am here, your loyal supplicant, your servant, tell me your will . . . I am sorry I ever doubted you were with us, I'm so sorry, it's just the End Times I know . . .'

Angelica's nose was pressed into the gravel and she could taste dust in her mouth, but her whole body thrilled with joy and gratitude.

When they came, the words shimmered like an aural heat haze, not emanating directly from

311

the being on the throne, but made up of the very particles and ions of the atmosphere, soft at first, then louder and clearer.

*Kill her. Kill her. Kill her. Kill her.*

'We will only be five then,' Angelica said timidly. 'Is that acceptable?'

And it came again: *Kill her. Kill her. Kill her. Kill her.*

The next time Angelica looked up, the sun streamed right into her eyes, nothing blocking it. The vision had vanished.

She got up, brushed the dust and dirt from her legs and breasts, and ran straight home feeling as though she was flying. As usual, Sekhmet had provided her with all the answers. It was incredible how, whenever she faced a problem, the Goddess told her exactly what she wanted to hear.

\*　　　\*　　　\*

That evening after meditation Angelica stood up and held out her hands to her Sisters, palms upwards, a beatific smile on her face. When she spoke, her voice rang loud and clear around the marble atrium.

'I have amazing news,' she said. 'We have all been shaken by recent events, the loss of our dear Sister Cindy, and the worry that the prophecy might not be fully fulfilled, when Kate Maddox declined to join us, and Junko departed. And Sister Heather being away from home at this crucial time . . . it isn't easy for any of us. But Sekhmet wants us to be flexible, and above all, loyal. We are so close now! I can smell the meadows of the Golden Age, the freshness of a new world, can't you, Sisters? I can see our palace, feel our eternal joy! Pain is a necessary part of the birth of the new order. I think we just didn't realise how much pain . . .'

'What's up, Dadi?' asked Simone.

Angelica paused for dramatic effect, then fell to her knees, her white robe spreading out behind her as she turned to the statue of Sekhmet.

'She appeared to me in person this morning! On the road, about two miles south of here!'

Brandi and Preeti both gasped and gazed wide-eyed at the statue as if expecting it to nod in agreement. Angelica noted that Simone's eyes remained downcast, and she did not react at all, which annoyed and displeased her.

'Don't you understand the significance of this?' Angelica addressed her comment to Simone, who somehow managed to nod and shrug simultaneously.

'What did she say?' Brandi asked reverentially.

Angelica beamed, her eyes shining with excitement. 'It is all as decreed. Our faithfulness will be rewarded—I confess, Sisters, I had suffered a brief crisis of confidence when we lost Sister Cindy—but *it was a test.* And we have passed! The Goddess told me that it is all right, the Transformation can still take place with the five of us, provided that Sister Heather completes her mission and returns to us.'

'What about Maddox?' Simone said, unsmiling.

'In Kate Maddox,' Angelica announced, 'we have our ultimate gift to the Goddess. Sekhmet wants her dead, as a final test of our loyalty and, in Her generosity, to put our minds at rest that Maddox can't somehow find a way to stop the

313

cleansing plague. Maddox can never be one of us—
the Goddess has examined her while she is here
and found her wanting. The trial is cancelled. A
blood sacrifice is all we need. Nothing can stop the
progress of the Golden Age now. Nothing!'

Simone got up, her sandals slapping on the
polished marble floor as she walked straight across
the ankh symbol and strode out of the room. The
three other women stared after her, aghast.

Preeti jumped up and made to follow, but
Angelica gripped her arm. 'What is going on?
What's the matter with her?'

Preeti hesitated, fixing her brown eyes on
Angelica's furious face. 'Forgive her, Dadi, it's
last-minute nerves, that's all. She . . . uh . . .'

'What?'

Preeti darted a glance at Brandi, who nodded
encouragingly.

'Promise you won't punish her for it?'

'It depends. *What has she done?*' Angelica's grip
tightened and Preeti pulled her arm away, rubbing
her biceps. Angelica's voice was ice-cold.

'Nothing, well, not nothing, it's just that . . . she
called her folks in LA, wanted to speak to them one
last time. To say goodbye.'

Angelica's hands flew to her mouth, but she
immediately regained her composure. She pulled
herself up to her full height before marching out
of the room. Brandi and Preeti scurried after her,
almost running to keep up.

'Did she tell them where we are?' spat Angelica
over her shoulder.

'No, Dadi, I swear—that's why she's so upset.
They were dead. No one answered at her folks'
house but she got hold of a cousin who told her.

The cousin was sick too. Can we go meditate with her? She's grieving.'

'She should know better than to allow such base, earthly emotions. And you—why didn't you tell me about this?'

Brandi and Preeti exchanged glances again. 'It only happened this morning while you were out on your run. Simone was going to tell you herself. She's really sorry, Dadi, she knows it was wrong. But she hasn't jeopardised us in any way.'

'*Hasn't jeopardised us?*' shrieked Angelica, stopping suddenly in the hallway, and turning to face them, all her joy and bliss from earlier having evaporated. 'What do you suppose Sekhmet will think of this? You are my chosen ones! I won't have you making her angry!'

'What are you going to do, Dadi?' Preeti asked, in a small voice, anxiously fingering the ankh around her neck.

'My whole life has been leading to this and I will not allow any of you, or Maddox, to *fuck it up* for me. The Goddess is demanding blood, and I am going to make sure she gets it; Maddox's blood, first thing tomorrow. Now . . .' She sucked in air. 'Get out of my sight.'

47

Kate sat on the edge of her bed, staring at the grey shapes in the darkness, too tired and scared to think straight. She had spent the last couple of hours standing on a chair beneath the window, trying to loosen the bars. But it was hopeless, as were her

315

attempts to find a weapon in the room. The chairs were solid and heavy to lift, the bed wouldn't come apart; there was nothing. The nearest thing to a weapon she possessed were her shoes, and they wouldn't be much use against the Sisters' guns.

She considered screaming to attract attention, then trying to overpower whoever came to the door. But, aside from being armed, these women—with the possible exception of Preeti—were all strong, much stronger than her. In the end, she decided that her only hope would be to somehow convince them that she had seen the light and decided to join the sisterhood, that Sekhmet herself had spoken to her. If they fell for it, that would buy her some time. But from what she'd heard Angelica say in the corridor outside her room, it seemed they had made up their minds.

She had a matter of hours left, then dawn would come and, with it, her death.

The prospect left Kate feeling oddly numb. As she sat, chin dipped to her chest, she felt herself drifting to sleep, as if she was shutting down, her exhausted brain unable to cope. It felt like a dream when, in the near darkness of her room, she saw a figure moving swiftly towards her.

When she opened her mouth to scream a hand clasped over it. Kate tried to shake her head, to bite, to push the hand away, but a voice whispered in her ear, 'Be quiet. If you scream, they'll kill us both.'

Kate stopped struggling. It was Simone. Her breath still smelled of chewing gum.

'If I take my hand away, are you going to scream?'

Kate shook her head. Her heart was going crazy,

beating so hard it seemed to be trying to smash its way out of her chest.

Simone pulled her hand away and, in the same moment, flicked on a torch. Dazzled, Kate screwed her eyes tight.

'Sorry,' Simone whispered.

'What . . . what's going on?' Kate asked in a whisper of her own.

Simone sat on the bed beside her. 'Was it true? What you said about the rats?'

'What?'

'The rats. You said that they'll, y'know, take over the world.'

Kate swallowed. Her mouth was desert-dry. 'Yes. When there are no people left, the rat population will explode.'

'A plague of rats.' Simone shuddered. 'I hate them. Nasty little fuckers.'

Kate didn't know what to say.

Simone went on: 'They're fixing to kill you in the morning. Going to sacrifice you to the Goddess. I'm not sure exactly how Dadi Angelica is planning to do it, but I'm guessing it's going to involve knives and incantations and shit.' She sighed. 'I'm sick of it. All the killing. I really thought it was the truth, y'know? The prophecy, it all seemed to make sense, though I've figured now it seems to change all the time depending on what Angelica wants to happen. She talks a good game. Guess she had me under a spell. I didn't realise she was crazy as a motherfucker.' Her laugh was low and mirthless.

Kate shivered. Simone had taken out her gun and was fiddling with it in her lap, the torch resting on the bed beside her.

'I like this world, Dr Maddox. That's the other

317

thing. You ever been to LA?'

Kate said that she had.

'Yeah. But I bet you never been to the part of LA I'm from. Compton. It's got a bad rep, and a lot of it's deserved, with all the gangs and drugs and shit. I was desperate to escape and . . . well, we ain't got time for that story now, but it led me here, to Angelica. Only, it's like you were saying earlier—I got people, people I care about . . .'

Kate couldn't believe it. She had actually got through to Simone. She had thought Preeti was the soft target, but she had been wrong.

'That ain't right,' Simone said in an almost inaudible, little-girl voice. 'I did have people I cared about. Not any more. They're all gone.'

Simone sniffed and Kate thought she might be crying, though it was too dark to tell. 'It's too late for my folks. But maybe it's not too late for the rest of the world.' She picked up the torch and said, 'I'm getting you out of here. But you have to do exactly what I say. If they catch us, they'll kill us both. I'm supposed to be on watch tonight so the others are in bed.'

'Thank you,' Kate whispered.

'We ain't out of here yet. Come on.'

They crept out of the room. Low lights were burning through the house. All was silent. Simone, with her torch tucked into the combats she was wearing—the Sisters wore a uniform of army pants and a black vest when they weren't floating around in their robes—led Kate down a hallway lined with pre-Raphaelite paintings, mythical scenes featuring tragic, pale-skinned women languishing in boats, or languorous in beds.

The ranch's corridors were long, with block

318

parquet floors so highly polished that even in the dim light they were almost reflective. Simone hustled Kate through a reception area, where light flooded in through a huge glass atrium, and individual and beautiful pieces of furniture—a scrolled, engraved armchair, marble statues of female nudes, a mahogany table with ornate legs and a glass top—were arranged artfully around the walls. Kate looked longingly at the enormous rough-hewn timber front doors, which were secured shut by an intricately fastened iron bar. They looked as though they had been plundered from a medieval castle.

But there was no time to appreciate these fleeting impressions—Simone led her on, through a smaller corridor that continued into the other side of the house.

Suddenly, they froze. Someone had moved in one of the rooms above. It had sounded like a chair scraping.

'Shit,' Simone hissed. 'Someone's awake. We gotta hurry.'

Kate felt sick and cold, but filled with hope. She could taste freedom. If she could get away, she could find Paul and Harley, track down Mangold and make him tell them how to stop the virus.

She followed Simone into the dining area, a vast room with a solid oak table at its centre. Beyond this was the kitchen and the back door. Through the windows, all she could see was the black velvet sky, dotted with stars.

Simone pulled Kate through the room, treading softly, cat-like, holding on to Kate with one hand, gripping her gun in the other. Kate didn't know how many of her colleagues at the lab Simone had

319

murdered with that gun, but right now she had to put her faith in this woman. She was experiencing an intense form of what she later realised was Stockholm syndrome, a sudden rush of gratitude towards her kidnapper. But what she mostly felt was terror beyond anything she had ever known.

If this went wrong, she would be dead. She prayed that Jack would be safe, that Vernon would look after him if she wasn't around. Images flashed through her mind: Jack giggling uncontrollably as she tickled him, frowning as he coloured in a picture for her, rubbing his tummy as he ate cake . . . a kaleidoscope of memories that threatened to turn her inside-out with pain. She forced herself to push them away, to concentrate on the task at hand.

They finally entered the kitchen and Kate's heart leapt into her mouth. There was somebody standing by the back door, disguised by shadows. Simone raised a stiff arm to stop Kate from walking any further. The figure by the door stepped unsteadily towards them.

It was an old man, wisps of white hair floating on his liver-spotted pate, his shoulders hunched with age, swamped by a huge pair of pyjamas.

'Beautiful night, isn't it?' he said, turning towards them. His eyes were glazed and his voice dreamy.

Simone's eyes flicked up to the ceiling.

Kate was paralysed with fright and surprise. The sight of him was so utterly incongruous. He was clearly no physical threat—but what if he woke the others? She braced herself, expecting to hear more noises from above. But the house remained silent.

The man came closer to them. 'How are you, my dears?' He didn't seem surprised to see either of them.

Kate tried to stay cool. 'I'm . . . I'm fine, thank you. Simone here was just showing me the house.'

'Ah. Grand place, isn't it? It used to belong to my daughter, God rest her soul.'

'Kate, we need to go,' Simone hissed, agitatedly fiddling with her gun. For a moment, Kate thought Simone might shoot him, or use the handle of her pistol to knock him out. Instead, she said, 'Sorry, sir, but we gotta go.'

She hurried a bewildered Kate out of the room, back the way they came.

'We're going to have to go out the front door,' she whispered. 'That means we gotta pass the main stairway, and it's impossible to open that door quietly. It has two locks and three deadbolts. Actually . . .'

As they entered the front hall, from which a staircase snaked up to the floor above where Angelica, Brandi and Preeti were—hopefully— sleeping, Simone went over to a side window.

'OK, we're going to go out here.' She turned the silver key that sat in the lock and pulled down the handle, pushing the window open. 'Go on,' she hissed.

Kate had to step on to the lower part of the window and pull herself out before jumping down. She stumbled as she hit the ground, and unwittingly let out a small cry, immediately putting her hand over her mouth and looking around.

Simone jumped through after her and grabbed her arm, pulling her along into the garden.

As they passed the kitchen, Kate looked up and saw the old man gazing out at them, his brow furrowed.

'I shoulda knocked him out,' Simone said. 'He could go upstairs and wake Angelica at any moment, if he realises what's going on. Maybe I should go back and . . .'

Kate opened her mouth to ask who the man was, when Simone whispered urgently, 'Come on, quick.'

They ran silently, following the side of the house until they found themselves on the edge of a great expanse of lawn. The moon was full and illuminated the grounds. About one hundred metres away, a dark line of trees marked the edge of the woods.

'You need to go into the woods. Keep heading in that direction and eventually you'll reach the road. Follow the road—it will take you into town. But if you hear any cars coming along the road, you'll need to hide, OK?'

Kate looked up at the house and, in that moment, a light came on in one of the rooms.

'Shit.' Simone saw it too and she swiftly grabbed Kate again and pulled her behind a high bush, concealing them from the house.

'Go, now. I don't want them to discover you're missing till morning. But first, you need to hit me.'

'What?'

'We gotta make it look like you overpowered me.' Kate realised Simone hadn't really thought this through. 'I'm gonna say I heard you cry out and went to your room, and as I came in you pretended to be sick. So I . . .'

'You leaned over me to check my temperature and I grabbed your gun. Took your torch too.'

Simone unclipped the Maglite from her belt and handed it to Kate.

'Then you pointed the gun at me and made me lead you out of the house.'

322

'At which point I hit you with it and knocked you out.'

Simone nodded. 'OK, do it.' She handed Kate her gun.

'Now?'

'Yes. Go on, quick. That old bastard might have already woken them up.' They both looked up at the lighted window. There were no signs of life. Yet.

'What about you? Are you going to stay?'

'Don't you worry about me. I need you to find a cure for the virus, OK?' she said. 'Don't want them goddamn rats taking over the world, do we? Now, do it, please.'

Kate lifted the gun and Simone bowed her head.

But before she could strike the blow, Kate had to know something. 'Who was the old man?'

'Him? Oh, pay no attention to him. He's crazy. Come on, what are you waiting for? Do it.'

Kate swung the gun as hard as she could. It connected with Simone's skull, making a sickening hollow sound, and she dropped to the floor like a rock, landing face down on the grass.

Kate hesitated for a second then, still holding the gun, turned and ran across the lawn towards the wood.

When she was halfway across, she heard a woman's voice cry out, 'Hey.'

Kate didn't dare turn and look. She kept running, expecting to feel a bullet between her shoulder blades at any moment.

## 48

Kate ran the last thirty metres across the lawn in a panic, waiting for a bullet that never came. She didn't hear any more cries or voices, but that might have been because of the roaring sound in her head, like a seashell turned up to eleven. Simone's gun was heavy in her hand. Kate hoped Simone would be OK, that the Sisters wouldn't see through her story and punish her.

When she reached the edge of the wood she stopped running and stood bent over, hands on thighs, catching her breath. Nausea bubbled inside her. Her knees ached and she had a stabbing pain in her left foot. I'm too old for this, she thought. Thank God she had taken up running last year to stay fit. But this was very different from her morning jogs along the banks of the Isis, iPod plugged in, looking forward to a well-earned breakfast when she got home. She had never had to run for her life before.

As soon as she stepped between the trees, the moonlight that had illuminated her way lost its power and she found herself in darkness. She hesitated between two tall trees, the ground soft beneath her feet, and looked back towards the house. No signs of life, apart from the lights that burned in the downstairs rooms and an upstairs bedroom. Kate had never seen the exterior of the house before and she was shocked by its grandeur and scale. It must be worth millions. To the far left of the house, Kate could make out stable buildings. There were several sports cars and a

Jeep parked by the front gate, which stood as high as a double-decker bus. Kate wished Simone had given her the keys to one of the vehicles rather than sending her into the woods, but she guessed that opening the gate would have been too noisy and risky.

OK, she told herself. You need to keep moving. They could start coming after you at any moment. They might even be in there, preparing, now. Zipping up their boots. Loading their guns.

She took a deep breath and entered the wood, deliberately avoiding the path. Feeling confident now that the light wouldn't be visible from the house, she flicked on the Maglite she had taken from Simone and stuck the pistol into her front pocket. On her first day as a prisoner at the house, the Sisters had given her a pair of loose-fitting trousers and a beige long-sleeved T-shirt to wear; the same clothes she was wearing now. It was cool in the woods and goosebumps rippled across her arms, the fine hairs there standing erect.

*Stay calm, Kate. You can do this.*

She headed into the trees, with no idea of the best direction to take. But she decided to try to go in a straight line, to get as far away from the house as possible. She didn't know how deep the woods were. Were there animals living here? Were there bears in California? She remembered asking Tosca McCarthy that question, on the car journey to the lab, but she couldn't remember the answer. It seemed like a lifetime ago already. All she could recall was him hamming it up, singing 'Lions and tigers and bears—oh my!' Poor Tosca. What a waste of a life. A twig cracked behind her, and she jumped—but it was only a squirrel, flying up a tree so fast its feet seemed to barely touch the bark.

Don't be frightened of animals, she said under her breath. It's the Sisters you need to be afraid of. She had a horrible sense of danger lurking close by. Hearing rustling in the trees somewhere to her right, she stopped dead, breathing hard. She tried to tell herself it was only squirrels, or birds, but her legs felt like jelly. The woods were so dark and in the torchlight the twisted branches of trees seemed to be reaching towards her, trying to grab hold of her; faces appeared out of nowhere, shapes on tree trunks morphed into mouths frozen mid-scream.

Kate leaned against a tree, taking deep breaths and counting to ten. She felt utterly paralysed by something deep inside her, a primitive fear of this dark, forbidding place, even though she had barely gone any distance into the wood. Telling herself to get a grip, she tried to picture what this place would look like in the daytime with sunlight streaming through the pretty trees, casting its rays upon half-concealed woodland flowers, maybe a deer stopping to nibble at a patch of grass. The image made her feel better.

Regaining her strength, drawing on that kernel of determination at her core, she carried on, shining the torch on the ground, using it to pick out a safe path over gnarled tree roots. She thought about Jack, pictured his happy face. He was such a good boy, even if he had inherited his father's habit of whining if things didn't go his way. Over the last year, she'd developed a sense that he was growing up fast, that he wasn't her baby any more. If I don't get through this, she thought, I will never see him again. He will grow up without a mum.

*If Watoto doesn't get him first*, a voice whispered

in her ear.

She shook away the thought. But she had no idea what had been going on in the outside world since she'd left the lab. How far and fast had the virus spread? How long did she have to find a cure?

*Just concentrate on getting out, Kate.*

She put her head down and carried on, accustomed to the chill now, her heartbeat slowing to a steady pace. Her senses were heightened, like those of an animal. Every sound around her, every brush of a leaf or branch on her face made her flinch.

After a while, she became aware that her back was aching from being so tense and that the sky was getting lighter. She could now make out shapes without the torch. Dawn was breaking. Right on cue, the woodland birds began to wake up, and the sound of their chirruping and cawing warmed her, gave her hope.

Until she realised how much easier it would be for the Sisters to find her in daylight. She still hadn't heard any sign of them pursuing her. Perhaps they were still in their beds. The shout she'd heard must have been a false alarm. Perhaps Simone had come to and, deciding on a change of plan, shot them all in their beds—just as Angelica had told her they'd done to the people at the lab.

More likely, though, they were waiting for first light to look for her, assuming she wouldn't have got far in the dark. And now the woods were springing to life before her eyes, emerging from beneath the cloak of darkness like a Polaroid picture developing before her eyes.

She felt very scared again.

Ahead of her was a clearing, about six metres in

327

diameter; Kate entered it and paused. How far into the woods had she come? It was impossible to tell, neither could she judge how far it was to the road Simone had told her about, or what direction it was. She was reasonably confident she'd been heading in a straight line, but it was equally possible she'd been walking in a circle. Maybe she could climb a tree, try to get a better look, although it would take ages and . . .

She heard a voice.

A female voice, somewhere behind her. Perhaps two voices, one of them issuing orders.

Oh . . . fuck.

Trying not to panic, she started to jog, heading out of the clearing into the thicker trees, away from the voices. It was much lighter now, and she dropped the torch, needing her hands to push aside thick undergrowth as she forged her way deeper into the woods. A few minutes later she cursed herself for dropping the torch: if the women found it, it would tell them where she'd been.

I'm going to die, she thought, and was almost overwhelmed by an urge to lie down and give in. But she forced herself to take more deep breaths, squeezed her eyes shut and counted to five, found that inner strength and kept going.

She heard a woman's voice again, swearing, like she had caught herself on something sharp. Kate hoped it was something really sharp. She jogged faster, sensing that the trees were thinning ahead of her. Hope flared violently inside her. Please let it be the road, she prayed.

But it was only another clearing, with a thin stream running through it, filled with muddy water. A steep bank angled down towards the stream, with a matching bank on the other side. She was going to have to descend the bank and jump across, or follow the stream left or right, hoping she could cross it at an easier point. She heard movement not far behind her. Oh God . . . She couldn't risk being this exposed. She had to cross.

Tentatively, she began to descend, placing her feet sideways, using her arms for balance. One step, two steps, three. Then, without warning, the mud beneath her feet crumbled and she lurched forward, windmilling her arms before landing flat on her face in the water. She immediately pulled herself out—no real harm done—but she was soaking wet now. There was water in her shoes, her trousers, her underwear, dripping off the ends of her hair. She spat muddy water and began to climb up the other bank.

Until she heard a voice.

'Where is that bitch? Those footsteps sounded close.'

Kate froze. She couldn't see her but she identified the voice, mainly through a process of elimination as she knew the other women's voices better. It was Brandi. Kate hopped back over the stream in an ungainly crouching position and flattened herself against the bank she had just descended.

She won't be able to see me from where she's standing, Kate thought. But if she starts to come down the slope, I'm dead.

Unless . . .

She reached into her pocket for Simone's pistol. It wasn't there.

Her stomach lurched and she looked down. There it was—lying in the stream, an inch below the rippling water, gleaming like a black stone. It was only a few feet away, but if she stepped across to get it she would expose herself to the woman above.

She went down on her knees, wishing she could bury herself in the dirt. She couldn't hear Brandi. Had she gone? She didn't dare breathe. Instead, she counted: one, two, three, four, deciding that if she reached twenty she would risk it, she would creep across to the stream and retrieve the gun. Twelve, thirteen, fourteen. She braced herself. Fifteen, sixteen . . .

'Well,' Brandi said. 'Look who it is.'

## 49

Harley shook Paul awake, his hand on his shoulder.

'Uh. Kate . . .?' Paul's eyes were glued shut with sleep and his back and neck ached from where he'd slept sitting up in the passenger seat, his chin on his chest. Outside the car, the moon was full and bright and a chorus of cicadas throbbed in the background.

'Sorry, Paul. I'm your less attractive partner.' He handed Paul a polystyrene cup of steaming, flavourless coffee that Johnston, the prison guard, had fetched for him while they waited. 'But I've got good news—clearance for Diaz to be released has just come through. Johnston's bringing him out now.'

'Finally! Thought we'd have to hang around here for ever.' Paul sipped the coffee. He needed to pee, badly. 'Have you heard anything about Kate? Have they found her?'

'No—not yet.'

They had agreed that their first priority should be to get Diaz working on the vaccine, rather than joining in the search for Kate and Junko. Not that Paul felt up to doing much of anything right now. It was as if something nasty had crawled into his mouth while he slept and made a nest in his throat. He swallowed and it hurt, and his nose felt bunged up. His head throbbed.

'You OK?' Harley asked, eyebrows scrunched with concern.

'Yeah.' Just tiredness. Please let it just be tiredness. 'Feeling like crap after a night in this luxury accommodation.'

Harley smiled then looked over his shoulder. 'Here comes our man.'

\*       \*       \*

Half an hour later, the three of them were sitting in a diner. They were the only customers. They had driven past half a dozen closed diners and restaurants and a deserted McDonald's Drive-Thru before finding this place. The sole member of staff, who Paul guessed must be the proprietor, appeared to be trying to carry on as if everything was normal.

'None of my staff turned up this morning,' he said before taking their orders. 'None of my regulars neither. But life goes on, huh? What can I get you folks?'

Diaz, who was close to drooling as he perused the menu, ordered the biggest breakfast available. Harley opted for granola and yoghurt. The only thing Paul wanted was a decent cup of coffee. He was feeling increasingly rough as the morning went on. But he tried to ignore it, to focus.

'Tell us about Mangold,' Harley said as they waited for their food. That had been Diaz's second demand: that they take him to see Mangold. Paul had almost punched the air—this old man knew where Charles Mangold was. He had been following the right trail.

'Down to business. I like that.' Diaz laughed and clapped his hands as the proprietor put their drinks on the table. 'You already know, I assume, that Mangold and I worked together at Medi-Lab? We were partners. But when the company got closed down, Mangold put all the blame on me. He said I had been solely responsible for conducting the research. That I was the one who had breached bio-security protocols and let the virus escape from the lab. All bullshit. But Mangold was the man with the money, the reputation, the connections. Not some Mexican lab-monkey like me. So when they needed a scapegoat, naturally they targeted me.'

'I don't understand,' Paul said.

Diaz leaned forward. 'There were things in that lab . . . valuable research. Knowledge. Things that the US Government wanted to get hold of.' He tapped the side of his nose.

Paul looked at Harley, expecting him to scoff at this, to refute the conspiracy theories, but instead he nodded.

His voice shaky, Paul said, 'Including Watoto and its cure?'

Diaz grinned. 'No, no—that was our secret. Project Hadza. There were other viruses, a whole cocktail bar of designer diseases. We were breaking new ground all the time. We were the best.'

332

Paul felt himself go cold inside. This would have been around the time that Gaunt was running the labs at the Cold Research Unit, using it as a cover for his secret experiments with deadly viruses—research that had been financed by Mangold. The CRU and Medi-Lab were almost like twin labs, one on each side of the Atlantic. And now Diaz was saying that the US Government had been involved in a cover-up.

'So . . . what? They hired Mangold and put all the blame on you?'

'Exactly,' Diaz nodded, pointing a gnarled finger. 'And they sent me away so I couldn't talk about it. That's why they gave me such a long sentence.'

'Mangold was working for the Government?' Harley said.

Paul turned to him. 'I can't believe you didn't know that already.'

'Of course I didn't.'

Paul stared at him. He didn't know who, or what, to believe.

'Do you want to hear the rest of it, or are you going to keep sniping at each other all day?' snapped Diaz. He paused to make sure he had their undivided attention, then continued: 'I didn't hear from or about Mangold for several years. Then, out of the blue, he called me. Asking for help.'

The diner's proprietor came over with their food. The benefits of being the only customers: hyper-fast service.

'Help?' Harley asked. 'With what?'

Diaz savoured a mouthful of egg, served sunny side up. 'This is the best meal I've had in years. You've no idea—'

Impatient, Paul tapped the table with his fork.

333

Kate was out there, in danger, maybe even dead already—please, God, don't let that be true—and this old man was more interested in his breakfast.

'OK, OK. Mangold was experimenting with a virus, something called Pyrovirus. And it had gone wrong—he had contracted it himself, and he had no vaccine. He was so desperate that he called me, begging for my assistance. Of course, I told him to fuck off.'

'But he survived?' Paul asked.

'Yes. But the rest of his family—his wife, his daughter—caught it and died. All except his granddaughter.'

'And what was her name?' asked Paul.

Diaz took another mouthful of his breakfast. He didn't answer straight away.

'Watoto broke out on an Indian reservation, didn't it? That's where Mangold will have unleashed it, knowing that visitors to the casino would catch it and spread it far and wide. I checked on a map after I first heard about the outbreak: that reservation is very close to the town where Mangold's daughter Tara lived, a place called Feverfew. It can't be a coincidence. That must be where Mangold is living.'

They rose to leave, Harley paying the bill on the way out.

'You didn't tell us the granddaughter's name, the one who survived,' Paul said.

'Oh—didn't I? Pretty little thing, she was, when she was a kid. Her name was Angelica.'

## 50

Brandi stood at the top of the bank, looking down at Kate, a smile on her lips and a gun in her hand.

'Nice try, Doctor. But Sekhmet is waiting for you.' She gestured with the gun. 'Come on.'

Kate glanced back at the stream. Could she grab the gun before Brandi shot her? And would it even be working now?

'What the fuck are you waiting for? Get back up here now or I'll sacrifice you right here myself.'

'Angelica wouldn't like that,' Kate said. 'Neither would the Goddess. She'd be displeased with you.'

Brandi's face twisted with anger and she pointed the gun at Kate's head.

'How dare you speak about—'

She didn't finish the sentence. Kate watched with shock as Brandi tumbled down the bank and landed beside her.

Sticking from her back was a hunting knife.

'I didn't enjoy that,' Simone said, skipping down the bank as steadily as a mountain goat. She had a bruise on her forehead from where Kate had hit her with the gun. She noticed Kate looking at it. 'You didn't hit me very hard. I was out for ten minutes. When I got back to the house the old man had woken Angelica up but she couldn't understand what in hell he was raving about. Then she saw me and I had to pretend to collapse, to buy you more time.'

'Thank you.'

'Ain't no thing. I liked Brandi. She was cool, y'know?' Simone gazed at the dead woman, lying face down in the stream, her hair snaking like weeds on the surface of the water. She crouched to pick the gun out of the water. 'I think you've fucked this piece.'

'Sorry,' Kate said quietly, unable to take her eyes off Brandi's corpse. So much death. And she was still in danger.

'I need to get you the fuck outta here,' Simone said. 'Before Angelica and Preeti find us.'

Kate hesitated. 'There are only two of them now. Why don't we stand and fight?'

Simone looked at her like she was crazy. 'You and me take on Angelica? Uh-uh. Sorry, honey, but you're too much of a liability, and she's ex-CIA, she can handle weapons like you wouldn't believe. I need to get you outta here. Follow me. And try not to fall on your ass.'

She led Kate up the bank, checking back over her shoulder every few seconds.

Kate heard voices. 'Oh my God, they're coming.'

Simone grabbed her hand. 'Quick.'

She led Kate into a thick patch of trees, ducking and weaving in order to avoid the branches and keep as quiet as possible. Kate followed suit. She heard a cry of dismay from behind her and realised Angelica and Preeti had found Brandi. Simone paused and looked back.

'Shit. I don't know if we're gonna be able to outrun them.' She looked around, in search of inspiration. 'OK, follow me, we're gonna double back.'

'What?'

'Just do as I say. And keep moving.'

They took a turn to the left, struggled through more thick undergrowth before hitting a path.

336

Simone broke into a run, Kate following, adrenaline giving her speed. She couldn't hear Angelica or Preeti but expected them to burst out of the trees at any moment. They kept running until Kate's lungs burned and her legs ached. Sweat soaked her back and dripped into her eyes. But she kept going.

Simone veered off to the left, leading them back in the general direction of the ranch. They crossed the stream at a point where it was only a foot wide, but Kate was so tired that she almost slipped in her wet shoes, and barely avoided falling in again.

'I need to rest,' she panted.

'You want them to catch us? Come on, Kate. You got a son, yeah? You wanna see him again?'

Yes, yes, I do. More than anything, Kate thought, and sheer determination kept her going, back through the trees until, eventually, they were in the open again, on the lawn that ran down to the ranch.

'Keep a lookout for the old guy,' Simone said.

They jogged towards the house. There was no one in sight.

Kate didn't understand why they were going back to the ranch—surely that was the least safe place of all. Maybe they were going to get weapons. Or call the police. But then she realised Simone was leading her to the stables. They stopped outside the stable door and Simone pulled it open, disappearing inside after saying, 'Wait here.'

A long five minutes later—during which Kate pictured her own death at gunpoint many times—she reappeared, leading a beautiful chestnut horse with a white blaze on his nose, and white fetlocks. The horse eyed Kate dismissively.

'This is Egypt,' Simone said. 'She was Cindy's horse.' A darkness crossed Simone's face and Kate had a horrible feeling that Simone was about to change her mind and exact revenge for the awful death Kate had condemned Cindy to.

Instead, she said, 'You know how to ride, don't you?'

## 51

Heather opened her eyes and was hit by a wave of pain like an electric drill grinding into her skull. It was dark and it took her a moment to remember where she was; then it came back to her and she pushed herself on to all fours, the motion causing a lurch of sickness and a second blast of white-hot pain.

She wiped the vomit from her chin and let herself breathe for a few moments, feeling the pain, riding a third wave as it pulsed through her body. It was like surfing; you just had to take control, harness the power. Take the pain and make somebody else pay.

Those bitches.

The motherfuckers who had attacked her and stolen her car.

*The whole damned world.*

She pushed herself to her feet, staggered, closed her eyes and found her centre of gravity. After the attackers had left her for dead, she had lain unconscious for a long time—she didn't know how long. At one point she had awoken and, like a wounded coyote, crawled into the nearest building, an abandoned warehouse.

Now it was dark outside, and she surveyed the spot where her SUV had stood. Long gone, along with the two bitches, the hot daughter and the once-hot mother. Had the gangbangers taken them, or had they got away? Hopefully they were already dead.

She wandered for a while, disoriented and hungry. She came across a locked up grocery store and smashed her way in, liberating a large bottle of Sprite and a pack of smokes, along with a couple of Snickers bars that she stuffed greedily into her face. There were flies buzzing around and she realised that the mom and pop who ran this place might not have deserted it. Curious, she checked upstairs and, sure enough, there they were—in bed together, stiff, cold and surrounded by used Kleenex.

In their tiny kitchen, she found a lovely new knife with a six-inch blade. She tested it on her forefinger and sucked the blood.

A thought struck her and, back downstairs, she checked under the counter. Yes. As she had hoped, there was a baseball bat, kept to deter robbers. The first weapon she'd ever used, back when she was eleven and her little sister's cat had peed on her bed, the last time it had ever peed anywhere.

Now all she needed was a car.

Leaving the store, with the bat held over her shoulder, she spotted a beautiful car across the street, a white Porsche Cayman, with the hood up. There was a woman sitting in the passenger seat and a man in his thirties bent over the engine, a look of blank incomprehension on his face. The woman in the car—a glossy, rich-looking bitch— kept sticking her head out the window and talking to the guy, which made his face contort with irritation. Heather strode over.

'Problem?' she said, as she reached the car.

The guy, who Heather vaguely recognised, looked her up and down—a dismissive look she had been on the receiving end of her whole life. 'We're good, thanks.'

Heather pulled a face and leaned under the hood, pressing her shoulder against the guy's. 'Doesn't look too good to me.'

She could see the problem—a loose cable. Elementary stuff, but this guy was probably used to getting his ass wiped for him. She clucked her tongue. 'Shit, looks pretty fucked to me.'

'Really?' He turned his face towards her. He was interested in what she had to say now.

A whining voice came from the car. 'Ryan, what's going on? I feel sick.'

'Chill, babe,' he said. 'We're trying to fix the goddamn car. Piece of shit. Should have stuck with the Lamborghini.'

Heather smiled to herself. This was going to feel good. She pointed to the cable. 'Check this out.'

As Ryan scrutinised it blankly, she stood upright, swiftly pulled away the metal support arm and yanked down on the hood with all her considerable strength.

It smashed on the back of Ryan's neck, breaking it. His body jerked like someone had shoved a thousand volts up his ass, then went still. Heather lifted the hood just enough to pull him out, his head flopping like a rag doll's as she chucked him to the ground, then casually plugged the loose cable back in

'What the hell?' the woman in the passenger seat

340

screeched. She pressed the button to wind up the window but the engine was off. Heather grabbed her by her perfect hair, pulled her head through the window and whipped her newly-procured knife out of her back pocket.

'Please,' whined the woman. 'I have money. I can give you anything. I'm famous.'

Heather was not in a good mood. She had been left for dead by those gangbanger motherfuckers, she'd lost the bitches, Paul freaking Wilson was way ahead of her and someone had jacked her car. Forgetting her own role in the spread of the virus, she blamed Los Angeles. She had always hated this fucking city, with its New Age crap, its endless influx of pretty little things, the bullshit movies, even the fucking roads. And this whinging, rich, privileged princess—whoever the fuck she was, pop star, model, actress, what-the-fuck-ever—represented at this very moment the whole stinking city.

Saying 'I'm famous' was not the smartest move ever.

Heather opened the door and dragged the princess out by her blonde hair, throwing her to the ground. The bitch lay on her back, staring up at Heather, who stood astride her, thumping the baseball bat against her open palm.

'Take off your clothes,' Heather commanded.

'What?'

'Why do dumb sluts like you always do that? I tell them to do something and they say "What?" Take off your clothes. All of them. Let me see those famous tits of yours.'

As this scene unfolded, both women became aware of a group of young men appear from round

341

the corner, six of them, holding back, watching. Baseball caps, shades, menacing scowls. They didn't look like they were on their way home from Sunday School.

Sobbing and sniffing, the blonde took off her clothes, hesitating before removing her bra, until Heather pointed the knife at her and said, 'Do you want me to cut that thing off?'

Heather swallowed. Fake tits. Still hot, though, not as hot as Angelica.

'Lie on your front,' she said.

The woman obeyed.

Aware of the men watching from the corner, Heather crouched beside the princess and grabbed her by the calf, holding her down. Using her new knife, she sliced through her Achilles tendons, first the left, then the right.

The famous princess screamed.

Heather stepped over her and climbed into the Porsche. The keys were in the ignition. Good. She looked out at the blonde, rolling around in a pool of her own blood. The men were coming closer now, like hyenas waiting for the lion to leave the zebra for dead.

'Have fun,' Heather called out the window, and the roar of the engine drowned out the woman's screams.

She drove through the city, feeling a little better.

The Porsche was exactly like the car Cindy had driven, the one that Heather had coveted for so long. Angelica had favoured Cindy, even though Heather had been her best friend back when they were kids. When the playground bullies picked on Angelica, it had been Heather who came to her rescue. All through her long recovery after the illness that killed her parents, Heather had been there for her. She'd have gone on being there for her, but after school Angelica left town to start a new, secret, Heather-free life. Unable to face being in Sagebrush without her, Heather had joined the Marine Corps Women's Reserves. And she'd almost succeeded in forgetting her best friend, until two years ago, when Angelica showed up again. With plans. Plans that involved Heather, in a starring role, and the love she had felt all those years ago, that had been hiding dormant somewhere inside of her, bloomed like blood on a white sheet.

Angelica had first mentioned Sekhmet after the sickness that almost killed her. That was when the visions had begun. Heather would listen, enjoying the stories—thinking that was all they were. And, although she would never admit it, she still thought they were only stories. But what stories! And look what they had done, causing all this—she gazed out across the great city of deserted streets, smouldering embers, fires and sirens and the dead and dying. All this was real. Very real.

Now Cindy was dead. She had been weak, unlike Heather, who was a survivor. Soon, when there was nobody left, when all the men and all the beautiful women were gone, she would take her place beside Angelica. Then finally Angelica would see what she had been missing all these years.

She took out her phone, which had both a sliver of juice left and a sliver of signal, and called Angelica. The phone rang a dozen times, and Heather—who had lost all track of time—realised Angelica was probably asleep. She was about to hang up when she heard that honey-and-barbed-wire voice:

'Hello?'

Angelica sounded so upset that Heather wanted to reach through the phone and embrace her. 'What's the matter?'

The answer came in a torrent that Heather struggled to make sense of: 'It's a test, Sister, that's all. Sekhmet is testing me one final time before the End Times finish, to make sure I—we—are all worthy of her. We have to prove ourselves worthy of her. This is the last hurdle, I'm sure of it. She couldn't just hand us the Golden Age on a plate, no, no, that wouldn't be right, would it? The future of the entire civilisation of the world is at stake here, of course she's going to push us to the brink, isn't she?'

'Yes, of course,' Heather agreed, a frown deepening in her forehead. 'What's happened?'

'Maddox has escaped.'

'How the fuck did she get out?'

'I've been asking the Goddess for answers, but she won't answer. Maddox killed Brandi—knifed her in the back and left her dead in a ditch.'

For all that she had liked Brandi, Heather felt no emotion whatsoever at the news of her death. 'Don't worry,' she soothed. 'I'll be back at the ranch by morning, and I'll help you find Maddox—she won't have got far. Stay calm, Dadi. Like you say, this is just a test. Everything's going to plan. *Om Shanti.*'

'*Om Shanti*, Sister Heather. Thank you. May the Goddess go with you.'

\*         \*         \*

344

An hour later, Heather arrived at the prison gates.

'Camilo Diaz? Well, ain't he just the most popular guy on the block,' said the voice on the intercom at the gate. 'You've missed him. He got let out. Guess they need scientists at the moment.'

'Did he go with a man called Paul?' Heather asked, inwardly cursing the fucking gangbangers who'd screwed it all up for her.

'I'm sorry, who are you?' the crackly voice enquired.

'Never mind,' said Heather, crashing the car into reverse and executing a furious three-point turn.

She parked outside a deserted McDonald's Drive-Thru and thought about what to do next. With no way of knowing where Diaz had been taken, her best course of action would be to head back to the ranch. At least there she could help Angelica and the others hunt down Maddox.

Then she would scalp her, gut her and leave what was left of her out for the birds. Make the bitch pay for this wasted trip. A few hours of torture would make her feel so much better.


52


The horse was huge. It was chestnut-coloured, with a distinctive white flash on its face, and stood around sixteen hands high. Kate had no chance of getting her foot anywhere near the stirrup that bumped against its fat middle. She'd nodded when Simone asked if she could ride, but she hadn't been on a horse for twenty-five years at least.

She remembered trotting around a paddock on a compliant piebald pony at the age of about ten rising up and down obediently in the saddle on the command of the instructor, calling 'Walk on!' in a shrill voice.

This was a whole other kettle of fish.

Simone locked her fingers together and stuck them near Kate's knees. 'Hurry. I'll give you a leg-up then I have to go, and so do you. Angelica will kill me if she sees us. Turn left out of the gate and keep going for about three miles—you'll come to a place called Feverfew. Keep out of sight as much as you can.'

Kate grabbed the saddle, put her left foot into Simone's hands, and just about managed to swing her right leg over the horse's back, scrabbling to slide into the saddle properly. She still only had one foot in the stirrup, and was practically lying on her stomach across the horse, clutching handfuls of its mane, when Simone slapped it hard on the rump and it set off at an unfocused canter towards the ranch gate. Kate didn't have time to thank Simone, and didn't dare swivel round to wave her gratitude—all her energy was concentrated on not falling off.

'Egypt!' she gasped. 'Slow down!' It felt like she was on a bucking bronco in some Western movie. She managed to grab one of the reins and pulled, but Egypt immediately started to turn—back towards the ranch. 'Shit! No, not that way!' she begged, gathering up the other rein and heaving on them both. Egypt snorted furiously at her, but straightened up and slowed to a trot. Kate made a monumental effort to get in synch with her mount. 'Up, down, up, down, up, down,' she chanted to herself, as Egypt careened out of the gate and turned left of his own accord, much to Kate's relief, as she was pretty sure that, had he wanted to go in the other direction, there wouldn't have been much she could have done to persuade him otherwise.

She pondered Simone's words, as she and Egypt settled into an uneasy sort of rhythm on the empty road: *Keep out of sight*. How the hell was she meant to do that, on a horse this size, if a car came by? Forest pressed in on either side of the road, too dense to try and manoeuvre a big horse through.

After a few minutes, during which time Kate's thighs and buttocks started to ache violently at the shock of the unfamiliar exercise, she saw a road sign: FEVERFEW—1 MILE.

'OK, good, nearly there,' she panted, risking taking both reins in one hand to give Egypt a brief pat on the neck. 'Good boy.' His flesh felt hot, as did hers—the sun was beating down on her bare head and forearms. She allowed herself a moment to relish freedom and the great outdoors after days of being locked up at the ranch and, before that, stuck in the lab. The air was so fresh up there, especially after the grim taint of Junko's final breaths, and the too-recent memory of all the other deaths she had witnessed over the past week. Poor Junko, she thought again. She vowed to do whatever she could to give her a proper funeral, when all this was over. If it ever would be over . . .

Shaking off the maudlin thought, Kate forced herself back to the present. What did she need to do when she got into town? She had no money, phone or ID on her—would there be a police station there? All she needed really was a phone, to make a reverse charge call to Paul. But then how would she *get* to him? Were buses and trains still running? She hoped he had escaped from California and had somehow got to Dallas to be with Jack. 'We might have to ride to Dallas, my friend,' she said to Egypt. 'Best conserve your energy.' She refused to even allow the thought that Paul might be sick, or dead.

She heard the sound of a car engine behind her in the distance, and froze in the saddle. Were they coming after her already?

Desperately she yanked on Egypt's reins, trying to haul him off the road but, as she'd already suspected, the forest was too thick. Egypt couldn't figure out what she was doing, and reared up angrily, catching Kate's arm on the spiky point of a branch, ripping a long deep cut across her forearm near her elbow. There would be no point in trying to outrun them on horseback. There was nowhere else to go.

Kate was about to jump off the horse and run into the forest when suddenly the vehicle rounded the corner and was upon her, a rattly old pick-up truck driven by an enormously fat man wearing a face mask and denim overalls. He slowed down and stared curiously at Kate, but did not stop, leaving her shaking like a leaf, blood dripping down her arm, feeling as though she was going to throw up. She spurred Egypt into a canter, praying that there would be no more unexpected surprises.

The forest began to thin out, and Kate turned a corner to see a valley below her, with a few blocks of houses on either side of what passed for a main street. There was a crossroads, and a railroad track, and not a lot else. The chances of finding a police station were slim to none, she decided.

348

'Stay still a minute,' she instructed Egypt, pulling on the reins. He shuffled his big feet, complaining, but obeyed. Kate examined her arm, which was beginning to throb badly. The cut was oozing blood at a steady rate, soaking through the beige three-quarter sleeved top that Brandi had brought her when she first came to the ranch and that, along with the matching beige cotton pants and espadrilles two sizes too large, she'd been wearing ever since. She needed a bandage.

She yanked hard at the seam on the blood-stained sleeve, but nothing happened. Cursing, Kate tucked the reins under her leg to keep them at hand, and peeled off the top, clenching the saddle hard between her aching thighs to maintain her balance. She was past fretting about whether anyone would see her sitting on a horse in her bra—in the current circumstances people had more important things to worry about, like trying to avoid catching Watoto. At least that was one problem she didn't have. This was the second time she felt grateful for having caught it as a kid, after she'd discovered that Gaunt tried to kill her with it at the Cold Research Unit.

Using both hands, Kate was able to tug hard enough to rip the sleeve right off the thin top. She wrapped it several times around the cut, tying the ends and using her teeth to pull the knot tight. The fabric smelled of the ranch—a sweet, faintly cloying scent of lily and incense, and it made her shudder. She tried to pull off the other sleeve too, but the stitching held firm and wouldn't budge, so she put the top back on as it was. Feeling more conspicuous than ever in her one-sleeved top, she picked up the reins again, kicked Egypt into motion and rode into town.

The clip-clopping of Egypt's hooves was the only sound penetrating the eerie silence. Kate felt like a cowboy in a Western movie. Main Street was deserted. Every establishment she rode past was closed. There was a small restaurant, a bank, a drug store, a store selling crafts and—ah! She spotted a phone booth on the corner outside a tiny cinema.

She steered Egypt towards it, throwing the reins over the top of the Perspex hood of the booth to tether him, and leaned down in the saddle far enough to reach the receiver. Wedging it between her shoulder and ear, she managed to punch in the numbers 011 8000 REVERSE that she had taught Jack to use in case of emergency, though she had never had cause to do it herself during all those years she lived in the US, gripping on to the hood with her free hand to keep her balance while Egypt fidgeted beneath her. Out of the corner of her eye she saw a white Porsche pull up behind her, but paid no attention to the muscly woman with short dark hair who climbed out of the car, and didn't notice how the woman's cold eyes fixed unmovingly on her back.

## 53

Paul waited outside the diner, beside the car. Diaz was in the back seat, dozing after his huge breakfast, his hands on his belly, while Harley paced up and down talking into his phone. Paul could only make out snatches of the conversation, the occasional exclamation of surprise. Finally, he put the phone away and came over to Paul, shaking his head.

'Well?' Paul asked impatiently. 'Do you know where he is?' He was by now convinced that if Mangold was behind the outbreak, he must have Kate. He would have been behind the bomb at the hotel, and the raid on the lab. Paul didn't know who else was involved—was Mangold's granddaughter somehow mixed up in this too?—but there was no doubt that Mangold had achieved even more than his old buddy Gaunt in unleashing hell upon this earth. Paul bounced from foot to foot, desperate to get moving.

'We have an address for Mangold's late daughter, Tara—a ranch outside Feverfew, in Cherry Valley, about a hundred miles from here. And get this—' Paul sneezed and Harley looked at him in alarm. 'Are you feeling all right?'

'Yes, I'm fine. It's . . . an allergy, that's all.'

Harley backed away, trying to make it look like he wasn't scared. 'OK. Well, listen to this—I ran the name Angelica Mangold, to see if the address was registered as hers, and an alert came up. That's what took so long: I had to wait for someone from the Agency to call me back.'

'The Agency?'

'Yes, the CIA. Angelica Mangold was a CIA officer. And she's been missing for the past two years. Presumed dead, in fact. She was operating overseas—in Tanzania—and broke contact. Nobody has seen or heard from her since then.'

Paul scratched his head. His scalp was so sensitive that even the slight rake of his fingernails hurt. 'So, according to Diaz, Mangold was recruited by the US Government to help them develop

351

viruses—biological weapons, in other words. And judging from your reaction, that doesn't strike you as too far-fetched. No, don't interrupt. And now we find out his granddaughter was working for the CIA. My God.'

He sneezed again. His body was screaming at him: go to bed, rest, turn out the lights. And he was scared. If he had Watoto, the clock was ticking fast. They had to get Diaz to Mangold fast, so Diaz would give up the cure. And if Diaz messed them around, they would just have to extract the information from Mangold, using whatever methods Harley and his colleagues had at their disposal.

He found a tissue in his pocket and blew his nose, then opened the car door. 'So we've got the address—come on, let's go.'

Harley walked round the car and climbed in. 'Mangold's daughter died years back, but there's no record of the property being sold.'

'Did you say it's a hundred miles away? That'll take what—ninety minutes? Can't you get us a helicopter or something?'

Harley sighed. 'It would take as long for it to get to us—assuming there'd be one free. They're all being used for border patrols and to airlift sick VIPs to out-of-state clinics.'

'For pity's sake.'

'I know, right.'

'Well, you'd better drive fast.'

As he sank into the passenger seat, Paul's head was thumping with pain, his throat full of razor blades. How much worse would he feel in an hour or two, by the time they got to Mangold's ranch?

352

The answer crept up slowly as they covered the miles between Long Beach and Feverfew, Harley driving, not saying much. In the back, Camilo rolled the window down and stuck his head out like a dog. At least somebody's happy, Paul thought miserably.

With each passing mile, he felt more and more sick. In his increasingly feverish imagination he could picture the virus populating his body like an invading army, battling his beleaguered defence force of antibodies, slaying them in silent combat, advancing on all fronts. His head was Baghdad under aerial bombardment, his nose and eyes were the damp trenches of Belgium, his skin burned like a napalm-scorched jungle. He shivered in the passenger seat, barely aware of the passing scenery, occasionally opening his eyes to take in the deserted highways, cars parked by the roadside with the bodies of entire families inside, nightmarish visions that might or might not have been hallucinations. At one point, they passed a line of tanks, a helicopter floating above them, but then minutes later he was unsure whether he'd imagined it.

He dozed. In his shallow sleep, he dreamed he was a soldier in some unnamed war zone, far from home, the dead and dying all around him. He was writing a letter to his sweetheart, telling her how much he missed her, how he wanted to come home soon. Stephen was there, lying on the bunk next to his. A telephone was ringing not too far away. Stephen appeared to be sleeping, but when Paul looked closer he saw that his brother's skin was charred black, his hair burnt to the roots, the stench of cooking meat rising off him. Suddenly his eyelids sprang open and his eyeballs swivelled towards Paul, then he opened his grotesque, lipless mouth, and said, 'Hey, are you going to answer that?'

Paul opened his eyes, with no idea where he was. He could hardly breathe. But the phone was still ringing.

Harley said, 'Are you going to answer it?'

Paul groped in his pocket and pulled out the iPhone. It had two per cent of charge left. He thumbed the screen and said, 'Hello?'

A robotic voice said, 'You are being called reverse charge by—' and then Paul heard the sweet, sweet sound of Kate, saying her own name. 'Do you accept the charges?'

'Yes, yes, YES,' Paul said, as loudly and clearly as his aching throat and fuzzy head would allow. Just hearing her name cut right through the fuzziness like a shot of pure adrenaline.

'Oh, Paul, Paul . . . It's so good to hear your voice.'

'Kate, baby, my darling, how are you? Where are you?'

Beside him, Harley jerked to attention.

'I'm in a place called Feverfew. I—'

She stopped talking and he thought she must have got cut off. But then he heard another voice, a woman's voice. He couldn't make out what she said.

'Kate? Hello? Hello?'

She was gone. He threw the phone down into the footwell with frustration and anger. His body was rocked by a sneeze.

In the back seat, Diaz said, 'Was that the famous

Dr Maddox?'

Paul was too upset to reply.

Harley asked him gently, 'Where did she say she is?'

'Feverfew.'

Harley nodded excitedly. 'Bingo.' He floored the accelerator and they hit 100 mph on the empty road. 'We're almost there. Let's go and get her.'

## 54

After twenty hours almost continuous driving, it was fair to say that the novelty of life on the road had worn off. Jack and Bradley sat in the back of the car throughout the night, alternately dozing, playing on Bradley's DS, and randomly punching each other when the boredom became too overwhelming. An increasingly morose Riley sat hunched over the steering wheel, smoking out of the window and listening to vintage heavy metal CDs. By the time they reached Tucson, Bradley and Jack could sing most of the lyrics to 'Bring Your Daughter to the Slaughter'.

'Are we nearly there yet?' Bradley enquired, not for the first time, as they passed through Riverside with the Airstream rumbling along behind them.

'I swear to God, if you ask me that one more time, I will make you eat that frickin' DS,' Riley growled over his shoulder. 'Get some sleep—it's like five a.m.'

'But are we?'

Riley ignored him.

'Are we, Riley? We must be nearly there now. I

355

can't wait to see Dad, can you, Riley? Do you think he'll let me and Jack have a go on his motorbike? He's got a Triumph,' Bradley informed Jack.

'Cool,' Jack said. He too had been wondering when they would get there, or if this endless drive would somehow keep going, probably until he was an old man. If he'd known it would take this long, he never would have let Bradley talk him into it. It was only the thought of seeing his mum that stopped him from crying and demanding to be taken back to Dallas—although the worm of doubt twisting in his gut wouldn't go away. What if Riley didn't take him to the lab? What if he couldn't find it?

'Riley,' he ventured. 'Do you think your dad will know how to find my mum?'

'Jeez, you kids with your endless QUESTIONS! Brad, we are totally nearly there—seriously, we're about, like, one hour away. And Jack, yeah, I guess my dad will know. Kinda depends on whether or not he's sick. He's not answering his cellphone and he still hasn't called me back, and I've left a bunch of messages. He might be out of town but I know where he keeps the spare keys, so if he ain't there we can crash at his place till we figure out where your mom is.'

'What's he like?' Jack was curious.

'He's awesome,' said Bradley. 'He's got all this grey curly hair, and he's really really tall—'

Riley laughed. 'He's, like, five ten. That's not *tall*.'

'He's tall to me. And he plays guitar in a band, and he's famous because he makes movies, and he won an Oscar once.'

'What's an Oscar?'

'It's a golden statue about this big, and you get to be on TV when you win one, and he keeps it on top of the cabinet in his bathroom. Oh, and he has a sausage dog called Martha. He's nicer than your dad.'

Jack considered this. 'My dad's nice.'

'Hmm. Sometimes, maybe. But he yells a lot.'

'All dads yell.'

'Mine doesn't. Does he, Riley?'

'He might, when he realises that we've driven all this way when I should've taken you kids home,' said Riley, flicking his cigarette butt out of the window. He had decided against topping up the credit on his cellphone, to avoid any more aggressive calls from Vernon, or pleading ones from his mom.

The next time he turned round, both boys were fast asleep again, leaning into each other with their small heads resting together. Riley shook his head. 'Fucking kids,' he said to himself.

\*     \*     \*

Half an hour later Riley stuck an unlit cigarette behind his ear and whistled softly. 'Shit, check it out.'

Bradley and Jack woke up and looked. 'What's that?' Bradley asked.

'County border. It sure wasn't like this last time I went through.' He scratched his head. Great rolls of barbed wire had been wrapped round fence poles on either side of the road, stretching into the distance, and increasingly large signs issued warnings: 'LOS ANGELES COUNTY UNDER

357

QUARANTINE—NO ENTRY', 'OBSERVE BASIC HYGIENE', 'STAY HOME AND DO NOT PANIC' 'IF YOU GET SICK, CALL MEDI-DOC AND DO NOT LEAVE YOUR HOME'.

'No cars going the other way,' Riley observed. 'Means they ain't letting people in or out. Shit.'

Bradley gripped the back of Riley's seat. 'We can't get in?' he asked, in a very high-pitched voice, his bottom lip already trembling. Jack's heart sank into his sneakers. Surely they wouldn't have to turn round and go home, after all these hours of driving?

'Don't worry, kids. I have a plan,' Riley said, but he didn't sound too confident. He slowed the car and trailer right down as they approached the roadblock. An armed guard stopped them, a machine gun held tightly against his chest. The boys could see, on the other side of the roadblock, a huge queue of stationary vehicles, some honking their horns, people in masks leaning out of open windows. 'Don't say nothing, guys, or I will hurt you. Got it?'

'Got it,' chorused the boys.

'County's closed,' called the man with the gun, who was also wearing a mask. 'Go home.'

'Ah, sir?' Riley said, in a more polite voice than either of the boys had ever heard him use. 'Actually, we have to come in. My dad lives in, um, like a totally remote cabin in the Santa Monica Mountains and I have to get these here boys back to him. He's expecting us. He's stocked up on food and stuff. It's safe out there—his nearest neighbour's, like, forty miles away. Our mom wants us to go there so we don't get the virus.'

The guard leaned down so he could see in the car's rear windows. Bradley and Jack both smiled at him, but, even through the mask, they could see that he wasn't smiling back. His black skin gleamed with sweat, and his biceps were bigger than Jack's waist.

'I can't let you boys in,' he said, speaking loudly to be heard over the thumping of helicopter blades overhead. 'Got my orders.'

'It's not like we're going to LA or anything,' Riley protested. Bradley opened his mouth to correct him, but Jack pinched his leg hard, and he closed it again. 'Could you just check with your superior, sir? I mean, surely we'll all be safer in a cabin in the mountains than we would be anywhere else? These kids need to get someplace safe till this thing passes, and we've been driving for days now . . . Got no food left, and hardly any gas money neither. Could you consider making an exception for us? Please?'

The guard narrowed his eyes. He looked as though he was about to speak again, when the sound of a gunshot exploded next to them. He swung round to see one of his colleagues lying on the ground, just as a flatbed truck full of young, smartly dressed men smashed through the barrier and accelerated away at high speed, one of them still shooting out of the passenger window. The guard raced over to his colleague, while four or five other guards opened fire on the truck. The helicopter swooped down low, executed a 360-degree turn, and took off after them.

'Fuck,' said Riley. 'Frat boys gone mental. Get your heads down, and hold tight, now!'

In the commotion, nobody noticed as Riley put

his foot on the gas and did exactly the same as the truck had done, only in the opposite direction, without firearms and considerably more slowly, as he was dragging the Airstream in his wake. The car broke through the barrier with a crack, and Riley drove as fast as he could into LA County, hunched down in his seat.

'Riley!' screeched Bradley. 'They've got guns, they're gonna kill us, what are you DOING?'

'Shut up and keep down!' Riley yelled back.

But there was no sound of further gunshots. No helicopter, no sirens, no police cars. Riley drove on, forcing the ancient car's engine up to sixty miles per hour, as it strained and complained in a high-pitched whine that drowned out the sound of the boys' fearful sobs.

After fifteen minutes of anxiously looking in the wing mirrors, Riley finally slowed down. 'Shit. We only friggin' made it,' he crowed, slapping the steering wheel. 'Come out, boys, we're in!'

'We're in!' echoed the boys weakly, as they scrambled back up to their seat, white with shock and tension. 'Nobody shot at us!' said Bradley, sounding almost disappointed. 'Wow, Riley, that was COOL!'

'Hell, yeah,' said Riley, cackling with relief. 'Hollywood here we come!'

\*      \*      \*

In the dirty house by the freeway, Lucy slept sporadically throughout the night, aware, even in her sleep, that she was starving and her arms numb and aching. Finally, as the sun shed its dawn filter and began its cruel blaze through the dirty window, she knew she had no chance of any more rest. She rolled over and looked at her mother, who was flushed, sweating and muttering to herself. At first Lucy thought it was the effects of the sun's rays—but then she realised her mom was burning up with fever.

'Oh no,' she whimpered. 'Mom. Wake up!' She crawled over to Rosie and tapped her mother's shoulder with her chin. 'Wake up, please!'

Rosie moaned and opened her eyes. They were glazed, the pupils massively dilated.

'We need to get out of here,' said Lucy. 'You have to get to a hospital, now. Get up.'

\*      \*      \*

Lucy and Rosie left the house and weaved back to the freeway. Rosie had not thought it possible that she could walk a step further, with her numb hands still tied, feeling the way she did—but Lucy had dragged her, clamping her teeth on the sleeve of her dress and physically pulling her along.

The freeway was even emptier than it had been the day before, and the morning sun beat down on their bare heads. Sweat was dripping off Rosie, and the pair of them walked in grim silence.

Finally, a car came over the brow of the hill behind them, a lone vehicle pulling a battered silver trailer. Lucy suddenly ran out into the freeway and stood in the middle of the lane, planting her legs wide.

'Lucy!' Rosie shouted, but only inside her head—the words wouldn't come out. The car was coming fast, too fast—Rosie had a brief flash of the student in Tiananmen Square standing in front of the moving tanks—she tried to run after Lucy, but fell. She couldn't get up, and she couldn't look. She turned her face away in defeat and waited for the impact. 'Better than getting the flu,' she muttered to herself. 'Better than that . . .'

\*        \*        \*

'SHIT!' Riley shouted, stamping on the brake so hard that the car and the Airstream almost jackknifed. The boys in the back woke up and screamed as they slewed across two—mercifully empty—lanes to avoid the young girl who was standing in the middle of the freeway.

They skidded to a halt in the slow lane, and Riley gaped in astonishment at the girl. She was totally cute. About his age, denim mini over long legs, ripped T-shirt with an authentic-looking bloodstain image on it, and awesome messy auburn curls. 'Cool,' he muttered. She wasn't even waving—but then she turned slightly to show him that her hands had been tied behind her back.

'Whoa,' he said. Her lips were moving but he couldn't hear anything.

'She's saying "help",' said Jack.

'Go help her, Riley,' said Bradley. Both boys were gripping the back of the driver's seat.

Riley scratched his head. 'I dunno,' he said uneasily. 'We're nearly there. I can't pick up no hitchhikers. It's dangerous.'

'She's crying,' Jack pointed out.

'Oh, for fuck's sake,' Riley capitulated. She was

362

a total fox, though, it was clear even through the shock and tears on her face. Perhaps if he helped her, she'd let him have her number. 'Stay there, you two. Do NOT open the doors or windows, OK?'

He got out of the car and gingerly approached the girl.

'Hey.'

'Hey,' she replied, now sobbing. 'Please, help us.'

'Us?' He looked around.

'My mom's over there. We got attacked. This crazy woman tied us up. She cut me, look.'

Shit, thought Riley. Those were *actual* bloodstains on her shirt.

'We need to get to a hospital. Please could you give us a ride? Please?' She looked imploringly at him. They were still standing in the middle of the empty freeway.

'We better get off of the road,' Riley said uneasily. 'My kid brother's in the car, something might come.'

'What's your name? I'm Lucy. We won't bother you, I swear,' she said. 'We could just ride in your trailer, if that's OK? You won't even know we're there. My mom really needs to rest, she's—ah—she hit her head when we got attacked. All we need is for you to cut this tape off my wrists, and drop us near a hospital. Please?'

Riley later wondered if he would have been so accommodating had the girl not been so beautiful. But at that moment he knew he couldn't leave her there.

'I'm Riley. You go get your mom, I'll get some scissors for your wrists. You can ride in the trailer.'

Lucy broke into a fresh storm of tears, and Riley blushed to the roots of his hair. She stumbled off

363

the freeway and Riley watched her for a moment, her long legs as wobbly as a colt's, her wrists tied tightly behind her back. He felt a surge of protectiveness that for one second made him feel more manly than he'd ever felt before—and then made him want to jump back in the car, lock the doors, and drive away as fast as he could.

But instead he ran to the Airstream, opened the door and found a pair of scissors in the drawer. When he came out again, a woman was standing with Lucy. He could tell that she was Lucy's mother—same colour hair, same pretty face. She would have been a bit of a MILF, if she hadn't been in such a state. Sick dribbled down her front, and she had a black eye.

'We need to get her to a hospital,' Lucy repeated. She turned her back to Riley and stretched out her arms. He carefully cut the tape binding her wrists, and was rewarded with a faint but still dazzling smile. Lucy rolled her elbows round and round, stretched out her arms above her then rubbed her wrists. She held out her hand for the scissors.

'I'll do Mom's in the trailer. You need to get going before you get in trouble for stopping on the freeway,' she said.

Riley snorted, suddenly shy. 'I reckon the Highway Patrol got other things on their mind,' he said. 'But yeah. We should hit the road again.'

'Thanks, Riley,' she said, smiling that smile again. 'I'd kiss you, but I'd better not in case you got the Indian flu.'

Riley saw her glance at her mother, and it occurred to him how red her mom's eyes were, and how much sweat beaded her forehead. He stared for a moment. But he couldn't leave them, not now

364

. . . Anyways, they were almost at his dad's. And Lucy and her mom would be out of the way in the trailer . . .

'Jump in, then,' he said.

## 55

Kate was leaning down into the telephone kiosk, clamping her thighs tightly across Eygpt's broad back so that she didn't slide off. She didn't notice anything at all until she felt the cold muzzle of a pistol stuck into her side, and a heavily muscled woman ripped the phone receiver away from her, leaving it dangling.

The woman stroked the horse's mane and murmured in his ear, 'Easy, Egypt. You don't have to worry about this bitch lady no more. Heather's here to take you home.'

She pointed the gun at Kate's face. 'Dr Maddox, I assume? Well, well, well. My day just got a *whole* lot better.'

\*     \*     \*

Five minutes later, Kate sat in silence in the passenger seat of the low-slung Porsche. The woman had handcuffed her arms behind her body, so she couldn't lunge for the door handle and try and jump out. She had no option but to sit back and await whatever fate they had in store for her back at the ranch.

There was no way she'd ever escape a second

time. She felt like crying—she'd been so close to freedom! Paul had sounded really sick on the phone. What if he had the virus? What if she never saw him or Jack again? I couldn't bear it, she thought desperately.

She took a deep breath, collected herself, and decided to try something. '*Om Shanti*, Sister,' she said to the woman. 'I'm on your side, you know. What is your name?'

The woman turned and looked at her through narrowed eyes. 'Sister Heather. Nice try, Maddox, but don't think for a moment I'm gonna buy that bullshit. I've already talked to Angelica.' After shoving Kate in the car, Heather had stood outside for a moment and made a phone call. 'And I gotta tell ya, she's pissed. Angelica doesn't get angry very often, but when she does . . .' She grinned and drew her finger across her throat.

Kate slumped down in the leather bucket seat, watching the trees flash past in a blur of dark green. She was out of ideas.

\*       \*       \*

'Ah, the faithless "Sister" Kate. Back so soon?' said Angelica, unsmiling. It didn't surprise her that Maddox hadn't got far—the Englishwoman looked as though she'd spent her life in the lab, and never even set foot in a gym. She looked pale and defeated and Angelica curled her lip scornfully. To think she'd believed that this might have been the seventh Sister! It was a fluke that she'd maimed Cindy in the lab, and a downright miracle that she'd managed to kill Brandi, a seasoned fighter, in the woods. Although something was bothering her about Brandi's death . . . She couldn't put her finger on it yet, but she would, given more meditation.

After Heather's call, Angelica had positioned herself in the high-backed gold velvet throne in the vast entrance hall, her arms resting on the chair's arms, her robe arranged so that its sleeves draped artfully down the sides. To assuage her anxiety, she had put on her ceremonial robes. They were made of a heavy cream silk shot through with gold threads, and had wide gold satin cuffs and hems. It always made her feel calmer and more in control when she donned them. And knowing that Maddox would once again be under her control was like a shot of valium coursing through her veins.

She turned towards Heather, who was dragging Kate by the hair. 'I hope you're about to tell me that Paul Wilson is dead.'

Heather's face immediately fell. 'I'm sorry, Dadi,' she said, her head bowed. 'I still haven't found him. But I have brought you Maddox. And I've left Egypt tied up at Feverfew, in Main Street. He seems OK.'

Angelica sprang out of her throne. '*What?* You've been away all this time, with no results? I have to know he's dead! What's the matter with you? Do you even know where he is?'

She slammed her fist into her thigh, panic and rage coursing through her. Why was nothing going right? Surely the Goddess couldn't be testing her this much, so late in the Cycle? 'Sekhmet, why? Why are you doing this to us?'

Preeti rushed over to Angelica and knelt beside her, holding her hand and stroking it with both her own.

Heather, her face twisted in a belligerent scowl, dragged Kate to the grand staircase, unlocked one of her handcuffs, passed the chain through the banisters and secured it. She couldn't resist giving Kate a savage kick in the ankle before turning back to Angelica.

'I tracked him down all right. He went to Glencarson to visit Diaz. I missed him by minutes. You don't know what it's like out there. It's chaos on the roads. Borders are all shut. People are going crazy . . .'

Angelica snatched her hand away from Preeti's soft pawings. All these lieutenants, so carefully chosen for their strength and courage and faith, trained and groomed for months and months, a crack team—but now look at them! The team was cracking up. Preeti was weak, Heather was inept, Simone was acting strange and distant—in fact, where the hell was she? Brandi and Cindy dead . . .

'How the fuck did he find Diaz? What does he want?' Angelica screeched.

*     *     *

Kate's entire body recoiled when she heard Paul's name, and she felt as though a bolt of lightning was zigzagging through her. Chained to the bottom banister, she could hear everything that was going on, but it was hard to see without craning her head round like an owl, and she didn't want to draw attention to herself. But even unsighted as she was, the tension in the room was obvious.

'Where's Simone?' Angelica demanded. 'Simone!'

Kate heard a door open and close on the floor above, and the sound of soft footsteps. Simone seemed to glide down the stairs, the picture of beauty and elegance in her white robes and serene expression. She looked like a catwalk model, even with the large bump on her forehead.

'Yes, Dadi, sorry, I was meditating and—'

She looked down the stairs, straight into Kate's eyes, and panic and horror flitted across her features. Kate looked away immediately, thinking, shit, no, Simone, don't look at me like that, she'll know, she'll be able to tell you helped me, then we're both in for it, why didn't you run when you had the chance?

Suddenly it was as if everyone in the room was suspended in time, frozen in a tableau of terrible dawning comprehension. Kate prayed that Angelica hadn't seen the look. She tried to make herself invisible, to shrink into the banisters and vanish, taking Simone with her . . .

\*     \*     \*

Angelica saw the look. In that split second, everything fell into place. How Maddox had managed to get out of the house, escape into the woods, saddle up Egypt and escape. Worse—far worse, how Brandi, her loyal and trusted servant of Sekhmet, had died.

'Sister Simone,' she said, slowly, calmly. 'How exactly did Sister Brandi die?'

Simone walked over and stood before Angelica's throne, her arms folded, eyes defiant. Her jaw moved up and down from her constant, irritating

369

gum-chewing, a habit Angelica had been unable to rid Simone of, in the same way she had never really embraced the elocution lessons and shed her ghetto talk. She realised now that she should have seen it as a sign, that Simone was not pure of heart, that she had never truly cast off her old self. But she had loved her, like all the Sisters.

Angelica had to look up to see into her beautiful smooth-skinned face, the perfect planes of her cheekbones and arch of her eyebrows. How could Simone have done this to her? To Brandi?

Simone affected surprise at the question. 'I don't know . . . I wasn't there, remember? You'd sent me out to search along the mountain road. I assumed that Maddox had shot her.'

Angelica narrowed her eyes. 'She wasn't shot. When Sister Preeti and I carried her body home to prepare it for the burial ceremony, Sister Preeti had to remove a knife from her back. I didn't make the connection at the time, but I have now: it was your knife, wasn't it? You stabbed your Sister.'

Preeti gasped.

Simone laughed, but it was forced. 'Don't be ridiculous, Dadi! Why would I stab Brandi? I loved the bones of that girl.'

'Let me see your knife, then.' Angelica held out her hand. 'I assume you have it under your robes, as always?'

Simone delved slowly into the split in the side seam of her robes—robes were worn over other clothes, so the knife should have been in its sheath around Simone's waist. Then she stopped.

'It's not there,' she said. She pointed at Maddox. 'She must have taken it. I ain't seen it for a day or so. I was gonna ask if anyone had found it.'

370

Angelica looked at the Englishwoman, tied to the balustrade like a dog on a leash, twisting her neck round so she could see what was going on. She felt like twisting that neck right round, until it snapped. 'Well? Maddox? Did *you* kill our Sister Brandi?'

*    *    *

Kate strained her head to see Angelica's face, and studiously ignored Simone's. Preeti was crouching at Angelica's feet, her hands covering her mouth, her eyes two dark 'o's of horror. Kate knew that the danger she was facing had escalated to a new level. Before, she had been collateral damage. Now, it was personal. She got the impression that Angelica didn't really care which of them had actually killed Brandi. What mattered was that she knew that Simone had helped her escape, so even if Kate *had* stabbed Brandi, Angelica would still blame Simone.

Kate hesitated. A large wilted petal dropped off a lily in one of the huge vases next to the staircase, and the silence in the room was so intense that they all jumped slightly at the soft sound as it landed on the parquet floor.

If she said no, Simone would probably be killed instantly, executed as a traitor.

If she said yes, they would probably both die anyway.

She ought to say no. She had to stay alive to find the vaccine, to find Paul and Jack.

But Simone had helped her. Simone had already saved her life once. How could she repay that with a death sentence?

She opened her mouth, still not knowing which of the two words would come out.

'It was me. I killed her, OK?' shouted Simone, her voice harsh in the stillness. 'I didn't mean to. I'm so sorry, Dadi, I was aiming at Maddox, but I was running at the time, and tripped over a root as I threw the knife, and it landed right between Brandi's shoulders. I was too ashamed to tell you. I'm sorry I lied. I've been up there for hours, begging Sekhmet's forgiveness . . . Please say you forgive me too?'

Simone fell to her knees and clutched the hem of Angelica's robes.

'But you helped Maddox escape,' said Angelica flatly.

'No! I swear—ask her. I didn't. She took my gun and hit me with it. I didn't want to tell you because I should never have left my gun, not even for a second . . . Ask her!'

'She didn't,' said Kate. 'I took her gun and knocked her out with it.'

The sound of soft sobs filled the room—Preeti was crying. Kate felt a momentary flash of optimism—the more division and conflict there was between the remaining Sisters, surely the better it would be for her chances of escape? But Angelica's next words extinguished all hope:

'Sister Heather, take Maddox and Simone away and lock them in the basement. They are traitors, and traitors must die. The ceremony will take place in an hour's time; you and I will officiate. Go put on your ceremonial robes. Sister Preeti, take the Jeep to Feverfew and bring Egypt home. Leave the car there. And pull yourself together, woman. This is your last chance to grow a backbone, do you hear

372

me? If Sekhmet is telling me I chose badly, that my Sisters are not up to the task they have been set, then I will suffer the consequences. I don't need you—any of you! I will fulfil Sekhmet's prophecy even if I have to do it by myself. Now get out of my sight, all of you.'

Preeti left the room, stifling a sob, and Angelica turned to Kate and Simone as Heather strode over to them, her eyes dark and murderous.

'There will be no more delays, Maddox. It is time for you to die. Both of you. And not just because Sekhmet demands your sacrifice.' She marched up to Kate and screamed in her face. 'I demand it too!'


## 56

Heather was grim-faced, refusing to meet Simone's eyes as she shoved her and Kate down the stairs and handcuffed them to a pipe.

'You could have had everything,' she hissed to Simone. 'But you've fucked up big time.'

'Heather, you gotta help us. Angelica's crazy. Come on, Sister, we're friends.'

Heather grabbed Simone by the throat and pushed her against the wall. 'I was never your friend. And I'm not your Sister any more, ya hear?' She spat on the floor at Simone's feet. 'You're nothing to me now but a walking corpse.'

With that, she marched out, leaving Simone and Kate alone in the velvety, laundry-scented semi-darkness.

'Why didn't they gag us too?' Kate asked, after a while. She'd grown so used to her hands being bound that she wondered if it would feel strange were she ever to find herself in a situation where she was able to move her arms freely. She and Simone were tethered to a hot-water pipe running along the wall of the basement. It scorched Kate's wrists whenever she accidentally touched it.

Simone, who still appeared shaken by Heather's violent outburst, shrugged. 'No need. Not like anyone can hear us down here anyways. Shit, woman, we are fucked.'

'I thought Angelica was bad enough, but that woman—Heather—is even scarier.'

Simone looked at the floor. 'She's angry because I betrayed Sekhmet.'

'I thought you didn't believe in all that.'

'I don't. At least, I don't think I do. Hell, I don't know what I believe. But shit, Kate, what if it *is* all true? I mean, I felt it. I really heard her, I heard Sekhmet talk to me. She chose me, through Angelica. Nobody ever chose me for nothing good before.'

'Simone, listen to me. You were brainwashed. You didn't hear her speak to you, not ever, because she doesn't exist. That milkshake thing that Angelica made you take every morning? She tried to force me to drink some. I'm certain it had something in it, something that gave you hallucinations, or delusions. Made you believe in Sekhmet. It's not your fault.'

Simone was silent for a moment. 'The vitamin,' she said eventually.

'That's what she called it, was it?'

'Yeah. Tasted awful, but she made us drink it. Said it was essential for muscle tone and concentration.'

374

'Hmm,' Kate said.

'I thought it was the real deal,' Simone said bitterly. 'Sekhmet, the Golden Age, the whole thing . . . I totally believed it. But you're right—Angelica ain't nothing but a psycho murderer.'

The two women sat in silence for a moment. Kate tugged the handcuffs, wriggled her hands, but there was no way they were getting free.

'Do you think the virus has spread—round the world, I mean?' Simone asked. 'I ain't seen a TV or the internet since this thing started.'

'It could have done. I don't know.' Kate pulled hard against the pipe again but it remained immovable. 'It would only take one sick person to get on a plane and then . . . it's totally out of control.'

'So you and those guys at the lab were trying to find the cure for it?'

'Yes. We were so close, too. Junko had just figured something out, something that might have held the key—but she's gone.'

'What about other scientists, in other labs?' Simone sounded hopeful. 'It can't have only been you working on it.'

'I'm sure it wasn't,' said Kate. 'But we were the best hope—well, until you lot arrived and killed most of us.'

Simone hung her head.

'And if Angelica goes ahead with this . . . sacrifice, or whatever shit way she wants to dress up our imminent murder, then the chances are that there won't be a vaccine, and this thing will get completely out of control.' Kate shook her head in despair. 'Do you think she's really going to go ahead with it?'

375

Simone laughed, mirthlessly. 'You've seen what she's like. She don't give a damn about nothin' apart from Sekhmet's supposed fucking will. She does whatever she thinks Sekhmet says . . . Actually, Sekhmet says whatever Angelica wants to hear.'

'Where did she get it all from, anyway?'

'Visions. Dreams. Says Sekhmet's been talking to her since she was a kid. Her granddaddy had this gold statue of the Goddess that he brought back from Egypt. Angelica used to play with it when she was a little girl. If I'd known she was so fucked in the head, I wouldn't have gone near her. But then, I guess, we were all fucked in the head otherwise we wouldn't have gotten taken in.' Simone rattled her own handcuffs, her biceps straining as she pulled against the pipe. 'Angelica didn't tell us about the virus, of course, not for ages . . .'

There was a faint scratching sound from inside the walls. Simone froze.

'Was that a rat?'

'Well, at least you won't be around to see the rats taking over,' Kate said. 'And you won't die of the virus, either.'

'That's good, about the rats. But I don't have to worry about the virus—we're all immune. Part of our initiation ritual to become a Sister of Sekhmet: Angelica gave us the virus and then the antidote, to make sure we'd be immune once she'd released it. Though we didn't know that at the time.'

'Do you know where she got hold of it? Did she take you to a lab or a clinic somewhere?'

'She did it right here. Don't know where she got the stuff.'

'What can you remember about it?'

Simone snorted. 'I ain't no scientist, all I know is

376

that Angelica gave me a shot. But it worked damn fast, I know that much. One minute I thought I was gonna die, then I had the shot—next day I was well enough to go for a walk in the yard.'

'And Angelica called it an antidote, you're sure about that?'

'Yep. I'm pretty sure she did.'

Kate pondered this. 'That's strange. Because an antidote is something you give for a toxin or a poison, not a virus. With viruses, you use a vaccine for someone who hasn't had the virus yet, or an antiviral drug for someone who's already got it. It's weird that she referred to it as an antidote.'

Simone made a face. 'Her brain is screwed. Maybe she made a mistake. Or maybe I mis-remembered.'

Kate rattled the pipe with renewed vigour. Simone must have got it wrong. Whatever it was that stopped the virus, it was fast-working. She wracked her brains to think what could have been used to create the antivirus, something Angelica had access to that she, Kate, never had . . . It could save millions of lives, if only she could figure it out. Assuming she could stay alive long enough to be able to try. 'Come on, Simone, you've been trained in combat and survival—surely you can get us out of here?'

'I think I'm pretty much all out of ideas, honey. We could try and shift this pipe, but I don't reckon it'll budge.'

'Let's pull, together. We can't give up, not now.'

They both heaved and strained, leaning as far forward as the handcuffs would allow, but the pipe did not give an inch.

'Can we overpower them when they come for

377

us?'

Simone shrugged wearily. 'Doubt it. Angelica and Heather are both crack shots, Preeti's there as back-up, and we're cuffed. We don't stand a chance.'

'Don't be so negative,' Kate said. 'I thought your meditation was all about acceptance and tranquillity?'

'Fuck that,' said Simone.

They slumped back against one another. Kate could smell the other woman's sweat and perfume, her solid presence, and she felt overwhelmed with pity and sympathy for her.

'Simone—I just want to say . . . thanks. Thanks for helping me escape, twice. I'm so sorry this has happened. But don't blame yourself for any of it, OK? You're a good person.'

'Oh, can it,' said Simone.

If she ever got out of this, Kate promised herself, and things returned to normal, she was going to take a break; a real break, with Jack and Paul. And the next time she saw Paul, she would ask him to marry her.

If she ever saw him again.

Who was she kidding? Defeat flooded through her as the reality of the situation struck her afresh. She slumped back against the basement wall, her wrists aching as much as her head and heart.

At that moment, the door at the top of the basement steps creaked open. Light flooded in, and Kate screwed up her eyes to make out the hunched shape of an old man standing there. It was the same man she and Simone had seen in the kitchen when Kate had escaped.

Simone suddenly sat up straighter. 'I'll handle

this,' she hissed.

The man must have been in his mid seventies, with long threads of white hair combed across his scalp, and huge ears. A pair of rimless glasses perched on his rather bulbous nose. His mouth was set in a frown.

'Dr Mangold, sir?' called Simone, and Kate gasped.

Mangold! *This* was Mangold? So Paul had been right all along. Kate felt as if she had woken up from a nightmare, only to find that the first bad dream was wrapped in another. She had first heard the name Charles Mangold eighteen years ago, the summer of the fire at the Cold Research Unit. Clive Gaunt, the man who'd murdered Paul's twin brother, had told them that Mangold had helped fund their work creating killer viruses. Kate couldn't speak. All she could do was watch as Mangold walked unsteadily down the basement steps, looking puzzled.

'Over here, sir—we've, ah, got a little problem.'

'So've I. I can't find my damned bedroom.' He spoke in a cracked drawl, and Kate fleetingly imagined he must have been quite an attractive, charming man once. To the outside world, at least. Nothing charming about what he had done with his life. What an odd thing to say, though. Kate wondered if she had misheard. Or was he suffering from dementia? She had seen it in Aunt Lil. Was Mangold suffering the same fate?

'Dr Mangold, we appear to have got ourselves chained to this here pipe,' said Simone, smiling sweetly at him. 'Do you think you might help us? There are some tools on that wall . . . Please could you see if you could maybe find a hacksaw?'

'A hacksaw?' Mangold turned and started to walk towards the far side of the basement.

'That's Angelica's grandpa,' Simone whispered. 'He's nuts. Harmless, though.'

Kate leaned the back of her head against the damp concrete wall, trying to take it all in. So Angelica was Mangold's granddaughter. That would explain how she had got hold of this strain of Watoto and the 'antidote'. She wondered how long Mangold had been 'nuts', as Simone had put it. Did he have dementia, or was it something else? But even after Mangold had gone mad, he would still have had money, resources, contacts, all exploitable by Angelica . . .

Mangold drifted back across the basement to them, empty-handed, and Kate heard Simone hiss quietly with frustration.

'What am I doing down here?' he said, gazing down at them. He seemed entirely unsurprised that they were chained to a pipe.

'Helping us, sir,' said Simone. 'You were gonna help us?'

'Ah yes,' he replied. 'I'll go get Angelica.'

'No!' Kate and Simone said together. Kate looked anxiously up at the open basement door. Someone could come along at any moment.

Mangold stared at Kate for a long time, then he pointed a bony finger at her. 'I remember you,' he said.

'We met, briefly, in the kitchen last night, sir,' Kate replied, her mouth dry with tension.

'No. Before. You were a little girl. I remember talking to your father about this, Miss Carling.'

Kate gasped, shock flooding through her.

'He gets muddled with names,' Simone said.

380

'Carling is my maiden name,' Kate managed, the words sticking her tongue to the roof of her mouth.

'Yes, yes, Derek Carling, I remember. You had a beautiful house in the English countryside. Roses growing in the garden. You and your cistern, er, sister, running about. Leonard took me to visit you once or . . . maybe twice. Your mother brought us homemade lemonade.' He licked his chapped lips.

'Small world, huh?' said Simone. 'His long-term memory is pretty good.'

'And I visited you in Africa too. In your village in . . . What's that place called?' He rubbed his forehead.

'Tanzania?' Kate asked slowly.

'Yes, that's right. Tanzania. Camilo and I went out there, looking for . . .' He stopped mid-sentence and leaned forward, gazing down on them. 'I'm so sorry about what happened to your parents. You are beautiful, like your mother.' He winked at her. 'I was always a little sweet on Francesca, I must confess.'

Kate's heart was beating so fast she thought she might collapse. 'No, you didn't know my parents. You can't have.'

'Oh, but I did. Your . . . daddy . . . a fine virologist. One of the best.'

'He wasn't a virologist, he was a foreign aid worker.'

'Um, sir?' Simone interrupted, fidgeting with impatience. 'Could you help us out here, and then we could continue this chat later?'

'One more thing before you do,' Kate said urgently. If Mangold's long-term memory wasn't too patchy, there was a chance that he might be able to tell her. 'How did you discover a vaccine for

Watoto?'

He laughed, and for the first time, sounded completely *compos mentis*. 'Oh, Miss Carling, your father would be proud of you. I've known for years. And when we wanted to recreate the cure, Angelica was kind enough to provide the seeds of what I needed.'

There was a screech from the top of the basement stairs. As if summoned by the sound of her name, Angelica flew down the steps and grabbed Mangold by the arm. 'Grandpa! There you are! What are you doing down here? Come on, let's get you back to your room.'

'I was *looking* for my room,' he grumbled sulkily. 'These here ladies need our help.'

'Yes, yes,' Angelica said, leading him away. 'Let's get you sorted, and I'll be right back to assist them.' She glared at Simone and Kate with an expression that said she'd be happy to shoot them then and there, and shepherded Mangold up the stairs, locking the door behind them.

The basement was thrown into pitch darkness again.

Kate slumped against Simone, Mangold's words whirling around her head, almost managing to distract her from the fact that they had just lost their opportunity to escape. So Mangold had known her parents in Tanzania? He said her dad was a virologist—but that had to be his memory playing tricks. She had been very young when Watoto claimed both her parents, but not so young that she hadn't known what her father's occupation had been. No one had ever said anything to her about her dad being a virologist too. It had been her parents' friend Leonard who had inspired her to study virology—or at least, that was what she'd always believed. Mangold's dementia, or whatever it was, must have made him confuse Leonard with her father. All the same, there was something about the way he'd said, 'Your father would be proud of you.'

'Shit,' said Simone into the blackness.

## 57

By the time they arrived in Feverfew, Paul felt like death would be a merciful release. The sickness had taken over his whole body until all he was able to do was sip from a bottle of water Harley had bought from a vending machine beside a shut-up shop a few miles back. He felt alternately sweaty with fever and shivery with cold.

But his determination to find—and rescue—Kate kept him going, and gave him some strength.

Harley checked the GPS and drove down a long mountain road until the ranch gates came into view. The sky was beginning to lighten, the stars winking out, birds filling the air with morning song. Harley pulled up by the side of the road, out of sight of anyone looking out of the ranch windows, and they sat in silence. It was beautiful here, Paul thought, so peaceful. But if everything they believed was correct, this place was the cradle, the source, of all the death and pain he'd witnessed since coming to America.

Including his own death, in all probability.

Diaz dozed in the back seat, a trail of drool on his chin. Harley, who had been wearing his flu

383

mask for the whole journey, turned round and said, 'Camilo—we've arrived.'

The old man blinked as he woke up, wiping his mouth with his sleeve.

'So . . .' he said, smiling grimly.

Paul turned round in his seat. 'Whatever happens next,' he said, 'you need to tell us how to stop the virus.'

Diaz unfastened his seat belt and opened the door, getting out of the car. Paul and Harley followed suit, Paul's legs almost buckling as he stepped on to the hot asphalt.

'Camilo,' he said in the strongest voice he could muster.

'Yes, of course. Don't worry. But I want to see Mangold first. Then I will tell all.'

'You'd better.' Assuming the man was telling the truth, Diaz was his only hope of survival. If there was some cure that could be created in—well, how long did he have left? A day or two? Would that be long enough? He couldn't worry about it now. At this moment, the most important thing was getting Kate out.

Harley had been on the phone while Paul was talking to Diaz. He slipped his phone into his pocket and said, 'Back-up is at least an hour away. Probably two. Every spare person we have has been sent to LA to try to help the situation there. We should wait here until they arrive.'

'No,' Paul said, trying to keep the desperation out of his voice. 'I have to keep moving. I need to make sure Kate is all right.'

'But, Paul, you're not well. You need to rest.'

'Resting isn't going to do me any good. If you don't come with me, I'll go on my own.'

'Don't be foolish.'

Paul stepped towards Harley, acting much harder than he felt. 'Listen—you brought Kate and me over here. It's your fault we're in this mess. And I am not going to sit here while we wait for back-up that might never arrive.'

'You never want to sit tight, do you, Paul? If you hadn't run off in the first—'

'What? If I hadn't done that, we wouldn't have found Camilo. We wouldn't have a clue where Kate or Mangold or his granddaughter were.'

Harley sighed. 'OK, OK. Let's take a closer look. Just hold on one minute.'

He got back into the car and opened the glove compartment. A few moments later he reappeared and handed Paul a small black pistol. Paul took it, felt its weight in his hand. Harley produced another gun from inside his jacket.

'This is against every procedure in the book, but . . . I guess these are extraordinary circumstances. Do you know how to use a gun?'

Paul nodded.

'Got one for me, young man?' Diaz said.

'No way,' said Harley. 'You wait here, in the car.'

'Don't be ridiculous! I came all this way to see Mangold. You're not leaving me here now.' He folded his arms and Harley sighed again.

'Great,' he said. 'What a team. Me, the walking dead and a cast-off from *Dad's Army*. Come on.'

Harley set off down the hill towards the ranch, Paul and Diaz following close behind. Paul sneezed. Every step hurt. *The walking dead.* You said it, Agent Harley, he thought, stroking the trigger of his gun with a fingertip. But if I can stay upright long enough, maybe I can take a few of the bastards with me.

*   *   *

They stood at the gates of the ranch, looking in. The gates were black wrought iron, fifteen feet high and surrounded by an equally high fence, with a brick wall running along its base. Beyond the gate, a path led past some stables towards a magnificent ranch house. Behind where the three of them stood now was a wood, the trees standing like sentries, watching them.

'Now what?' said Paul. On a post beside the gate was an intercom with a keypad. Above the intercom button was a small camera lens.

'I don't know,' replied Harley. 'Hang on, what's that?'

All three of them turned. It took Paul a moment to realise the sounds he could hear were those of a horse's hooves on the road. It was coming from somewhere just beyond where they'd left the car, and getting closer.

'Quick,' whispered Harley, dashing across the road into the trees.

As they watched, the horse came into view, ridden by an Asian woman wearing black leather. She pulled the creature up beside the post, pressed a few buttons on the keypad and waited while the gate opened. She rode through and directed the horse towards the stable on the right, vanishing from view. A couple of minutes later, they watched her go into the house and shut the door behind her.

Paul, Harley and Diaz emerged from the trees.

'We have to get in there,' said Paul. His head was swimming and his eyes were so sore he could barely see. But he felt desperate to find Kate. They were so close.

'One-three-seven-six-E,' said Diaz.

Harley turned to him. 'What?'

'That's the code to open the gate.'

Paul was astonished. 'You could see that from where we were standing?'

Diaz shrugged. 'I may be an old man, but I have the eyes of an eagle. And I could see the pattern of her fingers as she pressed the buttons.'

'Amazing.'

Harley pushed the buttons on the keypad. The gate opened and the three of them slipped through, the gate automatically shutting behind them. There was a white Porsche parked in front of the house, and they ducked behind it, peering through the vehicle's windows at the front door.

'OK,' said Harley. 'You two wait here. I'm going to go see what I can see.'

Keeping low, Harley jogged off down the left side of the house, his gun in his right hand.

He'd no sooner disappeared from sight than the front door of the house opened. Paul and Diaz shrank down; then Paul carefully raised himself into a crouching position so he could see through the rear window of the Porsche. He almost lost his balance, but steadied himself against the door, his head throbbing, white light pulsing at the edges of his vision.

The Asian woman came out of the house, followed by a stunning woman with hair the colour of wheat.

'That's Angelica,' Diaz said calmly in Paul's ear.

And then, side by side, two more people emerged from the house, handcuffed. One was a

387

beautiful black woman who looked like she'd just been told she had a terminal illness. The other was Kate, looking pale and strained, but defiant.

Paul had to clasp his hand over his mouth to stop himself from crying out her name. Behind Kate and her handcuffed companion came a fierce-looking white woman with short hair, who had a gun trained on their backs. Apart from Kate, they were all clad in long robes of either gold or white. Kate was wearing unfamiliar pale brown clothes and, oddly, her shirt only had one sleeve. The sight of her bare arm touched Paul deeply. There was a bloody bandage tied around her forearm. What had happened?

The blonde spoke: 'Bring them round here, Sister Heather.' She gestured to the right, the opposite side of the house to the one Harley had gone down. 'Sister Preeti, you decided to join us after all, I see. Give me your gun.'

'Yes, Dadi Angelica . . . I want to prove to you that I am your humble servant. I am not afraid. It is Sekhmet's will.' But Paul saw that the Indian girl, Preeti, was shaking like a leaf.

'I'm not going to harm *you*. Only the traitor Simone and the English bitch.'

From his position twenty feet away, Paul could see that Angelica's face was twisted with anger and hatred, but she appeared to be trying to look serene. It was as if her face was fighting a battle with itself. The calm side was losing. She looked completely mad, and the madness disfigured her beautiful face as dramatically as scar tissue would have done.

The party went round the corner of the house, the short-haired woman, Heather, jabbing a gun

388

periodically between the prisoners' shoulders.

Paul gestured for Diaz to wait. To his surprise, the old scientist assented. Leaving the cover of the Porsche, he jogged slowly towards the house, throwing himself against the wall and peering round the corner. His fever was getting worse by the minute and he felt as if he was trying to run through storm waves rather than across flat ground. The wall rippled and undulated against his body, and he had to grip on to it to stay upright. Sweat trickled into his eyes and he blinked away the stinging sensation.

At first he couldn't believe what he was seeing: Kate and Simone, as he had heard Angelica call her, were on their knees on the grass. Angelica and Heather were standing behind them, guns pointed at the backs of their heads. Heather was grinning. Angelica looked insane.

It was an execution.

Paul pressed himself against the wall, heart thumping so fast he thought he might have a cardiac arrest, sweat pouring off him. He raised the gun Harley had given him and released the safety.

He could hear Angelica chanting in a sing-song voice: 'Oh, great Sekhmet, Goddess of Pestilence, lady of the plague, who has guided and sustained us, who has blessed us with her love and her light, we, your humble servants, offer to you a sacrifice. The traitor, Simone, who like Judas was sent to betray us, and your enemy, Kate Maddox, who would undo your great work. Sekhmet, please accept this—'

Paul stepped round the corner, holding the gun out with both hands. His vision was blurred but he somehow managed to keep the gun steady.

'Put the guns down,' he shouted, hoping Harley would hear.

Several things happened at once: Kate looked up and gasped, 'Paul!' Preeti reached inside her robe and produced another gun. She squeezed off a shot at Paul. The bullet struck the wall beside his head, and he threw himself behind the corner, the sudden movement causing the world around him to explode in a burst of stars.

'Kill her now,' Angelica screamed, and another shot went off.

Paul roared, 'No!' and thrust his head back round the corner, expecting to see Kate lying dead on the ground. But at the same moment Kate had also cried out, the same word: 'No!'

It was the other woman, Simone, who had been shot.

She was on her side, blood pooling around her, her dead eyes open and staring right at him, piercing his heart. He couldn't see Kate's face, but her shoulders were heaving as if she was crying. He retreated behind the wall again. His hands shook and nausea swept over him. The air swam around him, but he forced himself to step out from behind the corner, heart pounding when he saw Preeti running towards him. Behind her, Angelica had her gun against the back of Kate's head while Heather was close to the wall of the house, moving swiftly towards him, that malevolent grin still etched on her face.

Paul raised the gun, his arms shaking, pure adrenaline keeping him going.

Preeti raised her gun too, her fear gone, her face twisted with hatred.

He shot her in the chest. Blood bloomed across

the front of her white robe and she dropped to the ground.

'Good shot, young man.'

Paul turned round, and Diaz smashed a rock against his forehead.

## 58

Camilo Diaz dropped the rock, which landed with a thump next to the unconscious Paul's head, then stooped and picked up Paul's gun. Shame this had to happen—he quite liked Paul Wilson. But he would be dead from the virus soon, anyway.

'High Priest.' He looked up and saw Angelica's ugly friend, Heather, the one who had stuck next to her like a shadow her whole life. She walked over and pointed her own gun at Paul, who was already stirring, his eyes flickering, too dazed to move.

'When the sacrifice is done,' Heather said, 'I'm going to torture this motherfucker until he begs for the flu to take him.'

'Do as you wish,' Diaz said dismissively.

She bowed to him. 'I'm sorry that I couldn't prevent Wilson reaching you at the prison. We were worried that he might have found out that you were working with us.'

'How could he have known that?'

'Forgive me. We had no idea how much he had learned in Sagebrush. We didn't know if he was aware of Angelica, and her visits to the jail. We decided we couldn't take any risks.'

Diaz nodded. Ugly but thorough. 'Well, it turns out it was fortunate that Wilson did show up. It was taking longer than expected for everyone at the prison to die.'

'With respect, perhaps you should have let us break you out of there.'

That had been what Angelica had wanted to do. Bomb the prison or storm in with all guns blazing. But Diaz knew it was too risky. He, or one of the women, could have been injured. Instead, at the same time the Sisters had unleashed the virus, Angelica had visited the prison and sprayed it into the air using a perfume bottle, close to several of the guards. This was to ensure the guards and other prisoners were among the first victims of Watoto. The plan had been that, once they were all dead, or too weak to stop him, Diaz could simply walk out of the prison and join the women here. But in the end, Wilson and Harley had simply given him a ride to the ranch.

'No. It has all worked out perfectly. There was no need.'

He was tired of talking to this troll because, standing a few metres behind her, wearing ceremonial robes, was his angel, his little beauty. She was holding a gun to the head of an attractive woman with brown hair—Dr Maddox, he presumed—but he only had eyes for Angelica.

He still remembered the first time he had seen her, when she was a baby. She had radiated beauty even then. Mangold was so lucky to have been given such a gift, a granddaughter whose eyes shone with precocious intelligence. As she became a toddler, then a small child, a schoolgirl, her radiance had become even brighter. But Mangold, that fool, never noticed; he was too obsessed with his viruses, his stupid game of trying to create the ultimate virus, played out with his friends around the world, like that walking cadaver Gaunt. And Mangold's daughter—Angelica's mother—was a drunken slut who neglected her little darling, the father absent if he was even known.

Camilo had decided to take that precious little creature under his wing. He took Angelica on expeditions to galleries and museums where he introduced her to the Ancient Egyptians, the mythology seizing Angelica's imagination from the moment she first saw those wonderful relics and heard the stories of the gods and goddesses. He took her to fine restaurants and walked with her through the park. She was the daughter he had always longed for, and he was the father she deserved. He loved her and she worshipped him. Now here she was, all grown up; stunning and so powerful too. Of course, he had seen her numerous times over the years, as she had visited him at the prison, pretending to be his granddaughter. But every time he saw her, he felt a great rush of emotion.

'Angelica,' he beamed, walking over to her and leaving Heather to watch Paul.

Angelica bowed and proffered her gun, holding it out towards him on two open palms.

'Your Holiness—you can carry out the sacrifice.'

He wanted to embrace her, but it would have to wait until after the sacrifice.

'With pleasure,' Diaz smiled, sticking Paul's gun into the waistband of the too-small jeans Paul had lent him. He stroked Angelica's cheek and she closed her eyes, her face alight with an expression of bliss. She kissed the back of Diaz's hand as he took her pistol.

393

He turned his attention to Maddox, who stood straight, a look of defiance on her face. Another attractive woman. Sweet Jesus, he had missed women!

'Who are you? Angelica's sugar daddy?' Kate spat.

Diaz reached out and touched Kate's hair. 'Beautiful,' he said. 'No, don't worry, Angelica, not as beautiful as you.'

'Take your hands off me.'

Diaz sighed, a sound like a man enjoying that first taste of beer after a hard day at work. 'Dr Maddox, I am a great admirer of yours. Your paper about Watoto was almost brilliant. You were so close, you and Dr Larter. That's why I instructed Angelica to kill you both.' He realised with a start that he'd almost forgotten something. 'Where's Mangold?'

'Inside,' Angelica replied.

'Will you fetch him?' he asked. 'I want to . . . see him. I have some things to say to him.'

'Can't you kill Maddox first?'

Diaz stroked Angelica's face again. 'Sweet, sweet girl. So . . . lusty. Be patient. You were always impatient when you were a little girl, never willing to wait for anything.'

Angelica entered the house, leaving Diaz guarding Kate.

Diaz was amused by the look of contempt she gave him, until she spoke. 'Like children, do you?' she asked. Her eyes shone with fury.

'How dare you accuse of me that!' Diaz yelled, sticking the gun in Kate's face.

Standing over Paul, Heather whispered to Diaz, 'Do it.'

394

'That's not what it sounds like to me,' Kate said. 'All this talk of when she was a little girl.'

Diaz's pulse rate had accelerated dangerously. 'That poor child had nobody who gave a fuck about her except me. I was the only one who was kind to her.'

'Kind, eh?'

'I am not a paedophile! I loved that child like my own flesh and blood. I still love her. And she loves me like the father she never had.'

It was outrageous, yet another sign of a ruined society that deserved to be destroyed. A man couldn't even show affection to a young girl without everyone thinking he was a pervert. His feelings towards Angelica were pure. He had hardly ever . . .

Maddox interrupted his thoughts. 'Who the hell are you, anyway?'

'My name is Camilo Diaz. I was Charles Mangold's partner at Medi-Lab, the head of research. I was also supposedly Mangold's best friend—but the son of a whore betrayed me. He let me take the rap for the crimes committed in those labs. I was only ever doing what he instructed.'

Paul Wilson had dragged himself into a sitting position, clutching his bloodied head. To Diaz's surprise, he called out weakly but clearly: 'If you loved Angelica so much, why didn't you help the Mangolds when they contracted Pyrovirus?'

Diaz felt a grudging respect for the man. Others would have rolled over and given up.

'Because I *couldn't* help,' he replied. 'I didn't know how to treat what they had. It broke my heart, thinking of poor Angelica suffering because of what her bastard of a grandfather had done, playing with things he didn't understand, unable to cope without me to hold his hand. And, anyway, they survived. The two of them.'

'They had Pyrovirus?' said Kate. 'That . . . explains a lot.'

He knew what Maddox was alluding to. Pyrovirus was a type of viral encephalitis, causing swelling of the brain. It was a rare virus, spread by mosquitoes and usually found, like Watoto, in Africa. It was fatal in about fifty per cent of cases, and those who survived were rarely the same; their brains were damaged. Some survivors were unable to function afterwards. Others were driven insane.

Like Angelica and Mangold.

A few years after recovering from the disease, Angelica had come to see him. She was sixteen and allowed to visit him in the prison on her own. She told him he was the only man who had ever been kind to her. She remembered their outings, the trips and educational visits. But even though she was more beautiful than ever—a stunning young woman—her personality was different. She was harder, colder, and there was a madness in her. Something dark—and he had seen an opportunity.

He remembered Angelica's fascination with the Ancient Egyptians. On her second visit to the prison, he noticed she wore an ankh on a chain. He went away and did some research using the prison's decent library.

The next time she visited, he introduced her to the idea of Sekhmet. He explained to her that this Egyptian deity was the lion-headed goddess of healing who was also known as the Lady of Pestilence. She could prevent plagues, but also send them against her enemies. Diaz told Angelica in murmured conversation that Sekhmet had visited

396

him in a dream and told her that she had great plans for Angelica.

Every time Angelica visited, Diaz fed her more stories about the goddess and her plans, her love for Angelica. Soon, Angelica began to dream of Sekhmet. Not long after, her dreams became visions. She was a believer, and Diaz knew that her personality was strong enough to convince others to 'believe', too. He continued to feed ideas to her— ideas that would eventually lead to his freedom and his revenge against the country that had imprisoned him and the man who he held responsible.

He also knew that the key to this lay in the new strain of Watoto he and Mangold had developed at Medi-Lab, along with the cure. The Pyrovirus meant that Mangold could no longer continue his work for the government, the work he had been recruited to do in exchange for his freedom. He was too erratic. But Diaz was confident that if he sent instructions through Angelica, Mangold would be able to recreate the strain again. Or perhaps he still had samples, kept over from Medi-Lab.

Then Angelica had hit him with a bombshell. She was joining the CIA, having passed their recruitment process. Sekhmet had told her that if she was to become the ruler of the earth, a living deity, she needed to train, to build the skills necessary to be a great warrior and leader. She had decided the Agency could do this better than anyone else. Before Diaz could stop her, she was gone. Into the bosom of the loathed CIA. He could see the warped logic behind her actions—the story he had fed her about Sekhmet had grown and distorted inside her own damaged mind. Now it was her duty to lead seven Sisters to fulfill a great prophecy. Diaz didn't see her for over a decade. It had hurt so much, and he believed he would never see her again. He thought he had failed.

But then, one glorious day, she returned. Her eyes were crazier than ever. She was leaner and harder and wearing a disguise, using a new fake name to visit him. She told him that she was ready, that she had also persuaded her grandfather to help her, and had begun to recruit her seven Sisters, her own small army.

Soon, she would be ready to unleash the plague and make the prophecy real.

Diaz had been thrilled beyond words. At last he would be able to get out of that shithole. At last, he could be with the girl he loved like a daughter. At last, he could have his revenge on the USA and Charles Mangold.

And, speak of the devil, here he was.

His old friend Mangold.

Walking to his death.


## 59

Paul watched the scene unfold before him with astonishment and confusion. He had liked Diaz. Trusted him, even. Now he wanted to kill him. But he felt worse than he'd ever felt in his life, incapable of killing anyone, his head pounding, sweating and shivering at the same time. His body had become his enemy. Only adrenaline and fear were keeping him from falling unconscious again, and it took all his concentration to follow the conversation.

He looked up as Diaz said, 'Hello, Charles.'

Angelica walked out of the house, with Mangold beside her. She was carrying a set of ceremonial robes and she strode purposefully towards Diaz, stretching out her arms for him to take them.

Mangold's face was creased with confusion, but when he saw Diaz he seemed to have a moment of crystal clarity.

'Camilo? What are you doing here?'

'I came to say hello,' Diaz said.

Mangold walked closer to him. 'And you're not angry with me?'

'Oh, I'm angry,' Diaz said, curling his lip. 'I also came to say goodbye.'

He raised the gun and shot Mangold in the stomach. Angelica gasped and dropped the robes. Beside Paul, Heather clapped her hands with glee. Mangold toppled to the floor, clutching his guts as if he was trying to keep the blood inside his body.

Diaz turned away from him and back towards Kate. He gestured to Angelica. 'Come here, my darling girl. Let's remove the one last person who can stop us.' He winked at Kate, so Angelica couldn't see. 'The person who would defy the will of the Goddess.'

Kate said, 'He doesn't believe, Angelica. He's trying to fool—'

At that moment, two things happened. Paul gathered every final ounce of strength in his body and grabbed the gun from the distracted Heather. And Harley—whom everyone, including Paul, had forgotten about in all the commotion—came running round the corner of the house, pistol raised. He must have been watching the whole time, figuring out the best course of action.

Paul struggled with Heather, clinging to the gun, both of them holding on to it with two hands. She screamed in his face but he wouldn't let go. To his left, there was a blur of action: Diaz shot at Harley but missed; then Angelica aimed at Harley, but Kate threw herself against Angelica's legs, knocking her off balance, sending the shot wild.

Harley shot Diaz in the chest. The old man dropped silently, landing flat on his back.

Angelica screamed, 'No!'

Heather finally managed to wrest her gun from Paul's weakened grip, swivelling to take aim at Harley. But Paul shouted, 'Jason!' and the agent dropped to one knee, squeezing off a shot at Heather. A perfect shot that hit her in the upper chest and sent her sprawling, lying still in the dirt.

Harley then trained his gun on Angelica, who had her own gun aimed at the kneeling Kate. 'Drop it,' he ordered.

Angelica looked at him, then at Paul. She pushed her gun against the nape of Kate's neck, in the exact place that Paul loved to caress while Kate was driving. He remembered the feel of her silky hair against his fingers, and the way she'd rub her head deeper into his hand.

'*Drop the gun*,' Harley repeated, walking closer to her.

Angelica shook her head, her eyes darting left and right.

She grabbed hold of Kate's hair and pulled her to her feet, the gun still resting against Kate's neck. She repositioned herself so Kate was between her and Harley, meaning he didn't have a clear shot. Heather's pistol was under her body, as was Preeti's. Diaz had taken Paul's own gun away after

400

he had hit him with the rock.

She knows, Paul thought, that if she shoots Kate, Harley will kill her.

He had to act.

He managed to stand up, staggering forward with his palms out. 'Come on. Angelica.' His voice shook. Kate was looking at him, her face ashen. She stood in a puddle of Simone's blood. 'Put the gun down. You can't win. Let Kate go and we can talk.'

Angelica laughed. 'You expect me to believe that? You expect me to believe you won't kill me immediately?'

Paul stepped closer, as did Harley, the two of them approaching Angelica in a pincer movement. Angelica looked over her shoulder at Paul.

'Back off or I *will* shoot her.'

'Kate, I love you,' Paul said.

She gazed at him, drinking him in with her eyes. 'I love you too.'

'If you hurt her . . .' he said to Angelica.

Angelica gave him a look of utter contempt. 'What are you going to do to me? Hold me down and rape me? That's what you'd like to do, isn't it? The High Priest told me that that was what most men would want to do to me, that he was the only man who would ever love me purely.'

Paul's mouth opened in surprise. 'Angelica, he was using you. Not all men are—'

Before he could finish his sentence, he saw a movement to his left. It was Mangold. He was still alive and trying to get to his feet. His stomach was a mess of blood, his shirt dripping red. His weather-beaten old face contorted with pain and confusion.

'Grandpa!' Angelica cried.

401

'Let Kate go, and we can still save him,' Harley said. 'We can get him to a hospital.'

Angelica looked from Mangold to Harley then back to her grandfather. She seemed to be battling with her thoughts.

Then she shot Mangold in the chest. Another hole blossomed above the one in his stomach.

'No!' Paul shouted. No matter what he thought of Mangold, and what he had done in the past, Mangold knew how to stop Watoto—assuming the madness hadn't overpowered him. Diaz was dead, and Paul had no idea how much of their scientific knowledge the two old men had passed on to Angelica. Plus, he couldn't see her being very co-operative. Maybe Mangold was too crazy now to help, but he might well have been their last chance.

Angelica turned her gun on Harley—and Kate flew at her back, launching her whole body at the blonde, wrapping her arms round her and clinging to her. Angelica grunted and tried to wriggle from Kate's grasp, attempting to swing the gun against Kate's head, but Kate held on. Harley sprinted over, as did Paul—although his was more of a lunge than a sprint—and between the three of them they wrestled Angelica to the ground, pinning her against the grass. She bucked and writhed and swore at them until Harley said, 'Stop struggling or I'll blow your fucking head off.'

Then she went limp, and Kate climbed off her.

'Kate, my darling . . . oh, sweetheart, are you OK?' Paul hugged her tightly, kissing her hair, inhaling the warm familiar smell of her. She kissed him back. They were both crying.

After a few seconds, she gently pushed him away, and looked into his face. 'Oh, no. You're sick.

You've got Watoto. Oh, Paul . . .'

'Mangold,' he said. All the adrenaline was flowing out of his body. 'He knows the cure . . .'

Kate ran over to where Mangold lay on the ground, on his back. The entire front of his shirt was now crimson. But he was still breathing. Kate knelt beside him.

'Dr Mangold . . . Charles, you're going to be OK, we'll get an ambulance.'

Mangold opened his mouth and groaned. Blood trickled out.

'The cure,' Kate urged. 'Tell me, please!'

Mangold coughed, blood splattering the front of her T-shirt. He rolled on to his side, gasping, his breathing shallow, and raised an arm, pointing to the garden that led down to the woods.

Kate leaned in closer. Mangold was trying to say something.

'Charles—what is it?'

Mangold's voice was very soft, rasping with his last breaths.

'There . . . there . . .' he said, before falling silent.

Kate collapsed into a heap.

Paul looked over. That was it. Mangold was dead. Diaz was dead too. And with them, the secrets of how to stop Watoto. He closed his eyes and let the sickness carry him away.

60

All the mingled hatred and loyalty that had made up Heather's lifeblood seemed to have frozen, stilled in time and space by the paralysis of her

403

body. *Is that it?* she thought, as she lay in the heat and dirt.

She waited for Angelica to rush over to her, to stroke the hair back from her sweaty brow, kiss her gently into the next world. But nobody came.

Heather heard more shots and hoped, not that Angelica had taken down Wilson, Harley and Maddox, but that Angelica herself had been killed. Then they could still be together. They would simply go into the Golden Age sooner than they had thought. Hand in hand into eternity. That was how it should be; Angelica and Heather, an eternal partnership, an unbroken chain. Heather wasn't a poetic woman, but her love for Angelica made her soul sing new and glorious words.

Heather tried to turn her head, to see where Angelica was, but her muscles wouldn't obey her commands and nothing moved except the slow flow of blood from the hole in her chest.

Sekhmet, she implored, don't make me go there alone.

And yet even as she said the word, she knew it was all lies. She almost laughed at how gullible she'd been. For she *had* believed it. She had, because Angelica had.

Heather felt a faint flash of pride. She had been more loyal to Angelica than anybody had ever been to a loved one. She had killed, maimed, fought for her. So what if Sekhmet was a fairy tale? If it had earned her Angelica's love, then it didn't matter.

Angelica had loved her too . . . hadn't she?

As the heavy shutters of Heather's brain slowly closed down, and the pain overtook her, she remembered Angelica's smile, her touch on that hot afternoon in the motel, her kisses.

404

As she slipped from consciousness, she saw a figure moving towards her. She struggled to concentrate for a final moment. It was a woman with the body of a lion, supple and sinuous. The Goddess! She was real! And she was here to carry Heather into the afterlife. How had she ever doubted?

'Sekhmet . . .' she tried to say, a bubble of blood on her lips.

But as she spoke she realised—oh, such sweet realisation—that the Goddess bore Angelica's face. Angelica *was* the Goddess.

'I love you, Angelica,' Heather murmured with her last breath, trying to reach for her.

Angelica bared her teeth. 'But I never loved you, bitch.'

Everything went black.

## 61

'Sweetheart . . .'

Kate bent over Paul, who lay on the sofa in the living room of the Sisters' ranch, wrapped in a fleece blanket she had found in a cupboard upstairs. He was shivering, his nose streaming, skin so hot you could make toast on it.

'I'm going to find the cure, I promise, I promise, and then we'll make you better.'

Paul gripped her hand and attempted a smile. 'Kate, I . . .'

She shushed him. 'Don't try to talk. You've exhausted yourself. You need to sleep.' She held a cup to his lips, gave him a drink of water. He squeezed her hand again then closed his eyes. She stroked his forehead.

'Have you . . . spoken to Jack?' he croaked, his eyes still shut.

'I haven't been able to speak to him for the last couple of days. I'll try later. It's been so awful not having access to a phone.'

His lips moved, but no more words came out.

'In the meantime, I'm going to work on making you better. At least now we know an antivirus exists. Turns out that Mangold had a lab here—I'm sure it must be in there somewhere.'

Harley had found the small but well-equipped lab in the basement, near to where Kate and Simone had been held. While he was busy calling in BIT back-up to deal with the corpses and airlift Paul to a hospital, Kate had started to search the lab, looking for anything that would give her answers, or at least clues to point her in the right direction. But what she hadn't told Paul was that so far she had found nothing except a few live samples of Watoto-X2—and some frozen samples of what looked like sperm. No sign of a vaccine or the antivirus that Simone and the other women had been given; she had described it as an antidote, but that must have been a mistake. The existence of this antivirus gave her hope that she could save Paul, but it seemed that Mangold and Angelica must have destroyed it after they had used it, presumably to prevent someone like Kate coming along and finding it. So Angelica had been prepared, despite her conviction, for things to go wrong. She'd been cautious.

Kate laughed bitterly. Yeah—cautious enough to have blown up a hotel full of virologists and

406

massacred the team at the Sequioa lab.

Angelica was locked up now, in the very room where she had kept Kate prisoner, her hands cuffed behind her as Kate and Simone's had been. Harley had tried to interrogate her, to find out what she knew about the antivirus, but she refused to say a single word. Kate doubted that her knowledge would be technical enough, anyway.

Kate stood up, massaging the small of her aching back, just as Harley entered the room. She'd have to go back to the lab later and have another look—there was a ton of papers she hadn't had a chance to skim through yet.

'How is he?' Harley asked, his voice muffled through the biohazard mask Kate had made him wear, even though they both feared it was like closing the stable door after the horse had bolted.

She put her finger to her lips, not wanting Paul to hear, and gestured for Harley to follow her out of the room into the front entrance hall. The bodies of Simone, Preeti, Heather, Mangold and Diaz still lay outside on the veranda in the baking sun. Kate had covered each of them with a sheet, but Harley had instructed her not to move or touch the bodies. Kate wished that Angelica was under a sheet on the veranda too. She might be their prisoner, but it was small consolation when the plague she'd unleashed still stood to wipe out most of the Earth's population unless they could find the cure.

Unless she, Kate, could find the cure.

'He's bad,' she said to Harley, who had the look of a man trying to stay cool when he was trembling inside. She paced the room, weak with exhaustion but determined not to let herself rest until the cure had been found.

She turned on Harley. 'Angelica and Diaz unleashed this virus, and you and your lot were helpless to do anything about it. Even though Angelica was one of your lot.'

'Not quite,' he said defensively. 'She was ex-CIA.'

'And Mangold was working for the CIA too, wasn't he?' She rubbed her forehead. 'I need you to tell me everything you know, Jason.'

'OK. But, listen, I've been on the phone to my director, Nicholas Lepore, and back-up is on the way. More agents, to deal with Angelica. And scientists to help you.'

'Who are they? The B team? Have you had them in reserve all this time?'

'Kate, please, there's no need to take it out on me.'

She took a deep breath. 'OK. But, come on, tell me what you know. I assume you've also been talking to Lepore about the Mangolds?'

Harley perched on the arm of an antique chair. A huge gilt-framed depiction of Sekhmet covered most of the wall behind his head. 'Yes,' he said wearily. 'But you have to understand that there are levels of classification that go deep. It's not like there's some central computer system that contains every piece of information about anyone.'

He looked up and, seeing how Kate was looking at him, continued hurriedly. 'OK, this is what I've been able to find out. Back in 1990–91, Mangold and Diaz were carrying out illegal tests at Medi-Lab. At the time, nobody knew about the work they were doing on Watoto—Diaz called it Project Hadza.'

'Hadza? That rings a bell.'

'Really? Well, seems like Mangold and Diaz were testing all sorts of nasty stuff. Marburg, Ebola, West Nile, rabies and a whole range of hybrids and designer viruses. A lot like Gaunt at the CRU.'

Kate shook her head.

'Then in '91 a lab assistant at Medi-Lab got sick and died, and that's when the CIA got involved.'

'But nobody knew about them having a vaccine for Watoto?'

'No. Not according to what Diaz told us, and not according to what I've just been told.'

'I wonder what else they created in that lab . . .'

Harley shrugged. 'I guess we'll never know. But—all this is highly classified, Kate; I'm only telling you in case it helps in some way—it seems that Mangold did a deal: his freedom in return for signing up to help with a top-secret biological weapons research programme.'

'And Diaz took the fall?'

'That's right. No wonder he was so angry with Mangold—and with this country.'

Kate wracked her brains to try and remember where she knew the word Hadza from. A long time ago. 'So then what happened? Has Mangold been working for the CIA for the last twenty-odd years?'

'No. Apparently, he left fifteen years ago. Moved back to his house in Utah and became something of a recluse. That must have been when he and his family contracted Pyrovirus, and Mangold and Angelica became mentally unstable and started worshipping this Egyptian goddess.'

'If I ever hear the name Sekhmet again . . .' Kate said, glaring at the picture on the wall. 'Hold on.' She went into the other room to check on Paul. He was asleep. She laid her palm against his forehead, and it came away soaking wet. She kissed him on the top of his head, then crept back out of the room.

Harley looked pensive.

'What is it?' Kate asked. 'You look like you've got something on your mind.'

He walked over to her and, to her surprise, took hold of her hand.

'What are you doing?'

'I just wanted to say I'm sorry.'

'What for?'

His eyes looked wet over his mask. She had never seen him like this before. Usually, Harley was Mr Straight-down-the-line; unemotional; like a civil servant who happened to work in an interesting government department. 'For getting you and Paul into this mess.'

'You were only following orders, weren't you?'

'Yes, I know, but . . . It was me who suggested recruiting you.'

Kate raised an eyebrow.

'I knew you were an expert. And I guess . . .' He stopped himself. 'After the thing with Gaunt, I was asked to put you and Paul under surveillance. To make sure you didn't say anything to anyone about the Pandora virus and break the Official Secrets Act. But then I got called away to join BIT and the surveillance ended. And I thought it would be . . . good to have you over here.'

Kate pulled her hand away.

'I'm sorry.'

'I could be back in England now,' she said. 'Me and Paul, with Jack. Safe.'

'Nowhere's really safe . . .'

'Everywhere is safer than this.'

Harley looked ashamed. 'I don't want Paul to die either, Kate. I never had much time for him before, but I've come to respect him. And I respect that you love him.'

Kate's face reddened with anger. 'If you don't want him to die, then stop all this bullshit. Keep talking to me. Help me work this out. It's in your interest too—you're the one who spent several hours in a car with him when he was at his most contagious.'

He hung his head. 'I know. That's why I wanted to take the chance to say I'm sorry—while I still can.'

'And stop saying you're bloody sorry.'

'OK . . .' He straightened up. 'So, Mangold, he must have kept samples of Watoto-X2 and the means of stopping it all that time. Frozen, I guess?'

Her anger subsided. 'I don't know. When I saw Mangold in Angelica's basement he said something to me . . . what was it? Oh yes; I asked him if he knew how to stop Watoto, and he said Angelica had been kind enough to bring him the seeds of what he needed. That was all I could get out of him, but it struck me as a strange thing to say when talking about creating a vaccine.'

Harley waited for her to continue.

'What did Diaz tell you? Didn't you quiz him on the way down here?' she asked.

'We tried, but he refused to talk. He said he wanted to see Mangold first, didn't want to risk us going back on our promise. He knew that bit of knowledge was his only leverage.'

'He didn't say anything at all?'

Harley thought. 'When we interviewed him at the prison, he mentioned you. He'd read your

411

paper. He said you were getting close.'

She sighed. 'Another one.'

'He said something else.' He furrowed his brow. 'What was it? Oh . . . yes, something about how you were going to find the satellite.'

Kate, who had turned away to look out of the window, whipped round to face him. 'What?'

'He said—'

'I heard you. The satellite. That must be . . .'

She fell silent, her brain buzzing, pathways opening up. A satellite. That must be it. That was the ghost Junko had talked about, the something she had seen beneath the microscope but had never been able to figure out. A satellite virus. But what about it? What did it do?

Surely . . .?

Excitedly, she returned to the window and looked out at the garden. And it came to her: where she had heard the word Hadza before, and she was thrown back in time to another place, a hot, dark part of her history.

'Yes! That's got to be it!'

'What has?'

She didn't answer. Instead, she ran over to the door, yanked it open and ran outside, heading straight to where Mangold's body lay, covered in a sheet. She lay down on the ground beside him, on her back.

Harley caught her up. 'Kate, what on earth . . .?'

She was following what would have been Mangold's line of vision as he'd said his final words. She found herself looking at the garden, at the field of red and white that stretched towards the woods.

'What did Mangold say right before he died?' she asked, already knowing the answer.

412

'He said, "There, there".'

She jumped to her feet. 'Jason, I know what he was looking at. What he was talking about. Get on the phone to your boss. Tell him we don't need a team of virologists here.'

'Really? Why not?'

'We need a botanist.'

## 62

Before Harley could react, Kate broke into a run towards the meadow, the tiredness in her legs forgotten as she experienced that wonderful sensation that happened so seldom in the lab, always after weeks or months—even years—of creeping towards an answer. She could feel the passageways in her brain opening up, ideas and memories and realisations waving at her, vying for attention, and another part of her mind crying out, *Of course*!

She reached the edge of the field of flowers. Thousands of the small red-and-white star-shaped blooms stretched from here towards the edge of the trees. She had seen them whenever she had looked out upon the grounds, had walked past them on her way back to the house with Simone only this morning. And she had thought she recognised them—somewhere, deep in her tank of memories, was an image of plants exactly like these. Instinctively she had known that she was supposed to be afraid of them, that she should steer clear of them—but she hadn't even stopped to try to remember why.

Harley caught her up and stood behind her, breathing heavily.

She crouched beside the flowers, examining the whole plant. Beneath the crown of flowers, a thick stem led down to a bulbous pod. 'Did you call for a botanist?'

'No, not yet. Kate, I'm completely lost.'

'Then follow me.'

She stood up and broke into a jog, back towards the house, heading straight for Mangold's lab.

'You'll need to wear a protective suit as well as that mask. God knows what Mangold had lurking in this lab,' Kate said. She opened a couple of drawers, then spotted a cabinet in the corner and pulled it open. 'Ah-ha, here you go.'

Harley suited up while Kate rifled through drawers, scattering paperwork across the benches, hundreds of pages of notes scrawled in Mangold's spidery handwriting. She was about to give up when she found a manila envelope that looked about twenty years old. In it were several black-and-white A4 prints that had been produced from a microscope.

'There you are,' she said. 'You little bastard.'

'Kate . . .?'

She gestured for Harley to look at one of the prints.

'What am I looking for?' he asked.

'You won't be able to see it,' she said. 'But the thing that really puzzled me about Watoto-X2 was how quickly it kills compared to the original.' She paused, thinking about Paul in the other room. How long did he have?

'Isn't it simply a stronger strain of the virus?'

'That's what we thought. But it looks identical

to the original strain, the one I had when I was a child.'

Harley nodded.

'So . . . I think this is the answer. For the last year or so, when Isaac and I were studying Watoto, we kept seeing a trace of something on the edges of Watoto's outer shell.'

She looked up and saw that Harley was confused. 'Viruses have an outer shell, a kind of coat, made of protein. In our paper, Isaac and I reported that we kept seeing a "ghost"—a trace of something on the outer edges of the shell that would appear fleetingly then disappear. We could never work out what it was.'

'Right.'

'Junko worked it out first. She was talking to me about "the ghost", which Isaac and I thought must be some kind of contamination, right before Angelica and her cronies turned up at the lab. She never got the chance to tell me more . . .' She trailed off for a moment. Junko's body was out there somewhere. Had they buried her or just dumped her remains with their other victims? Picturing another kind of ghost, wandering the grounds, unable to rest, Kate shivered.

'Go on,' Harley urged.

She pointed to the relevant part of the picture. 'But, as Diaz said to you, what we were actually seeing on the edge of the Watoto virus was a satellite virus.' She knew Harley wouldn't understand. 'Think of Watoto as being like planet Earth. And attached to it, like our moon, is a tiny satellite.'

'OK . . .'

'The satellite exists on both Watoto and

Watoto-X2. It's always been there. The difference is that, with X2, there is something inside the satellite—and that's what kills victims of Watoto-X2 so quickly.'

Harley squinted at her. 'What, like another virus? You mean, there are two viruses?'

'No—not really. I think the satellite actually contains something else. A toxin. A poison. When Watoto-X2—which is basically the original Watoto with the additional poison attached to it—enters the victim's body, it releases this poison into the bloodstream. And this poison kills the sufferer before the Watoto virus itself gets a chance. That's why people die so suddenly and the fatality rate is so high. The antibodies that might have some chance of fighting off Watoto never get a chance to do their job because the poison sneaks in round the back, as it were, and kills the victim first. That's what caused the seizures. And—oh yes! That's why Mangold told Simone they were giving her an antidote. Because you need an antidote to fight a poison.'

'OK—that makes sense. But what is the poison?'

Kate stood upright, her aching back forgotten. 'You know that when I was a child I lived in Tanzania for a while and caught Watoto?'

'Yes. Of course.'

'And Diaz told you that he and Mangold were working on something they called Project Hadza?'

'Ye-es.'

She smiled. 'Well, Hadza is the name of a tribe in Tanzania. They were the people my family were living with. It's been so long since I heard that word—and I was a child back then—that I didn't remember immediately. But then it came to me.'

416

She could picture the people now; she had an image of a young boy with a bow strung across his back. A hunter.

She went on. 'And that made me make the other connection. Those plants out back, with the pretty flowers—I knew I recognised them. They used to grow all around the village where we stayed. The Hadza had a name for the plant that I can't remember, but my mum called it a mamba rose.'

So strange, she thought, how life went in circles. So strange to be, in her mind, back in Africa, the hazy memories of heat and light through dappled leaves and the sickness that had claimed her parents: memories she had repressed for a long time because they were so unbearably painful. The first of so many losses: Mum, Dad, then Stephen, Isaac, Junko—and now, unless a miracle occurred, Paul too. She swallowed hard.

'The Hadza would use the sap from the plants to poison their arrowtips. I remember them warning us that the plants weren't safe, that we should be careful of them. And Mangold told me that he and Diaz had been to Tanzania. He said they were looking for something. Obviously, from the name they gave their project, it had something to do with the Hadza.'

'Couldn't they have been collecting samples of Watoto?'

'Maybe. But they did something to Watoto to make it even more deadly. And we know from what Diaz said that it must be something to do with the satellite virus. I'm willing to bet that they added the poison from the mamba rose, creating a version of Watoto that carries a satellite genome containing the toxic gene from the plant.'

417

Harley looked confused again.

'You don't need to understand the science. All you need to know is that the thing that makes Watoto-X2 so deadly is the poison it carries around with it, which comes from that plant growing out back.'

She gestured for him to follow her out of the lab, and he stripped off his protective suit, leaving it in a crumpled heap on the floor.

'So what happens now?' he asked. 'How does this actually help us find an antidote?'

'Well, the first thing we need to find out is whether there is an existing, known antidote to the mamba rose toxin. We should be able to look it up online, unless the internet is down here too.'

Harley thought for a moment. 'What resources do you need? Ideally? I'll get them for you.'

'The first thing I need is to talk to a toxicology expert.'

'OK.' Harley reached for his phone.

Kate looked into the room where Paul was still asleep. He was shiny with sweat, his skin as pale as an albino's.

'You're trembling,' Harley said softly.

'I'm really scared, Jason. Because even if we find an antidote to the toxin and get it here straight away, that won't stop the Watoto virus itself. All it will do is buy Paul time by stopping the poison. It will give him an extra couple of days, but Watoto itself still has a mortality rate of around seventy per cent.'

'So by finding the antidote we would be reducing his chances of dying from ninety-nine per cent with Watoto-X2, to seventy per cent with plain, unadulterated Watoto? That's still pretty good,

Kate.'

She stared at Paul, chewing her thumbnail nervously. 'Not good enough though.'

\*       \*       \*

While Harley got to work, making one call after another, Kate crouched beside Paul, stroking his brow, murmuring soothing words he couldn't hear.

Harley came over and held out the phone to Kate. 'I've got Professor Simon Black at the Center of Toxicology in Dallas. There's one in San Francisco but, not surprisingly, it's shut.'

Kate took the phone and found herself talking to a man with a gravelly Texan accent. She explained about the mamba rose, what she needed, could hear him tapping away at a computer.

'Well, now,' he said. 'This is real interesting.'

'Tell me,' Kate urged.

'The mamba rose is an extremely toxic plant. Hunters in Africa use it to dip their arrow tips in.'

'Yes, I knew that. But what about an antidote to the poison?'

He paused. 'Jeez. That sure is interesting.'

This was maddening. 'What is it?'

'It's quite a remarkable plant. The antidote to the poison, which is in the sap, is actually contained in the same plant—within the stem. Do you have access to this plant now?'

'Yes. There are thousands of them growing here.'

'OK. Well, I can talk you through how to prepare and administer the antidote. Though I need to make a phone call first, to check a couple of things.

419

Is that all right?'

Kate felt on the verge of tears. 'Yes, yes. But please, be as quick as you can.'

She handed the phone back to Harley and walked straight through to see Paul. As she entered the room, he stirred, then opened his eyes.

She knelt beside him. 'How are you feeling?'

His voice was hoarse and weak. 'Like death.' He attempted a smile. 'It's definitely not man flu.'

'I've got some good news. We've found an antidote . . . It's complicated, but I'm just waiting for a call back.'

This time, he managed a proper smile. 'That's amazing. I knew you'd do it. You're brilliant, Kate.'

She tried to smile back. How could she tell him that, while they had identified an antidote to the poison that Watoto-X2 carried, there was still no cure for the virus itself?

'Listen, Paul,' she said, 'when we get through this . . . You know what you asked me before, back in England, about marrying you? The answer is yes. I want to.'

'You don't have to say that, just because I'm sick.'

'No. I made up my mind while we were apart. I was being stupid before. I want to do it. I want to be with you for ever.'

He squeezed her hand. 'You'd better get me that antidote then. Hey, don't cry.'

She couldn't help it. She held on to him as the tears came, pressing her face against his burning hot shoulder. Paul held her back, not speaking. In the distance, she thought she could hear a phone ringing. But she didn't want to let Paul go. He had to survive. He had to. She needed him. And the sick

420

irony was, she had only fully realised that when she was on the brink of losing him.

From behind her, she heard Harley say, 'Er, Kate? It's Professor Black.'

She extricated herself from Paul—the front of her shirt was damp from his sweat and her tears—and crossed the room to take the phone from Harley, taking it into the entrance hall so Paul wouldn't overhear.

'Professor Black.'

'Doctor Maddox. I made my calls, and I can tell you how to prepare the antidote.'

'That's wonderful.'

'But while I was waiting for my contact to call me back, I did some more digging around to see what else I could find out about the mamba rose. I've come across something . . . well, it's kinda unconventional. Possibly a load of BS, if you'll pardon my French.'

She waited for him to continue.

'I found a research paper online written by an anthropologist, name of James Martens. This paper has recently been added to the online archive of the American Journal of Anthropology. An abstract came up when I googled mamba rose and virus, so I bought the full paper. It appears Martens stayed with the Hadza tribe in Tanzania for a year back in the seventies. It's a fascinating account.'

Kate felt herself growing impatient again. 'Yes?'

'Hmm . . .' There was a pause, as if he was scanning through the article as he spoke. 'Yes, here we are: Martens writes about how there was an outbreak of a disease among the tribesfolk. They had another name for it, but the symptoms sound exactly like Watoto. Identical, in fact. And Martens

421

wrote that the Hadza had a cure for it.'

Kate was suspicious. 'A cure? If there was some kind of folk cure for Watoto, I would have heard of it.'

'Not necessarily,' Black said. 'This paper was obscure—it was only added to their online archive this year, and it doesn't actually mention Watoto by name, so you would only have found it if you were searching for the mamba rose—which you wouldn't have done before, am I right?'

'Yes . . . that's right.' She felt her excitement growing.

'Virology isn't my field, but can plants be used to tackle viruses?'

'Well, as yet no one has discovered an antivirus that is derived from a plant, but there's an awful lot of research going on. The US Government has set up an agency called the Natural Products Branch—I assume you've heard of it? They've been carrying out a huge screening programme, because there are millions of plant chemicals out there—a whole world of undiscovered treatments. No antivirals yet, but plenty of antimicrobials . . .' She purposefully moved the conversation on. 'But what was this cure the Hadza came up with?'

'Get this.' He paused for effect. 'They used the mamba rose plant. Martens writes that the tribesfolk made a medicine from it which they gave to the victims of the virus, and within about twenty-four hours they started to get better. They almost all made a full recovery.'

'But the poisonous sap should have . . .' She broke off. She was going to say it should have killed them, but as she spoke, the solution had come to her.

'You're thinking exactly what I was thinking,' said Professor Black.

'That the medicine contained both the poisonous sap—and the antidote for the poisonous sap.'

'Yup. So the sap contains some kind of antiviral agent that stops Watoto.'

'And the other part of the plant makes the sap safe. Oh my God.'

Kate's mind raced. If this was true, then it would be the answer she had been searching for. But how far could she trust the account of some obscure anthropologist who had published a research paper, what, almost forty years ago? Could it really be possible that this plant contained an antiviral agent that would stop Watoto? Kate was more open-minded than many of her peers: she believed, as she'd told Black, that there could be many ways of tackling viruses that had yet to be discovered. Some using high-tech methods, but it was equally possible there might be others that relied on natural sources. This wouldn't help them create a vaccine—but an antiviral could be used to help anyone who had contracted the disease.

'Does it say anything else about James Martens on that site?' she asked.

'Yep. I'm ahead of you. I did some googling. Mr Martens was a lecturer in anthropology at Dartmouth College in New Hampshire. Retired a few years ago. He's on Facebook.'

Kate almost laughed. 'You're kidding?'

'I already checked out his page—looks like he uses it to keep in touch with his grandkids and former students. I sent him a message asking him to get in touch with me. He messaged me back right before I called you. He's expecting your call.'

'Professor Black—'

'Call me Simon.'

'Thank you so, so much.'

He gave her the number for James Martens and she ended the call. Harley was standing behind her.

'What is it?' he asked, when he saw the excitement on her face.

'I need to call New Hampshire. Now.'

\*       \*       \*

James Martens was polite and helpful. He reminded her of some of the academics she had worked with at Boston; well-spoken and keen to share his knowledge. He remembered his time with the Hadza tribe as clearly as if it was last week, he said, even though he was finding it increasingly hard to remember what he'd done the day before.

'They took the entire plant, dug it up, roots and all, and kind of crushed it in this big pot,' he said. 'Then they took all the . . . juice and injected it into each of the sick people.'

'Injected it?'

'Yes, they had needles and syringes that they'd got from the great armies of missionaries and aid workers who were constantly tramping through the place.'

'Yes. Of course.'

'So, yes, they injected them. I couldn't believe it. I knew they used the mamba roses to poison their arrows; I thought maybe they were trying to put the people out of their misery, like some form of euthanasia. But then they got better. I'll never forget it.'

Kate described to Martens the exact symptoms of Watoto, from beginning to end. 'Are you sure that fits what these people had?'

'Absolutely. Pretty rare disease though, isn't it?'

'It used to be. It's in the process of wiping out California.'

'What? The Indian flu?'

'Yes. It's not flu—it's a new strain of Watoto.'

'Holy . . . Of course I've heard about it, it's all over the news. They just reported the first couple of cases here—but no one said anything about it being Watoto.'

That meant, Kate realised, that it had spread across the whole country. It must be in Dallas by now. She had been completely cut off from the world for days, not even a week yet but it felt like much much longer. She needed to talk to Jack.

Kate spoke to Martens for a while longer before disconnecting and handing Harley back his phone. She gave him a rapid summary of what she'd learned.

'So, in a nutshell, we need to crush one of those plants that's growing out back and inject it into Paul?' Harley said, his tone sceptical.

'If we can believe any of it. First I need to run tests, to identify the compounds and agents in the plant, to work out the dosage. I can't simply mix it up and inject it into him.'

She went to the doorway and looked in at Paul. He was sweating so much he looked like he'd just got out of the shower. The room stank of sickness.

Harley followed her over. 'How long do we have?' he said in a low voice.

'When exactly did he start displaying symptoms?'

'Yesterday afternoon, when we left the prison.'

425

Harley checked his watch. 'It's just gone noon now. So, less than twenty-four hours ago.'

'The police officer they brought to the lab had been showing symptoms for seventy-two hours when he died. That means we should still have up to forty-eight hours, depending on Paul's underlying health, which is good. But in some cases the toxin is released early, so we can't really be sure.'

'OK. Tell me again what you need.'

Kate thought. 'The first thing I need is a better lab. The one here is ill-equipped and cramped. I need a team—the best people who are still alive. I'm going to need some rats or monkeys. And I need a load of those plants from out back. Roots and all.'

'OK.'

'And I'm going to need a lot of coffee.'

Harley smiled. 'All right. Let's get you back to Sequoia, we'll use the lab there. It's the best in the country.'

Kate looked over at Paul again. 'I wish Isaac were here, that that bitch hadn't killed him.'

'Hmm, Angelica. There's another problem—I'm afraid we're going to have to take her with us. All the prisons in this area have been shut down by the virus. I just had a call from HQ to say that they can't spare any more agents, so she's in my care for the foreseeable.'

'As long as she doesn't come anywhere near me.'

Kate sighed as Harley took out his phone and started making more calls. She went over to Paul.

'Hold on,' she said, not knowing if he could hear her or not. 'I need you to fight it, Paul. I'm going to make you better.'

426

It had always been a personal battle. Kate Maddox versus Watoto. The virus had taken her family, consumed most of her adult life, almost killed her twice. Everything that had happened in her life so far had been leading to this moment.

This was the final round.

## 63

The birdsong in the Sequoia forest sounded the same and the great trees stood as firm as they had for centuries but, to Kate, everything felt different this time. Even the lab was different. When she turned towards the place where Simone had tackled Junko to the ground and cracked her head open, an innocent shadow appeared as a pool of blood. She kept replaying Cindy's scream as the liquid nitrogen had ruined her face. And there, in the isolator behind a thick shield of glass, was where Officer Buckley had died, writhing in agony induced by the toxin from the mamba rose, his body already ravaged by Watoto.

Now Paul lay in his place. And if Kate and her new team didn't work as fast and hard as any team had ever worked, he would suffer the same fate.

Harley's superiors, working with the CDC, had mobilised everyone available, flying in a team of virologists and technicians from around the country in private jets: Philip Davies from Seattle, Elaine Manning from Chicago, and Dee Delaney and Victoria Danes from the CDC's HQ in Atlanta. They had all been frantically yet fruitlessly working on a vaccine since the outbreak began. Along with the virologists were two botanists and a toxicologist.

Upstairs, Angelica was being held under armed guard in one of the rooms where she and her 'Sisters' had slaughtered the sleeping occupants: Tosca McCarthy, Kolosine and the others. Even the housekeeper, Adoncia, had been murdered.

While she had been waiting for the new team to arrive, Kate had been in with Paul, who was barely conscious, whispering soothing words, urging him to be strong, to fight it, even though she knew that wouldn't do any good. You can't appeal directly to antibodies. But having her near, holding his hand, seemed to help.

The other huge worry on her mind was Jack. She had called Vernon's landline. It went straight to voicemail. She tried his mobile. Exactly the same. It had been like this for hours. This was all wrong— Vernon was one of those people who had to be surgically removed from his cellphone.

A spasm of panic almost made her double over.

'What's the matter?' said Harley.

'Can you keep trying to call Vernon for me? I need to know Jack's safe. Something's not right.'

Harley passed a weary hand across his brow. 'O.K.' He looked as though he was about to add 'I'll add it to the list', but thought better of it.

'I have to get into the lab now,' she had said. 'But please, tell me as soon as you hear something.'

As soon as the new team were in and suited up, she kissed Paul and made her way into the lab. Four pairs of eyes looked at her expectantly. She already had everything set up.

'OK,' she said, standing before them. 'My name is Dr Kate Maddox.'

They introduced themselves in turn.

428

She nodded briskly. 'I hope none of you are expecting to get any sleep tonight . . .'

*       *       *

By the time she left the lab, the sun was coming up. Harley staggered to his feet as she entered the room. He had dark shadows under his eyes, as if he hadn't slept either and had been waiting for her all night. Apart from a cat-nap in the helicopter on the journey up here, she hadn't slept in over thirty-six hours. She felt light, on the brink of delirium, but she was buzzing with adrenaline and excitement.

'Well?' Harley asked.

She sat down. 'Can you get me a coffee? I feel like I'm about to pass out.'

'Sure.' He hurried out and headed to the kitchen, returning a few minutes later with a steaming mug.

Kate sipped the coffee. The sky outside the window was lightening, the birds starting to sing again. She looked up at Harley and said, 'It seems to work.'

Lost for words, he stepped towards her as if he was going to embrace her, then thought better of it at the last moment, stopping awkwardly a few inches from her.

'Have you managed to get hold of Vernon?' she asked.

He shook his head. 'Still no answer.'

'What's going on? He *always* answers his mobile. Something must have happened—it's been two days. Has the flu got to Dallas? You have to find out, Jason—do something!'

Tiredness and panic were injecting aggression

429

into her voice, and Harley held up his hands.

'Kate, I will. I'm trying to help.'

She gave a tight-lipped smile. 'I'm really sorry. It's just that I'm exhausted—and so worried . . .'

'I know. I'll find out, leave it with me. I'll keep trying the phones, and I'll see if I can get someone to go round. But tell me about the antivirus.'

Kate tried to ignore the pain in her chest, the deep, gnawing anxiety that wouldn't fade until she knew that Jack was all right.

She gulped her coffee. 'We took the samples from the plants and extracted the toxin and the antidote. That part was pretty straightforward. The tricky part was testing it on the rats, because when we injected the toxin first they would die before we got the chance to give them the antidote.' Kate grimaced. She disliked testing on animals, found it the hardest part of her job. 'The answer was to give them both at the same time. The antidote from the upper part of the plant cancelled out the toxin from the sap.'

Harley nodded.

'So then we started trying to isolate which part of the sap was acting as an antiviral agent against Watoto. Or rather, finding out if it worked in the first place. We . . .'

'Are you all right?' Harley reached out a steadying hand, alarm on his face.

'Yes, yes . . . I can't stop thinking about Jack.' She took a deep breath. 'Jason, it was so tense in there. This was our only chance. If Martens, that anthropologist, had been wrong, or if he'd exaggerated about what he'd seen in Tanzania . . .'

'Was he?'

'No.' She was still surprised by what they had

430

found. 'We were able to isolate an agent . . .'

She saw Harley's face immediately switch into his 'uh-oh, science' mode. She smiled faintly. 'Don't worry, I'm not going to bore you with the details. Long story short: the sap contains an agent that works on the Watoto virus. Fights it. Stops it. Again, we tested it on the rats. I had already given them the virus, and they were sick. But the mamba rose appears to stop the virus in its tracks.'

'"Appears to"?'

She twisted her hands together. 'Normally, we would want to continue monitoring the rats over a long period to check that it had worked and to see if there were any side effects. But so far, the antivirus works. On rats at least.'

'That's amazing, Kate.'

'But we still need to test it properly. We need trials . . . We have no idea if this will really work on a person.'

Harley opened his mouth, then closed it.

'What were you going to say?' Kate asked, already knowing the answer because exactly the same thought had been running through her mind.

'Well—what about Paul? Surely he doesn't have that long before . . .' He stopped. 'You don't have time to carry out rigorous trials, do you?'

'I know, I know. This goes against everything I've ever learned, ever practised.'

'Do you think it will work?'

'I don't know. If we get the dosage wrong . . . If we get *anything* wrong, it could kill him. Maybe we should wait, carry out more tests, get some monkeys . . .'

Harley's phone chimed in his pocket. He silenced it and stepped towards Kate. This time, he took hold of her upper arms and looked her in the eye.

'If it was me in there, I'd want you to do it. To take the chance.'

Kate nodded. He was right. If it was her, if she only had this chance of surviving, she would grab it. Risk it.

She extricated herself from Harley's grip and, ignoring the wave of fatigue that almost toppled her, strode from the room.

\*     \*     \*

'Paul, Paul . . .'

She gently shook him awake. His eyes were glazed, his breathing shallow and wet.

'I need your permission to try something,' she said.

Paul opened his mouth to speak but nothing came out. He nodded towards a glass of water on the side, and she lifted it to his lips.

'We think we've found an antivirus. We've tested it on rats and it seems to work, but it's risky. Normally, we would—'

'Give it to me,' he whispered.

She looked up at him.

'But, Paul, I think I should—'

He cut her off. His voice was so weak she had to lean closer to hear him. 'I trust you, Kate. If you think it's going to work, I'll risk it.' He coughed. 'What have I got to lose?'

'It could kill you. I don't want to use you as a guinea pig.'

'If you don't, Watoto will kill me.'

'It's only a seventy per cent chance . . .'

'Only.'

She nodded. 'I'm frightened to try it, Paul. If I inject you and it doesn't work, it will be as if I killed you.'

He looked into her eyes. 'I'd rather die trying.' He started to cough again, his eyes screwed shut, wincing with pain. He gripped her hand and attempted a smile. 'And if it doesn't work, I guess I'll get to see Stephen again.'

Kate squeezed his hand back.

'Are you sure?'

'Yes. Do it.'

She left the room and returned a minute later. She took his bare arm, surprised again at how hot his skin was. The strength in his muscles, in those arms that she loved to feel wrapped round her, was absent; his strong hands were curled like dead spiders. She was amazed her own hand wasn't shaking. But as she prepared the injection, she wasn't a lover, or a nurse. She was a scientist. Beneath the fear, she had faith in what she was doing. It took a moment to find a vein, then slipped the needle in.

Now all she could do was wait.

\*     \*     \*

Harley was shouting at one of the junior officers when she emerged from the room.

'What is it?' she asked.

'Kate, I'm sor—'

'What is it?' She had a feeling of sick dread that he was going to tell something had happened to Jack.

But it wasn't as bad as that. Terrible, but not as bad.

'It's Angelica. She's escaped.'

## 64

Nothing could have prepared the three boys for what they saw when they finally entered the city of Los Angeles early on Tuesday morning. They were silent as Riley drove at ten miles an hour through deserted streets. Almost every shop window was shattered, and their tyres crunched over a million pellets of broken glass. Rubbish piled up on the sidewalks, but you didn't have to look too closely to see that some of it wasn't trash at all, but dead bodies. Smoke rose and mingled with the smog from a hundred unattended fires, from braziers on street corners to whole apartment blocks, shooting flames high into the air.

The smell was terrible—death and rotten food, blood, smoke and dirt. Riley closed all the windows and air vents, and popped down the locks. It immediately became unbearably hot in the car, but neither Jack nor Bradley complained. They sat holding one another's hands, without even noticing, staring open-mouthed with horror out of the windows. There was a bewildering and discordant backdrop of noise that filled every last cranny of their heads: a cacophony of never-ending alarms— car alarms, security alarms, smoke alarms—swirling and shrieking, seeming to press in on them.

A man lay dead in the middle of the street, blood from several bullet holes in his chest congealing in a dark puddle around him.

'Don't look, kids,' said Riley in a strangled voice, but of course they did. Jack retched, but managed not to vomit. He pulled his knees up to his chest and put his hands over his ears, burying his face.

'Shit,' Riley said. 'I don't have room to drive around him.'

'Can we turn around?' whispered Bradley, who had also turned green. 'I don't feel good. My head hurts.'

Riley shook his head. 'No space. Can't back up with the Airstream neither.'

The man was spread-eagled right across the centre of the narrow one-way street, although his blood had oozed from one sidewalk to the other.

'I don't want to walk from here,' Bradley added. 'My legs are aching.'

'We ain't walking nowhere,' Riley said. 'Close your eyes, both of you.'

Jack and Bradley did as they were told. Riley turned the steering wheel to the right, mounted the kerb, and drove as close to the looted storefronts as he dared—but they still felt the bump and crunch as he drove over the dead man's feet and ankles.

Bradley was crying. 'I want Mommy,' he said. 'It's awful here.'

Jack had his hands over his ears, and his eyes tightly shut.

'Come on, squirt, we got this far—look, we're almost in West Hollywood, and that's where Dad lives! We're real close now. Look out for signs for Wilshire Country Club, OK, 'cos his house is right by there. South Mansfield Avenue. First to spot it gets . . . shit, I don't know. I ain't got nothing left to give you. Gets a popsicle at Dad's, I guess. We'll be

OK when we get there.'

He seemed to be trying to reassure himself as much as them.

They drove on, past a field hospital that had been erected in a park, dark green army tents and lines of sobbing masked people outside being herded in, or pushed in wheelchairs, by soldiers in full protective suits, armed with machine guns. Even from the moving car, Riley could see the terror in the eyes of the sick people, like they knew that if they went into one of those tents, they wouldn't be coming out alive. Riley shuddered and drove faster. It was only when they had got a few blocks past it that Jack spoke. 'Those ladies wanted to go to a hospital.'

Riley had forgotten all about the hot girl and her mom in the Airstream. He hesitated. He couldn't turn the vehicle round.

'It's not far,' he said. 'They can walk from Dad's. I don't reckon it's safe for us to stop near so many people with the flu.'

'There's the turning to Dad's street!' Bradley said a few minutes later, pointing with a shaky hand. 'It looks different,' he added.

The formerly quiet, tree-lined road with its Spanish-style bungalows and neat front yards had turned into something resembling a war zone. Trash cans and cars had been overturned. A school bus blazed, watched by a small gang of young men with bandannas tied across their noses and mouths. Two of them were sitting on the sidewalk, cleaning their guns. They were big, muscle-bound guys with tattoos and shaved heads, but they looked sick and scared.

'That's Daddy's house,' Bradley informed Jack,

436

as Riley pulled up a little way along from the gang near the school bus. 'We're here.'

Riley put the car into 'park' and they all gazed at the detached, modern sandstone house. It looked untouched by riots and fire, and its large pillars, flanking the front door, were reassuring. Riley turned to face the boys. His eyes were red-rimmed with stress and fatigue, and acne stood out angrily on his cheeks. 'OK. This is what we'll do. I'm gonna go ring the bell. You two stay right here in the car with the doors locked. I'm gonna bring you out something from Dad's house that you can tie around your faces as a mask—a shirt or a tea-towel or whatever I can find. But you don't get out till I give you the signal. Got it?'

The boys nodded fearfully. Riley pulled on his denim jacket and buried his nose and mouth in the crook of his elbow. He leapt out of the car and dashed up the marble steps to the front door.

Jack and Bradley watched from the back seat as Riley kept his finger on the buzzer. Over the background noise of all the alarms, they could hear the high-pitched frantic barking of a small dog.

'Martha,' said Bradley. 'That's good. It means Daddy's home. Look, Riley's getting the spare key.'

They watched as Riley, with his arm still over his face, delved into one of two large terracotta pots of pampas grasses on either side of the porch. He pulled out what looked to Jack like a large pebble, and turned it over. 'It's in that fake stone. Cool, isn't it?' Bradley said, with a ghost of a smile.

Riley extracted a key from a small compartment at the back of the stone, opened the front door and vanished inside, holding up his palm in a 'wait' gesture at them. Seconds later he appeared again at

437

the top of the steps, and vomited copiously over the balustrade into one of the pampas grasses.

'Oh no,' Jack said. 'I hope he hasn't caught the flu. We'd better go help him.'

'We don't have masks on,' Bradley said. 'So hold your breath, OK?'

The boys ran up the steps to where Riley was still leaning over the edge of the porch. Jack tentatively rubbed his denim-clad back, but Riley straightened up and grabbed his arm, tears and snot and puke all over his face. 'I told you not to get out! Don't go in there!' he shouted, but it was too late to stop Bradley, who had rushed in calling 'Dad! Da-ad? We're here!'

Then he screamed.

\*     \*     \*

Riley, when he had recovered enough from the sight of his father's bloated corpse to be able to move without throwing up, marched the boys upstairs to the room that his dad called 'the world's smallest cinema', Martha the dog yapping hysterically at his heels all the way. He grabbed the nearest Disney DVD that he could find, shoved it into the home entertainment system and turned up the volume. It was *Fantasia*, to which both Jack and Bradley would, under normal circumstances, have objected strongly. But they sat down on the leather sofa in front of the huge screen and stared with blank, horrified eyes as pink elephants cavorted and whirled. The smell of dogshit permeated the entire house, but at least it masked the other, worse, smell.

'Stay there,' Riley ordered, in a voice muffled slightly by the cloth he had tied over his mouth and nose. 'Keep the door closed. Don't move until I come back for you. If you have to use the bathroom, use that one—' He pointed at the small en-suite off the room. 'Do NOT leave this room. I'll be right back, I'll go get you a drink.'

Riley bounded down the stairs on legs that felt like rubber. His heart was pounding so hard that it felt like it had been replaced with an enormous beach ball that had no room to move in his chest. He saw his dad's feet sticking out from behind the kitchen island, and it reminded him of the other dead man, the one whose feet he'd run over. Without looking again at his father's face—one glance had been enough to confirm that he had clearly been dead for some time—he grabbed his ankles and dragged him with great effort across the room, negotiating around two runny piles of dog shit, into the utility room off the kitchen, where he left him next to the washer-drier. He closed the door behind him, retched, and threw up again in the kitchen sink. After he'd cleaned up the dog mess, rinsed his mouth and the sink, and scrubbed his hands more thoroughly than he'd done for years, an investigation of the refrigerator revealed a carton of serviceable-looking OJ, and a half-full bottle of Chardonnay. Riley unstoppered the wine and downed its contents in four huge gulps, Martha sticking so close to his ankles that he risked tripping over her at every step. He filled two glasses of OJ for the boys, a bowl of dry food for Martha, which she fell on ravenously, and returned upstairs.

'OK, kids?' he said, holding out the juice.

Jack took the glass, but didn't drink any. Bradley

was unable even to reach out for his. His small body was trembling uncontrollably, almost convulsing. Riley looked at him more closely and saw that his eyes were red and his nose streaming—he had attributed it to tears, but now, laying a hand on his forehead, realised that his brother's temperature was sky-high, and he was almost catatonic.

'Fuck!' Riley said, in a panicked whimper, putting the OJ down on a shelf. 'Oh Jesus, no, no, no. Oh fuck, Brad, man, I'm so sorry, this is all my fault . . .'

He turned and thumped the wall hard with his fist, leaning into it, his shoulders shaking. Jack just stared at him, and then at his friend, and then at the garish swirling colours of the cartoon.

Riley took a deep, sobbing breath and turned back. He picked Bradley's limp body up in his arms. 'Jack, pal, I'm sorry but I think Bradley's got the flu. I'm gonna have to put him in another bedroom so you don't catch it too.' If you haven't already, he thought but didn't say. If we haven't all caught it.

Jack didn't speak.

'OK, buddy? He'll be down the hallway—but listen, you have to stay here. You can't hang out with him any more, not till he's . . . better. I can't look after two sick kids.'

Jack nodded briefly.

'Will he die?' he said, so quietly that Riley barely heard him.

'Nah, man, of course not,' he said, negotiating Bradley through the doorway. 'It's only a spot of flu, don't you worry.'

Jack stared down at the glass in his hand as though he'd never seen orange juice before.

440

Riley laid his brother on the bed in the spare room, wet a washcloth and placed it on his burning forehead. Bradley barely stirred. He looked so tiny on the huge king-sized bed, and Riley remembered when he was first born, the shock of his helplessness, and Riley's own resentment that there was a rival for his parents' affections.

'You're a royal pain in the ass, you know,' he whispered, dabbing beads of sweat away from Bradley's cheeks and neck. 'Please don't die. Please, Brad. Mom will kill me if you die. And, well, I guess I'd miss you . . .'

But Bradley couldn't hear him. He had slipped quietly under a thick comforter of unconsciousness.

## 65

Kate sat next to the isolator, watching Paul's chest rise and fall. He was deathly pale, but seemed to be sleeping peacefully. She leaned her forehead against the cool glass and felt her own eyes begin to drift closed. She felt so tired it was as though each individual blood cell inside her was aching. How long would it be before she knew whether it had worked? Whether she had saved Paul's life . . . or killed him?

Her thoughts shifted to Angelica. She could hardly believe that the agent who had been guarding Angelica had let her escape. Apparently, she had begged him to let her use the toilet. Surely it was the oldest trick in the book? His excuse was that, as they were so short-handed and there were no female agents to help, he had allowed her to close the door of the toilet. Of course, she had immediately squeezed through the window and shinned down the side of the building. She was long gone—into the woods, they assumed—before the agent even noticed.

Harley had been furious, but Kate had tried to calm him. 'What can she do now?' she said. 'All of her disciples are dead. Diaz helped guide her, and he's gone. She knows we are working on a cure. She's been beaten. If I was her, I would run ten thousand miles in the opposite direction.'

A rapping noise startled her—one of the medical staff who had arrived yesterday along with the virologists. She jerked awake again.

'Dr Maddox, Agent Harley needs to talk to you urgently.'

She left the lab, feeling her heart tug as if it were attached to Paul by an invisible thread, and found Harley outside, gesticulating excitedly.

'Kate, come quick, I've got Vernon on the phone!'

Adrenaline coursed through her body, animating her exhausted limbs like a sugar rush. She grabbed the phone, tripping over her words in the rush to get them out.

'Hello? Vernon? Finally! Where have you been, why haven't you answered your phones? How's Jack?'

Vernon spoke so quietly that Kate could barely hear his reply over the hiss and crackle of the phone line. 'I've been at the hospital. Shirley's been in and out of there all week. She's got a perforated

442

bowel.'

'Sorry to hear it. Is Jack OK?'

'He—ah—yes, he's OK, last I heard . . . He and Bradley stowed away in Bradley's brother's Airstream. They went on a road trip, Kate. I was at the hospital with Shirley. I didn't find out until the next day, and then Riley—Bradley's brother—said he was bringing the boys home. But he didn't.'

'What! Where did they go? You're telling me our eight-year-old son is out there, no one knows where, in a country with a deadly virus rampaging through it and thousands already dead?'

Her voice cracked and her throat tightened as the possibilities flew in a loop through her brain: dead from flu, kidnapped, hit by a car, lost, sick, alone . . .

There was a long pause, which in itself was unusual—Vernon's most common response to any hint of a challenge was to rebut it and fight back even harder.

'Vernon?'

She heard a deep sigh.

'They were heading to, ah, California. To see Bradley's dad . . . in LA. And to try and find you.'

'LA?' Kate's stomach roiled and churned, and she thought she was going to be sick. 'But Bradley's mother had called the police, right?'

'The thing is, Riley told his mom that he was bringing the boys home. That ought to have taken a day at most. Only . . . he didn't show up, and his cellphone's switched off.'

'Shit. How old is this Riley?'

Vernon hesitated, and Kate knew he was going to lie to her.

'Twenty-five.'

'I don't believe you.'

'Jeez, Kate, I don't know exactly. He's old enough to drive. He looks about twenty. Don't panic, if something bad had happened, I'm sure we'd have heard about it.' But the note of abject panic in his own voice belied his words.

'Vernon, something very bad *has* happened. Is happening, right now. Do you have any idea of the chaos and anarchy going on out there? Did they reach Riley and Bradley's Dad's place? Why didn't they call?'

'Their mother has been calling and calling her ex, but it always goes straight to voicemail, and his cellphone is switched off. We need to keep trying—it would've taken them twenty-four hours to get there, assuming they made it through the roadblocks in the first place. But you know what? I bet Riley's just headed off to Big Sur or down to Mexico with the boys to avoid the shitstorm he'll be in when he shows his greasy face back here . . .'

Vernon's voice cracked and, to Kate's amazement, she realised he was crying. She had never heard Vernon cry before, not when Jack was born, not even when his mother died. 'I'm so sorry, Kate,' he sobbed. 'Our little Jackie, out there, with all this—this—sickness and death everywhere . . . I'm so scared. What if we never see him again? It's too late! It's too late, for all of us!'

Tears filled Kate's eyes. 'Don't, Vern, please. I'm really trying to hold it all together here. Jack needs us to be strong. And listen, it's not too late. I've found a cure.'

She thought of Paul lying in the isolator and prayed she wasn't tempting fate, telling Vernon about the treatment. 'We've got to pray that Jack

444

is safe, and at Bradley's dad's place. He'll call when he gets there, I'm sure he will . . .'

Vernon gave a shuddering sigh, followed by a lengthy wet sniff. 'So, Dr Kate Maddox saves the world, huh?' But he didn't say it as nastily as he might usually have done, and Kate realised that, despite the snideness of the comment, he was actually paying her a compliment.

'Kate, I'll call you the second I hear anything, I promise. You available on this number from now on?'

'Yes, while I'm at the lab. I'll give you Harley's cellphone, although there's no reception here, only the landline.'

Kate dictated the numbers. 'Can you give me the licence plate of the car he's in, and the Airstream's? Oh, and Bradley's dad's address too . . .'

'I'll go next door now and get the details from Gina.'

After she hung up, Kate sat rocking herself back and forth, arms wrapped around her head as if they were all that was holding her soul inside her body. She stayed there for several minutes, trying and failing to think rationally and calmly over the shrieking panic. A knock on the door broke her train of thought. It was Harley.

'What's the matter?' he asked immediately, seeing the expression on Kate's face.

'Jack's run away. We think he's in LA at his best friend's dad's place.'

'Oh shit. I'm sorry, Kate. We'll find him. Trust me.'

She nodded slowly. 'I want to come. Can we go now? I don't want to leave Paul, but I have to get to Jack. The team here know what they're doing—and anyway, it's a waiting game from here on in . . .'

He nodded. 'I'll pull rank and get a helicopter.'

\*     \*     \*

As they left the building, after giving strict instructions that if Paul's condition changed at all they should contact her, Kate made a vow to herself. If they all survived this, there would be no more guns, no more helicopters. The most exciting thing they would take would be the bus.

And if Paul and Jack didn't survive, she would drag her ruined heart around the globe, do whatever it took, to find Angelica—and make her pay.

## 66

Jack froze, the TV remote in his hand, when he heard the persistent ringing of the doorbell. It must be the police, come to put me in prison for running away, he thought, his throat dry with fear. He clicked the off button on the remote, slid off the shiny leather sofa, and looked around the room for a place to hide. Shaking, he dropped to his hands and knees and crawled round to the back of the sofa. There was a small inverted triangular space behind it, just about wide enough for him to shuffle backwards into. He squeezed in there and crouched, shivering like a wet puppy. Why were so many bad things happening?

'I want my mummy,' he whispered under his

breath. Why had he ever thought it was a good idea to come on this trip, with dead people everywhere? He wanted his mum. *Mummymummymummy*. He missed her with a passion that felt like the worst sort of hunger. Leaning forward, he rested his forehead on the floor, amongst all the dust balls, letting his tears leak silently into the carpet. When he was little, he'd had a robot called Billy, and he used to pretend that Billy could protect him, fire his lasers at the bad guys. He wished Billy was here now, instead of gathering dust under his bed back in England.

Behind the sofa and through the closed window, Jack could hear distant shouting voices, a woman and a man. He tried to listen over the insistent drilling of the bell. He thought—but surely he was wrong—that he heard his name being called. He listened harder. Yes, there it was: *'Jack! Jack!'*

Fresh tears filled his eyes. He shot out of his hiding place at top speed and ran down the stairs two at a time, his heart leaping with joy and gratitude.

'Mummy!' he screamed, hurling himself at the front door. 'I knew you'd come!'

\*　　　\*　　　\*

Lucy stared vacantly out of the Airstream window at the dark-haired woman in glasses who leapt up the steps to the front door, shouting for her son. When the door opened and one of the little boys who'd gone into the house that morning threw himself into her arms, Lucy turned away and looked at her own mother.

She thought of all the packed lunches her mom had made for her. All the rows they'd had, the tears they had shed, the hugs, the songs, the laundry and the miles walked up and down grocery-store aisles. Lucy knew the pattern of every freckle on her mom's arms, the same as her mom knew the name of every boy Lucy had ever liked.

When Lucy was little she used to lie in her mother's big bed with her, tracing a soft path between each freckle, while Rosie giggled and squirmed like a child at the touch of Lucy's soft forefinger. Lucy remembered harsh words and apologies, laughter and linked arms, DVDs on the sofa and being told off for letting stray popcorn kernels slip down between the cushions.

Who could she tell her problems to now? What would she do with all her mom's things? How was she going to get home? How did you organise a funeral, when you were sixteen and had no other family?

All these questions felt far too big to answer. She supposed she should go and get help, tell someone. But if she told someone, they would take her mom away and she would never ever see her again.

Lucy lay down on her side next to her mother, reached out, and held her cold, dead hand.

\*     \*     \*

Kate made sure that Bradley was as comfortable as he could be, and that Riley was calm enough to be left alone with him. 'It's just while Jason here walks us to the helicopter,' she explained. 'We have to get back to the lab. Look, Jason has keys to the house. He'll be right back, I promise you. Another helicopter is coming for you guys, an air ambulance, so sit tight for a little while longer. Bradley will be OK, trust me.'

Riley had just stared at her with a blank expression. He would not let go of his little brother's hand.

As Kate and Jack left the house, Kate wondered if Bradley really would be OK. She was about to ask Harley to call Vernon so he could tell the boys' mother what had happened, when she heard Jack give a worried exclamation.

'What's the matter, sweetheart?'

He paused, staring at the Airstream. 'I forgot about the ladies,' he said. 'Riley helped them. He gave them a ride 'cos they needed to get to a hospital. We did pass one, but Riley didn't want to stop by then 'cos it was too scary. Do you think they're still in there?'

'Why did they need to go to a hospital, Jack? Did they have the flu?' Kate's heart sank.

'I don't know. I don't think so. The girl didn't. Her mum looked poorly, but the girl said they'd been mugged and her mum had a bump on her head. The girl had blood on her T-shirt.'

'You two stay here,' Kate said. 'And keep your masks on. I'll go and check they're OK.'

'Don't be long,' said Harley, grasping Jack's shoulders.

Kate cupped her hands round her eyes and tried to peer in the Airstream window, but the glass was tinted and she couldn't make anything out. She turned the door handle but it was locked, so she knocked instead.

'Hello in there? Do you need any help? I have

449

the antivirus, if either of you needs it—please open up.'

*     *     *

Lucy heard the woman knocking and calling, and didn't move. Her limbs felt heavy and lifeless, and she wondered if it was the start of the flu. She hoped so. If not, she was going to get those scissors that she'd cut the tape off with, and slice open her veins.

'I have the antivirus!' the woman repeated. Lucy sighed. She didn't care about getting the stupid antivirus, which probably wouldn't even work—hadn't they said on the news that there was no cure for Indian flu? But she supposed, much as she wanted to, she couldn't stay in there for ever with her mom's dead body, and at least this woman was offering to help. Lucy doubted that any of the other people roaming the streets of LA would be so willing.

Slowly she lifted herself off the bed and plodded to the Airstream door.

'Hi,' the woman said gently. 'My name is Kate Maddox. Are you and your mum OK?'

She had an English accent, like the man who had caused all this trouble. If Paul hadn't come into the diner, they wouldn't be here now. Her mom would still be alive, Lucy was sure of it. She wouldn't have caught the flu if that Heather woman hadn't come looking for Paul.

Lucy stared at her. Why did her name sound familiar?

'Is your mother all right, Lucy?'

450

'She's dead,' Lucy said flatly.

Kate Maddox gazed sympathetically at her. She had nice eyes, Lucy thought, brown, sorrowful. She was about her mom's age, maybe younger. Lucy swallowed hard at the effort of admitting Rosie was dead.

'Oh, honey, I'm sorry,' Kate Maddox said. 'We need to get you out of here. You're at risk too—we need to vaccinate you as a precaution. Come into the house and wait—an air ambulance is coming to take the boys to the nearest emergency room. There's a field hospital round the corner, but it's not accepting anyone else.'

'Are you a doctor?' Lucy asked.

'No, I'm a scientist, I—'

Lucy started. She gripped the doorframe of the Airstream. Suddenly she knew where she had heard that name before: the crazy lady who had broken into their house and kidnapped them, the so-called Sister Heather—*she* had said the name Kate Maddox—Dr Kate Maddox. Kate Maddox was Paul's girlfriend!

'What?' Kate stopped mid-sentence at the expression on Lucy's face.

Lucy raised a shaking hand and pointed at her. 'You? If you hadn't brought your DUMB boyfriend over here and then LEFT HIM to go to some DUMB lab so that all he had to do was come into my mom's life and flirt with her and put us both in danger by getting some CRAZY woman with a knife who threatened to cut off my tits and kidnapped us so Mom caught the flu and now she's dead and it's *ALL YOUR FAULT, YOU BITCH!*'

Her voice raised in pitch, higher and higher, until she was screaming the words out. She flew down

451

the metal steps of the Airstream and flung herself at Kate, desperate to blame someone, shrieking like a banshee, trying feebly to claw at Kate's face and hair. The man holding the little boy released him and ran across to drag Lucy away, as she continued to flail and yell. 'I SWEAR I'M GONNA KILL YOU AND YOUR DUMBASS BOYFRIEND! YOU WAIT AND SEE! IF IT'S THE LAST THING I EVER DO, YOU'RE DEAD!'

The man was holding her tightly, pinning her arms to her sides, and she collapsed into him, her legs giving way, letting him hold her as she sobbed and sobbed.

*　　　*　　　*

Half an hour later Kate sat beside Jack, his head resting on her chest, in the same helicopter that had brought her from the lab. They were with an FBI escort, a young agent with grade-one hair and a jaw that could win sculpture awards.

Harley was staying behind to make sure the air ambulance turned up for Bradley, and Riley and Lucy were going to accompany them, having been given the antivirus as a precaution.

Kate still felt shaken from the confrontation with Lucy. The girl's mother must have been the woman who answered Paul's phone that time. And they'd ended up in the trailer pulled by the same car Jack was in? Later, after Paul had told her the whole story, Kate would figure out that Rosie must have caught Watoto-X2 in her home town, probably from someone who came into the diner. For her symptoms to have been so advanced that she died before they could help her, that had to be the case. But this poor girl wasn't to know that.

Jack, thank God, thank everything, was showing no sign of having Watoto, although his exposure to Bradley meant there was a very high chance that the virus was there, inside him, preparing to do its deadly work.

Now she felt more anxious than ever about the effectiveness of the antivirus. She needed to get back to the lab, to carry out tests on Paul and check his progress.

The chopper lifted off, its roar deafening as they ascended above LA, the Hollywood sign clearly visible below them.

She looked down at the city, at the smoke that rose from burned-out buildings, at the empty streets, the abandoned cars. So much destruction. So much death, in such a short space of time. All because of one woman's warped vision of a cleansed world, a vision born of her own confusion and vulnerability, and another man's hatred and pain. When she thought about what Angelica had been through, what had caused her mind to snap, she almost felt sorry for her.

Then she thought of Junko, of Tosca, of Bradley, and of the grief and fury of a sixteen-year-old girl who had just lost her mother.

*Almost* sorry. But not quite.

Outside the helicopter, the sun was shining. From up here, Kate could see the ocean, as vast and beautiful as ever. Her armed escort sat opposite her, a frown etched deep in his face. She hugged Jack tighter and closed her eyes. Paul's ashen face swam into her vision.

She felt chilly—probably from exhaustion and

shock. She looked around and saw a bundle of blankets piled up beside a first-aid kit. Just the thing. She gently extricated herself from Jack's grip and crossed the inside of the helicopter, stooping as the ceiling was too low to stand, to lift one of the blankets from the pile.

There was a sudden violent movement from under the blankets.

Angelica leapt up at her.

## 67

Kate jumped back—banging her head on the hard metal ceiling, her heart bursting into overdrive—as Angelica flew at her. The blonde wore a snarl of hatred. But instead of attacking Kate, she knocked her aside and launched herself at the armed agent as he tried to unfasten his belt and pull his gun. Angelica swung a fist at his hand, knocking the gun from his grasp, making it spin away beneath the seat. In one swift motion she grabbed his throat with one hand and drove her other fist down into his lap, smashing his testicles against the seat. He screamed and as he doubled over in pain she scrambled over his seat and grabbed him from behind, her forearm round his throat, squeezing until he went limp. Then she dipped quickly and grabbed the gun from beneath the seat.

She crouched on her haunches behind the seat and pointed the gun at Kate, who had instinctively thrown herself in front of Jack. He was silent, his eyes squeezed shut, like this was one incident too far. Too much for him to take.

'Land the helicopter,' Kate shrieked at the pilot, who was craning his neck trying to see what was going on.

'No!' Angelica shouted. 'If this helicopter dips an inch I'm going to shoot you in the head.'

'Then we'll all die,' Kate yelled. They were both shouting to be heard above the din of the helicopter's blades.

Angelica shrugged. 'I'll be in Paradise. Sekhmet will see to that.'

'But . . .' Kate began, then realised it was pointless trying to reason with Angelica. On the other hand, if she could keep her talking for a few minutes, maybe she could figure out what to do. Or the agent might regain consciousness—she didn't think he was dead, though he might never be a father, poor guy—and take Angelica by surprise.

'Why didn't you run off?' Kate shouted. 'Escape when you had the chance?'

Angelica brushed her hair from her eyes. She was so extraordinarily beautiful. She could have achieved great things. Well, no doubt she would see almost wiping out the human race as a pretty awesome achievement.

'Because I wanted him,' she said. To Kate's horror, she pointed at Jack.

'Jack? Why?'

'Because I want you to know what it feels like, bitch. You took away everyone who loves me.'

Kate shifted slightly to the left, ensuring Jack was fully out of Angelica's line of sight. If she was going to shoot him, she would have to shoot Kate first. Which would spoil her plan to make Kate suffer.

'Everyone who loves you? Not everyone you love?'

Angelica stared at her uncomprehendingly.

'You loved Diaz, didn't you?'

'I don't want to talk about him with you.'

'And what about Mangold? Your grandfather?'

'Him? I never loved him. He betrayed Camilo. He stopped being my grandfather the moment he did that.'

'But didn't you look after him for years?'

Angelica glared. 'He was useful. And, anyway, he never loved me. He was more interested in you.'

Kate thought she must have misheard in all the din. 'Me? What are you talking about?'

'You don't know anything, do you? About your family, your parents?'

Kate felt herself growing colder 'No—tell me.'

Angelica laughed. 'I'm sick of talking. Stand aside. Let me see the boy.'

'No!' Behind her, she heard Jack whimper. 'It's OK, darling,' she called, wishing she didn't need to shout.

'It's not OK,' Angelica sneered. 'Come on, Kate. I'll make it quick. He will hardly feel it.'

'You'll have to kill me first.'

Angelica stared at her, chewing her lower lip. 'No, I want you to watch. I want you to see his little chest explode, his heart stop, the life leave his body. And as the son of a godless whore, he won't be going to Paradise.'

'You'll have to go through me to get to him.'

Angelica looked her up down and smiled. 'Very well.'

But first, she took hold of the unconscious agent's head and twisted it rapidly, breaking his neck with a sickening crunch. Jack whimpered and peered out from behind Kate.

456

'Close your eyes,' she yelled.

Angelica climbed over the back of the seat, her eyes fixed on Kate, but as she was halfway over, Kate moved forward and grabbed her, pulling her over and swinging her arms so Angelica landed on the floor. Immediately she dropped to her knees on Angelica's back, the blonde wriggling like a landed fish in an effort to get her off. Kate went for the gun, trying to wrest it from Angelica's grip, but the woman elbowed her in the stomach, winding her and causing her to tumble to the side.

'Mum!' Jack cried.

Angelica sat up and pointed the gun at Jack's face. He screamed.

The sound electrified Kate. She aimed a punch at Angelica's face, connecting with her nose. Blood exploded in the air between them. Angelica spat and tried to hit her over the head with the gun, but Kate ducked to one side, pitching her assailant on to her front. Kate frantically looked around for something to use as a weapon. The fire extinguisher. She shuffled across the seat towards it and managed to unclip it, but Angelica grabbed her legs and pulled her back on to the floor and crawled on top of her. Then Kate felt the tip of the gun's barrel against the nape of her neck.

'I've decided against keeping you alive to watch the boy die,' Angelica said. 'But be assured. I'm going to hurt him first. He'll be screaming your name when he—'

There was a loud bang and Angelica stopped talking. Kate felt the weight on her back lessen as Angelica fell to the side.

Kate twisted free and looked up. Jack was holding the fire extinguisher. He was panting. And

Angelica lay face down on the floor, blood on the back of her head.

'Oh, Jack,' Kate cried, grabbing hold of her son and hugging him tightly.

'I saved you, Mum,' he said.

'You did. You're so brave, so clever.' She squeezed her eyes shut and pulled him close.

'Everything all right back there?' the pilot shouted. 'I've radioed for help.'

'Yes,' said Kate. 'It is now. But we're going to need an ambulance when we land, and police, and—'

A great rush of cold air filled the cabin and Kate looked up, momentarily lost.

'Oh no.'

Angelica wasn't dead, just stunned. She had risen and made it over to the door, which she had thrown open, so the side of the helicopter was a gaping chasm, the sound of the blades above now deafening. Angelica crawled quickly back across the floor and grabbed Jack by the ankle, pulling him towards the door. He screamed. Kate yelled. Angelica was laughing hysterically.

'Sekhmet,' she shouted. 'I offer you this child, this sacrifice, so that—'

Angelica had Jack's legs, Kate his arms, and each was pulling him. He stared into Kate's eyes, pleading. But Angelica was stronger. Jack was being pulled closer and closer to the door and the five thousand foot drop.

She managed to pull Jack's arm to the side, so he could grab on to one of the seat legs. 'Hold that,' she shouted. 'Hold as tight as you can. I love you.'

She roared and leapt over Jack, bundling the unsuspecting Angelica against the door, her back smashing against the metal, forcing her to let go of Jack's ankle so he could scramble away. But Angelica pushed and Kate lost her balance, rolling towards the door.

The opening gaped. Six more inches . . .

Angelica scooted across the floor so she could push Kate out. But the helicopter tilted suddenly to the right and Kate tipped back inside the cabin. She grabbed hold of one of the seats.

'Roll left,' she screamed, and the pilot obeyed, pitching hard to the left. Angelica grabbed hold of the opposite seat leg and Kate kicked out at her as hard as she could, her foot connecting with Angelica's fingers. Angelica shouted out with pain and let go, rolling back towards the door. But the pilot—who couldn't see what was happening—straightened the helicopter just as Angelica was about to fall through the exit.

'No!' Kate screamed. 'Left again.'

The chopper pitched left, but Angelica had grabbed hold of the door handle. Her legs slipped through the gap, dangling in mid-air, but she clung on, screaming. Kate looked around her. There, wedged beneath the seat, was the gun. Kate grabbed it and cocked it.

Angelica saw.

'No!' she shouted. 'Please.'

Kate raised the gun and pointed it at Angelica's head, as steadily as she could with the wind roaring around her and the helicopter swaying, Jack crying as he clung on beside her. But all of that disappeared as she pointed the gun at Angelica's face.

For Isaac. For Tosca. For Junko. For Simone. For Rosie. For all of the people who had died

459

in LA.

*For herself.*

'Say hello to Sekhmet for me.'

She squeezed the trigger.

460

# EPILOGUE

Kate and Jack stood in the Departures lounge of LAX, Kate holding tightly on to her son's hand tightly. For once, he didn't try to wriggle away. He had been subdued ever since the big scene in the helicopter, unsurprisingly, but she was confident he would be OK once they got home. There were still several weeks of the school summer holidays left and she was going to make sure he had the time of his life. Whatever he wanted to do, they'd do it. Even if it meant eating at McDonald's every day.

After all the things he'd seen, there'd be trips to a child psychologist too. They said children were adaptable, stronger than adults gave them credit for—but Jack had been through so much. He was bound to need counselling.

She peered up at the board, waiting for their gate to be announced. She couldn't wait to get on the plane, knowing she wouldn't be able to relax until they were back on English soil.

'Are you OK?' she asked Jack.

'Mum, you've asked me that, like, a billion times.'

'Sorry. I just wanted to make sure.'

He nodded and smiled up at her. 'Yeah, I'm fine.' He paused and looked over at a store selling CDs and video games. 'Can I get a new game for my DS? For the flight?'

She couldn't say no.

'Come on then. Let's see if they've got any good ones.'

While Jack browsed the shelves, Kate looked

461

around. LAX was quiet. The airports had only reopened a short time ago, with a limited number of flights out of the country and strict medical screening of passengers. Nobody with any sign of a virus was being allowed out. Apart from that, she got the impression that the survivors of the pandemic wanted to stay at home. Los Angeles may have been deeply wounded, but its people were resilient. And they were dreamers; life's optimists. They would recover, rebuild. Soon enough, life would return to normal.

Which was what she wanted, more than anything. Normality.

Jack found a game he couldn't live without and hurried over to her. She paid for it, thrilled to see a smile on his face, trying not to worry about the game being too violent, and they left the shop.

Paul came out of the Gents opposite the store, spotted her and came over. She took his hands in hers. He was still fragile, but getting stronger every day. And some of the colour had returned to his face. Looking up at him now, she thought how gorgeous he was and how glad she was that he was hers.

'I was thinking,' she said. 'I could really do without any excitement for a while.'

'What about our wedding?'

'Hmm. Well, that's the kind of excitement I can handle. But promise me something?'

'Anything.'

'If you ever see Harley again, run in the opposite direction.'

Harley was back in San Francisco, helping to organise the clean-up operation. After they'd got back to Sequoia, and found that Paul was making

462

a good recovery, Harley had started to show symptoms himself, so had been given a dose of the antivirus.

Kate kissed Paul lightly and he snaked his arms round her. She wanted to take him to bed. She whispered in his ear, 'Can't wait to get you home, Mr Wilson.'

'And I can't wait to get home, Dr Maddox.'

He reached out an arm and pulled Jack, who was busy scrutinising the box of his new game, into a family huddle.

'Your mum's a heroine, did you know that, Jack?'

'Yeah, she's pretty awesome.' Jack extricated himself and rooted in his backpack for his DS.

'For a mum,' Kate smiled. 'But I'm not a heroine. I was only doing what I had to do.'

'You saved a lot of lives, Kate. Including mine.'

She was about to protest, to tell him that she could have identified the poison and its antidote straight away, if she'd spotted the satellite virus sooner. But then she thought, no. I'm not going to protest. I did it. I beat Watoto—for now. And I saved us. I saved Jack—and he saved me, too.

The treatment was being produced and distributed at a rate that the CDC called 'unprecedented'. Only a microscopic amount of the sap, and the antidote that counteracted the poison, was required for a dose, and almost every mamba rose in the world was being processed. They were calling it 'green gold', and Tanzania, where the plant grew most abundantly, had grown rich overnight, with the United States and other Western countries paying huge sums for the plant because they needed it now, couldn't wait to grow

463

it. Although there was still no vaccine to protect people from contracting the virus in the first place, anyone who tested positive was being given a dose, stopping the illness in its tracks and radically cutting the death rate.

But Watoto (the media had finally stopped referring to it as Indian flu) was still killing people, and it was still out there. Finding a vaccine, eradicating the disease once and for all—consigning it to history like smallpox—would be the next step. Kate vowed to continue her work. She would never give up, not until Watoto was wiped from the face of the planet.

TV stations worldwide had been desperate to talk to her—the woman who saved civilisation. There was talk of a Nobel Prize. But she didn't want the attention. And she didn't feel like celebrating.

They walked over to a row of seats and sat down, Jack flipping open his video game.

'What are you thinking?' Kate asked Paul. He kept slipping into an introspective gloom, which he then always denied.

'Nothing, honest.'

She grabbed his wrist to stop him turning away and he admitted, 'I feel guilty, that's all.'

'About Rosie?'

'Yes.'

They had already had the conversation about how it wasn't his fault, about how she must already have caught the virus by the time he met her. Of course, she wouldn't have spent the last days of her life being terrorised by Heather, miles from home—but Kate was worried that Paul's guilt was combined with something stronger. That he was

464

secretly grieving for Rosie, that he had been a little bit in love with her. It was a difficult one, and she didn't know exactly how to deal with it, even though she had made Paul deal with far worse—her grief for his dead twin, and her uncertainty as to whether she'd been attracted to Paul merely because he resembled Stephen, that it was a way of keeping Stephen in her life.

Why did it all have to be so complicated?

'It's not your fault,' she said, reassuring him, avoiding that other conversation for now. She looked away.

Five minutes later, it was Paul's turn to ask her what was wrong.

'Nothing.'

'Come on—you've got that look on your face. Is it about Rosie?'

'Actually, no.' It was true. 'I was thinking about what Mangold said when I met him—about how he knew my parents and how my dad was a virologist. My dad wasn't a virologist—he was an aid worker. It doesn't make sense.'

'The old bastard was probably lying.'

'I don't know. I realise he wasn't fully *compos mentis*, but he sounded so convincing, and he knew their names. And Angelica backed it up. She said I don't know anything about my parents.' She looked at Paul. 'What was my dad really doing in Tanzania? And if the local people, the Hadza, knew the cure for Watoto, why didn't they give it to us?'

Paul shook his head. Kate was about to speak again when a blur of movement caught her eye, followed by a man's shout.

She grabbed Paul's arm.

A woman was running through the airport,

security guards close behind her. One of them accelerated and grabbed her. As the woman tried to wriggle out of the guard's grasp, she sneezed, hard, and Kate realised why they'd been chasing her. All around, people jumped to their feet and scattered. The woman looked up from her position on the floor and caught Kate's eye, crying with stress and fear. Kate wanted to say, It's OK, even if it's Watoto you've got. You'll live. There's enough antidote for everyone.

'There's our gate,' Paul said, pointing to the departure board. 'Come on.'

The three of them stood up and headed towards the gate, leaving the security guards to haul the woman away, all the people around giving her a wide berth.

Kate stepped on to the travellator that carried them down towards the departure gate. She couldn't stop thinking about Mangold and her father. One day, she knew, she was going to have to search out the truth. But that would have to wait. Right now, as she glided along with Paul and Jack beside her, all she cared about was getting on that plane.

She had beaten Watoto, her personal nemesis. But there were still plenty of other viruses out there, all those potential pandemics, the mutations, and the people in this world who knew how to harness nature and turn it bad.

But she didn't want to think about that right now.

Because she had her boys beside her, and they were going home.